From the bestselling author of
Romancing the Stone
comes a new tale of adventure and romance...
The Legend Makers

The fortune-teller looked off into the distance. "You are going to the Oriente. I see you in the rain forest. There is a man there. Handsome and quite enamoured of you."

"Michael?" M.J. asked.

"Yes. You will need his protection." Martita rubbed her arms as if to warm herself. "There is great danger in the Oriente. Always has been. But now, especially for you."

"Why me? I have nothing to do with anyone who lives here."

Martita continued as if she hadn't heard M.J.'s question. "I am to warn you about the Oriente. There are many, many legends in the rain forest. But it is important for you to pay particular attention to a more recent legend."

"Sort of my own personal legend?" M.J. asked cockily.

Martita ignored M.J's tone and continued. "You come here to look for oil. Many have come before you. There is a legend of a woman and two men who came to the Oriente in 1933. All three died mysteriously. It wasn't nature that consumed them, but greed."

M.J. swallowed hard. "They killed each other over oil?"

"That and gold. Martita leaned forward and her ink-coloured eyes seemed to completely fill her face. "I am told to warn you that, if you persist on your current path, death awaits you in the Oriente."

Catherine Lanigan is a master storyteller of more than ten bestselling women's fiction novels—including the novelisations of the hit films *Romancing the Stone* and *Jewel of the Nile*, starring Kathleen Turner and Michael Douglas.

When not writing, Catherine enjoys entertaining her friends with innovative gourmet meals.

Already available in
MIRA® Books

DANGEROUS LOVE
ELUSIVE LOVE
TENDER MALICE
IN LOVE'S SHADOW

CATHERINE LANIGAN

the legend MAKERS

MIRA® BOOKS

*MIRA is a registered trademark of Harlequin Enterprises Limited,
used under licence.*

*First published in Great Britain 2000
MIRA Books, Eton House, 18-24 Paradise Road,
Richmond, Surrey, TW9 1SR*

© Catherine Lanigan 1999

ISBN 1 55166 517 4

58-0003

*Printed and bound in Spain
by Litografia Rosés S.A., Barcelona*

ACKNOWLEDGMENT

My deepest appreciation goes to so many people for contributing their time and personal "legends" to this novel. Without the expertise of geologist James Honert, the scenes in this story would have lacked the background and accuracy that you, the reader, deserve. Sincere gratitude goes to Prentis B. Tomlinson, Heather Tomlinson and Lace Honert for their contributions to this story. Thanks to Glenda Reed of Benz Energy, who answered my frantic overseas calls and mangled faxes.

Thanks to Miriam Clingersmith, our travel agent, who got us in and out of South America when it seemed a hopeless task.

In Ecuador, I wish to thank: Dr. Francisco Acosta and Mrs. Martha Acosta; Mrs. Guadaloupe Romoleadux; Carmen and Pablo Marcel, owners of La Vina restaurant; Mrs. Isabel de Ponce; Emile de Raschle and Mrs. Kirstin de Raschle, managers of the Hotel Oro Verde, for more stories than this one novel could ever hold; Mr. Francisco Espinoza, for his story about El Dorado; and a hug to Mr. Benito Velasquez and the entire staff of the Hotel Oro Verde—now the Suisse Hotel—for taking care of us and our golden retrievers, Beau and Bebe, and for helping us make our Ecuadorian home as welcoming as our Houston home.

And finally, to Jim Alexander, the best half of myself, for taking me on a silver plane to see "the other side."

This book is dedicated to Dianne Moggy, my muse, mentor and angel, who enthusiastically allowed me to write about my mythical and, I've found, quite mystical South American home—Ecuador.

In appreciation

A heartfelt hug to Naki Vastakis, whose personality is brighter than the sun and who inspired me to somewhat "invent" M. J. Callahan.

1

→ ←

Amazon jungle, 1997

They were the gatekeepers. The protectors of the jungle. The immortal guardians of the universe, so they believed. They called themselves Uma men, or followers of the ancient Andean god Uma, the hideous, scathing god of destruction who cleansed the earth of evil the night before the feast of Corpus Christi.

They were twelve in number, like the disciples the missionaries had described to their forefathers generations ago, two from each of the six tribes that comprised the peoples of the Oriente. Cofan, Siona-Secoya, Achuar, Shuar, Quichua and Huaorani. They acted as one mind, one soul, creating an awesome power.

Unschooled and illiterate, they rejected the contemporary world in its entirety. Wearing only loincloths for protection, their bodies were the sole sheaths for their thoughts. Shamans all, the Uma men moved stealthily through the rain forest, their brown bodies painted amber, white and green, looking like patches of dappled sunlight rather than human beings. Their nomadic lifestyle kept them apart from their families and ignorant of the outside world. They seemed to appear at will and vanish from sight like morning mist. Though they developed their talents of extrasensory perception and focused concentration, their narrow righteousness flawed their worldly perspective like rust collecting on iron.

Uma men fashioned their weapons from living plants and animals and ate uncooked flesh to best assimilate the soul's power into themselves. Feeding was a spiritual as well as physical necessity.

Uma men were responsible for keeping the ancient teachings alive through meditation, incantation and thought transference. They dared not write their actions in hieroglyphics, which would only diminish the power of the group. For their survival and the completion of their purpose as gatekeepers, it was imperative that the mind of the group remain whole. They did not believe in the possibility of their own deaths, and their fearlessness made them ruthless.

It was this zeal and intensity of purpose that caused them never to think of themselves, their needs, hungers or thirsts, but to hold holy their special destiny as they stalked their prey.

Grinding, smashing sounds bellowed from monster machines as they bulldozed their way through thick sections of liana vines, mangroves, acacias and rubber trees. Toucans and parrots fled to the skies. Snakes slithered silently into the forest floor while iguanas lumbered away on short stubby legs to the cacophony of screaming monkeys.

The faces of the Uma men contorted as they internally assimilated the dying breaths of rare orchids, laurel and even insects they knew cured diseases when blended according to ancient formulas. For years they had been fighting the invaders with prayers and the force of their combined wills. But their old tactics were as powerless as the delicate hecate and the blue-flowered sucupira.

They slipped between leaves and fronds like day shadows. A flit of light, a mere rustle of breeze.

Like the Spanish conquistadores, these men on their metal machines had come to destroy.

The gatekeepers waited patiently as the trio of workers finished their task, then stopped for their midday meal. The trio laughed among themselves as they passed around tin plates of food harvested from tin cans and paper boxes.

In unison twelve flints struck stone, and sparks ignited dried moss, then a stick, then more moss, creating torches. Twelve flames touched the earth, spreading cleansing crimson fingers that snaked toward the trio, surrounding them in a circle of death.

The gatekeepers walked behind the wall of flame, moving closer to their prey before flinging their torches at the men's backs, striking clothing, setting the men on fire.

The human screams were no more, no less painful to the Uma men than the dying trees. All living things were equal in the universe.

One by one the gatekeepers placed hollowed-out reeds to their mouths and blew deadly poisoned darts at the invaders.

The victims dropped quickly to their deaths beside one another, the jungle flames consuming them in a funeral pyre.

The Uma men were silent as they turned placidly away from their victory and vanished into the jungle like the spirits they believed themselves to be.

Mistakenly, they thought they had vanquished an enemy. Having rejected the modern world, they knew nothing about satellites or television or telecommunications. They didn't know that their story would travel to other continents and become a challenge for others. They didn't know the media would make martyrs of the three dead men.

The didn't know they had become legend makers.

2

*Y*ou *have been hired.*

The words jumped off the computer screen at M.J., who blinked twice before bringing herself out of her three-second-long semiconscious state. "No way!" she said, grabbing the sides of the monitor and kissing the screen. "Dreams of a lifetime don't really come true, or do they?"

She reread her e-mail from Texan Oil Company.

```
M.J. Callahan
Stewart Energy
2 Le Grande Plaza
12th Floor
San Francisco, CA
94920


Dear M.J.

  After careful review of your geological
credentials and résumé, we are happy to
inform you that you have been hired to as-
sist our head exploration geologist, Mi-
chael Hunter, on our currently scheduled
assignment in the Oriente fields in Ec-
uador, at our agreed-upon salary, terms
and conditions. Having newly acquired
Block 23 from the Ecuadorian government,
```

it is imperative you leave for Ecuador immediately.

Our team is headed by the owner of Texan Oil Company, Travis Kincaid, who is currently domiciled in Lago Agrio. You are to meet with Michael Hunter and leave out of Houston in six days. Please confirm via e-mail your acceptance of this letter as soon as possible so that I may arrange your travel schedule, tickets and hotel reservations in Quito.

Once I receive your reply, I will overnight our contract and a check to you for your traveling expenses. Please sign all copies of the contract, keeping one for your records and overnight back to us.

I hope the urgency of our situation does not cause you undue problems with Stewart Energy. If you are unable to meet our time frame I am afraid we must hire someone else.

I look forward to your speedy reply.

Sincerely,
Albert Pinchon
Personnel Director

M.J. was incredulous. The exhilarated pounding of her heart nearly drowned out the sound of her assistant Eloise's voice. Why Stewart Energy had ever hired the woman was beyond her. Eloise could barely run a computer, much less understand the intricacies of geophysics. Many a day M.J. was convinced Eloise was the embodiment of the seven plagues of Egypt. M.J. tried to be sweet to the poor woman, but in the back of her mind there was something about Eloise she didn't trust. Probably her very green, envious eyes.

"You okay, M.J.? You look like you just saw a ghost," Eloise said, staring a bit too intensely through her glasses.

"Huh?" M.J. snapped off the monitor. "I'm fine." She smiled too broadly, too quickly, her eyes darting from Eloise to the screen. The smile vanished. M.J. had never been good at lying. Oh, she could mold the truth a bit, embellish, even commit grave sins of omission. But out-and-out lying was a tough call. So was keeping a secret.

"So, did you see?"

"No," Eloise replied coolly, placidity resting on her seamless face.

Eloise could lie with the best of them. M.J. had always been awed by talent, any kind of talent. And Eloise was a master at this.

"You're not impressed?" M.J. asked, throwing a disdainful flourish into her voice. She placed her hand protectively over her heart for added dramatic measure. As far as M.J. was concerned, everything about her life was theatrical. If it wasn't, she made certain it was cued up, rewritten, blocked out and vividly executed. Nothing was as sad to M.J. as the mundane. She was extraordinarily emotive, and it was imperative that the entirety of her life be, as well.

"Like I said—"

"Oh, get out," M.J. replied and depressed the monitor button. "This is as good as it gets, Eloise, and you can't tell me that drool in the corner of your mouth is due to my new box of Girl Scout thin mints. You want my job."

Eloise nearly drew blood biting her tongue, keeping her exhilaration in check. "You're not really going to Venezuela?"

"Deliver me." M.J. rolled her eyes in her best thespian manner. "Ecuador," she corrected.

"Same thing."

"Hardly," M.J. replied, downloading her acceptance letter and typing an affirmative reply to Albert Pinchon. She sent the e-mail, yanked a tissue from the square box on her desk, handed it to Eloise and said, "On second thought, take the whole box. You'll need them when they pass you over for my job." M.J. rose. "It's one thing to wish for something. It's another to do it."

Eloise glared at her as she left to tell her superior she was resigning from the company.

"You can't go to South America!" Claire, M.J.'s elder sister wailed, standing in the center of myriad 1920s and thirties travel and movie posters that covered the walls in M.J.'s bedroom. She was sputtering so rapidly she didn't pay attention to Clark Gable's face publicizing *Mogambo* or Elsa Martinelli, who oozed sex appeal wearing a pair of very tight black Capri pants for the African-based movie *Hatari!*

"You can't chuck four years with a company to go chasing some fantasy! You've never been out of California! What do you know about international travel?"

M.J. flung a brand-new pair of khaki safari shorts in her suitcase, price tags intact. A matching blouse, knee-high socks and a leopard-print scarf followed. Out of her jewelry box she withdrew gold hoop earrings. "Do you think these are too much?"

Claire's eyebrows arched skeptically. "I rest my case. You haven't got a clue what you're doing."

M.J. shoved the earrings into the breast pocket of the blouse. "Okay! So, I have an image issue. I'm working on that." She put the scarf back in the bureau drawer.

"This isn't a movie, M.J. You're going to the Amazon jungle!" Claire reminded her.

"Right." M.J. snapped her fingers, dashed to the bathroom and returned with twenty-three bottles of various vitamins and herbs she believed she couldn't live without. She packed with lightning speed, talking even faster. "I've been prepared for this longer than you know. I renewed my passport last year on the off chance that something like this would come along."

"But you have a great job. Secure. Safe."

"What's so safe about Stewart Energy? Eloise is always hanging around waiting for me to make a mistake so she can move up. And if it wasn't her, it would be someone else just like her. It's the nature of the beast. Besides, when I went to Mr. Wells and told him about Ecuador, he didn't have a problem with my quitting."

"Why am I having a hard time believing this?"

"Thickheaded?" M.J. chuckled quickly and retrieved a fist full of Victoria's Secret lingerie from her drawer.

"And what are *those* for?" Claire demanded.

"Oops. Sorry. Didn't know I had 'em, did you?" She put them back.

Claire was at the end of her patience. "M.J., please..."

"Okay! So, Mr. Wells wasn't exactly fine with it. But he did say he would give me a leave of absence for six months."

"Thank God not everyone has lost their mind around here. You can go back. That's a relief."

M.J. chewed her bottom lip, sheepishly looking away from Claire's penetrating gaze. "I, uh, told him I couldn't promise I'd be back."

"What?" Claire threw her hands in the air and grabbed her hair. "You make me crazy! You've always made me crazy! Why are you doing this to me?"

M.J. stopped abruptly. "You? This has nothing to do with you. This is my life we're talking about here."

"Yes, but I've been responsible for you ever since Mom died."

"You mean since Dad died," M.J. said sadly.

"Left. He left, M.J. Why do you insist on pretending he's dead? The truth is, he was a quitter."

"Don't even say it! I'm not a quitter like him. I am not guilty for his leaving," she affirmed to herself. "I am moving out of my going-nowhere career. My going-nowhere life. I'm making reality out of my lifelong dreams. I am the master of my destiny. Creator of my fate. I hold the cards here, not some nitwit middle manager at Stewart Energy. I've been gifted with this opportunity and I'll be hanged if I'm going to let you or anyone else talk me out of it."

Claire tried to touch M.J.'s shoulder, but her sister scooted from her caress. "I understand. Having no one is tough. I remember before I married Robert and had the girls—"

M.J. cut her off. "Oh, spare me the husband and kids routine, Claire. Just because I'm not married and could care less if I ever was does not mean I don't have a life. Life is *supposed* to be an adventure. Biting off all the excitement I can chew." M.J.'s eyes grew wide with rapture. "I want to go places, meet people who are shaping the world, making things happen. I want to know what it's like in the rain forest. I want to talk to every cockatiel who'll look my way. What do these exotic people think about all day? I want to exchange ideas. See what kind of men and women these other geologists are. Why, Michael Hunter is world renowned. He's been everywhere you can think of, searching out new oil reserves that will heat your home so you and my nieces don't freeze in the winter. Did you ever think of that?"

"No," Claire answered lowly.

"Don't you see, Claire, I'll never be happy, much less fulfilled, if I don't jump out there and try."

"South America is so far away, M.J.," Claire said sadly.

"They do have telephones, you know. It's not the end of the world."

Skepticism rang in Claire's voice. "If being two miles

up in the Andes on the other side of the equator isn't the end of the earth to you, M.J., what is?''

M.J.'s eyes leveled on her sister as she answered honestly, "Here.''

"Argh! You're slamming me again!'' Claire sputtered. "Will you never stop?''

M.J.'s shoulders heaved with exasperation. Her conversation with her sister was as confrontational as ever. How many times would M.J. have to assure Claire that she was not responsible for their mother's death from cancer last year? Claire had nursed their mother, Ruth, for two years, exhausting herself, alienating herself from her husband and children, and nearly had a nervous breakdown before admitting she *needed* M.J.'s help.

M.J. had been consumed with her career at the time, and though she'd helped Claire on weekends, the fulltime care of Ruth was impossible without hired help. Fortunately, M.J. had finally started earning enough money to be able to procure a day nurse. However, the nights and weekends had been long, tedious and unbearably painful emotionally.

M.J. had forced herself not to cry in front of her mother, saving her tears for the drive to the office or behind the closed bathroom door. Most nights she cried herself to sleep. The nurse told M.J. that Ruth was lingering long past her time. Her stubborn willfullness was causing her needless suffering.

M.J. begged her mother to give up the ghost. But Ruth was not a quitter. She was strong and clung to every breath of life she could take. Pain-filled or not.

For a year after the funeral M.J. struggled with her memories.

"I've asked the doctor to double your morphine dosage, Mom,'' M.J. had said, holding her mother's hand.

"I wish you hadn't done that.'' Her voice creaked the reply.

Tears flooded M.J.'s eyes. "It hurts me to see you suffer."

"I know, dear. I wish it didn't. That's the part I hate. I never meant for any of it to turn out this way. My life, I mean. Yours."

"There's nothing wrong with my life. I'm just fine," M.J. assured her, though a smile would not come.

"I should have remarried. Provided more security for you girls."

"Why would you do that? So another man could leave you, too?"

"What makes you think that?" She looked at her daughter with milky blue eyes, dulled by too much heartache.

M.J. looked away, grinding her jaw. "I really hate him, you know. For what he did."

Ruth rolled her head on the pillow and looked out the window. "It's almost spring. Your father loved the spring. He was so romantic then, bringing me tulips and apple blossoms he stole from the neighbors' yards." She lifted her thickly veined hand to her gaunt cheek and stroked herself. "He said the sweetest things. He made me feel so pretty." Her sigh was shallow but hopeful. "He made me feel so alive."

M.J. bolted out of her chair. "How can you talk about him like that? The man was a creep. He was no hero. Not yours. Not mine. And he's not coming back. Ever." She fussed with medicine bottles. She moved the glass of water, repositioning it three times, wanting desperately to fling it out the window. She wanted to strike something, and quickly.

Ruth closed her eyes. "Let's not argue."

"We weren't arguing," M.J. replied, pulling the quilt to her mother's chin. "I didn't mean to argue."

How long do we have, Mom, before I can't do this for you any more? How will I feel when you are gone? What will it be like

*when they come to take you away from me? Will it be worse
than this burning in the pit of my stomach? Will I still choke up
every time I look at your photograph? And why am I always
wanting to fight with you about him? What's the matter with
me that I can't let a dying woman have her fantasies?*

Ruth's eyes fluttered as sleep settled gently over her.

"That's it, Mom. Dream pretty dreams. Anything you
want."

M.J. closed the door quietly, wondering what she
would find the next morning.

*How can she stay alive for a man who never cared about her
in the first place?*

M.J. looked at Claire's anxiety-riddled face. She'd
never noticed how Claire's guilt rode openly on her
shoulders like a demon, causing reactions and decisions
that probably weren't part of Claire at all. Even worse,
M.J. had been judging her on them.

"Don't be afraid for me, Claire. I'll be fine. I'm the one
who's afraid for you."

Claire's eyes softened to a peculiar shade of periwinkle
blue. "But you're the one who is alone."

"But it doesn't bother me. I like it. How can I go off and
change the world if I'm tied down with a family? I want
to make history, Claire. I'm no Madame Curie, but I want
to make a *difference*," she said with riveting earnestness.

Claire put her hands on M.J.'s shoulders. Her eyes
glanced to the wall posters. "This isn't a movie, and you
aren't the lead in the senior play."

Claire's tone was a touch too patronizing for M.J. "Aw,
man! Don't act like Claire again. Please? I was just getting
to like you."

"You are insufferable, M.J." She dropped her hands instantly.

"No, I'm going to Ecuador and you aren't going to stop
me." M.J. grabbed her favorite CDs, and put them and

her sunblock in the tote bag with an oversize can of insect repellent.

"You're gonna need a lot more than that in the Amazon," Claire warned.

M.J. turned what she hoped were understanding eyes to her sister. She was trying to be tolerant and patient—two elusive virtues. "I know my life doesn't make sense to you, being so totally opposite from yours. But it's what I want. Can't you let me have it?"

The battle of wills had exhausted Claire. "Is this what you really want, M.J.? Or are you running away again?"

"Again?"

"Look at you. You work with rocks and sand and soil. Inanimate objects. They don't make any demands on you, and you don't have to interact with them. You wanted to be an actress all your life—at least once Dad left, you did. But I always thought you were hiding behind the characters you imitated so well to keep yourself from admitting you were hurting. You've fantasized about adventures like Africa and the Amazon for so long, you've somehow managed to make this all materialize. But what you don't seem to understand is that this is dangerous stuff.

"I mean, if the pythons don't kill you, the drug dealers will. Have you even looked at a newspaper lately? Why, last month three loggers were burned to death by some rogue native tribe. Nobody seems to know who they are. And don't forget those oil men in that Venezuelan fishing village last year. I have every right to try to talk you out of this."

"I love you, Claire, but really. I'm like third fiddle on this thing, and maybe I have overglamorized my part. All I'll be doing is processing data, CAD programming, 3-D graphs, charting, applications and positioning. It's even tamer than what I do at Stewart Energy. Did. It's a nobrainer. I'll probably be stuck in Lago Agrio the entire

time. I'll never see anything more than a workstation."
She shrugged.

Claire was unsure. "So, basically, you're saying it's the
same job you were doing here, but just in a new office?"

"Yeah," she replied unblinkingly, believing what she
said was the truth, yet secretly hoping her future held
more. "I promise, I'm not running away from anything,
Claire."

"It's just that you've been so withdrawn since Mom
died."

M.J. was quick to answer. "Swamped and overworked,
yes. But not withdrawn. I'm sorry I missed Erin's birthday party last week."

"It just wasn't like you, is all. You've doted on her since
the day she was born."

"Because I love her." M.J. smiled, then hugged Claire.
"Now, cheer up. I'm going away for six months to do
some computer work. I'll come home with outrageous,
basically untrue stories to tell. Erin and Colleen will think
I'm a heroine."

Claire crumbled under M.J.'s charm. "Okay. Have
your adventure." She wagged her finger at M.J. "But I'm
still going to worry."

"I love you, Claire."

"I love you, too, M.J." Claire smiled. "About those earrings…"

3

Flying for M.J. had always been jaunts, never more than an hour or so within California. She hadn't thought much about the process until after she was airborne. While other passengers complained about the long flight, the lack of legroom and the undercooked meal, M.J. was riding higher than the stratosphere. She was going somewhere. Almost to the end of the earth, as Claire had said. Her exhilaration was unbounded.

As usual, she made a pest of herself.

"It's incredible, isn't it?" she bubbled to the middle-aged businessman sitting next to her.

"What is?"

"Flying. Screaming through the air at rocket speed, eating up miles in seconds, making the world shrink in time and space, bringing the foreign to the domestic…"

The man put his hand to his face. "Don't tell me, it's your first flight."

"Heck, no. I've flown before. Many times. Just not this far away."

"And where are you going?" he asked.

"Ecuador."

The man looked at his watch. "Only twenty minutes since our takeoff. You *do* have a long way to go!" He guffawed. "Take my advice, save all that enthusiasm for the last leg of your journey. You'll need it."

"Oh, I can handle it. I've waited all my life for this."

He rolled his eyes. "I couldn't tell." He spread out his newspaper, blocking her view of him.

"What's so bad about a little enthusiasm?" she whispered to herself and looked out the window at the clouds below.

Here she was, soaring through the heavens on her way to an exotic country. She was biting off her life in huge hunks, and it felt great. She felt powerful. Capable of righting wrongs. Able to change history.

Suddenly, her face fell. For no matter how high she soared in spirit or in a plane, or how fast she flew, she was still M.J. Not an angel. Not all that powerful.

She couldn't bring her mother back to life.

Then it hit her.

Am I running away like Claire said?

Changing planes in Houston turned out to be more confusing than M.J. had imagined. She not only switched airlines, but terminals, as well. Because she was flying to South America she assumed she would be departing from the international terminal. Instead, her flight was scheduled out of Terminal C, and because she'd brought two very heavy carry-on luggage pieces, she almost missed her plane.

She was breathless and anxious when she raced up to the podium to check in. That was why she didn't notice him watching her.

He wore a battered, sweat-stained white hat with a black band, jeans, hiking boots and a khafi safari shirt. His chest was broad, his shoulders even broader. The two-day-old stubble of blond beard told her he'd been flying through the night and into the day to make this flight with her. His blond hair was long in back, scraping his shirt collar. He smiled at her with a quirky, almost mischievous smile and shook his head when she dropped her tote, spilling brand-new lipsticks and mascaras on her way to the gangway.

Immediately, he bent to help her retrieve her possessions. "Did I hear right? You're M.J. Callahan?" He balanced a square gold-cased designer lipstick on his forefinger.

M.J. didn't like the smirk he gave her. Nor the flashing sexual broadcast he was sending with his deep-set crystal-blue eyes. She smiled back. She could feel herself being drawn into his gaze.

Why wasn't someone snapping their fingers to shock her out of this insane, overly reactionary response she was having to this man?

"I'm M.J." She heard her own voice purr. *What was up with her? She'd never acted like this around a man before.*

The sun shimmered off the lipstick case.

"Thanks, Mr. Hunter," she said, snatching it off his finger and shoving it in her tote.

"So, you know me?" he asked, his cocky smile brimming with a twinge of machismo charm.

"Of you. I know *of* you. Your reputation precedes you."

He preened.

She smiled in spite of herself. She'd never flirted so outrageously in her life.

"You can't be M.J."

"And why not?" she asked with justified impudence.

"Because he's supposed to be a guy. I mean, you're obviously not a guy."

"Nobody said your company was gender biased," she replied with a hand on her hip.

"We aren't. Normally."

"And this isn't normal?" She started walking away from him.

"Damn straight it's not." He chuckled, handing his

boarding pass to the attendant. "Travis Kincaid is going to go blind over this."

"What are you talking about?" she demanded as she held out her boarding pass.

He grabbed her hand, stopping her. "I'm serious. You can't go."

"What are you talking about?" Her face screwed up in anger. "Get out of my way!"

"I'm trying to help you," he started to explain before she cut him off.

"Who gave you that kind of authority, anyway? I don't see Travis Kincaid standing here." Her head moved from side to side. "I don't see anyone dictating to me but you, and just who do you think you are, anyway?" she demanded.

His eyes narrowed to icy slits. "Pardon me," he replied condescendingly. "It's just that I have a hard time imagining Travis Kincaid hiring a woman for this particular assignment."

"Actually, he didn't."

"What?"

"I mean, I haven't exactly met Mr. Kincaid."

Michael's blue eyes widened. "I was right."

"Half right, Mr. Hunter. Mr. Pinchon in your personnel department hired me. I was what you might call a 'rush job.' I had less than a week to quit my job and get to Ecuador."

"This is a nightmare," Michael said, taking off his hat and raking his hair. He replaced the hat with a slight backward tilt in order to better see her. "Mr. Pinchon—"

"Was acting on direct orders from Mr. Kincaid," she cut in.

"No way. I know Pinchon. He's one of the best in this field at matching personalities to positions. He would have taken one look at—" He looked at her bangle bracelets, matching leopard-print earrings and fashionable shoes. "No way. Period."

The chink in M.J.'s defense screeched as it widened. "I, er, uh, that is, we never met. Mr. Pinchon and I."

"Don't stop now," he said, exasperated. "I'm all ears."

"I applied by e-mail. He replied by e-mail."

Michael expelled a heavy sigh. "I really don't want to know any more. I'm convinced. There's been a mistake. A big one."

"Now, wait a minute," she said hotly. "I have every right—"

He interrupted quickly. "You bet you do. And you know what? I can see you're a big girl. Travis Kincaid will be putty in your hands. You'll figure out a way to change his mind. You can take care of yourself. Right?"

"Yes, I can." She smiled reassuringly.

"I was just trying to save you. Save you the bother and embarrassment of going all the way to Ecuador only to have Travis Kincaid send you straight back home."

"What's he got against women?"

Michael replied quickly. "A lot, actually, but that's another story, which has nothing to do with business."

"Then what makes you think you know so much about my situation?"

"Experience," he said with a cool twist of disdain and arrogance that gave worldly people like him the advantage.

Envy ate at M.J. She would have given anything to be as smug as Michael Hunter. Anything.

He was right. She had no experience with Travis Kincaid, the rain forest or bigger-than-life-itself men like Michael Hunter, not to mention just about anything else that constituted "experience." She was about as experienced in life as a newborn.

Her shoulders slumped, the fire left her eyes, and the venom dissolved in her mouth. She liked herself a bit better when she was shooting for effect. Michael Hunter had done a good job of stripping away her mask.

"Okay, I give. But really, why would he send me back? I have credentials."

"It's too dangerous for women in the jungle. They get hurt. Physically. They aren't prepared for what's out there."

She was undeterred. "Which is?"

He blinked at her incredulously then began blasting her with the ingredients of nightmares. "Pythons, piranha, pumas, quicksand, dangerous mountains, hostile natives…"

"Oh, those," she replied dismissively.

He winced. "I suppose you think those enthralling eyes of yours mask your true nature?"

She lifted her chin and looked at him straight on as if daring him to challenge her. "I'm not an idiot, is all."

Had she heard him correctly? Enthralling? He thought her enthralling? What was he trying to do, cause a meltdown? Well, it was working. She felt positively liquid.

"You can't bewitch me, so don't even try."

"I wasn't," she replied indignantly with an unwavering gaze.

He gawked at her, holding his breath.

She couldn't believe it. She'd done something, she wasn't sure what, to hold him spellbound.

Maybe he's just thinking this over. Whatever this is.

He pretended to clear his throat, as if he was thinking of something else. But she caught his eyes traveling the length of her, spending too much time where men usually did when assessing women. No matter how many times it had happened to M.J., she always wished she could smite them for their animalistic behavior. But the truth was that, secretly, it ratcheted her ego up another notch.

He's hooked.

Michael licked his lips before pursing them in a tight line as he remembered himself. "I just hope you don't turn out to be a pain in the ass."

"How rude! What makes you think such a thing?"

"Women like you think they're smart. Daring. In essence, you're foolhardy, and your naiveté could cause others to come to grave harm. I can handle myself. But what if your ineptitude endangers Travis, who hasn't spent as much time in the jungle as I have? He's my business partner. I'm used to standing night watch over my personal business interests. But I'm not a baby-sitter for people who think they're the next Indiana Jones."

"I'm not a daredevil!"

"Sure you are. I know because I'm one. But I've survived shipwrecks, plane crashes and lost communications under the sea. You're one of the new breed. All this 3-D technology takes the guesswork out of oil exploration. My bet is you're double-degreed like the other young geologists I've been seeing over the past three years. You probably know more about rock, shale and limestone than I ever would.

"But here's the deal. My exploratory instruments are my hands, eyes, nose and tongue. I can smell oil when it's a half a mile down. I can taste it, smell it in the air, the grass and sand. I rely on gut instinct, intuition." He took a deep breath. "I just know."

"Yeah? Well, I know I belong on this exploration just as much as you. I believe I have something to offer. Something to give," she said with sincerity.

Michael backed down, temporarily. Folding his arms, he said, "I'm curious. Since you don't have jungle experience, I assume you must be an expert linguist."

"No," she answered flatly. "But I bought some Spanish tapes to listen to on the plane."

He guffawed, twisting his shoulders away from her. "Oh, well then!"

"I'm a fast learner," she retaliated acidly.

"Look, this isn't a game, M.J." His eyes blazed a warning as if willing her to run back to San Francisco and retreat into the life she'd always known.

M.J. knew in that moment that perhaps she didn't have his experience and she certainly wasn't the legendary Travis Kincaid by a long shot, but what she did have was determination and persistence. She had put everything in her life on hold, or rather, in the past, chucking it all to make this trip. To go the distance. If Michael Hunter could make a name for himself blazing trails through uncharted jungles, mountains and the deepest fathoms of the North Sea in the pursuit of black gold, so could she.

M.J. felt a rush of confidence shoot up her spine. "Nothing about me or my life is playtime, Mr. Hunter. I was hired to do a job, and I intend to do just that. I have plenty of experience. It's just different from yours. Obviously, someone at Texan Oil saw that much. I guess the only thing left for me to do is prove it to you and Mr. Kincaid, as well."

She turned away from him and trundled down the gangway with her oversize, overweight bags.

Exasperation riddled Michael as he shook his head, but he couldn't help the encroaching appreciative smile at her retreating form. "What a ride this is gonna be," he mumbled.

4

Due to fog and poor visibility the plane circled Quito for one hour and twenty minutes before finding the necessary break in the cloud cover to land.

"At least they didn't send us back to Panama until tomorrow," Michael said as they disembarked.

"We could have just taken another flight," M.J. said, wondering why the thought of spending the night in a strange city with Michael Hunter bothered her. After all, she was in Ecuador with him. Going to the jungle with him. Yet there were no corporate affiliations in Panama. No boss. No Travis Kincaid lurking in the shadows to watch over them like a sentry.

Michael chuckled as he hoisted his backpack over his shoulder. "There is no other flight, M.J. This is a third-world country. But then, that's what you're here to discover, isn't it?"

"I guess so."

They tramped down the roll-up metal staircase and were met by armed guards checking passengers, pulling one or two aside, glancing at passports, telling the rest to continue toward the terminal.

"I hope Travis thought to have Paulo here."

"Paulo?"

"He's sort of a special envoy to make sure we get through customs and help us with baggage. Come to think of it, Travis was probably too preoccupied to remember."

"I can get my own bags. I don't need any help."

Michael chuckled. "Oh, believe me, I'm not worried about you."

"Good," she replied confidently, then walked into the terminal and headed to the back of the shortest immigration line.

Suddenly, M.J. was overwhelmed with the enormity of her situation. The signs everywhere were in Spanish. *Entrada. Salida. Peligrosa. Policia.* She could only guess at their meaning. And what if she was wrong? What if she did the wrong thing? Went in the wrong line?

She saw huge German shepherds and Rottweilers on metal chain leashes sniffing the carry-on bags of the passengers in front of her. What if one of those dogs smelled her chocolate diet cookies? What if they pulled her aside and started asking her questions?

Her anxiety escalated as four guards in uniform carrying automatic weapons entered the immigration area. She tensed. The line moved incredibly slowly.

She looked around for Michael.

He was gone.

He'd abandoned her.

Every instinct urged her to shout out his name. A half a dozen deep brown eyes peered suspiciously at her from under military caps. She felt perspiration erupt on her upper lip, but she kept her mouth shut and her eyes on the back of the tall man in front of her in line.

"Come on."

Michael's voice came to her like a rescuing angel from heaven.

"Where did you go?" she asked in a low but demanding whisper.

"I told you, to find Paulo."

"And did you?"

"Yes," he said, whisking her out of the line and past the immigration counter where a good-looking man in his late twenties dressed in jeans and a Nike jacket quickly took her carry-ons from her.

"Permit me," Paulo said with a brilliant smile. "Your passport, papers and claim tickets?"

M.J. dug them out of her purse and handed them to Paulo. "Thank you," she said with a rush of relief she hadn't thought was possible.

"I take care ebryting," Paulo said in broken English.

"Thank God Mr. Kincaid remembered," she said to Michael.

"Oh, he didn't. I called Paulo from my cellular. Luckily, he was here at the airport for a Maxus executive coming in on the American flight." Michael nonchalantly laid his palm on the small of her back, ushering her past the immigration officials toward the baggage carousel.

"Oh," she said, curious why she should like the way Michael took charge of a situation and the protective feel of his hand on her when she was struggling so hard to prove her independence and adventurous soul to the world. To herself.

The ride to the Oro Verde Hotel in the minuscule cab, though less than twenty minutes, was torturous for Michael with his long legs. "I'd rather arm wrestle a python than ride in these damn things," he said, working out the kink in his left knee.

M.J. extricated herself from the back seat, where she'd been jammed in along with her two overpacked bags. The cab's trunk was even smaller than the interior.

"Ditto," she said, performing a half back bend. "I think the plane ride was just as bad."

"Cheer up." He smiled charmingly. "It only gets worse from here on out."

M.J. returned the smile. "You're just baiting me."

He shrugged as they walked into the marble-floored,

etched-glass and eucalyptus-wood-trimmed elegant hotel lobby.

M.J.'s mouth gaped at the stunning floral bouquets, leather and tapestry upholstered furnishings and the elegantly dressed couples exiting the bar and gourmet restaurant. "Yeah, roughing it in third world countries..."

"Don't say it," he warned, stepping up to the long reception counter to shake hands with the manager, who seemed to know him quite well.

"Mr. Hunter! How good to see you again, sir. We have been expecting you. I understand the plane was late. Terrible weather. Terrible."

Michael took the pen and signed in. "Thank you, Benito. This is Miss M.J. Callahan. She is a new employee of Texan Oil. I believe she has a reservation?"

"Callahan. Of course, sir." Benito smiled graciously, though curiosity was strung across his face. He looked at the reservation card. "I am afraid we made a mistake. I was expecting Mr. Callahan. I put cigars in the room, as you requested."

Michael chuckled. "The joke is on us, Benito." He turned to M.J., mischievousness sparkling in his eyes. "The Cohibas are the best."

"I beg your pardon?" she asked.

"You do want the cigars, don't you?" he taunted.

M.J. had just about had all she could take from Michael Hunter. She was tired, very cranky and sore from being the butt of his jokes all day. She placed her totes on the floor and took the pen from the counter. "I would like a no smoking room, if that's possible, with a king-size bed. I toss and turn a great deal. Continental breakfast in the morning. Coffee with cream. And extra towels. I bathe at night and in the morning." She finished signing the registry.

"Very well," Benito replied and crisply rang housekeeping. He rattled off several phrases in Spanish. "Your room will be ready in fifteen minutes. I'm having fresh roses sent up, as well. Compliments of the hotel."

"That's not necessary," she said.

"Oh, but of course. For so pretty a lady, roses are always in order," Benito replied. "Perhaps you would like to have a glass of wine in the bar while I make ready your room."

"Thank you," she said with a smile and sailed away from Michael's probing eyes toward the bar.

The woman sitting on the leather banquette at the far end of the bar with an elderly man watched M.J. enter with almost rapt fascination. She inquired in Spanish about the woman. The impeccably dressed man in a custom-made wool pinstripe suit, monogrammed white shirt and black pin-dot silk tie shook his head. He did not know the American woman.

There was no doubt the young woman was American. She was too tall to be Ecuadorian. Her coloring was European, though not Spanish. And her style was unabashedly American, they agreed.

M.J. plunked her black leather purse on one of the three chairs at the round table. Smoothing her long hair from her face, she was already dreaming of the hot shower and shampooing she would give herself in only a few minutes. It seemed an eternity since she'd left San Francisco.

Claire's face flitted across her mind. As eager as she was to throw herself into her new adventure, she still missed her sister.

She glanced at her watch. Nearly midnight. Claire and the girls would be sound asleep. Dreaming. About her? Wondering if she made it to Quito safely?

I should call Claire, just so she doesn't worry, she thought.

Placing her hands on the arms of the chair, M.J. started

to rise, and just as she did, her eyes met those of the strikingly beautiful woman on the banquette.

Enormous ebony eyes, thickly lashed and heavily lined in kohl, peered at her out of a face so white, she reminded M.J. of a Japanese Kabuki dancer. M.J. guessed the woman to be well into her sixties, with hair so jet black she assumed it was colored.

The man sitting with the woman pulled out his wallet and laid several Ecuadorian sucres on the table. The woman didn't look at him as he departed. Instead, she kept her eyes anchored on M.J.

As if in a trance, M.J. continued rising and, losing all thoughts of Claire and her nieces, approached the woman.

"Hello," M.J. said, extending her hand. "I don't speak Spanish."

"I speak English," the woman replied.

"Pardon me for asking, but you were staring at me. Do I know you?"

The woman's full ruby red lips parted in a knowing smile. "Perhaps," she said.

"Excuse me?"

"We have never met in this lifetime, I can assure you. Please." She gestured with a delicate hand. "Sit down."

M.J. sat in the chair that had been occupied by the man. "Is there any other lifetime?"

The woman looked at her curiously. "I had not thought you so young."

"I'm twenty-seven," M.J. said proudly, almost arrogantly, as if she were entitled to more respect.

"Your birthday is in August."

"Yes. How did you guess?"

"I am Martita. You have heard of me, yes?"

"No. I have never heard of you."

The woman's beautiful face was radiant. "How refreshing. A neophyte."

M.J. was curious. She hugged herself and asked, "Is there a reason I should have? Are you famous?"

"Some think I am. Others should be so lucky as to come to know me."

M.J. didn't particularly like the mystery this woman wove around her like a brightly painted shawl. However, she found herself being drawn into the woman's sphere with each word they exchanged. "Are you an actress?"

"Odd you should choose that profession for me. Does it bother you so much that you are not?"

"What has my being an actress got to do with anything?"

"Has no one ever told you that the best way to understand another person is to listen to the questions they ask us?"

"No, but it makes sense," M.J. concurred.

"You did not follow your dream. You wished to be famous. So, you came to Quito, to Ecuador, to make a name for yourself."

"You can't know that."

Martita laughed. "People pay me to tell them such things."

"You're a fortune-teller?" M.J. gasped as if the words burned her lips.

Shrugging, Martita replied, "Why are you appalled?"

"I'm not in the least," M.J. retorted defensively, pretending a fearlessness she didn't feel.

Martita shook her finger at M.J. "This is why you are not an actress. You don't hide your thoughts as well as you think you do."

"I've been known to do a pretty good job of it."

Peering deeply into M.J.'s eyes, Martita said, "I see myself at your age when I look at you. That is what drew me to you when you first entered the room. I came here from Barcelona. I studied in Paris, London and Geneva when I was young. I never finished a course of study in my life. I flitted from one thing to another. I became bored so eas-ily. I knew things too easily. I knew history as if I'd lived it. I remembered books I'd never read, paintings I never painted. Then I realized I was able to foretell events. It frightened my friends, so I found I was best off among strangers. Quito was the farthest place on earth I could think of. It is the highest inhabitable city in the world."

"Well, my life is nothing like that. I have a job here—"

Martita cut her off. "I know." Her black eyes looked into the distance and then filled with streaks of silver light as if reflecting galaxies of stars. "You are going to the Oriente. I see you in the rain forest. There is a man there. Handsome. And quite enamored of you."

"Michael?"

"Yes, I feel the archangel Michael's energy around him. The warrior. Protector. The knight in shining armor."

M.J. felt herself being sucked into Martita's voice, her world.

"You will need his protection." Martita rubbed her arms as if to warm herself. Her eyes remained transfixed on some ethereal space.

"Why?"

"There is great danger in the Oriente. Always has been. But now, especially for you."

"Why me? I have nothing to do with anyone who lives there. I don't know anyone there."

"Do not be foolish thinking that danger comes only from humans. Only from this dimension."

Suddenly, M.J. felt as if she'd been jerked to reality by the collar. "That's preposterous. I don't believe in ghosts."

"It doesn't matter. Facts are facts. I am being told by your spirit guides that destiny brought you here, just as it did me."

"What are spirit guides?" M.J. asked.

Martita continued as if she hadn't heard M.J.'s question

or had no intention of addressing such naiveté. "I am to warn you about the Oriente. There are many, many legends in the rain forest. Some are tens of thousands of years old. Be open to all you will hear about the ancients who colonized here after the sinking of Atlantis."

"Atlantis? That's just a myth," M.J. replied dismissively, though her curiosity was definitely piqued.

"All myths have their basis in reality. Otherwise, they wouldn't exist in the first place."

"Is that true?"

"Of course. However, it's important for you to pay particular attention to a more recent legend."

"Sort of like my own personal legend?" M.J. asked cockily.

Martita ignored M.J.'s tone as information rushed through her like a freight train. "You come here to look for oil. Many have come before you. In the 1920s both Europeans and Americans flocked here searching for oil, but they kept their findings secret. They fought each other for space and grappled over the land.

"There is a legend of a woman and two men working for Standard Oil of New Jersey who came to the Oriente in 1933. All three died mysteriously. It wasn't nature that consumed them, but greed. Human frailties can be so delicious sometimes, yet deadly."

M.J. swallowed hard. Martita was giving her the willies but good. "They killed each other over oil?"

"That and gold. There is a great deal of gold here, according to the legends. Keep your ears open at all times, my new friend. You should also know that the legend says their spirits still walk the rain forest, helping to keep strangers out."

Martita leaned forward. Her ink-colored eyes seemed to fill her face as M.J. gazed into them. "I am told to warn you that if you persist on your current path, death awaits you in the Oriente."

Two hands descended upon M.J.'s shoulders, and their fingers squeezed her flesh ever so gently, but firmly. "And on that note, I say we hit the hay." Michael's cocky voice startled M.J.

She jumped up and slammed the top of her head into Michael's jaw.

"Ouch!" He withdrew his hands and rubbed his jaw. "Remind me next time to blow trumpets to announce my arrival."

"Michael! You frightened me!" M.J. retorted.

He pointed his finger at Martita. "I thought that's what she was doing."

Martita opened her palm. "I should be leaving."

Michael frowned and dug into his back pocket. "I should have stayed in my room. Had a Scotch. But, oh, no, my good Samaritan genes beckoned to me. I should help M.J. Make sure she's all tucked in for the night. I could have saved money and my face!" He groaned, handing Martita a twenty-dollar bill and rubbing his jaw sourly.

Martita rose and walked to the opening next to the etched glass. "You will remember everything," she said to M.J., more as a promise than a question. She hurried down the marble steps with the ease of a woman half her age.

"Michael! Must you continue this misplaced Father Knows Best behavior of yours? I grant you that for most mortals it is exciting to be in your presence. Voyeurism is a turn-on for some. But not me. I was doing just fine all by myself."

"Right," he said, stepping back as she bolted to her feet.

"I suppose now I'll never get to the heart of her message."

He rolled his eyes. "Sweetheart, you don't need a fortune-teller to know that the Oriente is no place for a woman."

"Dammit!" She stomped her foot.

"What?"

"I want to know the rest of the legend. What happened to those three people?"

"Oh, sorry. Is this the part where I have to finish your bedtime story for you?"

She huffed and folded her arms. "How is it, Michael, that we have only just met and yet you infuriate the tar out of me more than anyone I've ever known?"

"Luck?" He cocked an eyebrow mockingly at her.

"Oh, shut up!" She spun on her heel, ready to march away. Michael grabbed her elbow and yanked her back.

Her body slammed into his.

"Hmm." He chuckled, not bothering to disguise his sexual motivation. Before she could open her mouth, Michael said, "Lovers. They were lovers. All of them."

"What?"

"But not all at once. The woman was a journalist. She was supposedly covering what was to become the largest oil discovery of their age. She accompanied her fiancé into the Oriente. They were joined by a geologist or the banker putting up all the money for the drilling, I've forgotten which. They were inexperienced, like you. They trusted too much and didn't heed warnings when they should have."

"How did they die?"

"I'm not sure. Boat accident, I think. Probably eaten by alligators."

"How gruesome," she said, shuddering. "How sad." Inexplicably, her heart went out to them, these people from the past whom she didn't know, never would. Oddly, she couldn't get them out of her mind.

"Newspaper or magazine?" she asked as Michael

steered her out of the bar and across the lobby toward the elevator.

"What?"

"Who did she write for?"

"*Life*, I think," he said, watching the elevator door close.

"How do you know about this?"

"I read an article about them once when I was down here a dozen or more years ago. There's another one about a medicine man who—"

"Was she beautiful? Did you see pictures of her? What about the oilman? How old was he? Who was younger? The banker? I'll bet the banker was younger. Maybe he promised her a bunch of money. Do you think she was mercenary? Do you think she was just after the money and not his love?"

Michael held a computerized plastic card that served as a door key out to M.J. "Do I think you'd lose your head if it wasn't attached? Yes, I do."

"Oh, my key." She looked at it sheepishly. "I guess I'm a little tired or something."

He opened the door and handed her the card.

"Or something," Michael said, brushing her hair from her face.

She should have seen it coming, but she didn't. His fingers sank into her nape, gently pulling her closer to him. She should have been afraid, but the chills racing down her spine were born of anticipation, not fear.

"Michael…"

"You talk too much," he said, claiming her lips with his.

If M.J. had been kissed a lot in her lifetime, she would have said Michael's was an incredible kiss. But the truth was that, again, he was right. She'd always talked too much.

She did it purposefully to keep men at a distance. She

felt comfortable without a man in her life. She'd never really had one since her father left. It was best that way.

But now, Michael's lips told her of a new perspective she could have on life—if she wanted it.

He was commanding, forceful and bent on possession. His lips were full and hot, and they thrilled her like nothing she'd ever experienced. She had the sensation of going over the edge of a waterfall. She heard rushing sounds that nearly drowned out everything around her. She realized it was not water she heard, but her own blood pounding through her veins.

His arm tightened around her back and pulled her body closer to him. Next to him. Crushing her breasts into his chest. She could feel his heart as it slammed against his rib cage and was shocked that he was responding to her as much as she was to him.

She felt as if her muscles had lost all control. Her fingers went limp, and she dropped her purse to the floor. Putting her arms around his neck, she held him prisoner, as he was holding her.

His hand caressed the small of her back, then moved around to her rib cage. Then he moved his hand upward, closer and closer to her breast.

His tongue parted her lips, seeking the interior of her mouth. She felt as if lightning bolts were shooting through her body straight to the deepest core of her. She leaned her breast into his hand and felt his fingers sink into her flesh.

Never had anything felt so divine, so incredibly adventurous.

Your destiny has brought you to Ecuador, she heard Martita's wisdom-filled voice say.

Destiny.

Fate.

"Michael," she breathed through parted lips swollen from his siege. "I should go in...."

He pulled her closer, ignoring her words. His tongue plunged inside her, exploding yet another series of electric shocks. Every atom in her body craved more touching, more probing. More Michael.

Your destiny.

Words filled her brain just as sensations filled her body. She didn't know which to heed. She wanted it all.

"Michael..."

"I know," he said, panting like a caged animal. He kissed her bottom lip, pulling seductively on it. He held her face in his hands, holding her captive for yet another rapacious kiss. "I don't want to go," he said, making no move away from her.

"We shouldn't...."

"I shouldn't...." he said, and kissed her cheeks. "But I'm gonna."

"Michael." She opened her eyes.

"Leave, I mean," he said opening his own.

She was stunned at the desire she saw. He was smoky with it. It enveloped him like a powerful spell. It was as if they were bound together by it, transported to another world where they were the only inhabitants.

He was mesmerizing, intoxicating.

He was everything a knight in shining armor should be, and more, she thought. He had been foretold.

He smiled just then, as if reading her thoughts. It was the sweetest, most endearing smile she'd ever seen, and she knew she'd never forget it.

He drew her head down just enough to place a soul-felt kiss on her forehead. "I'll wake you in the morning," he said. "Sleep well, little girl."

Then he stepped back and gently pressed her shoulders toward the open doorway. "Take note," he said. "I'm not backing off. I'm not that stupid. I'm saving you."

"From what?"

"Why, from me."

"Oh," she said, grabbing the doorknob for support for her watery-feeling legs. She wasn't quite sure what had come over her. She was certain she hadn't wanted it to end, but somehow, Michael had had enough strength for the both of them.

She started to close the door, then stopped. "Michael?"

"Yes," he said, turning to face her.

"Are there any corporate rules about us? I mean, about what we are doing? Er, were about to do? Fraternizing, I mean."

"Yeah." He smiled wickedly. "It's off-limits." Then he winked at her.

"That's what I thought," she said and closed the door, knowing that for an adventurer like Michael Hunter her off-limits status only made her more enticing.

5

The dream began innocently. Michael was kissing her, and she was kissing him back. She remembered every exquisite touch, the taste of him, the smell of him and the pressure of his body against hers.

She remembered the sound of his voice, the brush of his breath against her neck and the way he pushed the hair from her face. She remembered his strength and his gallantry.

M.J. had wanted Michael in every way. She'd wanted to feel his bare flesh stretched alongside hers, had wanted to watch that smoky glimmer in his eyes turn to fire as they explored each other in intimate fashion.

M.J. had little experience with men because she set her sights so high. She refused to settle for anyone less than her one true love—her soul mate. She'd dated in high school and college, and experienced one serious though doomed love affair. After that she purposefully kept herself from committing to anything more than dinner. She found a lack of perfection in the men who asked her out. They weren't Mr. Right. They weren't *him*. She told herself that *he* was out there, somewhere, waiting for her. She knew she was buying into the Cinderella complex but she didn't care.

She was safe in her illusion.

She would risk her life for adventure, but she would never risk her heart. It was too dangerous.

Michael, on the other hand, was clearly experienced,

and her brain was on overload just thinking about the things he surely knew all the particulars about when it came to sex. Every cell in his body shouted it to her. Loudly. But was he the one?

As drawn as she was to him physically, she just wasn't sure.

Remembering his kiss, the tender yet confident way he pulled her into him told her that he would be gentle with her. He would not diminish her but rather show her the way.

In the dream, she allowed him to take the lead. He gave her time to explore her physical reactions.

"I want you to know everything I do to you," he said. "I want to please you, because pleasing you makes it all more exciting for me. I want to watch your every response to me. I want to make certain I am everything you've ever dreamed about."

"But you are, Michael. You are my dream."

He was kissing her again, and like flint against stone, sparks ignited inside her. It felt like the undertow in the ocean, pulling her into the sensation. Forcing her not to think, only to feel.

His lips clamped possessively on hers. She felt as if she were sinking into herself, into him. The pleasure was so divine.

His breath came in sharp, twisting pants as if he wanted to break away from her before they bonded, before the seal was permanent.

But he was as much a captive as she.

Humans could not create this kind of beauty, she thought. Only angels knew to sing this song, feel this much love.

His tongue melded with hers.

She placed her hands on either side of his face, wanting to memorize the movements of his jaw and lips as he brought her across the threshold of heaven.

He moved his head lower to nuzzle the column of her neck.

He flew her to the moon.

Soaring through the cosmos, she knew she'd never live on earth again. She would ride the stars with Michael.

"Oh, Michael, are you my destiny?"

Shadows passed over the silver full moon, contorting its landscape, making it look as if, indeed, there was such a thing as the man in the moon.

No, not a man in the moon, she realized. A woman.

Martita.

She looked more like a Gypsy than an aristocratic Spaniard. Her eyes were slanted, almond-shaped, and her hair was wrapped in a gold turban. She wore huge golden hoop earrings, and her mouth was much smaller, her cheekbones so high and sharp they looked as if she would slit her skin if she were to touch them. Martita wore a huge robelike garment that hid her hands from sight.

"My child," she said with a voice that sounded half like bells ringing and half like a computerization. "You may think this is a dream, but it is not. I have come to you in your sleep in order to let you know that you will always be protected. Your destiny is at hand. Look and you shall find it."

Martita disappeared.

Michael remained.

At the point where she thought she could not live through another second of pleasure, he gazed into her eyes.

In the dream his face became the moon, and then it mutated with shadows. Black ones. Red ones. She could not see him as clearly as before.

Suddenly, she realized she was sinking. No, not sinking, but falling away from him. She had committed to his kiss and it had ended just as she'd thought—in disaster.

She'd been wrong to trust.

Now she was going to die. Die for falling in love.

"Michael!" she screamed. "Save me!"

"Give me your hand," he called.

She reached toward him, but grasped only a handful of air. She was filled with terror. Gone was heaven. "Michael!"

"I'm here."

"Michael, I can't find you." Frantically, she grasped at the air around her, searching for him who had brought her this high. Who had touched her soul.

She clutched at nothing.

"Michael!" she screamed, and woke up.

Sheets formed a pink cocoon around her legs, and her arms were spread across the pillows. She was struck by the notion that she looked like a butterfly emerging from its past life as a caterpillar.

Her body was still on fire, still pitched to ultra sensitivity. If she hadn't known better she would have thought Michael actually had been here kissing her.

A bead of perspiration trickled down her temple as she looked at the lonely, empty space beside her in the king-size bed.

Michael had not come to her. No one had.

It was only a dream.

6

Before dawn M.J. and Michael were on a private plane headed to Lago Agrio. Reflections on her dream and its meaning were scrapped in order to pack, dress and slug down half a cup of coffee in her room. Though there was only a three-hour time difference between San Francisco and Quito, M.J. was feeling every minute of the jet lag.

Yawning, she dug in her bag for her ginseng capsules. "I could kill for more coffee," she said, half to herself and partly to Michael, who was going over a thick stack of projections and letters from Travis he'd intended to read earlier but hadn't.

"No problem. It's only a thirty-minute flight," he replied offhandedly. Then he glanced at her. "How can you justify caffeine and all those herbs you take? Obviously you are not a purist."

She shook her head, pulled out a huge bottle of vitamin B_{12}, one thousand milligrams each, and tossed two into her mouth. She swallowed them without water. "That would be too boring. Life is to be enjoyed."

His smile was infuriatingly sensual as he leaned across the narrow aisle between them. He touched her hand. "I like that you can be corrupted."

With lightning speed he placed a kiss on her cheek before she could protest, then went back to his paperwork.

"Michael, I think we should talk about—"

He held up his hand to stop her. "No, we shouldn't."

"You don't know what I was going to say."

"I have a good idea. You think we shouldn't get involved. No hanky-panky, no sex. No flings. No assignations. That I shouldn't look at you the way I do or even the way I intend to. That I should be a good little boy and keep my hands to myself."

She gaped at him. His eyes were intractable. "I came here for a job."

His hand darted to hers and held her tightly. "No, you came here for adventure. You said so yourself."

His eyes bore into hers. He was throwing the truth at her, and she didn't like it. She would have liked to shift the blame for last night's impetuosity on him. But the truth was that she'd wanted him as much as he did her. Neither of them had been fully prepared for the intensity of their attraction. M.J. wished she could shove those feelings down some internal elevator shaft and seal them away.

Unfortunately, just looking at Michael was enough to make her feel as if the top of her head was going to blow off.

He rubbed the edge of her hand with his thumb, creating a slow burn in her belly.

She squirmed in her seat.

Michael was so pleased with her reaction, he preened. "Adventure involves risk, M.J. I'll bet you've never risked a thing in your life."

"Sure, I have!" she replied indignantly.

"Name one thing."

She thought of the school trip to the Grand Canyon when she was ten that she didn't take because she was afraid to leave her mother. Of the bus ticket to Los Angeles when she was eighteen to try her wings at being an actress that she never used. Of Sam Watkins, the boy she nearly fell in love with when she was a freshman at Stanford, but whom she dumped because she was afraid of commitment. She thought of the million and one tiny chances she encountered every day that would involve her in someone else's life that she never took, all because she was afraid of losing.

Of losing herself to another. Of losing her heart. Of them losing their love for her.

"I might lose my job if Travis Kincaid disapproves."

"Your job?" He peered at her.

"Yeah." She smiled wanly, hoping he would understand.

He dropped her hand as if it were red hot. "Sorry, I thought last night meant something to you."

M.J. was stunned. "Are you saying it meant something more than a kiss to you?" Visions of her dream came back to her. She found it odd how real those scenes were, and she had a difficult time discerning between reality and fantasy. M.J. had never been more confused in her life.

Michael pressed his lips together as if considering his choice of words. "You know it was."

"I don't," she heard herself say. She pressed her fingers to her temple. This isn't happening. He's not saying these things to me. A man, a living myth among men, does not say to M.J. Callahan that he has found Mecca in her lips.

Her face was serious when she said, "I've always had difficulty with altitude."

"Got an excuse for everything, don't you, M.J.?"

"What I meant was…"

"You want me to tell you that I'm falling in love with you."

The words blasted her like a tornado. Had she not been seated, she would have lost her balance. How did he do that? Throw her left curve after right. And how dare he search her face with those blue lasers of his, peeling away her facades like thin onion skins? Who did he think he was, anyway?

"I don't need to hear anything of the kind."

"Sure you do. All women do."

She shook her finger at him. "Do not ever categorize me with the rest of my gender. I'm not like them."

"You're implying there is something wrong with women. I never said anything of the kind. But I find this fascinating that you think you are different. Better, perhaps?"

"No, just different."

"You don't want to be needed?" he asked.

She winced under his penetrating gaze. Feeling a sprinkle of nervous perspiration rimming her scalp, she broke his spell by looking out the window. She took a deep breath. "Where'd you learn this tactic—the CIA?"

He chuckled in spite of himself. "You're something, M.J. Callahan. I've never met anyone, man or woman, quite as intriguing."

"Really." She sniffed, glad to feel the heat under her fade.

"Fascinating."

"You're just saying that because I didn't sleep with you."

His smile was wickedly impish as he tugged on the brim of his Panama hat. "Okay. Have it your way." He crossed his arms, settling more comfortably in his seat. He closed his eyes. "Don't tell me you didn't dream about me last night."

"What?" *How could he know?*

"Admit it. You dreamed about me." Desire was in his voice. "You thought about how our lips felt pressed to each other. The taste of my tongue. My hand on your breast. You wanted more, didn't you, M.J.? You wanted to know what I look like naked. You wanted to know if I wanted to be inside you."

M.J. felt her body growing hot, coming alive just listening to him.

He opened one eye, shot her an incredibly seductive look and said, "You bet I do."

"Michael, we don't know each other, and I'm not in the habit of jumping into bed with every man I meet."

"I don't think that of you. On the contrary. But I believe there is something between us. Something mystical."

"Mystical?"

"Magical, then," he said earnestly. "I feel it. And I don't feel things like this. I'm a man of action, M.J. When I feel something is right, I say it. Do it. No looking back. I've lived my life by that tenet. And I have no regrets. Can you say the same?"

Her voice was a whisper as she answered truthfully, "No."

"I don't want you to worry, M.J. I understand what you are saying. I understand that you need time. Me, I know that life is a process of running out of time. I don't think like you do. I don't live like you do. You want assurances. Security. All women do. In that you are very much like other women. I'll give you all the time you need. We'll be down here months. Alone. Thrown together day and night. I'll show you that I'm right. There is something between us. I won't deny it. And soon you'll discover that you can't deny it, either."

Michael closed his eyes and placed his hat over his face, blocking the rising sunlight, his signal their conversation was over.

Pretty words, she thought. He sounded sincere as he spoke them. His unwavering eyes reiterated truthfulness.

So, why was she doubtful? Because she'd never had a man speak to her like this? And why was that? Had she ever given anyone a chance? she wondered, reflecting on her history with men.

M.J. had met dozens of men at work. Friends of friends. Claire's stupid blind dates she set up. But they'd all been too mundane, too ordinary for her.

The fact was, too many of them were like her, wanting

excitement in their lives and not knowing how or where to find it.

For far too long, M.J. had dreamed of a knight in shining armor coming to take her, the princess, away with him to his castle. He would be kind, handsome, thoughtful, powerful and wealthy. Perhaps M.J. had never met a man who intrigued her because she'd conjured a vision that didn't exist—except in the movies.

Maybe that was why she'd always wanted to be an actress. That way, she could pretend at life and never have to live it.

Michael Hunter was no apparition. He was real. And he was demanding real emotions, real decisions from her. He wanted her to respond to him not only with her body, but with her heart. He seemed at ease offering his emotions. He didn't care if she ripped out his heart and broke it in pieces. He didn't care if she used him, abused him or loved him. He was up for whatever she would dish out. And what was that?

What kind of man offered himself up like a sacrifice knowing he could be toast by morning?

Was he an idiot? Or just about the most courageous man she'd ever met?

Lord! No wonder the man was a legend. From the magazine articles she'd read about him, Michael Hunter had faced charging lions, killed alligators and strangled snakes. Taking on an inexperienced geologist who'd never been out of California must be child's play for him.

She could only wonder at the exotic women he'd known.

No, Michael Hunter was no idiot. She was the one who was a fool. Surely this was some kind of game he'd played often. She was just the next one up for grabs. Another notch on the gun belt.

She'd been right to keep him at arm's length. Or even

farther, if she could manage it. Who could believe a man like him? He was outrageous.

Common sense told her that he would use their months together in the jungle to bond with her, get her to fall in love with him and then, when the assignment was over, he would be off to the next adventure.

And M.J. would only be a part of the story that constituted the legend of Michael Hunter.

Steeling her resolve, M.J. promised herself she would not give in to Michael. She would assess their encounters. She would keep their relationship as close to business as possible. She would do everything in her power to return to California with her integrity intact.

As far as she could tell, she only had one tiny problem—keeping Michael Hunter out of her dreams.

7

―――▶ ◀―――

Base camp was situated just outside the town of Lago Agrio because Travis Kincaid was paranoid other oil companies, spies for European oil interests and bribed locals would sabotage his project.

He was right.

Not since the early 1930s had competition for South American oil fields been as intense as it was in the last days of the twentieth century. Venezuela had contracted most of their fields to large companies, as had Peru and Brazil. Only Ecuador entertained bids from small independent foreign companies.

By all measures, Travis Kincaid was considered by his peers to be a brilliant man. And incredibly savvy about foreign countries. Of the one hundred twenty-seven countries in the world, at his last count Travis had been to ninety-four. Still on his list to conquer for either financial or personal enrichment purposes were three in Africa, all in a state of violent conflict and therefore unappealing; two newly formed nations in what was formerly the USSR; a smattering of places either too close to one of the poles or located in Southeast Asia, which a military tour to Vietnam during the war in 1969 cured him of any desire to see more. He'd been to the Himalayas, and that was enough.

That he found himself, his circumstances and his only financial window of opportunity in the Amazon jungle at this juncture in his life was to him a twisted karmic joke.

He despised heat, jungles, poisonous snakes and, at the age of forty-eight, inconveniences of just about any kind.

His life for the past decade—since the oil crash of the late 1980s, which had bankrupted his company and his explosive, disastrous divorce that followed—had become a string of inconveniences enough to test even Job. But he'd hung in there.

He'd had no other choice.

Travis Kincaid was a survivor. He was a genius geologist, and he was legendary among petroleum companies around the globe. There were others who thought they were maverick entrepreneurs in the oil business.

But Travis wasn't in the oil business. It was in him.

He never had figured out when it was that he decided he wanted to be a geologist, needing to plumb the depths of the earth in search of crude.

But he did know it was in his genes.

His great-great grandfather Daniel had been a down-and-out immigrant Irish miner. A wastrel. He'd wandered the American west and half of Mexico searching for gold. He claimed that leprechauns were responsible for keeping the pot of gold at the end of the rainbow perpetually just out of his reach.

Travis's grandfather and namesake, Travis Daniel Kincaid, was fifteen when Daniel died, leaving him a small patch of land in northern California not far from San Francisco. This same patch of land covered one of the largest gold mines in California history. The family got rich and spent it rather than investing. The following generation of Kincaids found oil on that same Kincaid land.

Travis grew up in the 1950s listening to family lore about the gold they'd once owned and the oil company they had founded and sold to Standard Oil of California.

There was enough money to send Travis to Boston College, then later to Harvard for a post-grad degree, and finally to set him up in business in Houston in the late seventies—just in time for the oil industry to go bust in the 1980s.

When Travis lost his money, he lost his elegant, free-spending wife, Blane. After years of reflection and self-analysis, Travis was convinced he'd subconsciously set himself up to lose his fortune, which in turn caused Blane to leave him. She was the kind of woman who *had* to have money more than love, companionship or Travis. Blane stripped the seven-million-dollar house down to the switch plates and drapery rods, and hired the most expensive, ruthless divorce attorney in Texas.

She made Travis pay for his sin of canceling her credit cards and not providing for her future in the manner to which she'd become accustomed.

She bankrupted what was left of his assets after his company folded.

Travis scrambled for years, groveling for every dime he could lay his hands on. He suffered local jokes about his divorce. He formed alliances with men he wouldn't have broken bread with a decade earlier in order to earn a living. Stripped of ego, he learned humility.

He learned he was not as smart as he'd thought. His belief in love, loyalty and soul mates didn't make it so. He'd made a big mistake thinking Blane was his partner, his equal.

She'd told him when they were dating that she wanted a house and children, wanted them to be a family. But she'd lied. She said she'd follow him anywhere, but she feared flying. She had pretended to like camping, fishing, hiking and the great outdoors he communed with so easily. Once they were married, she never walked on grass unless it was clipped and mowed by the gardeners.

Blane was happiest when left alone in Houston with a stack of credit cards for companionship. True, she never complained about his extensive traveling. She was faithful to him. As far as Travis could tell, there was no time for a lover in Blane's shopping schedule.

When his money disappeared, so did his usefulness to her.

Travis put aside dreams of having a family, someone to love who would love him back. He told himself the woman's voice that haunted him during sleepless and incredibly lonely nights was a sexual fantasy. He'd never been able to focus on a face, not even a hair color. Even though there were times he believed she was seeking him as much as he was searching for her, she never showed up. No angel of mercy had appeared in his life. No princess called for him to save her. No women crossed his path. He realized women were all the same. Not that there was anything wrong with that. In the end, he supposed they had the right to seek out a man who could provide for them.

Unfortunately, Travis could barely provide for himself, and over the years his fantasies of a dream girl attenuated into the past like ghosts.

Then he had an awakening.

No matter what else he tried to do to make a new life for himself, he was a seeker of fortunes, and oil was in his soul. He swore he heard his grandfather's and father's voices in the middle of the night urging him to distant lands. Pressing him to try once again, just one more time. This time he would make it.

Often he thought he was insane. That he had lost his mind in the wake of his financial ruin. He sold his Rolex, his cars and even his wool overcoat in order to book air tickets to London, to Vienna, to Riyadh looking for investors.

At night he prayed on his knees for guidance and by day he followed his nose. It led him to Ecuador.

Like a fool, he listened to the legends about the mysterious Oriente. He hung out with locals in bars, in hotel lobbies, inquiring in his broken Spanish about the truth in the rain forest. Were the oil reserves as large or even larger than those in Venezuela? In the Middle East? Travis had read that the 1942 invasion of Ecuador by Peru which resulted in Ecuador signing away over two-fifths of its territory to its southern enemy, had been instigated by a rivalry between foreign oil companies wanting concessions in the Oriente.

In 1949, to staunch these rumors, President Galo Plaza shocked even his own countrymen by claiming, "The Oriente is a myth." There was no oil in Ecuador, never had been.

Travis remembered those tales of ancient lore and the lost city of gold, El Dorado, which the conquistadores had come to find four hundred years ago. The city was still to be discovered. Instead, the Spaniards found oil. It oozed through the surface of the ground. It squished under their boots when they walked across the Oriente. They watched natives evaporate the oil and use it for torches, medicines, waterproofing clothing and weapons. Finally, the Spanish anchored their great ships at the Santa Elena Peninsula, where the natives caulked their leaks and tarred the exteriors of their boats.

These stories were not legend. They were historical facts chronicled by ship captains for centuries.

Ecuadorians had been sitting on fortunes even then, but they'd always kept their discoveries a secret.

No one on the outside ever really learned the truth.

Not even in 1999.

Travis needed more than luck or a break; he needed a miracle. He'd invested everything he had in this project. He'd tried not to listen to his instincts, which somehow always led him to Ecuador. He struggled with a board who told him he would capsize his precariously funded fledgling company if he continued on his foolhardy path.

They told him he needed more help, expert help.

Jim Sloan, the CFO of Texan Oil Company, Travis's corporate right arm, hit Travis between the eyes when he said, "We think you should try to get Michael Hunter. He's been everywhere in the Amazon. He knows that basin like the back of his hand. With his knowledge he could cut months off exploration time. He's up on all the 3-D seismic technology."

Travis had bristled. "I can handle it."

"You've been the maverick long enough. There's too much work. And we need to move fast."

"Someone else, then," Travis countered.

"What's the matter with you, Travis? You and Hunter got some kind of bad blood between you that I don't know about?"

Nailing targets was Travis's arena, not Jim's. "Bad blood. Why, no."

"Good, because it's unanimous with the board. We want him and we've already sent him a fax in Tunis."

"He's in Africa?"

Jim shoved his hands in his pockets. "Yeah, he's sniffing around Algeria like I thought we should have been doing."

Travis shook off the derision he felt Jim was only too willing to layer on top of the I-told-you-so's. His smile was pinched when he replied, "Why don't you go ahead and say it? You've all been nervous as whores in church now that I've spent two years and a million bucks in Ecuador with no results. But I've finally secured the government concession."

"Yeah, but our lack of funds is just about equal to our lack of patience, Travis. It's our money. We want Hunter."

"Fine with me," Travis grumbled as he relented.

Michael Hunter proved expensive, wanting a third of the profits. They bargained down to a quarter. Michael's reputation as a crack geologist cum adventurer surpassed Travis's notoriety. Besides, Michael had no blight on his record, no failures. He was golden...at least to the investors.

The banks and investors weren't interested in the bad blood between Travis and Michael. But Travis remembered every detail all too well.

In 1991, still very much down on his luck from the oil bust of the eighties, Travis had pasted together a motley group of out-of-work geologists and middle managers, all victims of large corporate downsizing. They were broke but dedicated. They believed in Travis, believed he could make something happen.

But they were shorthanded. They needed Travis to continue to drum up loans, sell royalties, sell the company stock. He was too valuable to spend time exploring. The buzz back then was about the vast amount of oil in Maracaibo Lake, Venezuela. The latest geological surveys had shown that there were more oil reservoirs in Venezuela than anywhere else in the world, including Saudi Arabia. And it wasn't being tapped.

Travis had heard from an old friend of his who still worked at Shell Oil that Michael Hunter, Shell's best geologist, had up and quit. Hunter was bored. He wanted excitement.

Travis couldn't believe it.

He didn't care, because at that fateful moment, Hunter was just what Travis needed.

Travis offered Hunter the job of going to Venezuela. It was one of the biggest mistakes of his life.

Less than a year later his little company folded, and everyone was out job-searching again.

Travis had plunged into the study of the new 3-D seismic technology. He had to find a new method of exploration, one that was surefire. One that couldn't possibly miss.

The next time, Travis had to hit oil.

Two years later, in 1993, Travis learned that Michael Hunter had been part of a small oil exploration group out of California who joint-ventured with the Venezuelan government and succeeded in pumping a great deal of oil out of Maracaibo Lake.

Travis felt betrayed.

Ethically, Hunter had every right to seek other business partners. Travis knew his offer was small at best. In fact, after paying the debt service, it would have taken Hunter three years to reap the first dime.

But Travis's heart had been in that little company. He'd wanted success so desperately then. He'd needed assurances from…God, the cosmos, anywhere. His self-confidence had been lower than dirt at the time.

To this day, he still felt that kick in the teeth from Michael Hunter.

This time around, Travis was better funded, better prepared technologically. He thought he'd buried the hatchet between himself and Hunter at least halfway into the ground until the day he sat face-to-face with Michael Hunter in his office four months ago.

"Travis, your company appears to need my services. Your board and I have come to an agreement about the terms and conditions of my contract. I can't wait to get back down to Ecuador again. It's been two years since I've been in the Oriente." He leaned back in the leather wing chair, observing Travis's pinched expression with sharp eyes. "But you look as if you've just swallowed battery acid. If you've changed your mind, just say so."

Travis was out of his chair in a flash. His back to Michael, he stared out the window of the fifteenth-story office and angrily shoved his fists in his pockets. He shot Michael a glacial look as he faced him.

"Damn it, Michael, I'm just trying to figure out how long it will take you to fuck me this time."

"What the hell are you talking about?"

"Maracaibo Lake."

Michael stared at him, dumbfounded. "What about it?"

"I sent you there, and you made a deal behind my back on my time and my money!"

"Bullshit!" Michael bolted to his feet and slammed his fists on Travis's desk. Paper clips were elevated like Mexican jumping beans. "You had no business sending me there! You lied to me, you son of a bitch! I go down there and shoot my mouth off conning the officials, making them think your company hung the moon. I assured them that your financing was in place and then, when I get the whole damn thing together and they're ready to sign on the dotted line, you blink!" He pounded the desk again.

"I wasn't prepared to drill the whole damn country!"

"I told you from day one that these guys think big. Real big. Goddamn it, Travis, you left me out on a limb with egg on my face. I blew every connection I had there!"

"Bullshit! You turned around and contracted with Caloil."

"You bet your ass I did. But I worked behind the scenes, like a general in a war room. None of my Venezuelan contacts knew it was me they were dealing with. If they had, all bets would have been off," he said, slumping in the chair, his anger dissipating. "You have no idea how it killed me not be part of the…"

"The kill?"

Michael's eyes met Travis's. "Yes."

Expelling a sigh, Travis said, "I know what you mean." Slowly a smile crept onto his face.

Michael forced a half smile and extended his hand. "Guess we've been given a second chance."

Tentatively, Travis took his hand. "Looks like it."

"So, Travis. Can I trust you out there? You won't blink this time?"

"If I do, I'm dead."

* * *

It had been hard for Travis to admit he'd been in the wrong. Harder still was putting all his faith in Michael Hunter.

It was distrust that had brought him to hire M.J. Callahan.

Looking at the fax in his hand from Albert Pinchon in Houston, Travis was glad that M.J. Callahan, whose expertise in 3-D technology had put Stewart Energy on the map, was at least more reasonably priced.

Travis read the short description about Callahan and marveled that someone so young had risen the ladder so quickly.

"The guy must be a wizard," he said to himself, checking his watch.

It was almost six-thirty. The plane from Quito would be landing any second.

He reached to the old Formica-topped folding table behind him and switched on the gas camping stove under the pot of coffee he'd prepared.

Travis had become addicted to the smooth-tasting coffee he'd found in Ecuador. During the last stress-filled month he'd needed the coffee more than ever to help keep him awake during the long nights he was finishing his work so that when Michael Hunter and M.J. Callahan did arrive, they would not waste a single minute of time.

According to Travis's geological calculations, the oil fields in the Ecuadorian Oriente were at a crisis point, or "sizzle point," when the oil turns to gas and evaporates. The fields were about to implode. It was a rare geological phenomenon, but he'd heard of it happening. The oil reserves were so massive and the layers of rock and shale so volatile that the oil was in danger of sinking so deep into the middle of the earth that no amount of drilling would ever suck it out.

The oil would be lost to him and to Ecuador forever.

He wasn't sure if even a miracle could help him.

There was no question in his mind. Travis had run out of time...and money.

The weather change from Quito's cool mountain air to the steamy, sultry jungle was a huge shock for M.J. Sweat slicked down her back as she manuevered her luggage out of the cargo hold. "Is it always this warm?" she asked, not realizing Michael was watching her.

"It's not even seven o'clock yet, M.J. This is the coolest part of the day," he said condescendingly.

"I knew that," she snapped.

"Yeah, I thought so." He smiled, letting her struggle with her bags.

M.J. was a bit put out that neither the pilot nor Michael was helping her with her bags. Granted, Michael had his hands full carting all his computer equipment, but it seemed to her that he could have at least offered.

"Gustavo!" Michael shouted to an Ecuadorian man getting out of a Jeep Cherokee.

"Mr. Hunter! How nice to see you, sir," Gustavo replied, rushing up to Michael and taking his computer bag. "How was your trip?"

"Fine. Uneventful."

M.J. frowned. Uneventful. That's not what he'd been saying only moments ago to her.

"Have you met Mr. Kincaid yet?" Michael asked the driver.

"Yes, sir. He is a very curious man."

"How is that?" Michael asked.

Gustavo laughed. "He asks many questions about you, sir."

Michael laughed, too, as he tossed his bags and backpack into the rear of the Cherokee. Then he turned as if he suddenly remembered M.J. was with him. "Gustavo, this is Ms. Callahan. She will be accompanying me."

"Into the Oriente, sir?" Gustavo lifted his eyebrows, though he tried not to register surprise in his voice. He had been trained by Michael over many trips to Ecuador not to question or react to things he heard.

"Yes." Michael leaned closer. "She is not my girlfriend. She is working with me."

"Yes, sir," Gustavo said, and rushed toward M.J., taking her computer bag from her shoulder.

"Thank you very much. It's nice to meet you, Gustavo."

"Yes, missus." Gustavo hurried about his business.

M.J. climbed into the back seat of the Jeep. Michael had already taken the front passenger seat. She was struck with the notion that Michael was playing the role of the Great White Hunter. She wasn't certain if his behavior was due to her dismissive attitude toward his romantic suggestions or if this was normal for him.

One thing was for certain, time would answer her question.

"Is it far to the camp?" M.J. asked.

"Just the other side of town," Michael said as the Jeep wheels churned the mud on the unpaved streets of the town.

The marketplace was thronged with shoppers. M.J. thought there were more patrons going in and out of the four banks she saw than on the Friday afternoon drive-thrus in San Francisco. Natives, Americans and Europeans wore high rubber boots to protect their clothes and feet from the soggy dark mud.

"So much for my new espadrilles," she mumbled.

"You like Nueva Loja, missus?" Gustavo asked, looking at her in the rearview mirror.

"I'm sorry, I've only been to Quito," she answered.

"Nuevo Loja is the official name for this town," Michael explained. "It was changed to Lago Agrio, which means Sour Lake, by some Texaco oilmen about twenty, twenty-five years ago. It reminded them of their hometown by the same name. The new name stuck. Most of the natives call it Lago Agrio now."

"Not all, sir." Gustavo smiled and pushed his wire-rimmed glasses up at the corner brace, which caused them to sit cattywampus on his face.

"That's my man!" Michael laughed good-naturedly as they hit a particularly deep rut that jostled Michael and sent M.J. to the floorboards. "Buckle up, girl. This isn't Kansas."

M.J. pretended not to hear him and looked out the window at the cement-block houses with worn wood shutters. "This must be a very old town."

"No, it is new," Gustavo said.

Michael nodded. "This kind of intense heat and humidity will rot just about anything in six months. That particular *edificio* you're looking at is not quite a year old."

"But it's decaying!"

"Precisely." Michael smirked. "Makes you wonder what kinds of incredible artistry have been lost to rot and weather over the last millennium. Hell, the last ten thousand years. Yep, this place just gobbles up things, and people, leaving nothing behind. Not even a memory."

M.J. was struck at the wonder and respect she heard in Michael's voice. She was beginning to realize that if Michael Hunter had ever been in love in his life, it was with this jungle. It and those like it. This intimate detail increased her fascination with him. She couldn't help but wonder what his eyes had seen in his lifetime. What answers to life's mysteries he'd found.

She envied him.

He'd done something with his minutes and hours on earth. Her accomplishments, on the other hand, could be stacked on the end of a gnat's eyelash. She was going to have a difficult time measuring up. She was beginning to feel defeated before she'd even started.

"Don't tell me Travis rented this old slop house!" Michael said.

"Bought it, sir," Gustavo said. "It was a good deal, he said."

"Yeah, they probably paid him to move in," Michael said, getting out of the car and giving M.J. a clear view of her new home.

Home was definitely an exaggeration. The building looked like a half-story warehouse, with tin walls warping at the corners and a tin roof that she could swear was not attached but resting precariously on the base.

There was no glass at the windows, just screen covered in dirty tarp. A screen front door sat ajar, in total symmetry with the rest of the misaligned house. The thing looked as if a giant prehistoric monster had sat on it.

"Well, it must be quite safe here," she ventured, "since there aren't any locks or shutters."

Michael took two strides and loomed over her. His voice resonated warning. "Did you forget so soon? I told you, this is a third-world country. Folks around here have been known to throw a man down and pull the gold out of his teeth with screwdrivers and pliers. There are no damned locks, no infrared security system, no bolts, not even a door, because women aren't supposed to be here. You aren't supposed to be here."

He was scaring the living daylights out of her.

She felt her knees buckle, and she was shaking so much she nearly dropped her heavy luggage. She knew she must have turned white, but thank God the sun was out. Her fair skin would burn in a fraction of a minute, long enough to cover her fear. She wanted to stand up to him, show him she had courage, too. Purpose. Just like him.

Just like Travis Kincaid.

As if he knew she was thinking about him, Travis stepped out of the squashed-looking building.

"Hunter?"

M.J. peered around Michael to see a giant of a man stoop his shoulders and nearly bend at the waist to clear the doorway of the little house. He straightened, and sun glinted off the silver at his temples and the jet of his thick head of hair. His eyes were even more blue than Michael's and so clear they looked streaked with platinum to match his hair. His voice was commanding yet melodic, much like she imagined all charismatic leaders possessed. How else could they mesmerize their flocks?

Upon his emergence, he was quickly surrounded by a dozen or more natives, brown as berries, smiling at him, hands out for coins they obviously were used to receiving. Others awaited instructions.

He looked like Gulliver among the Lilliputians, and she wondered if he would think her one of the little people.

"Where's Callahan?" Travis asked, his eyes ricocheting off M.J. and back to Michael.

"I don't know how to tell you this, Travis, but..."

M.J. swallowed hard. She could see it in Travis Kincaid's eyes. The ax. Pink slip. Adios.

This was going to be tougher than she'd thought. Her only hope of staying was a strong offense. "I'm M.J. Callahan, sir." She stepped around Michael with her hand extended toward Travis. "I understand from Mr. Hunter that you don't allow women in the jungle, sir. Frankly, now that I look around, I can't quite blame you. It would be a real challenge being responsible for a woman's safety in a dangerous outpost like this."

She didn't so much as let him draw a breath before continuing. "Let me put your mind at rest. You aren't responsible for me. Neither is Mr. Hunter. I came here to do a job, sir, and that's what I intend to do. I was told by Mr.

Pinchon that you have a transcript of my résumé. That tells me that you were all for hiring me as long as you thought I was a man. I can take care of myself, sir. Always have. And I don't intend to stop now."

Silence.

"The way I see it, let's just barrel on through, get this job done and hit that well." She smiled broadly, making certain her feet were securely planted on the ground.

Travis shoved his hands in his pockets to avoid shaking hers. "Cute." He looked at Michael. "Now take her back to Quito."

"That's what I thought you'd say," Michael said. "I told her no way would Travis Kincaid ever allow a woman into his jungle. No matter how pressed he was."

Travis's frown was like the gathering of a storm. His dark brows rumbled together, and furrows streaked his forehead. His mouth curved down, and his full lips parted, ready to blast her again.

M.J. boldly took a second step toward Travis. She wasn't backing down. "I won't go, sir. And you can't make me." She started digging in her tote.

"The hell you say. It's my company."

She pulled out a stapled set of papers. "This is my signed contract, sir. Says here I have a job with you for a minimum of six months and as long as eighteen months if that is what is required by this project. Says here you have to pay me regardless. I've read a great deal about you, sir."

Her eyes were steady as she matched his glare.

"Go on," he replied dryly.

"*Time* says you're one of the last of the mavericks. It said you take all kinds of risks with other people's money. *Fortune* said you've run out of supporters. That this is your last stronghold. It's make or break time."

"What's your point?"

"You need me, sir. I'm well trained, competent and

even have a few risk-taker bones in my blood. But the real reason you won't send me away is simple."

"And that is?" His face was as hard as granite.

"You don't have time to replace me."

He snorted, glanced to the distance at the dark clouds. He raked his hair. "I'll have Pinchon's hide for this flagrant act of…of insubordination," Travis growled.

His cheeks burned a crimson color definitely not from overexposure to the sun. She started to hand him her sunblock then thought better of it. "It's not his fault, sir. He's never met me. I was hired by e-mail."

"He never met…" Travis rolled his eyes.

Michael moved closer to Travis. "She has no prior field experience, Travis, and as your partner, I cast my vote for sending her back."

"Traitor!" M.J. snarled at Michael, throwing her hands in the air. "How can you side with him? You lied to me, making me think you wanted me here with you, working side by side."

"I never said that, Travis," Michael replied with the narrowed eyes of a conspirator.

"You most certainly did," she countered.

Michael leaned toward her and in a whisper said, "I wanted you, yes. But not working with me. I've made no bones about the fact that you shouldn't be here."

Travis watched them sparring with an implacable, immovable expression on his face.

"I say can her," Michael said. "How much could it cost, anyway?"

"Too much," Travis said finally.

The sun came out from behind a cloud.

"She stays."

M.J. gasped and brought both fists to her sides. "Yes!"

Michael shook his head as Travis crowded his six-foot-two-inch frame through the doorway of the ramshackle tin hut. He took off his Panama hat, scratched his head and smiled at M.J. "When I'm right, I'm right. This *is* gonna be one nutty trip."

8

"You don't honestly expect me to sleep here, do you?" M.J. asked Michael as he hoisted her bag onto the mold-covered canvas folding cot. The legs were splintered, and several screws were missing. The cot sagged under the weight of her bag, then the canvas ripped ever so slowly, promising disaster.

"Look, you've caused enough grief, don't let your little victory go to your head."

"Little? It was major, and you know it. I triumphed. Vanquished the enemy. David met Goliath, and the rest is history," she said proudly, her eyes gleaming with the excited rush she felt.

"God, you have a lot to learn."

"Fine," she replied, still miffed at Michael. "I don't know what kind of game you're playing, Mr. Hunter, but I'll remember this defection of yours."

He exhaled heavily as if suffering a child.

Which he was, she thought.

He reached behind his back, pulled out an automatic pistol and held it up.

"Yikes!" Her head retreated between her raised shoulders like a turtle's. She stumbled backward into a wooden trestle table piled with geological maps. A coffee cup spilled dregs onto the paper. "Isn't this a little drastic?"

"Not at all," he replied calmly. "Ever see a Glock?"

"Only in the movies."

"Well, you have now. What's more, I'm going to teach you how to use one."

"I think I should tell you, I have a handgun issue I'm dealing with," she started to explain.

He took her arm, his eyes made steely by determination and said, "Not anymore, you don't."

He walked her out a rickety wooden door to a clearing that looked not unlike someone's unlandscaped backyard.

The sky still threatened rain, but she had to squint when the sun came out from behind a cloud. "I need my sunglasses," she said, starting for the door.

"Oh, no, you don't!" He chuckled pointing to the spot where she had stood. "Come back here."

She frowned. "This machismo power play of yours truly is not necessary. I simply wanted to make myself comfortable."

He ignored her. "See that bromeliad in the tree over there?"

"Uh-huh."

He lifted the gun, and with an ease that sent a chill through her bone marrow, he shot swiftly and accurately, blasting the flower off the tree limb.

"That was a perfectly good tropical flower!"

"Here," he said, holding the gun out to her butt first. "Let me see what you can do."

She cringed.

He shook the gun at her impatiently.

M.J. took the gun, which fit surprisingly well into her palm. "It's not as heavy as I'd thought."

"Try aiming. Then slowly squeeze the trigger. Let me see what you can do first."

M.J. raised the pistol, sighted it and fired. She picked off a drooping bromeliad leaf.

Michael gasped, "No way."

She smiled sheepishly. "Beginner's luck."

"Bullshit."

"So, I went to the State Fair. So, I tried my hand at the shooting gallery." She inspected the Glock.

"I know those little duckies were just metal, but still…"

He grabbed the pistol from her. "You little imp," he said, putting his arm around her shoulder and pressing her into his side.

She looked at him. "You look disappointed."

"I am. I was hoping you were the worst shot in the world."

"Why?"

"All those hours, my arms around you, helping you to steady the gun, get your aim precise…"

"I told you I could take care of myself, Michael, and I meant it."

"I'm beginning to see that." His eyes were appreciative and filled with sensuality as he looked at her. He lifted her chin with his index finger. "Since I won't be spending hours teaching you how to shoot, I guess there's nothing left but to cut to the chase," he said, lowering his lips to hers.

"Chases are highly overrated," she replied, opening her mouth to his.

Michael's kiss sent a tide of riveting sensations through her body. She flung her arms around his neck and pulled him closer. She heard him groan deep in his throat as she pressed her breasts into his chest, as if he was surrendering to her against his will.

When he parted her lips with his tongue, her body went limp. She sagged into him, demanding that he support her and be her strength.

He obliged.

His arms were like steel girders, the muscles taut and strong. She couldn't help thinking he was powerful enough to hold up a building. He was everything to her—as beautiful as Adonis and as powerful as Zeus sending thunderbolts straight through her heart to her loins.

She wanted him, and he knew it.

He slanted his mouth over hers, taking and possessing more of her, not asking if she wanted partnership. Michael was the adventurer laying claim to his lost treasure. And M.J. didn't care that she had no say in the matter.

Her body responded to his every breath. The rise and fall of his chest. The beat of his heart. The tensing of his muscles. Lips. Tongue. Arms. Breasts. Thighs.

They were one.

"M.J."

"Yes?"

"M.J. Callahan!"

"Yes?"

"I'm talking to you!" Travis's voice boomed.

The spell was broken.

Michael's lips were no longer ravishing hers. Instead, they were blithely speaking to a furious Travis Kincaid. "What's up, Travis?" Michael asked with an aplomb that disoriented M.J.

How could he descend from paradise to earth with all his faculties intact, especially when she was having a very difficult time simply standing up straight?

She smoothed a thick wave of hair from her face and shielded her eyes from the sun. "You need me, sir?"

Focusing on him, she realized Travis was barely holding his anger in check. "I'd like to speak to you in private, Miss Callahan." Mushrooms of dust exploded like miniature atomic bombs under his stomping feet as he disappeared inside the building.

"You think he's miffed?"

"Pissed, I'd say." Michael frowned. "I'll handle this."

"He doesn't want to talk to you, Michael. He wants to fire me. That much is clear." She shoved her sleeves to her elbows. "I'll be right back."

"Have it your way," he replied, bowing with a generous sweep of his arm toward the back door.

M.J. met Travis in his office, an area divided from the rest of the shanty by a suspended panel of tin.

Looking at the precariousness of the workmanship, she said, "I hope you didn't pay too much for this place."

"How I spend my money, Miss Callahan, is not your business."

"I just meant—"

His face was placid as he chopped the air, cutting her off. "I don't give a damn what you think, quite frankly, Miss Callahan. What I do give a damn about is your fraternization with my business partner. How long have you been sleeping with Michael?"

It was her turn to be incensed. "What makes you think we're lovers?"

"I have eyes," he said turning to the opening in the tin that served as a window. "Is he responsible for getting you hired?"

"God, no! I can explain," she began.

He interrupted her again. "Life is difficult enough in the jungle, not to mention this project, without throwing some sexual scenario into the fracas. This is precisely the reason I have never allowed women out here."

"Really? I thought it was because it was dangerous. Meaning life-threatening."

"That, too. You'll find that out soon enough." He took a step toward her, his anger hitting her like a hot wave from a blast furnace.

She was jolted backward, though she stood her ground.

"You have no clue what I've invested in this project, no idea what this means to me. It appears that this is just a paycheck for you, an experience flirting with the unknown, a trek into the jungle that you can go back and tell your friends in San Francisco about."

"Tiburon," she interrupted with only the slightest inflection of necessary arrogance.

He continued without missing a beat. "This is my *life*, Miss Callahan. Everything I've lived for since I was a kid is wrapped up in this deal. This may sound strange to you, but I know this is my destiny. Opening these new fields would create jobs for so many unemployed here. As far as I'm concerned, the most important benefit, and the one that drives me, is that with the money the government makes from my association with them, new schools can be built. High schools. Colleges. They can bring the internet here and improve communications. All those things are necessary to help wipe out the ignorance that keeps these people from seeking medical help when they need it. From knowing about proper nutrition. Laws. Hell, everything we Americans take for granted." Travis paced the room as he continued. "I've already spoken to the top officials here about the kinds of improvements we could make in the infrastructure. The roads are badly in need of repair. New rail systems would cut the air pollution caused by buses that do not have catalytic converters in half or more.

"Children that live on only a meal every other day will be fed because their parents will have jobs. I don't want to tear anything down in our pursuit. That's why this 3-D technology is so important. We don't waste time or valuable land space drilling where there is no oil or natural gas."

"Gas? You're going after that, too?"

"Do you realize that there is no natural gas line in this country? At home, you turn on your stove, heat water for tea and think nothing of it, don't you?"

"Yes."

"Here every stove, water heater and furnace, when they have one, which isn't often, is fueled by bottled gas from Houston, Texas. It is brought through the Houston

Ship Channel, down the Gulf of Mexico to Guayaquil on the coast, then by truck up the Andes and distributed throughout this country. It is the most primitive and inefficient use of manpower, not to mention the gasoline and diesel fuel being used by the boats, planes and trucks transporting the stuff to the consumer. In one fell swoop, I can change the way this country thinks about their lifestyle and their future."

This man wanted to send a riptide through the future, through history.

"You want to be a shape changer," she said in hushed, reverent tones.

"I want to change the world for the better. Yes. In a very big way."

"I owe you an apology," she said meekly, trying on the emotion for the first time in her life. She was amazed at how well it fit. "I'd read you were a deal maker. You make your millions, sell out and get out. That your scruples were in converse relationship to your bank account."

Travis laughed heartily. "Accurate description of the old Travis Kincaid."

"Old?"

He stopped pacing and looked at her. "The man I used to be before—" He stopped himself.

"Before what?" she asked curiously.

"Never mind," he replied and glanced away, but not before M.J. saw a pang in his expression, a wound so deep in his eyes, she winced and stepped away from him.

She didn't know what had come over her. She'd never felt someone else's pain before. She hugged herself, wondering if she could love it away. But it lingered, reminding her that she'd crossed some uncharted territory. She wasn't certain if she should press on, but she knew she couldn't go back.

M.J. wondered if Travis's reaction had something to do with his divorce. Perhaps he was still in love with his ex-wife. Maybe the rumor she'd heard that he despised women was true. Maybe she'd taken on more than she could handle with this assignment.

Maybe she should do as he suggested and go home.

She chewed her bottom lip pensively.

"He's charming, isn't he?" Travis asked.

"Who?"

"Michael."

She shoved her hands in her pockets. Just thinking about Michael made her tremble with anticipation. "Yes, very. Is that a problem?"

He faced her again and stood very close. He peered at her, and she got the distinct impression that Travis didn't care for her honesty. "Tell me it won't be. Like I said, I have a lot riding on the next weeks."

She inhaled deeply. "It's not a problem, sir."

His silence was as powerful and eloquent as the penetrating gaze he shot her.

He frightened her more than a thunderstorm or even the tornado she'd lived through as a child. And yet there was something about his refusal to waver from his commitment that instilled trust in her.

It was a strange feeling.

She shivered, but she wasn't afraid. Intrigued, yes, but not afraid.

M.J. knew she'd never known anyone like Travis. And probably never would again.

"I'd like to ask you a question, M.J." His voice nearly boomed. He was purposefully trying to intimidate her.

Her mouth was dry when she spoke. "Anything, sir."

A flicker of a smile curved his lips as he accepted her acquiescence. She realized with a jolt how pleasant his aristocratic-looking face could be. Not at all imperious and critical, as she'd thought.

"Why do you insist on calling me sir? It's rather formal, don't you think?"

"I hadn't thought about it, sir," she replied. Without thinking she continued. "It seemed appropriate for a knight…" Embarrassed, she placed her hand over her mouth, her eyes growing wide.

"A knight in shining armor?" he supplied, finishing the phrase for her.

She swallowed hard. She couldn't have said that. Not out loud. Not to her boss.

"I didn't mean…" Get a grip, she told herself. Recover. "Sir, you are the one who hired me. You do have the power to fire me. If I've stepped over the line with, er, Mr. Hunter, I can assure you it won't happen again. I take my work as seriously as you do. I mean, now that I'm here, I will. Er, I intend to, that is."

She straightened her shoulders, her eyes brimming with determination as she said, "My reputation isn't anywhere near yours, of course, but it's the only one I have, and I'm quite proud of what I've accomplished in my career. I'll do a job for you, sir."

His demeanor was stoic. He was all steel, determination and moral purpose when he finally said, "See that you do, Miss Callahan. Unfortunately, I have no choice but to believe you."

"Yes, sir," she said looking fondly toward the door.

"You can go."

M.J. left feeling repentant, fully intending not to do anything to anger Kincaid again. And that included kissing Michael Hunter.

9

——▶◀——

The Uma men felt the presence of their god. His pulse was always recognizable to the faithful. In his brain and soul were the makings of the future.

Their minds fastened on Uma's mind, probing it, seeking their orders, charting their destiny's path.

Gatekeepers cherished their assignment in life. They were loyal to Uma. They lived for him, they sacrificed their individuality for him and they'd proven they would kill for him.

As a unit, they tuned their collective ears, listening for the growing strength of Uma's thoughts. Their god was moving toward them from the west.

Soon the wailing of their people would end. The time of reckoning was at hand. Though plagues had eaten away at the flesh of their people, bringing heartbreak, suffering and excruciating pain to even the smallest babes, the new age had come.

The gatekeepers were the deliverers.

When Uma returned to the rain forest and made his presence known to them, revealed his fall and brought forth his power, the Oriente and all its peoples would be free. Souls would be renewed. Shining, they would light the earth, sending whorls of colorful thoughts to the heavens. There, with the stars and planets of all time, a new world would begin in the heart of the rain forest.

All humanity would realize the gatekeepers had not

failed. They were faithful to their path and to their destiny.

They would prevail.

Uma would prevail.

Looking at one another, no one spoke a word, but their conclusions were unanimous. The eldest Huaorani doused the fire, while the youngest Siona-Secoya gathered the poisoned darts they'd been making and placed them in a fat hollow reed for protection.

They broke camp.

As always, they moved like a voiceless wind toward the west. Toward their maker.

10

Travis Kincaid knew better than to approach Michael about his sexual liaison with M.J. Callahan. To do so would only challenge Michael, who would not hesitate to pick up the gauntlet. Hunter, he knew, prided himself on his prowess with women as much as he did his ability to find oil.

No, he'd made the right choice speaking to M.J. and intimating it would be her loss, her responsibility, if the romance continued. He'd guessed she would curtail her time alone with Michael, and she had.

He watched surreptitiously as M.J. purposefully situated her workstation in the shack's farthest corner, away from Michael's computer and away from Travis.

For three days she went to sleep after Michael and Travis had retired, and she was up, bathed, dressed and at work when they arose. She spoke only when spoken to and displayed none of the headstrong behavior he'd seen upon their initial meeting.

She acted like a dedicated employee, or one in fear of losing her job. Either way, Travis was happy.

He could find no fault with her work. In fact, her speculations were creative and backed up with mountains of information.

"Here are the graphs of the northern-most block of the Sushafendi, sir," M.J. said after compiling results for thirteen hours straight.

Bleary-eyed from staring at her computer screen too

long, she rubbed the bridge of her nose, then stretched her neck, dropping her head slowly from shoulder to shoulder. She took a deep breath before delivering the bad news. "I've gone over this a dozen times, sir, and I can't find my mistake. I'm sorry."

"Mistake?" Michael's head popped up from behind his monitor. "The whiz kid made a mistake?"

He ground his jaw, his eyes piercing M.J.'s accusingly.

She knew he was feeling shunned by her. But she'd had no choice. She peeled her gaze from his.

Travis said nothing, only scrutinized the data she handed him.

"I know you've acquired this area along the edge of the Sushafendi," she said, trailing her pencil along a border-line on the map. "And to be as accurate as possible, I surveyed the totality of this entire field owned by Petroecuador, but I think, no, I *know* I've miscalculated. I just can't figure out where."

Michael's curiosity got to him. He rose and walked over to her.

"Why do you think you've miscalculated?" Travis asked her.

"According to this, the Sushafendi contains over a billion barrels of oil."

"A billion?" Michael whistled.

Travis didn't respond. He didn't blink an eye or flutter an eyelash.

M.J. gaped at him. "You already know this?"

"Yes."

"What?" Michael exclaimed.

Travis looked even more surprised. "Michael, you know this, too."

"I don't," he protested grabbing M.J.'s charts and calculations. "How does she?"

M.J. shrugged her shoulders, palms up. "Beginner's luck?"

"Bullshit," Michael replied, narrowing his eyes suspiciously.

"Sharp girl," Travis said with respect.

A smile warmed M.J. She wanted to thank Travis for that, but thought better of it. After all, she was being paid well to be accurate.

"So what are you saying, M.J.?" Michael asked.

"That this field Mr. Kincaid acquired could easily tap into the Sushafendi. Bleed off it, to some extent."

Travis handed Michael the rest of the charts. "There's so much oil down here it spurts out of the ground like a cut artery."

"I've been here, remember? But a billion..." Michael was not convinced. He remembered too many legends about the Oriente. Too many conflicting stories. Too many false hopes and shattered dreams.

"I was in their data room," Travis said. "Trust me."

Michael rubbed his hands together gleefully. "That's a horse of a different color. Let's get on with it!"

"We will," Travis replied. "We head out at six in the morning. We'll drive as far into the interior as we can, but then we'll have to take a boat the rest of the way." He pulled a map off his worktable. "Down the river here."

M.J. squinted at the tiny squiggle on the map. "What river is that, sir?"

"It doesn't have a name."

"It's uncharted?" She gasped as visions of Amazonian horrors loomed in her imagination. She gulped. Was it possible Claire had been right and she'd bitten off too much adventure?

"It's a tributary of the Amazon," Michael said.

"Oh, lovely," she whispered. "You've been there?"

"Sure. So has Travis. Right?"

"Yeah." Travis groaned, rose and stretched. "It's gonna be a long trip. What do you say we call it a night?"

M.J. wished she could be as imperturbable as her cohorts, but no amount of bravado could mask her rising consternation. "Do you have aerials of the river? A Polaroid, perhaps."

They stared at her.

"I just need to familiarize myself with the layout. You understand."

Michael bit his tongue to keep from laughing.

"No aerials. No snapshots. No travel brochures. Sorry," Travis replied, and without another word or any apparent concern, he went behind the tin wall where he worked and slept.

She heard him unzip his trousers.

M.J.'s eyes moved slowly from Travis's wall to Michael's face. Dry lips stretched over her teeth in a nervous smile and got stuck. Her eyes were as wide and round as saucers. "Aunty Em?"

Michael finally broke into laughter. Placing his hand on her shoulder, he said, "I warned you."

She shook her head and, turning toward her moldy cot, said to herself, "I just wish Toto was here, is all."

There were no roads in the jungle.

They were lucky to find ruts, and most of the journey to the River of the Unknown, as Michael had dubbed it, was over low-growing grasses, thick walls of palmettos and tall, skinny trees that sprouted more vines than leaves.

"At least we aren't having to machete our way through," M.J. said as she clung to the overhead grip with both hands. Gustavo, sitting beside her in the back seat, was seemingly unaffected by the jostling they endured. He was to take the Jeep back to camp and meet them at the river again six days hence.

"That's only in the movies," Travis replied as he steered around a series of low, marshy spots.

"Well, this thing is going to need a new paint job when

it's all over," she said as the forestation grew more dense and limbs and fronds scraped the door panels.

Chuckling, Michael said, "If your calculations are accurate, Miss Callahan, a new paint job won't be a problem."

"Oh, they're right on," she assured him haughtily.

"Let's hope they are," Travis replied. "Because our first drilling site is the one you chose."

A lump rose in her throat, but she wasn't sure if it was pride or terror. "You don't mean CK-19?"

"I most certainly do mean CK-19."

"I thought we agreed it would be CK-25," Michael said, his voice raw-edged.

"I want to go farther upriver," Travis replied.

"But that's nuts. We'll be doubling back to the Andes."

"Almost that far, yes. But I have a hunch," he said.

M.J. couldn't help but notice the wistfulness in Travis's voice. She was also certain this argument was ongoing. From the intractable glare in Michael's eyes as he forced himself to remain silent, she suspected it wasn't over yet.

"Look, I'm the first one to believe in hunches," Michael began.

Travis cut in, "Sure, as long as they're yours."

"I *am* your partner," Michael reminded him.

Travis glanced at M.J.'s very curious eyes in the rearview mirror and replied placidly, "We'll discuss this later."

Michael stared out the window.

M.J. watched Travis's expression turn to granite. The discussion was over. They were headed for CK-19. Her chosen block.

And if they hit, her immortality.

11

—▶ ◀—

The four boats looked like ancient canoes fabricated out of eucalyptus wood, tree bark and woven vines. The boatmen were natives and spoke no English but rather a bastardized Spanish that was so clipped and harsh it hurt M.J.'s ears.

Travis had arranged the hire of the boatmen through Gustavo, and most of their supplies had been transported to the area the day before their arrival. Two canoes were to carry their clothes and personal items, portable generators, gas stoves, tents and the insulated coolers containing their food.

"Michael, you ride with M.J.," Travis said. "I'll guard the satellite phone and computers in my canoe."

"Sure," Michael said, opening the back of the Jeep. "What the hell is all this?" He pointed to M.J.'s over-packed duffels.

"My stuff," she said indignantly, wrestling with the heavy bag. She could tell from the censuring look on Michael's face that she'd done something wrong.

"I told you to pack light."

M.J. waved her arm at the assortment of goods scattered over the riverbank. "I saw all this stuff being packed yesterday. It didn't look to me like anyone else was cutting back. Besides, I couldn't leave these things in that rickety old shack. They'd be stolen!"

"What's going on?" Travis walked over to the pair, the satellite phone raised to his ear.

"Don't ask," Michael replied and hoisted his backpack out of the Jeep. He glanced woefully at M.J. "I'd like to see you get out of this one."

Travis's call went through to his offices in Houston. "Hi, Jerry. It's me. Listen, what did you find out from my attorney?" He turned his back to M.J. "And what did the Swiss banker say?"

M.J. pulled with all her strength on the bag, but it wouldn't budge. "How can a few measly vitamins and a couple pairs of hiking boots weigh so much?" She yanked harder, but she was so intent on eavesdropping on Travis's call that she lost her grip, stumbled backward over a rock and fell square on her behind. "Oomph!" She dropped her face to her hands. "This isn't going well," she groaned.

A hand rested on hers.

She jerked, opened her eyes and looked up.

"Let's get moving, shall we," Travis suggested.

"Fine." She smiled wanly.

When she stood, tiny rocks moved under her feet, causing her to lose her balance. She fell against Travis.

His body was as hard as a hundred-year-old tree trunk, she thought. And just as unwavering and cold.

He didn't reach out to steady her like Michael would have. He offered no assistance whatsoever.

"Sorry," she said, a bit disappointed over his indifference.

"You okay? You're not sick or anything?"

"I'm fine. Dandy. Just gotta get my stuff." She beamed brightly, trying to prove her self-sufficiency.

"Leave it. Michael's right. We haven't got room."

Incredulous, she spun in a circle, arms plastered tightly against her sides. Her face wrinkled. She smiled to smooth it, but it gnarled again with anger.

Travis's expression was implacable. "It can stay in the Jeep. Locked up. No one will take your things." He pulled his precious satellite antenna up again to make another call. "Take only what you need. Quickly," he said dismissively and sauntered away.

"But I need my herbs. My vitamins," she protested, but Travis was already out of earshot.

It took nearly an hour to load the boats and tie down the supplies and equipment. Then Travis gave last-minute instructions to Gustavo.

M.J. had rifled through her things, taking only the most essential, combining most of her herbs into a simple six-day supply contained in three plastic bags. She cut the four pairs of shoes down to one, but refused to give up her lipsticks or the pearls. "Nobody said I have to be *uncomfortable* on this trip."

She smeared three coats of sunblock on her face, neck and arms, then donned a long-sleeved cotton shirt over her athletic-cut T-shirt. She adjusted a wide-brimmed khaki hat on her head and settled into her seat in the prow of the boat, unaware she was being watched.

As the boats moved from the shore to the middle of the river, Michael sat on the seat behind M.J. studying the curve of her waist as it undulated into her hips. He wiped his wet palms on his trousers, knowing the afternoon heat had nothing to do with his discomfort. He rubbed the sweat from the back of his neck.

M.J. lifted her hair to apply sunblock on the back of her neck, and Michael remembered what it had been like kissing that neck.

"How many tubes of that stuff did you bring?" he asked, hoping the idle conversation would help him.

"Three. Why? You want some?"

She half-twisted toward him, the sun filtering through the fine cotton of her shirt, outlining her ample breasts.

He swallowed hard. "Only if you put it on me," he replied huskily.

"Michael!" A ripple of vexation shot up her spine. "You shouldn't say things like that."

"Like what I'm thinking?"

"Okay! Don't think like that, then."

"I can't help it. Just because Big Daddy told *you* to be a good little girl doesn't mean *I* have to play by his rules, too."

"What's gotten into you?"

He took a very, very deep breath, but it didn't help. "I don't know," he replied.

"Oh, Lord." She faced the front.

How did Michael do that? Make her feel as if he were touching her, kissing the back of her neck, when she knew full well he was at least three feet away. Okay, two feet. Less than arm's length. Close enough. Too close.

Beads of sweat trickled down the valley between her breasts, tickling her like Michael had in the dream. Like she wanted him to do to her now—right now.

She stopped herself when she realized that he was telling her he still wanted her and intended to do something about it. No doubt it would be tonight. Could she handle it?

If she had an ounce of restraint when it came to Michael, she might be able to argue with him. Resist him and beg him to focus on work, to forsake sex for the good of their careers.

Instead, she was already planning what she would wear when he came to her in her tent.

Pearls. I'll wear my pearls. Understated. Always chic. Elegant. And not flashy like gold so they won't attract crazed animals or jungle insects.

"How're you doing, Miss Callahan?" Travis's voice shattered her daydream, he was calling to her from his position just upriver.

"Just as I was getting to the good part," she whispered. She waved to him. "I'm fine, sir. Fine."

Travis waved back, then lifted his satellite phone to his ear. He proffered a smile, but it froze like ice on his lips, looking fake.

She frowned. *I'll bet he's never had a sexual thought in his life.*

The boatmen expertly guided the boats away from the low-growing vegetation.

"It's kind of eerie, isn't it?" she said to Michael. "Sort of like going down a green tunnel, not knowing what's on the other side."

"Oh, I wouldn't worry about the other side as much as I would the underside," he said nonchalantly.

She peered cautiously over the side of the boat at the murky water. "Underside?"

"Piranha," he said flatly.

Instantly, she reeled her hands in and held them under her chin. "Lord!"

Michael used the moment to reach out and touch her neck. He caressed her shoulder. "Don't worry, nothing will happen to you. I'm here," he said.

"Thanks," she replied with a nod. But she still held her breath, watching the water churn below them.

The river turned a bend, and the placid journey was over in the blink of an eye.

"Oh, my gawd!"

Whitecaps, whorls of fast-breaking water sucked them downriver, shoving the canoes perilously close together, threatening to capsize them. Then just as suddenly, M.J. and Michael were spun ahead, leaving all the others behind.

M.J. clung to the slats beneath her. Mangrove trees reached across the river with trunks and limbs like sea serpents climbing out of the ocean. Rocks appeared in their path. First one, not so large and easily navigable. Then another, much larger and more dangerous. Then an army of them, ready to attack.

"M—Michael? What'll I do?" she shouted over the mounting roar of the rapids. The boat was moving swiftly as if it had sprouted rocket engines.

"Hold on!" he yelled.

"I know that!" she retorted, wondering if he thought she was an idiot. Of course, he did. Both men did. Travis didn't want her here. Michael had wanted to send her back. *I say can her. Send her back home.* His words still cut a wide, painful swath through her brain.

Maybe she should have listened.

Smack! Crunch! Sounds of destruction diverted M.J.'s thoughts.

"We've hit a rock!" she warned.

The prow of the canoe shot toward the sky. It was as if they were taking flight. M.J. heard the boatman scream, but she couldn't turn to see him or Michael. She lost her grip, and only her feet touched the boat. She was being flung out of the boat straight toward heaven.

She tried to cry out, to release her fear. She thought she cried Michael's name. Her lips moved, but her vocal cords were frozen with terror.

I'm going to die! We're all going to die!

Her eyes widened as she looked only at the sky, not wanting to know how far down she would eventually have to fall. She felt weightless, like a spirit, as if she'd already left her body.

This is my fault. All of it. I picked CK-19 trying to show off my smarts. I could have agreed with Michael. Backed down. One block is as good as another down here. Didn't Travis say that in so many words? But no. I had to be right. I wanted immortality.

M.J. rose in the air as the canoe sailed out from under her. She flew toward the swirling water and the enormous rock ahead.

She hit the water's surface spread-eagle, as if her outstretched arms would grow wings…or fins.

The water stung the entire surface of her skin.

The last thing she thought as she sank below the surface was of Michael—his kiss, his hands.

"M.J.!" Michael screamed at the top of his lungs, reaching for her. His arms held only air as he careened back to earth.

The canoe slammed down on the river with a smashing sound that sent macaws, toucans and puff birds shrieking from the treetops.

Michael grabbed the paddle that had been thrown against him when the canoe fell. Straining his muscles, he fought the current and the whirlpool and righted the canoe. Then he pushed the boat toward where he'd seen M.J. enter the water.

"M.J.!" he screamed, paddling frantically.

She was underwater somewhere and astounded to find she was still alive. Temporarily dazed, she had no idea if she had been unconscious or for how long. Her lungs burned like fire. Her head pounded, and her shoulder felt as if she'd been shot. Her arms were useless appendages and did nothing to move her closer to the surface, to air, to life.

Hands yanked on her hair and pulled her from the rock that had almost killed her.

Rough hands tugged her, forcing her toward the light. Again she felt weightless. She couldn't breathe because her lungs had already filled with water. Everything around her looked black except for the light far in the distance above her. The pain was ebbing, the heat of it being replaced by a numbing cold.

Am I dead? Is this the tunnel of light the spirit experiences? Is this my angel? And what will my judgment be?

Just as M.J. resigned herself to death, her head broke the surface. Water rushed in her mouth. She choked, gasped, as blessed air fought for space in her waterlogged lungs. She coughed.

Huge hands held her rib cage and shoved her high above the breaking waters, into the light that hurt her eyes. Holding her high, the hands made it possible for her to fill her lungs again.

"M.J.!" Michael's voice was filled with relief and joy. "Oh, thank God you're all right!"

Michael! He saved me!

She wanted to assure him, shake her head, speak. See him. But she kept her eyes closed so her head would not explode from the pain.

The incredibly fast-moving water rushed around her, making even the simplest response a minor miracle. But she had to reassure him. She owed him that much. He had, after all, saved her life. "Fine," she said weakly as she was overtaken with a coughing spasm.

"Oh, Michael," she said weakly, putting her hands on his shoulders, clinging to him.

She opened her eyes then, to look at her rescuer, and was taken by surprise.

"Travis," she gasped.

He made no reply, though a dark curtain descended in his eyes. He looked away, toward the riverbank.

He fitted his crooked arm under her breasts, instructed her to hold on and began pulling her toward shore.

M.J. wanted to help, to help herself and be her own hero, but pain shot through every bone and muscle in her body. She couldn't believe a human could hurt so much. Surely her legs were broken, her arms, as well. She wondered if she would ever walk again.

"Relax," he said gruffly.

So she did, letting her body glide through the water like a rag doll.

Travis's legs were flapping frantically, moving them rapidly toward safety. "Hurry, we must hurry." He groaned, and she noticed the pain in his voice.

Has he been hurt, too? Why can't I help him? Why won't my

body work? He's going to think I'm a burden. He'll send me back.

Then she remembered Michael telling her about the man-eating piranha. If she didn't help Travis, they would be eaten alive. She willed her legs to kick. She didn't care if she was paralyzed the rest of her life. For the next few moments, until she knew Travis and she were safe, she would not accept that fate. She could help, she could kick, she would swim.

Travis was coughing water as he emerged from the river. His lungs burned from nearly drowning, but he was determined to save his employee. Fitting his hands under her armpits, he dragged M.J. as quickly as he could onto the shore.

She dug her heels into the muck as they climbed out. Exhausted, she collapsed beside Travis.

"M.J.! Travis!" Michael shouted from his canoe. He paddled the empty canoe until it came to a stop in the mud, jumped out, rushed toward M.J. and gathered her in his arms.

M.J. felt as if she would implode, her insides burned with so much pain. But she was alive! Travis was alive! Michael was alive!

"My God, I thought I'd lost you," Michael said, smoothing a clump of wet hair from her cheek.

Every cell in her body shrieked with pain. She couldn't talk, could only breathe.

Travis was gasping for breath, but managed to sit up and pull his knees to his chest. "Are you all right, M.J.?"

She nodded.

"Good." Water rattled in his lungs as he spoke.

M.J. realized when she heard his voice how close to death he had come for her sake.

Suddenly, she realized Michael had not jumped in the water after her, had not risked himself for her.

She stared at him.

As if reading her mind, Michael said, "Thank God for you, Travis. I was about to jump in to save M.J. when I realized my boatman was dead."

"Oh, my God!" M.J. exhaled in shock. "He drowned?"

"No," Michael replied. "I thought he'd passed out when we were in midair back there. But when his body fell into the boat, I saw that he'd been shot."

"Shot? How?" Travis asked.

"With a poison dart. There's a four-inch reed sticking out of his neck."

"God in heaven." M.J. slammed her hand over her mouth, her eyes round with horror. It was the last of Claire's predictions, the worst part of her nightmare come to life.

Michael looked at Travis's taciturn expression. "You're not in the least surprised?"

"They've been watching us since we set out on the river."

"What?" Michael sat on his heels.

"I didn't think they'd go this far," Travis replied, his eyes scrutinizing the shrubbery and landscape around them. "They're gone now. We'll be safe here for the night."

"You can't be serious?" Michael watched as Travis stood and motioned with his arm to the three remaining boatmen to join them.

"What did you think, Michael?" Travis said angrily. "Are you as naive as Miss Callahan? You knew full well this band of renegade natives was a possible threat. As far as I'm concerned, they've come, done their damage, and we probably won't be seeing them again."

Michael stood and faced him. "They killed one of their own. That wasn't their intention. That dart was aimed at me, and you know it. They'll be back, all right."

"Maybe, maybe not. Until then, we'll have to take turns on the night watch." Travis walked around Michael, waving the boatmen to shore and instructing them in Spanish to make camp.

Michael struck his foot against the ground. "I hate guard duty."

"Michael?" M.J.'s eyes filled with panic as the full meaning of their conversation registered. She shivered and hugged herself. "What renegades was he talking about?"

"Don't listen to him," he said, crouching next to her. He put his arms around her reassuringly. "He was just spouting off."

"No, he wasn't. Somebody killed the boatman."

"Okay, so there's this group of nomadic zealots that have been causing a little problem around here."

"You're saying murder is a little problem? No wonder you didn't want me on this project."

"Look, it's too late for 'I told you so.' This is something we're just going to have to deal with. Frankly, I didn't think they'd come this far west. Not to mention the fact that we aren't marauding the earth, chopping down trees or bulldozing roads. We could have been out on an afternoon boat ride for all they knew." He looked away from her and surveyed the forestation around them.

"Michael, you're very sweet to try to make me feel better, but I wasn't that out of it when you were talking to Travis. I know what's going on as well as you do." She wiped her hand across her forehead and realized she was more nervous than she'd thought. "I'll do my share. I'll keep watch at night, too."

Michael's eyes narrowed as he continued to look behind each frond and blade, searching, waiting for another attack.

"Nice of you to offer, but…" he said turning his gaze to her. "M.J.?"

There was no response. M.J. had passed out.

12

——▶ ◀——

The harpies from hell cast no worse curse upon the unconscious M.J. as did her own insecurities. It was her own psyche that dredged up the phantoms from the past, their ghoulish faces wrecking havoc upon her precariously mended heart.

"Daddy, don't go!" little three-year-old M.J. pleaded while tugging on her father's pant leg. "Don't leave us!"

He slapped her hand—hard. "Get off me, you brat!"

She remembered that his breath was foul-smelling, like the dragons in the fairy tales her mother read to her every night. Her mother told her she was like a little princess and called her that often. But her father reminded her that even princesses find themselves in danger. There was no telling when the fire-breathing, evil dragon would appear.

This time it was Christmas Eve.

Hands scooped her up and saved her—her mother's hands.

"Don't hurt the children, Sean! So help me God, I'll…"

"You'll what?" he taunted.

M.J. remembered her mother remained silent, but she was shaking like a leaf. "Go sober up so's we can have a happy Christmas," she said.

"I'm gonna have a real happy Christmas, Ruth, because I'm leaving. I told you when you got pregnant I didn't want these brats. But no! You said the priest would damn you to hell for doin' what I wanted. Well, know what? I got my life, too. And I didn't bargain for kids. I told you that when we met."

"It's not their fault, Sean!"

"No, it ain't!" he railed, then grabbed the malt Scotch bottle and went to the door. "It's yours. You just always remember how you had somebody who loved you once. You threw us away, Ruth. You did."

Sean Callahan left by the back door, which had never closed properly due to age and warping.

M.J. remembered that door always remaining open just a crack, its bolt unusable and impotent, in the hope that Sean would walk through someday.

That had been her mother's dream until the day she died.

Even when pitched at a fast rate, nuggets of truth did nothing to break through the resilient shadows of guilt.

M.J.'s truth was that she and Claire were responsible for their father leaving their mother. He had not wanted children. Ever. He was emotionally crippled, but her mother had not been able to teach him how to walk. Instead, he'd run.

"*Are you running away, M.J.?*" Claire's voice blew across the chasm of the nightmare.

Running? Like father, like daughter?

In the dream, M.J. heard Claire's voice intensify, then fade over and over again.

M.J. heard Michael's voice then, and the nightmare turned into the most delicious dream. It was his kiss that sent her to the stars like he had before. Among the galaxies she would surely find Claire. She'd be home again.

Then she heard the fortune-teller's voice. "*You must not deviate from your destiny, child. But if you continue on your current path, death awaits you in the jungle.*"

M.J. had not known what Martita meant, but in the dream, everything was becoming clear.

Her current path was one of not giving her love to a man. She could see that now, clear as crystal.

In the instant M.J. had this realization, she suddenly found herself under the sea, again searching for Claire's voice.

Where are you, Claire? If only I could find you, I could go home again.

In response, Claire's voice gurgled toward her.

M.J. reached out and touched it as if it were encased in a bubble. Capturing Claire's voice, M.J. realized she wasn't home at all, but that she had died. She didn't panic or protest. She accepted her death.

At long last, she was relieved.

She looked more closely at the bubble and saw that it held a caption of her life with Claire. Reaching further, she touched another bubble holding her mother on the day she died.

Suddenly, hundreds of bubbles floated toward her in the sea. She could touch her past—the good and the bad. But M.J. was unaffected.

Here, she was motionless. Emotionless.

Here, there was no agony over the love she knew she needed and the love that always remained elusive. Here, she didn't have to lie to Claire, telling her she didn't want someone to love, didn't want children. Here, the truth caused no pain.

And here, M.J. finally admitted to herself she was desperately alone.

M.J. didn't fear adventure because there was no one to mourn her if she risked too much. If the piranha ate her alive, no one would weep over her.

Except Claire. They were sisters, after all. Claire would miss her.

But Claire had a family. It wasn't the same, at all.

Just then an older man's voice called to her from far

above. It was raspy and raw, as if it had spoken too many words in its lifetime.

"Is that you, God?" she asked.

"Some say I am." The old man's voice became clearer.

"Am I dead?"

"No."

"That's a relief," she replied, struggling to open her eyes. Her lids were burning. So was her forehead, face and neck. She touched her palm to her cheek. "It's hot here, isn't it?"

"Yes," the old man said.

"Feels like I'm in hell."

The voice chuckled, but the laughter contained within was unused to expression and died quickly deep in his throat. "I've always found it to be."

It took a gargantuan physical effort for M.J. to open even one of her eyes a tiny slit. Everything was bleary, as if a white cloud surrounded her. "I thought hell was red."

A wet cloth of some kind was placed against her forehead, then it swiped down her cheek, neck and onto her chest.

It hurt to breathe.

The air was hot and wet. The cloth felt a degree cooler as it slid down her arms, over her breasts, her rib cage.

"Michael?" she asked.

"I'm not Michael. You don't know me."

Her mind was mush. She couldn't think in normal patterns and rhythms. She willed herself to wake up from the dream, but she felt as if she'd been drugged.

His voice was too old to be Michael's. Too old for Travis, also. Yet he spoke perfect English.

There was only one person it could be.

"Daddy?" she hoped.

"Is that who you'd like to see?"

"Oh, yes," she replied, forcing her eyes open.

"Then, that's who I shall be," the old man's voice said.

Vision came slowly to one coming back from the dead. The day had passed into night. The glow from an incandescent camping lantern made the white hair circling his face look like a halo. For a moment she thought she was seeing Jesus himself.

He had a beard, clipped ragged but short. On his forehead were painted golden Indian hieroglyphics that looked like dancing dolls.

His eyes were dark brown and twinkled at her with a gleam she wouldn't have thought possible in someone so old. She guessed him to be eighty or more. His face was round, not angular at all, and his lips, though not full, were still smooth and smiled at her with a grin that was almost impish.

"Well, I'm a better healer than I'd thought. Most folks would have taken you for a goner," he said, touching a very steady hand to her cheek. "Just as I thought, the fever is receding. You're going to be fine," he assured her with a gentle, affectionate squeeze of her forearm.

"Do I know you?"

His dark eyes were filled with light. A glow came to his face, and the lines that ran down his cheek and disappeared into the beard softened. It was easy for her to imagine what he had looked like when he was young. He was looking at her with the eyes of a young man, a man with hope. "You tell me," he whispered.

M.J. took a breath. Her lungs ached with the effort. She could feel every heartbeat. It was frightening to be so acutely attuned to every single body function. She was almost afraid to turn her attention away from her body for fear she would drop back into oblivion.

"I've never seen you before."

The disappointment in his eyes was so crushing, it pained her to watch. She wanted to close her eyes, but she was far too fascinated with this stranger.

"So much for that," he replied, this time faking his merriment.

"But you think you know me?"

"Naw," he snorted and dipped the rag into the water again.

Squinting, she studied the dancing figurines on his forehead. "Are they gold?"

He followed her gaze. "You are referring to my icons, I assume. Yes, they're gold. Leftovers from last Friday's tribal festivities."

"The natives have gold dust?"

"More than just dust. The ancients built a city of gold called Tomebamba, where Cuenca is today. The stone-masons built a massive temple of the sun, and the palaces had walls sculpted of gold. Of course, by the time the conquistadores arrived, it was a ghost town."

"I've never heard that story."

"Of course you have, my dear. I told it to you."

"Well, yes, now."

"No, long ago," he said, smiling wistfully at her.

"Long ago." M.J. was more confused now than when she'd been inside her dream. He wasn't making sense. Or she wasn't making sense of him.

"Isn't that why you've come back?"

"Come back?" She pressed her fingers to her temple. Surely, he meant come back from death's door. "My head…"

"It hurts, I know," he replied with so much empathy, she felt more soothed by it than the sweep of cool cloth across her forehead.

When he wiped her face, she noted the distinct odor of eucalyptus in the water. It filled her nostrils, making her feel measurably better. "I had terrible dreams," she said.

"I know," he replied. "I tried to keep you from going too far."

"Too far?"

"You know...to the end." He leaned closer. "You were there, you know. Dying. You weren't dead. Not really. I knew I could bring you back."

Weakly, she took his hand. "That was real?"

"Of course," he said mockingly. "You lived it. Bet I could describe every incident to you."

She watched his face. Who was this man who knew so much about her? About life and death? About her death, her nightmares? Was he an angel? Maybe he would vanish like those bubbles she'd been holding only moments ago.

Her brain functions slowed with each tick of the clock.

"What am I thinking? Of course you know what I dreamed. I talk in my sleep sometimes."

"You didn't say a word."

"Huh?"

"I have been where you were. I nearly died myself," he said. "I went to the edge but I came back. That's how I know what to do to help others. That's my destiny—healing."

She looked at his crudely made clothes. His shirt was white, not the purist white Americans have come to love but a homespun off-white, smeared with green stains. He wore shorts, trousers that had been cut off. Around his waist were several leather thongs forming a belt, and from it hung leather and cloth pouches. Some were tiny, some larger. Some were quite full. Over his shoulder he'd slung a wine bag or water bag. At first she thought he'd put a leather thong around his strong, lined throat, but then she realized a once white, battered Panama hat hung from the thong.

"You're a…"

"Medicine man," he said proudly. "Whites call me that. The natives call me Uma."

"And is that your name?"

For the first time, he glanced away from her. His eyes

were clouded, though she couldn't tell if it was sadness or deceit. "Yes."

"My name is M.J."

"Nice to see you again, M.J."

"Again?"

"I always see my patients in my dreams first. That's how I know to come to them. They call for me. Or rather, their spirits do."

"You live near here, then?"

"I live far away and near, too."

"Well, you must have been close by since I've only been sick since this afternoon."

"My dear child, you have been unconscious for three and a half days, from what I can gather."

"They...told you that?"

"Not in so many words," he said, taking a pouch off his belt, opening it and removing a pinch of what looked like ground-up tree bark.

He took a tin cup from the wooden fold-up table next to her cot and stirred the tree bark into the contents of the cup.

"Now, this will taste bitter to you, but don't worry."

"Worry? Me? Why should I worry?" She tried to push herself up, but clearly hadn't the strength of a wet noodle. "I wake to find a strange man in my..." She looked around her. "Where did this tent come from?"

He shook his head. "I haven't the foggiest. It was up and you were laying here when I arrived."

She ignored him and continued. "In my bedroom, to put the right spin on the whole thing. A man who, I might add, is bathing my very naked body and giving me some kind of voodoo potion that could be..."

"You talk too much," he said, putting a tin spoon to her lips.

"Travis said that."

"Ah, yes. Your companion."

"One of my companions," she corrected, staring at the amber liquid.

"Drink. It's the same stuff that made you well."

"What is it?"

"My God, but you're a difficult one, aren't you? Who told you being ornry was ladylike?"

"Nobody taught me to be ladylike in the first place."

The corner of his mouth curved up in such a fashion as to almost be sensual, she thought.

But that's impossible. He's old enough to be my grandfather.

"My child, you are the most beautiful woman I've ever met. Everything about you is a lady."

M.J. almost swooned with the compliment. "Oh, what a sweet thing to say."

"I'm sure you hear it all the time. Now drink."

"I've never heard it," she replied, then drank as he'd instructed.

It was his turn at astonishment. "Impossible."

"Okay, have it your way," she replied, her intractability returning and with it a smattering of physical strength.

"What's the matter with these young men that they can't see that?"

She smiled at him, and he leaned closer. She had to fight the urge to reach up and touch his scruffy cheek. She couldn't help thinking he looked like a cross between Santa Claus and...

My father—only older and much sweeter.

She pushed the dangerous thought from her head.

"Why are you being so nice to me, Uma?" she asked suddenly, feeling her mouth go dry as cotton and her lids slip slowly over her eyes. She didn't want to sleep. She wanted to wake up, to get well, to see Michael again and assure him she wasn't a burden. She wanted to tell him again it was not necessary to send her home.

She didn't want to go home. Not yet. She had so much living still to do.

She felt as if she were falling away and going back to that world far beyond this one. She lifted her hand, and Uma took it.

She smiled as she fell into a deep state of slumber.

Uma smoothed the same recalcitrant lock of hair from her forehead and cheek that seemed to bother Michael so much and said, "You've come back to me, my dearest Dorothy. I've always felt you would. Finally, the world is right again."

He stepped back from the cot, slipped under the tent wall and vanished into the night.

13

M.J. broke through the cloud of fever hovering over her brain. She felt a presence with her—a man—but she didn't know who. She could only hope. "Michael, is that you?"

He gathered her hand between his. "It's me, baby. Are you back with us?"

She heard the relief in his voice. "I can't see you." She reached out for him with her other hand. "What's the matter with me, Michael? Have I gone blind? What's happened to me?"

"No, baby. It's late. I've turned off the lantern is all."

"Oh, thank God." She felt tears fill her eyes, further distorting her vision.

The lamp came on, and she could see Michael's face. He hadn't shaved in days, or bathed. "Michael, you look awful."

"Thanks a lot," he quipped. "You're a fine one to talk." His smile was broad and happy.

She smiled back, but the effort exhausted her. She rubbed her temple. "Is he still here?"

"Who?"

"The old man I was talking to."

"There's no old man here. Only Travis and me."

"There was an old man," she said excitedly. "He had white hair and a beard and he made me drink some potion he stirred right there in that cup." She pointed to the little table, but there was no cup.

"You must have been dreaming, baby."

"It was no dream," she assured him.

Michael shot her a condescending look, and she frowned. "Michael, I would know if I had been conversing with someone. He held my hand."

"Sure." Michael laid his hand on her forehead, checking for fever. "Listen, M.J., you've been out of it for days. Recovery will take awhile."

"Oh, Michael," she replied weakly, "I feel so woozy. Did I have a concussion?"

"A big one, we think. But you contracted a fever somehow. Probably some kind of river contamination through the open wound in your leg."

"A wound? In my leg?"

He nodded. "Where the piranha got you good. Travis stitched you up."

"Stitched?" Her voice rose an octave. She tried to sit up.

"It could have been worse. I think he got you out just in time."

"I thought piranha only attacked if they smelled blood. Like sharks."

Michael caressed her cheek. "Let's not talk about it. You've been through enough."

"Michael. Tell me the truth. You're always saying I'm naive. Educate me."

"They'll attack anything that enters the water. You're just damn lucky you didn't fall into a school of them. There would be nothing left but your skeleton. It wouldn't take them even fifteen minutes. But with the water rushing around you like it did, you only picked up a stray. There's a three-inch-long chunk of flesh out of your leg near the ankle."

She put her hands over her face. Claire had been right. She'd put herself in harm's way and she had no one to blame but herself. She'd been a fool to come here, a fool to think she needed an adventure. She should have stayed in Tiburon, rented another video or gone to the movies with her nieces. Instead, here she was, proving that both Michael and Travis were right—women didn't belong in a jungle. "What have I done?"

"You survived. And I'm damn proud of you for it."

"You are?" She brightened slightly.

"You bet," he replied and kissed her cheek affectionately.

"But you scared the life out of me, young woman. Don't let it happen again. Okay?"

"Okay," she said, mellowing to the husky sound of his voice, the concern in his blue eyes.

She was lucky to have Michael. Lucky that Travis had jumped in that river knowing the risk he was taking.

M.J. was lucky to be alive. And living had never looked quite so precious to her.

She swallowed hard, mustering courage. "Michael, lift me up so I can see my leg."

"I don't think that's such a good idea."

Just then Travis entered the tent. "I thought I heard voices. That's plural," he said looking at M.J., relief in his voice but only the ghost of a smile fleeting briefly over his lips. "Lift her up. She might as well know," he said tersely.

Michael protested. "But it will be better in a few days, Travis. That's time enough."

Travis took a step forward. "Then I'll lift her."

"Never mind." Michael waved him away, slid his arm under M.J.'s back and eased her to a sitting position. Her leg was exposed to the air, though the rest of her was covered demurely with a sheet. "You want me to take the bandage off?"

Gazing at the gauze patch with trepidation, she answered, "Yes."

"Okay," Michael replied and carefully, so as not to

cause her pain, lifted the two large square gauze patches. "What the hell?"

M.J. couldn't see the wound because it was covered with a thick paste of grasses and mud. Little twigs and chunks of bark stuck out of the concoction. There was only one person who would have made this herbal plaster.

"I told you he was here!"

"Who?" Travis stepped forward and inspected the bizarre-looking remedy.

"She says a medicine man was here."

Travis faced M.J. "There's no medicine man around here," he said, then stopped and peered inquisitively at her. "Uma was here?"

Michael gaped. "No way."

Travis's eyes were locked on M.J. "Was he?"

"You know him, then?" she asked.

Michael guffawed. "He's a legend! A myth! A made-up fairy tale the natives pass around the campfire along with their whiskey."

"He *was* here. He told me he was healing me. He said he came to me every night!"

"That's impossible. I've been here at your side nearly the entire time," Michael was almost belligerent in his protest.

"Except during your watch. Then I was here," Travis said.

She glanced from Michael's incredulity to Travis's curious expression. Her voice was low but firm. "I touched him, conversed with him. He said that if it weren't for him I would have died."

Travis scratched his head. "All I know is that I didn't make that plaster. Maybe she did see someone."

"She's been out of it for days, Travis," Michael retaliated. "She was dreaming, I tell you."

M.J. frowned at them. "It isn't polite to speak about

someone in the third person. I'm fully conscious, and it wasn't a dream." She fell back on the pillow and flung an arm over her eyes. "Men," she groaned. "Both of you are too egotistical to admit that this feeble old man slipped one over on you. He came in while you were sleeping or when you went to the latrine. There's an explanation."

Travis snapped his fingers. "That call from Jerry. Last night. I was here, but then I left. Only for fifteen minutes, but still."

Michael rose from the folding canvas bench. "Now she's got you believing this bunk! I'm going to get a drink!" He stormed out of the tent.

"Michael," she called after him, raising herself up on one elbow.

Travis placed his hand on her shoulder and gently pressed her back to the pillow. "Leave him be."

"What's the matter with him? Why won't he believe me? I'm not making this up, you know. I have the proof on my leg."

"I think Michael is feeling a little guilty for not having saved you."

Her eyes sought his. "But you did."

"Yes," he said gruffly.

As she looked at him she thought she saw a flicker of desire cross his eyes. It was ever so faint, like the last flash before a lightbulb burns out. The side of his mouth curved into a quarter smile, but it died quickly as if frightened of detection. "You should rest."

"You believe me, don't you, Travis?"

"I don't think you're crazy. And someone was here. Whether it was Uma…"

"But he said that was his name. Why is Michael so sure that's impossible?"

"It's an old legend."

"Tell me, please," she pleaded.

Travis sat on the cot looking quite ridiculous, his long

legs bent at the knees standing higher than her cot. He rested his elbows on his knees and cradled his face in the hammock of his crisscrossed fingers. She'd never seen him this relaxed and wondered why that was.

"The man is immortal, or so the story goes. He's been in these parts for almost a hundred years, the natives say. Since that is nearly impossible, I've always thought this guy to be some kind of shaman who learned the tricks of the trade from his father, who probably learned the craft from his father. You know, a regular family business?" He laughed at his little joke, then continued.

"I've never seen the man, but I've heard stories at Lago Agrio, even seen the results of some of his ministerings among the boatmen. Gustavo has a tale or two about him." He shrugged. "Of course, no one's ever given the same description of him twice. He's tall, he's short. He's young, he's old—"

She interrupted. "He's quite old. Looks to be eighty, I'd say. White hair. Straight teeth, well cared for, as if he sees a dentist regularly. Lined face. But it's his eyes...they're as young as mine. Full of life. Vibrant. And his smile..." She touched her lips and realized she was rhapsodizing about him. "There's something about him—his energy, his concern—that makes him larger than life."

"He certainly impressed you," Travis observed.

"He saved my life." She reached out and touched his arm. "So did you."

His eyes locked on hers.

There. She saw it again. He was looking at her with an intensity she'd never experienced before. Not even with Michael. It shook her to her core. She felt as if he'd reached inside her and captured her essence, her soul.

Amazingly enough, she wasn't frightened as she'd been when Michael first announced his desire for her. She didn't feel like backing away. Instead, she wanted very much to entice him to further exploration.

His gaze was warm and friendly and not at all threatening. She could look at him for days, seeking this communion with him and never tiring of the process of their bonding.

Silence filled the tent, yet a thousand promises were felt in their minds. And hearts.

His face moved toward hers. The pools of his eyes offered a warm bath as they cradled her journey farther inside him.

M.J. had never seen another person's soul before, but Travis had opened his to her without warning, without hesitation.

The surprise of his gesture stunned and pleased her. She squeezed his long fingers, gently tugging on them, letting him know she welcomed his spiritual exploration of her interior, as well.

He moved closer.

There was no mistaking the vulnerability she saw. Flutters of temerity threatened to end their idyll, but his courage triumphed as his lips moved over her mouth.

"I owe you my life," she said so softly he nearly didn't hear her. "Always."

Travis's lips brushed hers lightly. There was no ravishing as there'd been with Michael, no possession.

He hovered over her, his breath mingling with hers, becoming one—one soul, one thought. He touched her lips again, but again only with a faint brush stroke. She wondered if perhaps this was a dream.

He wrapped his fingers over her hand, dwarfing it in his large palm. He brought her fingers to his lips and pressed his mouth to them. "Get well," was all he said and kissed her fingers one by one.

The electricity that passed through her nearly lifted M.J. off the cot. She felt the vibration zing from her fingers, down her arm and through her chest straight to her heart. It was the sweetest act a man had ever performed for her.

I will cherish this always.

Suddenly, he was on his feet. "I'll let you sleep," he said. "I'll get Michael for you."

"Michael?" She was confused.

"I have a lot of work to do. Unfortunately, we lost a lot of time because of…the accident. Four days now. It's imperative we get back on schedule," he said and opened the tent flap.

"Yes, I understand."

"Good," he said, and was gone.

14

Travis punched out the Quito telephone number of the doctor he'd been trying to reach since the accident occurred. He was more than frustrated; he was angry.

"Why won't anybody answer?"

Michael walked up, cut off the end of a Cohiba cigar and lit it with a butane lighter. "What's up?"

"I'm trying to get through to a doctor in Quito. I can have him flown out here to check on M.J."

"So, what's the problem?"

"I paid a fortune for this satellite phone, and I can't get a call through anywhere!"

Michael shook his head. "It's not the phone. It's Mardi Gras, the holiday. Lasts five days. No one is working. Especially not your doctor friend."

Travis rolled his eyes. "How could I have forgotten?"

"It happens. We're in the middle of nowhere. You lose your sense of time out here," Michael said, blowing out the expensive smoke and looking through the trees to the stars. "Incredible, isn't it?"

Travis punched the redial button. "What is?"

"That sky. I'm always amazed at the night sky in the southern hemisphere. I mean, stars are stars. But they're all turned around down here, and nothing looks the same." He blew out another mouthful of smoke.

"What makes you so philosophical tonight?"

Michael peered at the glowing ash on the end of the cigar. "You believe her story, don't you?"

Travis cocked an eyebrow. "No. I believe you mixed up that goo and smeared it on her."

"You're being facetious."

Travis took a step back. "You mean you didn't?"

Michael looked at his partner incredulously. "Aw, come on. Since when did I become a herbalist?"

"Bwana Hunter? I thought you performed all kinds of magic mumbo jumbo. That's why I hired you," Travis replied with a quirky grin. He lifted the phone to his ear—still no dial tone.

He shoved the metal antenna down and put the phone away.

"That's not why you hired me," Michael replied, looking squarely at Travis. "Is it?"

"What do you think?"

"I think you wanted to keep me close."

"Close?"

"Yeah, as in keep your friends close, your enemies closer," Michael chuckled nervously, hoping to pry the truth out of Travis.

Unconsciously, Travis dug in his heels. "Are you denying you wanted this assignment?"

"Not in the least. I wanted it very much."

Crossing his arms, then rubbing his chin, Travis said, "That's the part that confuses me a bit. It's not like you need the money—"

"You're wrong," Michael interrupted.

"How's that?"

"My Venezuelan partnership, over which you still seem to have your nose out of joint, wasn't all I'd hoped it would be."

Travis couldn't hide a derisive chortle. "They screwed you? Imagine that."

Michael held up his hand. "Oh, I know what you're thinking...just desserts and all that."

Travis grinned. "I was."

"I can tell." Michael sucked on his cigar. "I still like the adventure, you know. But the fact is, it takes money for safaris and explorations like this. Even for fun, it's not cheap. Because I know the jungles, because I know the dangers, I don't go off half-cocked without proper supplies and guides. I'd like to be able to do this the rest of my life. And that takes money."

"Don't I know it," Travis replied.

Michael looked at him. "But you, you do it for the glory."

"You make me sound noble," Travis said with surprise.

Michael shook his head. "Glory can get you killed, Travis."

Travis rubbed his elbows, not liking the other man's tone. "I need the money just as much as the next guy."

"Don't try to sell that crap to me. You've always thought it was your duty to play Santa Claus to your employees. Hell, you still wear your guilt over 1991. Anybody who knows you can see your failures listed one by one on your sleeve."

"You make me sound like a sap," Travis shot back.

Michael looked at the sky again, blew out smoke and smiled. "Not a sap, a survivor. Nothing beats idealism when it comes to survival."

Travis was so taken aback by Michael's praise he was speechless. Thoughtfully, he settled onto a folding bench next to the campfire. Michael had successfully chipped away at the distrust Travis had been feeling.

"I'm glad we're partners, Michael," he said, and for the first time, he meant it.

Michael stared at the fire, then at Travis. His face was intractable. "So am I. Maybe now you'll believe me when I say that, on the graves of all my ancestors, I swear I did *not* make the plaster M.J.'s been talking about. I didn't concoct any poultices. I did not visit her in the middle of the night, for any reason."

Travis knew he was telling the truth. "Then we have a problem."

Michael nodded. "A serious one."

Travis gazed in the fire. "Once I get hold of the doctor, I'll have him take her back to Quito."

Michael rubbed the back of his neck. "She's a nutcase, all right."

Travis was incredulous. "I don't think she's crazy."

"Then what the hell are you talking about?" Michael demanded.

"I don't think she got up from a raging fever, went out into the jungle and found all the proper herbs and bark and dirt and whatever garbage it took to make that stuff, plastered it on her leg, then got back in bed and proceeded to concoct the story about Uma coming to her in the middle of the night while I was out taking a leak."

Michael expelled a heavy sigh. "Look, there's no such thing as Uma. It was probably some native shaman who will show up in the morning with his hand out for money, whiskey or—" he looked longingly at his cigar "—or one of my Cohibas."

Travis clenched his jaw and stared at the fire thoughtfully. "Natives don't wear boots."

"Huh?"

"I checked the ground outside her tent. The underflap of the tent had been untied, and there are tracks leading to the tent and then away from it."

Michael's mouth formed an O.

"Besides, if he was native, he'd have spoken Spanish. M.J. doesn't speak it. Therefore, the guy, whoever he is, spoke English, at least enough for her to understand him and to have a conversation with him."

"This is nonsense. It's like looking for El Dorado or something. There is no gold. There is no Uma."

Chortling dismissively, Travis said, "No gold? You should spend some time with the Ecuadorian minister of mines and energy."

Michael threw his head back. "Aw, come on!"

"Seriously. There's been gold here for centuries, lots of it. And not just in veins, either."

Michael looked at him as if he were crazy. "Great. M.J.'s hallucinating and my partner is fantasizing."

Travis put both his hands in the air and said, "I know it sounds far-fetched, but while I was in Quito working to secure our contract with the government, I stumbled onto this guy, the owner of a restaurant, who led an expedition into the cordilleras back in eighty-three. He claims he saw El Dorado."

"What did he look like?"

"Who?"

"El Dorado. You know, the Gilded One, the Indian in ancient lore who lived near Bogotá, Colombia. During their pagan festivals, he plastered his naked body with gold dust and then threw himself into Lake Guatavita after the ceremony. They say that the townspeople pelted him with enough gold and jewels to fill the lake. The conquistadores spent decades looking for him but never found him.

"I've always contended that the Spanish were responsible for cooking up the story that El Dorado is an entire country, or a city at the very least, to make up for their failure at finding the Indian. They went as far as the Orinoco and Amazon valleys looking for some mythical city that never existed in the first place. Even Pizarro crossed the Andes from Quito right into this area chasing this tale. And look what it got him. Nothing."

Travis started to comment, but Michael waved his hand frantically in the air. "Trust me, I've heard them all. That Francisco de Orellano sailed down the Napo and the Amazon rivers. That Queseda went east from Bogotá looking for it. Even the Portuguese Pero Coelho de Sousa went north from Pernambuco searching, and even went so far as putting El Dorado on his maps as if it actually existed. Hell, El Dorado is responsible for half the exploration of South America. Don't get me wrong, Travis. If it weren't for a really good myth every now and then, human beings would be content to sit on their asses."

Travis was hard-pressed to hide his surprise. "You're right, Michael. I didn't know that much about El Dorado."

"I told you, I've studied it all," Michael boasted.

"Yes, you certainly have. I find it curious that you'd spend time doing so." Travis's eyes were piercing, accusatory.

Michael snorted. "You think I'm chasing gold? You know what, Travis? You need your head examined. I came down here to look for oil. Something I can see, smell and touch...drink, if I wanted to! I don't need to be chasing some mythological Andean city of gold, nor do I need to waste valuable time analyzing M.J.'s ghost or fantasy or whatever the heck it was. Okay?"

"You're right. No question about it, she's going back to Quito," Travis said with finality.

"Great. Then who's her replacement?"

"I haven't got one."

"So, we waste another month or more when we could be finished with this phase if we'd stuck with her."

Travis dropped his eyes to his hands. "We've lost four days between the boating accident and now her fever. We should have been much farther into the jungle by now. To make matters worse, my funding has fallen through."

"No way." Michael dropped his hand to his side. "You got the call from Jerry?"

"An hour ago. The European deal is kaput."

"Now what?"

"We either fold it all down or—"

"We press on," Michael interjected.

Travis nodded. "This is our last shot. Except that now the timetable is cut in half. We need to pinpoint our site from our maps as accurately as possible. I want to be running 3-D seismic equipment and setting our charges within two days. Then we'll translate the data on the computer, pick our final sites and get back to Quito with the results. And we pray we hit."

"Or?"

"Or, I'll be selling newspapers on the street corner, M.J. will be out of a job and you—" he picked up a burning stick and poked the fire "—you'll just go back to doing whatever it is you've always done."

Michael sank down on the ground. He stared at the fire for a long moment. "What I've always done."

"Yeah."

"I don't mind telling you I'm getting too old for this, Travis. It was a great gig when I was twenty-five, but I don't want to be scrambling for dollars when I'm…"

"My age?"

"Yeah. I look at you and think, man, I don't want to be like that cat, old before my time."

"Thanks."

"You're welcome."

Travis glanced at Michael. "I'll trek upriver tomorrow with two of the boatmen and scout it out. See what I can see. You stay here with M.J."

"Hold on. I say leave one of the boatmen with her, and I'll go with you. You take one section of the block, I'll take another. We both know how to set the dynamite charges and microphones. I know it takes time, but we can get the recordings and then analyze the computer readings back here at camp. That way, we'll cover twice the ground and not be gone from M.J. for too long."

"Deal," Travis replied, straightening his back. "Guess I'll turn in for the night."

Michael looked at his cigar. "I'll douse the fire when I finish this."

"See you in the morning," Travis said, and left.

Michael puffed on his cigar, looked at the stars and then at M.J.'s tent. He glanced at Travis's tent and watched his shadow against the tent wall as he took off his shirt, then stretched out on the cot.

It was Michael's turn to sit night watch.

He kicked dirt onto the fire, putting out the low flames, and with the keen eyes of a hawk, scoured the surrounding area. As if he had infrared vision, he looked past where the boatmen were sleeping in hammocks they'd stretched between tree trunks. His eyes went past the thicket of palmettos, past the trees and farther.

He was searching for mythical men who came and went like prayers, men who mysteriously transformed into the landscape. Who slipped into his camp, made strange poultices and healed dying women.

Men who were known to kill with poisoned darts. Dangerous men. Murderers.

15

M.J. awoke at dawn to the sound of the boatmen as they lugged equipment and supplies to the remaining boats.

With an energy she didn't know she had, she bolted upright, flung her legs over the edge of the cot, stood up and fell down.

"I'm paralyzed!" she bleated.

"What?" Michael, who was passing her tent, stopped instantly and ducked inside.

"Michael! My legs are numb!"

He put his hands under her armpits and dragged her onto the cot. "I should think so. You've been in bed for four days. I have a feeling it has more to do with lack of nourishment than a fatal disease."

She glanced through the open tent flap and saw one of the boatmen lugging Michael's computer equipment across the clearing. "You're leaving me?"

She looked so helpless he couldn't resist kissing her forehead. "Only for two days and one night. We'll be back by nightfall tomorrow."

She grabbed his forearm. "You promise?"

"Yes, little girl." He kissed her soundly on the lips. "I promise."

Travis pushed one of his long legs through the entryway. He took one look at Michael embracing M.J. and stopped cold.

A dreaminess had settled across her face as she looked

up at Michael. He pushed back a lock of her fever-damp hair.

She blushed. He smiled. Travis backed away.

"Travis!" M.J. called. "Don't leave without saying goodbye or good morning." *Something*.

She touched her heart absentmindedly and wondered why his leaving should bother her as much as Michael's. Brushing the thought aside, she realized the simple fact was, she was afraid to be in the jungle overnight by herself. Though it had never happened before in her life, she'd become dependent. Not just on a man, one man, but two of them.

"How are you today?" Travis asked, examining her pallid face. "You look weak."

"I guess I am," she replied, wondering why he was giving Michael such a cursed look. "I fell. Michael helped me up."

"Bad?" he asked, looking at a widening discoloration on her knee.

She rubbed it, wishing she could hide it somehow. That's all Travis needed—another excuse to substantiate his case that she should be sent back. "Not bad at all. My legs aren't used to walking yet, I guess. I'll be fine, sir."

"Let's hope so," Travis said dryly.

Her head was pounding. Reflexively, she pressed her fingers to her forehead, but remembering Travis, she quickly dropped her arm and feigned a healthy smile.

"I told her she needs some food," Michael said.

Travis nodded. "The cook made some stew. It's not bad. It's not good, either, but it will help. There's canned juice, too." He looked at her, checking her vital signs with his eyes. "Do you want some help walking outside?"

"I…"

Travis faltered. He realized he'd been looking too intently into M.J.'s astonishingly blue eyes. He ripped his eyes from her and said, "Michael, help her get settled. I had one of the men set up her computer on the generator." He glanced at her face.

M.J. was looking at him with the most curious expression, as if expecting him to say something meaningful.

"Only if you feel up to it," Travis added. "We're four days—"

"Behind schedule." M.J. completed the sentence for him. "I remember." *My fault. Again.* "You can count on me, sir."

Of all the things Travis Kincaid knew at that given moment, he knew he could *not* count on M.J. Callahan. He'd risked his neck to save her because she hadn't been smart enough to hang onto the canoe when shooting through the rapids. Only luck had helped him find her in that whirlpool. On top of that, she'd caused him delays so serious, he could lose his company due to her naiveté.

What he really wanted to do was throttle her, shake her hard and knock some sense into her. But he'd never laid a hand on another human being in his life and he wasn't about to start now.

Travis cleared his throat of the anger and frustration he felt damming up inside. They were emotions that did no one any good if brought out into the open. Emotions he was convinced he'd long ago buried when he'd lost Blane and lost his old company. Emotions that played no part in his very focused, business-oriented life.

It was a struggle for him, but he replied, "Good," then left.

Michael put his arm around her shoulder. "That guy has the worst sense of timing of any human being on earth," he said, taking her chin between his thumb and forefinger. "Come here, you."

He kissed her sweetly, compassionately, desperately.

It was the kind of kiss that let M.J. know he'd been scared out of his wits that something dire might have happened to her.

He slanted his mouth over hers and, despite her lack of energy and the exhaustion she felt due to the fever, she responded to him with every nerve in her body. He was bringing her back to life.

"Oh, Michael." She sighed and kissed him back.

She was amazed at the yearning she felt in her heart, the longing that pervaded her spirit. She'd always thought unconsciousness created a sense of timelessness. Yet M.J. felt as if she'd been asleep for a hundred years.

"You're back with me," he breathed seductively, sliding his hand under her shirt.

Erotic chills erupted on her skin. "Like Sleeping Beauty?"

"Yes," he replied, opening her lips with his tongue, sending tremors of pleasure to her core.

Her arms encircled his neck, and she pressed her body into him as their tongues made love to each other. He was in no hurry and urged her to enjoy this languorous dance. She memorized the sweet taste of him, the shape of the walls of his mouth and the powerful sense of becoming one that she felt as she breathed his breath, as he took in hers.

They were like one being, a perfect human conceived in love.

She was awestruck at the wonder she felt, and she thanked God for creating this most ingenious method to show humans how to contact the divine.

All her life, M.J. had never understood why her mother spoke about Sean Callahan with such rapture in her voice, such longing and hope in her eyes. To M.J., a man was a man was a man. One was not much different from the other, except in the way they dressed or the career they chose. Thinking this was precisely the reason M.J. had not chosen to pursue a man.

The mere idea had seemed folly, a waste of time. She told herself she didn't need attention and convinced herself she didn't want affection. She rationalized she was autonomous.

Now Michael was showing her there was no such thing as anonymity, that humans needed one another.

Michael needed M.J. The concept exploded inside her, making her legs weak. Yet it made her heart strong— strong enough to take a chance on Michael, on herself.

He sank his fingers into her hair, holding her steady, forcing her to take more of the passion he created like flash fires in them both. He needn't have worried that she would refuse him. As far as she was concerned, there weren't enough minutes in the rest of the days of her life to tire of kissing Michael.

He filled his hand with her breast, slipping his thumb over the nipple in a rhythmic motion that caused the bud to tighten and which, in turn, sent shocks of carnal lust riveting through her insides. She shivered.

His kiss became more rapacious.

"Michael, please…"

"I want you." His voice was guttural and low, like the voice of a jungle cat uttering a warning to his prey.

He was deliberate and urgent as he plunged his tongue into her honeyed mouth again and again. He was purposeful in his pursuit. He knew exactly what he was doing. And she was thankful to every woman who had trained him for this moment.

"I want you to miss me while I'm gone, M.J. Not just a little bit." He peered deeply into her eyes. "But a lot."

Plunging his tongue into her mouth, he kissed her like a man who believed he'd never return. She tasted the bittersweet of his thoughts and felt a tear spring to the corner of her eye.

Suddenly, it was as if she were sitting in the canoe in his place, watching him sink below the surface of the river, falling out of sight and out of reach.

She felt his terror because she knew how she would feel if anything like that happened to him.

Her fingers dug into his biceps hoping to hold him steadfast, hold him safe, even though they would be miles and hours apart.

"I'll miss you," she said as he slowly ended the kiss.

His eyes were demanding and intense. "You have no idea how much I'll be thinking of you. None."

He put his lips to her ear.

She closed her eyes.

"Tell me you'll always want me like this."

She was speechless. His words drilled themselves into the marrow of her bones. For as long as she lived, she knew she would never forget the inflection of his voice, the desperation and passion in his kiss.

She was silent, feeling all she could feel and knowing words were impossible.

"Tell me," he demanded.

"I...can't," she whispered. Then he cut off her protests with his lips, rapaciously claiming her one last time.

"I have you with me now. Forever," he said.

M.J.'s eyelids were weighted with desire. Only with a gargantuan effort was she able to open them. She felt as if he'd mesmerized her. She felt weak. Her legs were rubbery, and her mind wafted from illusion to reality. Michael's intoxicating kisses were the most potent drug she'd ever experienced.

"You okay?" he asked. His eyes were crystal clear, his smile indulgent and prideful.

"How can you be so lucid at a time like this?" she asked.

"Beguiled, are you?"

"Uh-huh."

"Good. I want you to miss me. It's important." He grinned impishly as he released her, then left her tent.

16

<hr>

Graveyards have more activity than camp, M.J. thought as she stared at her computer screen. She'd only been working for an hour, but it seemed like days. Her energy level was low, and her force of will was not enough to keep her going.

She rose from the camp stool and took a metal pot of hot water off the camping stove to make more tea. Then she heard what sounded like a rustling in the foliage along the perimeter of the camp.

She spun around. "Who's there?"

Her first thought was that Michael had come back early. Maybe they'd decided not to stay away all night.

Her eyes swiped across the clearing. The remains of last night's fire smudged a circle in the center. Two folding stools stood where Travis and Michael had left them.

Agli, one of the boatmen, sat with his back propped against the side of a huge mangrove tree, weaving what looked to be a thick rope out of jute. A thicket of low-growing grasses, vines and vegetation meandered down to the riverbank five hundred yards away. Clumps of tall trees surrounded the camp on all sides except the north, where they disappeared for a quarter of a mile and then began again. She had the odd impression that people had lived here once, maybe a hundred years ago. She knew how quickly the jungle devoured wood and mortar. People could have inhabited the area as little as a decade ago, only to have all evidence disappear.

Heck, they could have been here last week, and I wouldn't have a clue.

She heard the rustling again and her instincts went on alert—the hair on her arms stood on end, her breathing stopped and her hearing suddenly fine-tuned itself to catch the highest pitch and the lowest animal groan. She felt like a predator of a million or more years ago. Every sensation they must have felt when stalking wild game or being stalked by prehistoric dinosaurs, mastadons and jungle cats exploded inside her. She was one of them. It was if she could sense danger through her pores. Even with her eyes shut, she believed she could see movements she'd never noticed before. The flock of herons near the river that rose swiftly like an unfurled bolt of gauzy fabric toward the sun. The school of neon tetra feeding at the water's surface. The thousands of butterflies gathering on the humid sand of the islet in the distance.

She heard the buzzing of the pesky piums, small black biting flies that would have driven her insane if not for her insect repellent. Thank God Travis hadn't forced her to leave that behind—that and her sunblock.

However, none of these things could protect her from the presence out there in the heliconias and ferns. She could feel it, or him, thinking, planning a strike.

Functioning on adrenaline, she was reduced to an animal state of mind, unable to discern any human characteristics.

It wants to kill me.

She knew it, felt it. *But what is it?*

Her eyes did not serve her well. The jungle brush was too dense. Even though it was mid-afternoon, in this level of the jungle little daylight streamed in. She'd heard the tales of how easy it was for a seasoned nomad familiar with the terrain to get lost this far inland. Once away from the river, the jungle could swallow up an entire search party, let alone an ill-informed woman like herself.

Suddenly, she realized that the woods where Travis and Michael were headed were deadly. It was the first time she was truly afraid they might never return.

Though more faint this time, she heard a crunching sound, as if a foot or paw had crushed grass.

She cocked her head in the direction of the sound.

Puma? Tiger? No, that's India. Cheetah? No, Africa. Monkeys?

She expelled a huge sigh. She was doing it again, letting her imagination run away with her. There was no danger from predatory animals along the river. Hadn't Michael told her that most of the animals would keep their distance from camp? They didn't want to disturb her any more than she wanted to take tea with them.

Her eyes slid to the boatman. "Agli?" she called.

He was on his feet in a second. He raced toward her. "*Si*, Meesus." He waited for instruction with anticipation.

"Did you hear something? An animal?"

He blinked at her.

And well he should, she thought. He didn't understand English any more than she could speak Spanish. "*Tabien. No problemo.*"

He grinned, nodded frantically and went back to his work.

"So much for that," she said and took a herb tea bag from the Ziploc in her duffel.

She realized that if she were in trouble of any kind, she had no way to communicate with Agli. How would he know if she was dying or just needed water for a bath?

Agli had been posted by Travis and Michael to guard her in case of an attack of some kind. But how good was that? Some lion could be ripping her to shreds before Agli would figure out what was wrong.

She needed to devise a warning system between them. Some kind of special signal they would use in case of emergency. She stuck two fingers in her mouth and gave a blasting whistle.

Agli's head popped up, and he was on his feet in a flash. He dashed toward her, concern on his face.

"Yeah, that's it!" She walked over to him. *"Quando yo es peligrosa, yo,"* and then she whistled again. She'd mucked up her Spanish but good. However, Agli seemed to know exactly what she was saying.

"Si! Si!" He smiled and tried to emulate her whistle. He blew and blew but nothing happened. He seemed fascinated with M.J.'s ability to create a sound loud enough to disturb the hummingbirds.

"No, like this," she said, placing his fingers correctly under his lips.

Nothing happened, but Agli seemed determined to learn, his sense of humor bolstering him.

An hour later, M.J. was exhausted just watching Agli blow. He finally emitted a sound that, though not as strong as hers, would improve with time.

Through hand signals and spliced Spanish, M.J. and Agli formed an alliance. M.J. hoped she wouldn't need to use her new "security system," archaic though it was, but each time she heard an unfamiliar sound and felt that nagging, gnawing sensation in the pit of her stomach where fear bred, she knew she'd been smart to cover her bases.

Finally, M.J. brewed some herb tea and settled down to her computer.

"When Travis said he was four days behind, he wasn't kidding," M.J. grumbled as she pored over the stack of work Travis had left for her. While she'd been unconscious, Travis and Michael had ventured beyond camp, running preliminary 3-D seismic tests. They needed her to organize the computer data and analyze it. Diskettes had to be arranged according to location, then preference for drilling. However, even the simplest tasks overwhelmed her and it seemed that the geology maps floated in front of her.

Her mind was as dull as an overused knife. She found she couldn't remember even the basics. First was a list of the area's "charges," the rocks that would make hydrocarbons like shale and limestone. The maps indicated deposits by the colors she'd used—blue for shale, yellow for limestone. Then she looked for "reservoirs," the second step, places where any of the topography had been fractured by earthquake, tremor or faults. Sandstone layers had been drawn in red pencil. Lastly, she looked for the "traps," where porous rocks that could hold oil had been deposited from overthrusts. From her studies, she knew the area they occupied had a geological history of tremendous tectonic activity and anticlines.

She'd always been good at this kind of detective work. She'd dug up the original 1930s Royal Dutch Shell Oil maps and copied them before leaving San Francisco. Travis had current maps.

It was to their advantage that they would be drilling near areas that had been explored, and in some cases even drilled. The difference was that prior to 3-D seismic technology, all a geologist had to go on was 2-D, a process that gave internal geological readings vertically and horizontally, but not diagonally. With the new 3-D technology, the dynamite charges sent shock waves into the earth. Microphones picked up the waves as they descended and bounced off various rock layers. Ninety-nine percent of the waves were logged on the computer. The shock waves went into the earth in a cone formation, hitting the layers in a three-hundred-sixty-degree radius of reflections, as if there were thousands of microphones in the earth, hearing *all* the reflections, collecting all possible data.

As far as M.J. was concerned, 3-D was like having a CAT scan of the interior of the earth, whereas 2-D was only an X ray.

In the first tract of the block Travis and Michael had gone to, several wells had been dug decades ago, then abandoned. Travis and Michael were conducting cross-well tomography. They would send one energy source down a single well bore. Then a microphone was sent down a second well bore. They would set off a dynamite explosion in the first well bore and record the shock waves as they traveled between the two wells. The shock waves would tell of the kinds of rocks between the two wells, which would help when drilling. Collecting the shock waves through the rock was the easy part. The trick was correctly reading the physical properties of the myriad different kinds of rock.

That was where M.J.'s expertise came in. The computer would know exactly where the shock waves were coming from and their time of arrival, according to every kind of rock known to man. It was M.J.'s job to determine which rock densities to run on the computer. The densities would produce a three-dimensional image on the screen.

She would measure how fast the shock waves moved through the rock, then ascertain if the rock formations were the same from the first well to the next. Sometimes there was a reef or channel. By measuring the changes in seismic waves and how they acted, she could determine if a well were only a shelf of oil. Perhaps it didn't go as deep as it needed to to warrant the millions of dollars it would cost to bring the oil out of the earth.

She pulled up the first testings on the computer screen and began cross-referencing, but the forms and figures suddenly appeared animated.

"Maybe it's my electrolytes," she said, pinching the bridge of her nose. "I feel so woozy."

Having never worn glasses, M.J. knew the problem

was not her vision. Something else was causing this impairment. She closed her eyes, rubbed her neck and pressed her thumbs to the back of her head. "A little reflexology and I'll be just fine," she told herself as she went to work with her hands. "I am not a burden. I am an asset to this expedition." She rubbed furiously. "I am!"

Knowing tea would relax her, she downed the last of it and rolled her head up, down and around on her shoulders.

"That's better," she said to herself. As she picked up the second set of figures and graphs, out of the corner of her eye she saw what looked like a man dressed like a flowering bush dart from a huge rosewood tree over a patch of wild orchids to a wide-frond palm.

"Who's there?"

The sharp teeth of fear took a large bite out of her stomach.

"Don't try to hide," she warned in a quaking voice that carried no authority whatsoever. "I see you."

She rose slowly from her camp stool. Her legs felt wobbly.

All we have to fear is fear itself.

She put her fingers to her mouth and blew, but there was no whistle. *No whistle. No Agli.*

"I...I see you." She squinted at the palm. Everything looked incredibly normal. She rubbed her closed eyes and looked into the distance again. Then she looked at the palm and giggled nervously. "I'm losing it. There's no one there."

The jungle was silent.

"Is there?" she yelled, hoping to startle the man or animal or whatever it was out of its wits.

Hearing her shouts, Agli jumped to his feet and whistled a perfect trilling note. He did not move toward her, only whistled again, as if he knew how to play the game.

"Ugh!" She threw up her hands. "He doesn't understand at all!" She waved him away and went back to her work.

"What good is he, anyway?" she grumbled, and too quickly moved to her computer. Her legs were more than wobbly, they were giving way beneath her. Images on the computer screen were distorted, bending and cavorting like cartoon characters. She could not distinguish between the real and the unreal. Sounds warbled like old wax phonograph records left in the sun too long. The light in the jungle faded; and she couldn't help wondering if it was sunset already.

She collapsed to the ground, her head striking with a thud.

As Agli raced frantically toward M.J. repeating his whistle, he did not see the human figure moving behind the clump of acacia trees.

Neither Agli nor M.J. saw the burlap bag being untied and the fer-de-lance—an extremely venomous pit viper—slither into the grass toward the campsite.

17

━━►━◄━━

The dream seemed curiously familiar, yet M.J. knew she'd never experienced it before. She was in the jungle, then she was in the mountains. She was with two men, one with light hair like Michael and one with dark hair like Travis. She believed herself to be in love with both of them. They were climbing a precarious footpath up a cliff. One minute she thought she was herself, then she seemed to be someone else. But the other woman felt like her. She was a bit taller and slimmer, and her skin was not as sensitive to the sun. But why was she dressed in this ridiculously impractical white linen skirt and matching Panama hat?

In the dream she felt a tremendous sense of urgency, then alarm. The dark-haired man was threatening her, but she didn't know over what. She tried to defend her position, but when she did, he walked away from her. She was conscious of her need to open up to him, to admit her deep, abiding love for him. Somehow she knew that if she did, everything would be all right.

But she remained closed off to him.

Then a voice came to her from out of the distance.

"Dorothy, look around you. Tell me what you see."

"Mountains. A gorge below us."

"Look up. Look across," the voice urged.

In the dream M.J. tried to focus, but it was difficult. "There's a cave on the other side. No, it's not a cave, but a palace. Yes, I can see the towers. It's gold! My God, I'm in heaven! I've never seen so much gold. What it must be like to have that much gold."

"I will give it all to you, Dorothy," the voice said.

Suddenly, fear engulfed her. "I don't want it. I want to go home."

"I'll take you home," it said. "Come back to me."

Suddenly the voice dissipated and the sound of two men arguing increased. M.J. felt as if she were walking between two worlds—the real and unreal, heaven and earth.

The dark haired man walked to the blond man and began shouting. Suddenly, they tore at each other like jungle cats.

"No, stop!" she cried, but their punches were brutal, damaging. Deadly.

Frantic for all their sakes, M.J. tried to stop the fight by throwing herself between them. "Stop it now!"

A fist hit her in the jaw, and she stumbled backward. She could see over the cliff's edge to the gorge below as she continued her backward fall. Panic gripped her, and her eyes filled with terror.

She screamed, "Save me!"

Her arms flapped in the air as she continued to fall backward. She felt a rush of wind career up from the gorge and hold her suspended for a split second. Then another equally strong blast of wind, pushed her over the edge.

She fell.

I'm dying.

M.J. remembered the sensation, just like in her fever dreams.

This was a dream, wasn't it?

Her hand shot out, and she clutched a jutting rock.

No, this is real.

She cut her hand on the rock. Pain shot up her arm.

Blood seeped through her fingers, making the rock sticky, then slippery.

She heard herself scream the man's name, but when she forced her brain to recall the name, she couldn't.

Thank God. It is a dream.

The sun appeared out of nowhere. It struck her eyes nearly blinding her. She couldn't see the two men above her.

No, not the sun, but the reflection of all that gold. Golden walls. Golden cities.

"Dorothy!" She heard the voice again.

Her hand slipped. She screamed the man's name again. The blond man rushed to the edge of the cliff and reached out for her. He was there for her, but why? Did he love her? He was risking his life to save her. Odd, she hadn't thought him that noble. But then, he hadn't been given a chance to display his courage.

Until now.

"Help me!" she screamed, and as she did, M.J. felt herself coming awake.

She knew she was dreaming, but the fate of these people, of her other self, pulled her back to the netherworld.

Wind blew the man's golden hair. "Hurry!" He was anxious to save her.

As she struggled, reaching out for his hand, the dark-haired man's face loomed over the edge.

M.J. knew that, as long as she lived, she would never forget the demonic hatred in his eyes. He was no longer human, but possessed by some need to commit evil. He'd lost all his ability to love.

She'd no more finished the thought when the dark-haired man shoved the blond man over the edge, and her with him. Her eyes locked on her murderer. She watched his eyes turn from evil to terror as she continued to fall. She held the blond man's hand, sensing that he needed her strength more than she needed his.

She didn't feel the ground rise up to meet her. She was aware of dying long before impact.

She saw herself floating out of her body and saw the blond man's essence float out of his. Their souls made a pact never to leave the earth in anger again.

"Dorothy," the voice called. "Dorothy?"

Slowly, M.J. opened her eyes.

"Dorothy, you're back," the old man's voice said as M.J. came fully awake.

"Where am I?" She looked at the white swirls above her.

I always thought heaven would be white.

Shadows moved in and out of the white clouds of mosquito netting that cocooned her. Her eyes focused rapidly, but her mind was filled with pits and potholes.

The voice was still speaking to her. "In your tent." He clucked his tongue. "Don't those young men of yours know how to take care of you?"

M.J. pressed a palm to her forehead. "I feel awful. I thought I was dying. Do I have the fever again? Still?"

How much have I dreamed? How much was real? Was he here before, or is this still the first time? Did Travis and Michael leave? Did I teach Agli to whistle or was that part of the fantasy?

She tried to sit up and fell right back down.

"Not so fast, Dorothy."

I was right, I'm still dreaming. People are still calling me Dorothy. But maybe this is reality and my life as M.J. is a dream.

She smelled eucalyptus and knew she was in the jungle, not on a mountaintop. And the voice was Uma, the old medicine man.

"You're here again?"

"I'll always be with you, Dorothy." Suddenly, he leaned very close. "You saw it again, didn't you?"

"What?"

"The city, the city of gold!"

She shook her head. It was thick with cobwebs. "I didn't see any city."

Uma looked disappointed. "Oh, I thought I heard you talking about it in your sleep."

"I don't know what you mean."

He smiled like a mischievous child. "You were quite vocal...and descriptive."

Struggling, she smiled and licked her dry lips. "That's because I have a good imagination and excellent communication skills."

He smoothed damp hair from her face. "I think it's because you were reliving it."

His eyes were mesmerizing. She felt herself falling into them, falling asleep.

He shook her. "Hey, now. Don't do that. It's time for you to wake up."

"I'm tired."

"Later." He slapped her hand and rubbed her arm. "Come on. That's it. Open those pretty eyes."

M.J. needed to orient herself. "What time is it? What day is it?" She succeeded in sitting up.

Uma pressed his hand against her shoulder. "Not that fast! You need food and nourishment before trying to work again, otherwise you'll continue to faint." He clucked his tongue. "The next time you might open your leg wound. And I would have to start all over from scratch."

"Faint?" So, she had been dreaming.

"Yes."

She looked at him quizzically, then remembered the sounds from the bushes that had frightened her. "How do you know I was working?"

"I saw the papers scattered over the ground where you fell."

"You were watching me." She said it accusingly.

His smile was flip. "I told you. I'm always close by."

She realized he liked to play word games. His implications were not what they seemed. It was her job to unravel the mystery. "How close?" she asked drowsily.

"Why, I'm Uma," he boasted.

Her Irish ire brought her energy to normal levels faster than a B$_{12}$ shot. "You're not a god. You're a man!" She poked his chest, not only to make her point but to assure herself. "See? That's real flesh and blood. You aren't some apparition or ghost. You can't frighten me like you can Agli. He didn't go with Travis because he's afraid of ghosts. I can see it in his eyes. He was all too happy to stay here with me."

"Most of the Indians are afraid of the forest…and the beings that roam it."

"Beings? There's no one else here but you and I. Say, what have you done with Agli?" She put her fingers to her mouth and blew a shrill whistle.

"He's not coming."

"You killed him?" she screeched.

One bushy eyebrow cocked over a dark, twinkling eye, and he chuckled. "Good God, no. I simply gave him some of your tea."

"My tea?" She licked her lips pensively. Then her eyes became wide as saucers as the truth hit her. "You poisoned me!" She tried to get up, but he put his arms on her and held her down.

"Now, don't take it personally."

"Are you nuts?" She flailed at him, but he was twice her size and stronger. "You *are* trying to kill me."

He let her go. Because of the force she was exerting against him, she jackknifed off the cot, landing squarely on her backside.

"Fine, have it your way," he said dismissively, then lifted the mosquito netting and turned toward the back tent wall.

"Why don't you use the front door?" She snorted.

"Too civilized," he mumbled.

"Stop!" She slapped the earth and exhaled. "Okay. So you aren't trying to kill me. What *are* you trying to do?"

"Save your life, for one. Perhaps if you'd rested like I told you to do, I wouldn't have to put a sleeping potion in your water."

"My water and not the tea bag?"

"Everyone else drinks the jug water. You drink your water from those funny bottles with the pink nipples."

"Sport bottles," she corrected. "They're great for when I'm jogging."

"Jogging." He shook his head.

She waved her palms at him and lowered her head. "This is getting us nowhere." She stood, but slowly and very, very carefully. She took a deep breath to steady herself.

Putting her hands on her hips, she demanded, "I want to know how long you were watching me."

His eyes were deadly serious as he answered, "I heard Agli's call. He has a reed whistle that works a lot better than his hands. You were passed out when I got here."

"So, you weren't here when that noise was out there." She pointed out the door of the tent.

"Noise?"

She wished he wouldn't look at her as if she was making no sense. She knew full well she didn't make sense.

What was sensible about being in the Amazonian jungle to begin with?

"Why didn't I listen to Claire?"

He shrugged. "It's beyond me. Now, I have to be going. There are others who need me."

"You're lying," she said as if given an incredible revelation.

"Lying?" He faced her.

"Yes, there was a hardness to your voice just now that I've never heard before."

He walked toward her. "Are you sure?"

She felt cold. "Why, whatever do you mean?"

"You're too bright not to mean what you say. You talk in your sleep. I know about your nightmares. In fact, I have the ability to be inside those nightmares with you. Want to know what they mean?"

"Which ones?"

"The ones on the cliff, in which you were dying."

"I said that?" She looked at him, mystified.

"I was there, remember? What else did you see in the dream?"

"A cliff. Mountains. But it was like an old movie. I do that sometimes—put myself in my favorite Bette Davis black and whites. Claire says it's the result of an overstimulated imagination. I say it's one of my many talents. I wanted to be an actress when I was a kid."

Uma rubbed his whiskers. "There's no one you recognized from the dream?" He leaned toward her, his dark eyes peering into hers.

She didn't know what came over her. It was as if a click went off in her brain and the metal tracks of her life were suddenly switched to a new route by some invisible conductor. Uma's eyes were the same as the eyes of the man in the dream, the man who had murdered her.

She screamed.

He put his hand over her mouth. "Shh. You'll wake Agli!"

"That was my point!" she protested behind his hand before prying it away from her lips. She took a deep breath to calm herself. "Look, I'm not going to get hysterical."

"Thank God."

"I know about dream therapy. I know that my subconscious is working out my conscious mental and emotional dilemmas. My dreams are very symbolic. Sometimes I'm quite entertained by the way my mind works. I realize I was just acting out my frustrations and fears. The fact that you were there is only natural. You have come to symbolize life and death to me, what with healing me and all."

"I see."

She crossed her arms, observing him as he sat on a stool. She mulled over their conversation. "Wait a minute. What did you mean, you were there inside my nightmares with me?"

"Just what I said. I was inside your head, in your thoughts. I was dreaming the dream with you."

"That's impossible."

His smile was patronizing. "You don't know much, do you?"

She gasped. "You're being melodramatic."

He rolled his eyes. "Look who's talking."

How could he do this? Know her soul like this, her past, without her having told him things? What kind of person was he that he slipped in and out of their camp without detection? And just exactly how did he know to come to her? What clue would he have had that she would faint?

As far as M.J. was concerned, he was the person she'd heard rustling around in the shrubs just before she'd passed out. But she couldn't prove it, and he knew it. He was playing some kind of cat-and-mouse game with her, but she didn't know why.

"It must be pretty boring here in the jungle. Nothing to do. No entertainment," she said, hoping to provoke him.

"You don't know me."

"No, but I'm trying to," she said, pulling her knees to her chest and wrapping her arms around them. She rested her chin on her knees and stared at him. "Here's a deal for you. You quit lying and I'll shut up."

Throwing his head back, he roared with laughter. "You are a minx."

"Now there's a word," she said, laughing with him.

Suddenly, his smile disappeared. His eyes had that pained look she vaguely remembered seeing on his first visit. "It's from my generation," he said softly.

"You used minx to describe a jungle girl?"

"Oh, I didn't live here then."

"When was that?"

"In 1929. No, 1930, I believe. I'm not sure," he said with a faraway look that told her he was sincere. "I lived in New York and California."

"Oh, my God! Where in California?"

"Los Angeles. I love it there. Movie stars, yellow Duesenbergs and Bugattis, the trestles of wooden oil wells lined up in rows against the setting sun."

"You haven't been back lately, have you?"

"Uh..." He rubbed his chin. "Not for awhile."

"What did you do there?"

"Same thing as now, healing."

She lifted her chin. "So, what happened? Did you flunk out of med school or something? Couldn't get a gig in the States so you came down here?"

"Something like that," he said, staring brazenly into her eyes.

M.J. got the distinct impression there was nothing fatherly about his thoughts. "What?"

"You're more beautiful than I remembered," he said wistfully, as if he weren't actually in the moment with her but someplace else. Some time else.

"It was only yesterday. I couldn't have changed that much in a day. Besides, I was sick then."

He collected himself, cleared his throat. Then he placed his hands on his knees and started to rise. "I should be off."

"What kind of healing?"

"Pardon?"

"What kind of healing did you do in California?"

"I worked a lot with natural things—oranges, lemons, strawberries."

"To make cures?" she asked, noticing how uncomfortable her probing was for him, hoping that she could get to the root of this old man.

"It was just a hobby back then. I noticed that certain smells jogged people's memories. At the time, I had this silly notion that if we could unlock our past, we could discover the base of our inhibitions. It was during the time that Freud was gaining notoriety. Carl Jung was coming up about then, also. Folks were reading all about them, and suppositions flew like fodder around the cocktail parties I attended. I thought it was poppycock. I was pretty insensitive back then."

He paused thoughtfully then continued. "However, it was at those parties I observed that food and food smells always got people to reminiscing. A pumpkin pie reminded one person of Christmas with Grandma, another of a family fight, another of a funeral. That same pumpkin pie could be one man's Mecca and another's albatross. So I kept experimenting with my findings and I realized that food triggers, as I called them, could break through some fierce psychological barriers. Once a person confronts their demons, their fears dissolve. So, I mashed my oranges, mixed them with cinnamon and different spices and gathered a guinea pig or two. And I started annihilating devils.

"Then someone called me a charlatan. It got in the papers and I had to leave town. I went back east, got some more education, smartened up. Eventually, I found my way down here and taught myself how to heal the body, as well as the mind, and I've never looked back."

"Until now," she offered.

He smiled. "Until now."

"And the Indians, they think you have magical powers?"

He laughed. "Are you kidding? They think I'm a god. Their god, Uma."

"That's some delusional largesse you're perpetuating for yourself!"

He roared with laughter. "Yes, I suppose it is. But I am helping people. And I will until the day I die."

He reached in his shorts pocket and pulled out a beautiful orchid. "This is for you. I thought you might like it because the center is such an unusual pink."

She took it. "It's magnificent." She smelled it. "I love orchids. They remind me of…"

"Vanilla." He finished the thought for her.

"Yes! How did you know?"

"I know."

"But how?" she demanded.

"I just know."

"Are you psychic?"

"What's that?"

"You can read my mind," she said slowly, as if she knew his answer before he spoke. The corner of his mouth curled into an impish smile, reminding her of a leprechaun. "Are you Irish, too?"

"Welsh, actually," he replied and stood. "I think you've had enough for your lesson today. I do want you to rest."

"But my work." She glanced at the workstation Travis had set up for her.

"It can wait till tomorrow. Or next week, for that matter."

"Not likely. I have to get it done by tomorrow afternoon before they return."

"They're coming back that soon?" he asked.

"Supposed to."

"Don't count on it. This is the jungle. Count only on the unexpected," he said in a warning tone.

She shivered. He looked more dire than he sounded. "I expect you won't be far."

"That you can count on," he assured her. "Now, rest."

"Okay," she said, "but under one condition. That you answer my question. Can you read my mind?"

He walked over to her and touched her cheek. The sparkle in his eyes was so electric, so intense, that at that moment he was no longer an old man, but a young one full of life and promise. "I can do a lot more than that."

"Like what?"

"I adore your eagerness to learn, my dear. But all in due time." He trailed his finger to the edge of her jaw and brought it to her chin, holding her in much the same way Michael had before he'd kissed her.

M.J. didn't understand what happened at that moment, but it was as if she were transported to another time or dimension. He was young and handsome. She had the impression he was dressed in a dark tuxedo with a white starched shirt and black bow tie. His hair was raven. His dark eyes were the same, only the emotions were a hundred times more consuming.

He was in love with her, and there was definitely nothing fatherly about the way he looked at her.

His eyes were possessive and brimming with sentiment.

She felt as if she'd known him since the beginning of time. She trusted him, loved him. He was the teacher and she the pupil. He knew her thoughts and the words in her heart she'd never uttered.

He was handing her an orchid.

Vanilla perfume filled the air. His breath smelled of vanilla. Everything around her reeked of it.

As quickly as it came, the vision vanished.

"I'll teach you more tomorrow," he said.

M.J. blinked as a wave of fatigue swept over her. "How long before the aftereffects are gone?" she asked, opening her eyes.

But Uma had vanished.

Is he a magician or a fantasy like Travis and Michael claim?

Then she thought of Martita, her stories about oil and gold and death.

M.J.'s head ached from overuse. She dug in her bag for plain old aspirin to ease the pain, then grabbed her sport bottle and filled her mouth with water, remembering only after she'd swallowed that Uma had drugged her water.

"Bastard!"

She wiped the back of her hand over her lips, then walked outside the tent and emptied the bottle. She looked up and realized night had fallen.

Somehow, she'd managed to get through her first day without Michael and Travis.

She'd survived, but that was all.

Somehow she'd crossed time barriers and gotten caught up in Uma's memory of himself when he was young. What magic had he worked to do that, and what did any of it have to do with her? And why did he keep calling her Dorothy?

Was the answer simple yet more sinister? Had he poisoned her drink? Given her a hallucinogen?

Was it possible she'd never really had a fever to begin with? Maybe this creepy old man had drugged her, inducing her dreams with enough nightmarish qualities to make her doubt her own sanity.

And yet, how was it that he could be so sweet and gentle with her? How did he know to bring her an orchid? There was no way he could know orchids were her favorite.

M.J.'s thoughts left the past and focused on the present. Uma was more than different, more than special. He was annoyingly accurate about her. It was as if he could read more than her mind.

How was it possible for some hermit man in the middle of the South American rain forest to know so much about her?

"I'm only M.J. Callahan!" she protested.

For hours, she stared at the darkness, asking herself questions, but she got no answers.

Her mind was so filled with her problems, she did not see or hear the fer-de-lance as it crawled through the opening to her tent.

The snake was not looking for prey or food. He'd feasted well that afternoon on a rodent near the rosewood tree. He wanted a place to rest, and as long as no one bothered him, he would leave everyone alone. But a fer-de-lance knows one thing above all else—his habitat is the jungle where everyone sleeps with one eye open.

18

➤◄

"He was here! Look, he gave me this flower."

Michael looked haggard, as if he hadn't slept all night. Travis was more intent on the phone call he was making than on anything M.J. was saying.

"I'm telling you, Uma is a real person," she said unconvincingly, lowering her voice to a whisper when she realized no one was listening to her.

Michael walked past the stack of analyses and data M.J. had printed. "You got all that done?"

"I couldn't sleep," she replied, putting the orchid on the desk. For the first time she was disappointed in Michael.

Michael began riffling through the projections. "This is good work."

"You sound surprised."

He looked at her. "I'm not." He went back to reading.

Travis ended his call to Houston. "How are you feeling?" he asked, inspecting her like a microbe.

"Fine, sir," she replied, glancing at Michael and wondering why he seemed so disinterested in her. She'd been expecting exuberant hugs and at least a kiss upon his return. Reunion scenes in old movies flashed across her mind. There was no running into each other's arms, no breathless kiss—nothing. Just an intense scrutiny of her work.

"What happened out there?" she asked.

Michael still did not look at her. "Nothing." He tossed the papers down. "Not a thing."

"I—I missed you," she whispered.

"Huh?" Finally, he glanced at her, but only fleetingly. "Oh, yeah."

That's when she saw it—disenchantment.

Michael was wearing the same clothes as when he left. His hair, face, height looked the same. But he was changed. He was not the same person in the least.

He rooted through more papers, more calculations, as if expecting to find something he had missed. She noticed his hands were shaking. He raked his hair nervously.

Her instincts heightened. Something wasn't right about him. Something had happened out there, or not happened. Michael acted as if his plans, whatever they were, had gone awry.

And something told her that it had nothing to do with her particularly, only that she was a part of it.

But what? Part of what?

"Michael, if you'd tell me what you're looking for, I could help you."

"I'm not looking for anything," he said curtly, slamming the sheaf of papers down on the stack a bit too forcefully.

"Sure you are." She smiled sweetly.

He wiped his hands over his shorts pockets, as if they were covered with nervous perspiration. "Not at all. I was checking it out." His laugh was clipped.

He's lying.

But why?

Michael's eyes deflected off her face to an open map on the camp stool. He lifted it. "Planning to go to Colombia?"

It was her turn to laugh nervously.

You're overreacting, M.J. He's not the one who's being devious, you are. He's not sure if he can trust you.

She took the map from him. "I was studying it, was all. I was looking for gorges, interesting passages. Stuff like that."

"Why?"

They were in my dream. "After we leave here," she said, "I thought it would be fun to photograph these fabulous mountains...." Her voice trailed off. "Someday."

He smiled. "Oh." He started to turn away. "I didn't know you were interested in photography."

She shook her head. "I only use throwaways. I've never had anything interesting in my life to photograph. Until now."

"I see," he said, his eyes following the map as she set it down.

As much as she wanted to tell Michael everything about her dream, the mountain pass and the strange visions of golden cities, she knew he would think her certifiable.

And there was the fact that he was not dying for her kisses upon his return. Something was different between them.

"I don't give a goddamn about any of that!" Travis's cusses into the phone broke through M.J.'s thoughts.

She looked at Travis. *I wonder if Mr. Kincaid is behind the change in Michael's behavior. Just how much did Travis see before they left?*

Travis disapproved of her romance with Michael. She'd been warned. Maybe Travis had reprimanded Michael. Perhaps Travis had gone so far as to order Michael not to pursue her. Obviously, Michael had taken the warning to heart.

That had to be it. She wouldn't accept any other reason for Michael's sudden heartlessness.

She felt a radiating pang inside her. She didn't want to believe that Michael was no longer attracted to her. Not when she could think of nothing but being with him. And, of course, his kiss.

However, she was no fool, either. It was time she protected her heart. Michael was cool; she could be even cooler.

"You've accomplished a lot more than I'd hoped for," Travis told her after he hung up the phone.

"You said you were four days behind because of me."

"The accident," he corrected her.

"That's what I meant," she replied, walking to her computer. She ordered up a printout of her latest calculations.

"What's that?" Travis asked, pointing to the screen.

"A pet project," she replied smugly.

He gave a half smile. "On my time?"

"It's for you." She retrieved the first batch of sheets from the printer. "I got to wondering about some of these older fields that have been mined out."

"Really? Which ones?" He took the papers from her.

"Panacochi. Venturi."

Michael's head jerked up, and Travis looked accusingly at him.

"I never said a word," Michael said defensively.

Travis narrowed his eyes as he shuffled through her report. He raced to the last page, glanced at the bottom numbers and said, "You've been through my files."

M.J. was aghast. "I'm not a thief, Mr. Kincaid. I had no idea you were interested in the those fields. Many of these sectors have been abandoned for years, which anyone with half a brain would realize makes them all the more enticing. This technology could make fortunes just on those two blocks alone."

"I know that. But I have to make a mark first. I have to hit quickly."

"Why this incredible race against time?" she asked.

"Politics," he replied. "This government was bankrupted by its incumbent president just a year ago to the tune of two billion dollars, which he now has in his safe-keeping in Panama. A small country like this can't sustain that kind of loss without cracking at the seams. The people are desperate, and there's no money unless the new regime makes it the old-fashioned way—through business ventures. They're in the process of privatizing everything that was once government owned. It's a free-for-all here, and I'm scrambling against some very wealthy worldwide companies. However, the real issue is not the oil itself."

"What is?" she asked.

"It's hit critical sizzle. If the oil is not extracted soon, it will boil and turn to gas. Then no one will have the benefit of the rewards."

"I had no idea," M.J. replied.

"I've got just three months to find my site and cut my deal."

"No wonder this is so important to you," she said, feeling respect for his predicament. "Sir, I truly apologize for putting this expedition in jeopardy," she said sincerely. She whisked Uma's orchid off the camp table and crushed it into her shirt pocket.

Watching her gesture, Travis asked, "You really think Uma was here?"

Her eyes shot to his. He'd accepted her apology but he'd never admit it in so many words. This was his way of telling her they were equals, that he respected her. It was a big step for both of them.

She had to tell him the truth. "Sir, I'm not sure."

Michael gasped. "What the hell is with you, M.J.? Either he was or he wasn't."

"Truthfully, I have my doubts about my ability to discern certain things. I remember collapsing…"

"Collapsing?" Travis and Michael said in unison.

She nodded. "I'm not sure why. I think I drank some-

thing tainted," she replied, hoping to keep the veil of
guilt suspended yet a bit longer while she sorted out
truth from myth. "I had horrid nightmares. I dreamed I
was dying."

Michael went to her and enfolded her in his arms. "I'm
sorry, M.J. I had no idea."

Instantly, she was suspicious of him. Two seconds ago
he'd acted as if she didn't exist. Now he was holding her.
She glanced at Travis, who was frowning, and realized
that Michael's attempt to comfort her might be more for
Travis's benefit than hers.

*These two men are more dangerous than the jungle! And to
make matters worse, I really do want someone to hold me.*

"You were in my nightmare, Michael. At least, I think
it was you. And Travis, too. Well, the man had dark hair
like yours, anyway. You tried to save me, Michael, but I
fell anyway."

"Fell?"

"Yeah, over the cliff."

He held her closer. "You're shaking. This must have
been some dream."

"It was." She sniffed, suddenly fighting the fear all
over again. "It was so real to me. I could smell everything. Feel the wind. The pain...my blood. And I remember I was blinded by this golden light."

"What golden light?"

"From inside the mountain. I remember thinking it
was a lost city or something. We were so high up. I
couldn't imagine heaven being any higher."

Travis realized he hadn't breathed while she related
the story. "How high?"

"There were cliffs and a gorge below. I fell over the
cliff." She looked at Travis and trembled. "You pushed
us."

"I'm the villain? Gee, thanks."

M.J. felt as if she were inside the dream as she focused

on Travis's intractable gaze. "We died before we hit the bottom of the gorge."

Michael moved away from her, held her shoulders, and peered deeply into her eyes. "It was just a dream, M.J., and now you're here with us. Me and Travis. Look around. There are no mountains for miles, but if there were and you needed saving, I'd save you."

"I know you would, Michael." She smiled. She felt her fear melting. "I feel better."

"Good." He smiled back.

M.J. was smiling, but still, something was out of sync. Then she realized Michael's smile was not as warm as it had been before.

Was her overactive imagination at work again? Or had she been so mesmerized by Michael's charm that she'd imagined a sincerity in his kiss that had never been there in the first place?

Travis tore his eyes from M.J. and picked up a set of maps she'd been working on. "You've accomplished a lot more than I'd hoped for," he said again, clearly changing the subject.

M.J. kept silent but logged the compliment in her head, knowing it took a lot to win his approval.

Michael released M.J. and quickly gathered her paperwork and the folded map of Colombian mountains under his arm. He picked up a cardboard tube containing the geological maps they'd brought and said, "I'm going back. Now."

"What?" Travis shot Michael an astonished look. "You have to be as exhausted as I am."

"Time is of the essence. You said so yourself."

"Yes, but this is above and beyond—"

Michael cut him off. "Forget it. I'm going. I told you out there I wanted to set more charges, make more recordings. But you wanted to turn back. We left too soon. I'll take the boat boys, and Agli can stay here with you.

I've been known to cover some serious ground in a short amount of time."

"It's too dangerous, Michael. When M.J. is well enough—"

She interrupted, "What's any of this to do with me? I'm fine. I can travel. Let's just do it!" Enthusiasm fueled her fading dream. She was lit from within. She'd made a contribution and was nearly inclined to believe she was an asset to Travis.

Her eyes swept to Michael's face. His expression was cold, calculating as he picked through the new data.

She watched his hands flick through the pages, discarding, choosing ever so wisely. He took the newest map she'd drawn, that indicated the latest readings Travis had taken from his expedition last month. It showed a preponderance of limestone and shale and what she believed could prove to be a trap containing a great deal of oil. Two overthrusts in the area were sure-fire indicators that they were close.

Michael is good, damn good. But what's going on in his head? Why this much of a rush? Couldn't he rest for an hour or two? Spend some time with me? Doesn't he want to be with me? Is he running away? Or is he running to something? And why?

Michael caught her scrutinizing him. He smiled at her and she smiled back.

"I want a doctor to check you out," Travis said tersely.

"A what?" M.J. looked around, her eyes boring into her employer's face. "There's not a doctor within days of here."

"That's what I said," Michael replied, head down, still studying M.J.'s work.

Travis shook his head firmly and looked at his watch. "Actually, he should be arriving in little over an hour."

She slapped her forehead. "I do not believe this!"

"Me, either," Michael grumbled, gathering rations and supplies.

"You aren't flying a doctor in here?" She glared at Travis.

Michael chuckled and cocked his head. "Wanna bet?"

Holding up his satellite cellular, Travis replied, "I got through earlier today. He's flying to Lago Agrio from Quito, then Gustavo is taking him to the boats and he'll paddle up here just the way we came."

"Over the same rapids?" she asked.

"He's a buddy of mine. We went white-water rafting in Costa Rica."

Anger sparked inside her. She shook her finger at him. "You know what you are? Exasperating! You can see that I'm perfectly fine, the picture of health. I could do vitamin commercials. I finished all this work and then some." She grabbed a stack of papers for emphasis. "I could pack a duffel under each arm and make it miles into that jungle. I can handle my share of the load." She rattled off the last of her tirade, shoring up her shoulders and giving Travis a pouty glare.

"Yeah, and if anything happened to you down here, your parents would sue me and I'd be right back where I started," Travis said logically, infuriatingly.

"That's what all this is about? Money?"

"Yes, it is," he said icily, turning his back on her.

"Well, you needn't have worried because my parents are dead," she said, dropping her voice an octave. She would have argued more, but the lump in her throat cut her short.

She hadn't planned her defense. She felt as if she'd just buried her mother that afternoon, and the grief that flooded her annihilated her anger. There was no room for hate; her heart was too broken.

Travis stopped dead in his tracks. He stared at her and saw the pain he'd inflicted. "Well, then," he said, clearing his throat. "I guess the good doctor will have made a trip for nothing."

Travis went to his tent.

M.J. stared after him. "Heartless bastard."

Travis stomped around in his tent, digging in his bags. "I need Scotch. Lots of it."

He hastily threw clean T-shirts over his shoulder along with neatly starched and ironed jeans and shorts—luxury items left from his days in Quito. "Where is it?"

He found the bottle and plopped on the camp stool, scowling.

He could hear them outside—M.J. and Michael.

"Michael, please don't go right now. You—you need to rest. Look at you! You look like death."

"Thanks for the shot in the arm, but I'm going. Period."

"Michael, I was hoping we could talk."

"About what?"

"What happened out there? Did Travis say something to you about us?"

"No. There's nothing to say."

"This isn't rational. At least have something to eat before you leave."

"I don't have time."

"What you mean is, you won't take the time."

Michael stopped dead in his tracks. "Okay, then. I don't have time to make the time."

Travis didn't hear Michael's reply as they walked across the camp, but he was aware of the subliminal seduction in M.J.'s pleas.

She wanted Michael to sleep with her.

It had been a long time since a woman had approached him with that soft purr in her voice. A very long time.

Travis sipped Scotch straight from the bottle. He wiped his mouth on his sleeve and grimaced. "Why does it taste better at home?"

He paused and looked at the bottle longingly. "Home. Who am I kidding?"

He took another swig.

Peering out the tent opening, Travis watched M.J. steadfastly presenting one argument after another to Michael.

"Stay. Rest, Michael," she pleaded.

Michael's response was simple, "I gotta go."

"Fine, go ahead," she said, her voice quaking with emotions she didn't want to feel, didn't want anyone to detect.

Travis exhaled deeply.

M.J. heard him. Felt him watching her.

She glanced up.

He gaped at her with knowingness, with pity.

She knew then she'd failed to hide the melancholy in her eyes, failed abysmally to keep her vulnerability a secret.

"Damn," she mumbled to herself.

"Damn woman," he growled, then stood, lifted the bottle again and drank. "I should have sent you back!" he yelled.

She dropped her eyes and raced to her tent.

Travis flopped back on his camp stool. "Gonna get us all killed yet."

He blew out his lantern and stared into the black night.

19

M.J. felt the hairs on the back of her neck stand on end. It was as if someone had walked over her grave or was watching her.

She turned abruptly toward Travis's tent and saw him sitting there, his eyes intense lasers. He sucked in his breath.

Their eyes locked as they caught each other red-handed, observing each other, watching each other like bats.

"Meesus!" Agli's shout cut through the thick wall of banyan leaves like a machete as he raced toward camp from the riverbank. *"Medical es aqui!"*

Travis ran from his tent and raced toward the water.

M.J. fell into line beside Travis, but he jabbed his forefinger in the direction of her tent and ordered, "Stay here! You get into enough trouble wandering around."

"Wander? When did I ever…"

"Go!" he boomed.

"Okay!" She rammed her fists on her hips, thinking how opportune it was that the doctor had arrived just in time—before she strangled Travis with her bare hands. The doctor could pronounce him dead, sign the death certificate, lug his body back to Lago Agrio, and she'd have some peace of mind. "I can't wait to meet him!"

She ducked inside her tent and pulled the curtain of mosquito netting around her. She crossed her arms angrily as she tapped her foot on the ground. She heard Travis speaking.

"I can't thank you enough for coming out here, Juan Carlos, I've been quite concerned that the infection could cause serious damage."

As they approached the tent, the doctor spoke in near perfect English, letting M.J. know that he had undoubtedly trained in the United States. "Are you kidding? The last time I had a boat ride like that it cost me four hundred dollars for the river guide. But don't let that go to your head. I'm still charging you. Full price."

Travis lowered his voice, but M.J. could still hear him. "She's my employee. I'm responsible."

They entered the tent.

Juan Carlos was shorter than Travis, but above average height for an Ecuadorian. His eyes were honey brown, not dark at all, and his skin was clear and healthy. He smiled broadly when he shook her hand as she sat on the camp stool and deliberately flashed him a coquettish smile. She glanced at Travis, finding his uneasiness enjoyable.

"Ah! I see now why you are so concerned, Travis. If I had known you were hiding such a beautiful flower in the jungle…"

Travis was flustered as he placed his hands on Juan Carlos's shoulders, nudging him to get on with the examination. "Her leg, Juan Carlos, was severely injured. The piranha…" Travis bent and took her ankle, he twisting her calf to the light.

"Hey, watch it!" she warned with a grimace.

Juan Carlos nodded. "Better let me do that," he said.

"Oh, yeah. Sure." Travis backed away. "Like I told you on the phone, some old shaman sneaked in here, put some goo—mud, really—on her wound. I'm certain that is what has caused this redness. I think there was poison in it."

Juan Carlos delicately pressed his expert fingers into the flesh surrounding the wound. He opened his brown alligator medical bag, withdrew sterile gauze and alcohol, swabbed the area and then sat on his heels. "It's not infected, Travis. It's healing. The discoloration is part of the normal healing process."

"Are you sure?" Travis asked apprehensively.

For the first time, M.J. noticed he was gnawing the corner of his lower lip. Was he truly concerned about her? He'd made such protests to the contrary. Yet, intuitively, she believed Travis might consider her more than a company liability.

"That shaman probably saved her life," Juan Carlos said.

"His name is Uma," M.J. whispered, leaning toward Juan Carlos. She felt he was her ally.

"Not the legend Uma?" Juan Carlos asked, eyes widening.

"The same," M.J. replied.

"That's a myth," Travis replied dismissively.

"But Travis, you said—"

Travis interrupted her. "What do you know about him, Juan Carlos?" he asked.

He shrugged. "I grew up hearing tales about him. That he was immortal. Why, stories about Uma go back a hundred years. No, two hundred. He appears out of thin air and disappears just as mysteriously. Fifty years ago it was said he robbed from the rich to give to the poor, besides his healing powers." Juan Carlos frowned. "And the fool doesn't charge a fee. Guys like him could put me out of business. Ha!" He laughed and slapped his knee.

"So, you don't know who this guy really is?" Travis asked.

"Sure, I do."

"Who?" M.J. and Travis asked in unison.

"He's Uma. Where he came from I don't know.

Frankly, no one I know has ever actually seen him in the flesh. So, I took it for granted this was just a fairy tale, a jungle story to scare the uneducated Indians away from the deep forest."

"But he's sweet. Maybe he's trying to draw people in," M.J. offered.

Travis gave her a hard look. "For what reason?"

"Maybe he's lonely," she replied. She knew now was not the time to bring up the sleeping potion Uma had put in her water. She had no ill effects from it. Neither had Agli. So how bad could it be?

Juan Carlos and Travis laughed together. "Fat chance!" the doctor said.

Travis added, "He wants something. Nobody risks their life without expecting something in return."

"You did," she reminded him. "For me."

"If the guy is for real," Juan Carlos said, "I think he gets a kick out of perpetuating this fantasy. As long as he doesn't pose a threat to anyone's health, he's harmless."

"But how do we know he hasn't killed? Who's keeping head count? Who's monitoring his work, if that's what you want to call it."

M.J. watched Travis as his ire rose. She didn't understand him. "Why do you care?"

"What?" His eyes met hers.

"You heard me."

"I want to make certain he isn't demented. A kook who kills. How am I to know he didn't put poison in that concoction? All I had to do was wake up one morning and find you dead to prove my theory."

"Oh," she replied sheepishly. "I see what you mean."

"You're so enamored of the old guy, you aren't being realistic. Logical. You weren't thinking of all the possibilities."

"I owe you an apology, Travis," she said, hoping to cut off his wrongful thinking. She could never tell him the truth. Travis would have organized search parties to hunt the old man down. M.J.'s intuition told her Uma was a harmless old man. Travis was being overprotective.

Juan Carlos reached in his bag and withdrew a bottle of pills. "I'll leave these antibiotics with you, just in case. And here's a tube of antibiotic cream for the wound, though I don't think you'll need it. Whoever this man is, he knows what he's doing." Juan Carlos patted her hand. "I'm sorry about the scar."

"Scar?" M.J. was horrified as she examined her ankle again. She realized he was right. "I'll put vitamin E on it." She swallowed hard. It would be a reminder of her adventure that she would not cherish.

Juan Carlos rose and shook Travis's hand. "I'd better head back before night falls." He looked at M.J. "Keep it clean and covered. You'll be fine. It was nice meeting you, M.J."

She took his hand and smiled. "Thanks for the house call."

"Anytime."

Travis and Juan Carlos left. She heard Travis say goodbye, then give Agli orders in Spanish. She watched as he made a fire, opened cans, heated something and brought it to her.

"I made you some soup," he said, handing her a large tin cup. "Chicken noodle. My favorite. Here's an apple and some bread," he said, pulling them out of his back pockets. "Juan Carlos said you should eat."

"Thanks," she replied, slurping more ravenously than was polite.

"I'm fixing pork tenderloins and baked potatoes for supper. Consider this the appetizer."

"What? No chocolate mousse?" she quipped.

He looked apologetic. "I hadn't thought about dessert."

"I was kidding. I like the menu."

"The chops are just pan seared." He looked down, away, then back at her.

Why, he's nervous, about being alone with me!

He was giving her the sweetest compliment she'd ever received. And without knowing it, Travis had endeared himself to her in a way that a million compliments, gifts and flowers could never do.

A smile leaped to his face, and its power jolted her. She was guilty of being inside herself and her problems so much, she hadn't bothered to think of Travis as anything but her adversary. She was reminded of schoolboys who dawdle, anxiously looking for excuses not to leave.

"You like to cook? At home, I mean."

"Yeah." He shoved a single hand into his pocket and withdrew it nervously. "No, not really. I order take-out a lot."

"I love to bake more than cook," she said. "It's rote. All measuring and exactness. No guesswork. No creativity, though."

"I didn't know there was a difference."

"Huge," she said, wondering why she suddenly found his company so pleasant, wondering why he wasn't jumping on her about some screw-up.

Something had changed about him. Then it hit her.

Travis hasn't changed any more than Michael did. I'm the one who is changing. There are two men in my life and neither is what he seems. They are both complex and confounding.

"I don't eat much sweets," he was saying. "But I love ethnic breads. Russian rye, rosemary and sun-dried tomatoes, Greek pita." He shrugged. "Sorry, I haven't got anything close to that for tonight."

His eyes skimmed her face with an unreadable look, as if he were consciously keeping his thoughts secret.

She wondered if he could read hers.

"Well, I guess I'd better get started."

He started to duck out of the tent, then stopped and said, "I'll have Agli boil some river water for you—for a shower. That always makes me feel better when I've been sick."

"I'd like that."

He shoved his hands in his pockets and nodded. "Maybe you should rest until dinner."

"But I was going to show you something I found on the charts. It's a pocket—"

"Later," he interrupted. "After we eat."

"Okay," she said, and he left.

She finished the soup, then bit a large hunk out of the apple. Her stomach growled like a tree shredder, and she devoured the food as fast as she could. She felt like an animal surviving on instinct.

She heard Travis banging pots around, then heard the sound of meat searing in a pan. She leaned to the side of her cot, chewing on a hunk of bread, to get a better look at him.

Over the fire, buckets of water were suspended from metal hooks stuck in the ground for boiling. Purifying. All to keep her healthy, to keep her working.

Travis arranged serving utensils and plates on the folding camp table where they would eat. He went about his work methodically, as if the placement of these things mattered to him. He'd brought cloth napkins, a testament to his predilection for luxury despite his censure of her for doing the same. She thought of his admitted love for take-out food. It was her guess he probably frequented a gourmet deli. She imagined him bringing home poached salmon in dill sauce, a bottle of Chardonnay, perhaps, and setting the table for one.

Then she realized she did precisely the same thing, though she added a flower and a candle.

The same. Are we the same? It's possible. But not probable. Travis is Travis, a regular Simon Legree.

The aroma of cooking meat and potatoes filled the humid air. M.J. couldn't help thinking Travis was inviting every wild animal within miles to join them. Her saliva glands squirted just smelling the food.

She finished the apple and bread, then ventured from her cot. She sprayed her exposed skin with insect repellent, ran a brush through her hair, applied lipstick, then checked herself in her compact mirror.

"Good heavens, I've lost weight! And not in the right places," she shrieked, placing her fingers in the hollows of her cheeks. She looked different, older but not aged. Somehow the sharp elevation of her cheekbones made her look wiser. Then she realized she saw a new depth in her eyes, as if she'd seen things, experienced things, that had illuminated her soul.

I've seen death and come back to life.

It was an incredible revelation for a young woman who'd never before been out of California. She was finally growing up.

M.J. put her makeup away, smoothed the front of her rumpled T-shirt and wondered why she was acting as if preparing for a date with Travis.

"Nutty." *And stupid. He's my boss. He has to eat.* She paced the tent like Travis.

He's not doing this for you, M.J. You are not the center of the universe, of his universe. But I wish I was.

She stopped herself. *What am I thinking? More importantly, what am I feeling? Why is it so important to look pretty for him?*

"Stop this, M.J. or you'll make yourself crazy."

She left the tent. Travis was pouring himself a Scotch.

"Ah, just in time for cocktails, I see," she said, walking up to him.

What little sun was left could not penetrate the thick jungle foliage. The campfire threw golden orange shadows on their faces.

The weariness and stress she saw in Travis was camouflaged by a steadiness in his voice that had been missing earlier. "You shouldn't have alcohol on an empty stomach."

His eyes traveled from her face to her abdomen. Then lower, but only for a brief second. When he looked at her again, she recognized the smoldering passion she thought she'd seen before. He worked hard to hide his emotions, locking them away and then allowing them out at unexpected intervals when they were more likely to stun and confuse her.

The passion vanished in an instant, like a magician's trick. She wondered if, for Travis, emotions were precious treasures. In any case, he wasn't sharing.

"Then I'll save mine for after dinner," she quipped.

"Good thinking," he said.

She didn't know why she couldn't tear her eyes from his. She wanted to be composed, businesslike in her dealings with him, just as he was with her...most of the time. Maybe she'd been mistaken about the desire. Maybe it was she who desired him.

Travis was so different from Michael, so tight within himself. He kept his feelings and thoughts bound up, whereas Michael couldn't wait to declare himself. Travis looked as if he'd perish if he did. Maybe it was just as well he didn't.

And maybe Michael had moved too fast.

Finally, she managed to look away from him and at the pans on the fire. "Smells divine," she said.

"Thank God it's nearly done," he answered, pulling a revolver from his waistband. "I've seen at least a dozen pairs of eyes surrounding us."

"Yikes!" She hopped closer to Travis, her head darting around the camp perimeter. "And I thought the fish were dangerous."

"Let's eat. I'll have Agli wash up the pans quickly."

M.J. was still scanning the jungle. "What—what kind of beasts are out there, do you think?" Her voice squeaked.

"Rodent types, mostly."

She exhaled, relieved.

"And maybe a puma or two."

M.J.'s nerves jumped, and she clutched his forearm.

"I was kidding." He chuckled.

"Some joke," she replied haughtily, lifting her nose in the air. She let go of his arm.

Travis placed meat, potatoes and a small bowl of canned fruit cocktail in front of her. It was all she could do to wait for him to be seated. She didn't know which had built a greater hunger, the fever or her fear.

"Dig in," he urged.

She did. She cut, chomped, bit and swallowed. She didn't talk.

Travis held his tin cup with Scotch in both hands, elbows propped on the table, watching her.

"What?" she asked looking up.

"You're gobbling."

"I'm hungry."

He nodded, expressionless, then glanced away suddenly as if hiding something.

She stuffed her mouth. "You're mad at me."

"Yes."

"Why?"

"Do you have any idea how close to death you've come? Twice?"

"I'm okay now," she replied. "Thanks to you."

"You're an idealist," he said condemningly. "You go around thinking everything will be fine. The lame will walk, the blind see…"

"Justice will be served," she finished for him. Then she smiled and leaned back, swallowing a mouthful of food. "You know what angers you the most, Travis?"

"Do tell."

"You see yourself in me."

"Ha! Hardly."

"Sure, you do. You're a closet idealist. I hear you spouting bottom lines and revenues to those bankers on your cellular, but what you really want is to make enough profit to improve this country. Help these people build schools and hospitals. I've got your number."

"Here," he said gruffly, shoving his plate at her. "You can have mine."

"Oh, no. I couldn't...." She looked at the food longingly. Then she took the plate and stuffed her mouth again. She felt as if she could eat seven plates. All those nights and days of fever had left her hollow.

He put his Scotch down. "You make me feel guilty for even thinking about eating. You need this more than I do."

"I'm full. Really," she mumbled. She chewed and swallowed, then smiled at him. She knew she'd become the thorn in his side she'd promised she would never be. She'd slowed them down. She'd put them all in danger. He was right. She was inexperienced. She owed him for a lot more than just dinner.

She let her eyes settle softly on his. She had a million things she wanted to say to him right then, but all that came out was, "Thanks."

His eyes locked on hers and her heart stopped.

He's doing it again. It wasn't my imagination. It's like he can see inside me.

M.J. felt as if she'd been forced against her will to enter a dimension where her thoughts had no place and his emotions had all the power. She didn't understand. He was confusing her again. For an instant she thought she saw, felt, that he cared about her.

But that was impossible. Travis only cared about his

company, about the oil. He would never care about earthly things. People.

Suddenly, Travis's gaze turned from magnetic to icy.

Fool! Travis doesn't care about you. It's Michael who cares. Isn't it?

Her hand was shaking as she looked down and speared another forkful of food.

Travis nodded. "That's good. You need to get your strength back as quickly as possible. I've lost too much time. I need your conclusions and the graphs—"

"I'll do it," she interrupted. "I won't be a burden any more."

"Good," he said perfunctorily. He started to rise, then looked at her. "This is off the subject, but I'm curious about something you said earlier. In that dream you mentioned a lost city."

"Did I say that?"

"Yes. Specifically. What did it look like?"

"Travis, it was a dream."

"Hmm." His eyes flicked across her face, then to his plate. "You ever hear of the lost city of Atlantis?"

"Sure. Who hasn't?" She chomped, then her head jerked up. "It's in the Caribbean somewhere."

"You're thinking of Bimini. They've proven the temple columns some explorers claim to have seen from the air are definitely not Atlantean."

"I didn't know you were interested in such things."

"There's a lot of things you don't know about me," he said, then rushed on. "There are several legends about the lost continent. Half the archeologists who come to South America are hunting for its remains. Oh, they won't tell you that's what they're doing. But it's true. There's a fellow I met in Quito. He claims he actually found the lost city back in 1983. It's high up in the mountains, on a cliff. Just like you described in your dream."

"No way."

"Uh-huh."

"How's that possible?"

"The theory is that Atlantis was a large continent connecting part of the Mediterranean to the Yucatán. There were three cataclysms that led to its sinking. One theory is that this technologically advanced civilization went to war with itself using laser weapons and blew itself up. Another is that there were a series of earthquakes over time, the first around fifty thousand B.C., the second around twenty-eight thousand B.C. and the third and last around ten thousand B.C. With each destruction there was a wave of migration to other parts of the world.

"Some theorize that the Egyptian culture that produced the Sphinx and the great pyramids were actually Atlantean transplants."

"But the pyramids were built around thirty-five hundred B.C.," M.J. countered.

Travis shook his head. "Thank contemporary computers again for bringing new evidence to light. With the SkyGlobe program, archeologists can reconstruct the planet placements back in time to see their positions in ten thousand B.C. Know what they found?"

M.J. felt goose bumps on her arms and tried to rub them off. They remained. "Go on."

"The tips of the three great pyramids exactly line up to match the placement of the three stars in Orion's belt, which in ten thousand B.C. was located directly above the pyramids. The pyramids were a marking point on earth for the map of the stars."

"Oh, whoa!"

"The Egyptian government doesn't want to accept these new findings, probably for financial reasons, but as far as I'm concerned, facts are facts. So many mysteries, like how the pyramids were built, what the Sphinx represents and the complicated and accurate calendar system the Egyptians devised seemingly overnight could be easily explained once you accept the idea of Atlantis and these migrations."

"That's a lot to take in, Travis. Are there any others who can substantiate this evidence?"

"Of course!" He clasped his hands tightly and leaned closer, his enthusiasm boiling over. "I knew this guy, Bruce Bower, who in 1986 carbon-dated a rock shelter in Brazil to thirty-two thousand years ago. The red painted lines on the hearth go back to seventeen thousand years ago."

"So that would place cave art in South America at just about the same time as that of Europe and Africa."

Travis stared at her. "How did you know that?"

Shrugging, she replied, "Anthropology, junior year." She leaned forward, resting her chin in her hand. "Don't stop."

"The largest migration, however, was to Pikimachay Cave in Ayacucho, Peru and today the dating concurs the artifacts are fourteen thousand five hundred years old. The story that is most intriguing to me is the relocation of the firestone, or the great crystal, from Atlantis. Many historians say it was taken to the Yucatán and that there is a buried temple of records. In the records are the instructions on how to build a firestone but not the actual firestone itself."

"You believe there was an Atlantis?" she asked.

"Yes, I do. Why? Is that too preposterous?"

"Coming from me, no. From you, yes."

"What? Why?" he asked, sincerely surprised.

"Atlantis is so mythical. You're factual. Scientific. Structured."

His eyes probed hers as she told him what she thought of him. It shouldn't have shocked him, but it did. He was a robot. Closed off. Unemotional. He was a tough nut to crack, and she knew it. "Isn't everything in this world a myth until we prove it otherwise?"

"Yes." She smiled at him. "Yes, it is."

"Good. To further convince you, have you ever read Plato's stories about Atlantis?"

"Maybe in college. I'm sure I have. I took Greek philosophers."

"How about Ignatius Donnelly's *Atlantis, the Antediluvian World*, printed in 1882? Or Lewis Spence's 1924 *Atlantis in America*? Spence made sense to me. He drew some interesting correlations between similar customs and legends of the Native Americans of North and South America and the natives of Egypt and Africa. Then there was the whole Theosophist school of thought, which in the 1920s was incredibly hot."

"Who were they?"

"They came up with the theory of Lemuria, a continent that at one time composed all of Africa, Asia, the Indian Ocean and parts of the Pacific. These people all scattered to the east when their continent began sinking, and they wound up in what is today Arizona. They were the ancestors of the Hopi and Navajo Indians. James Churchward was another popular writer about Atlantis. His findings were based on a bogus translation of the Mayan *Troano Codex*."

M.J. was awestruck. "So what have you done, devoted your life to Atlantis mythology?"

A smile flickered on his lips. "Silly?"

"No. No!" She tilted her head, assessing him. "Intriguing. I just thought I was the only person I knew who found value in fantasies."

His expression was firm. "Not the only one."

She couldn't imagine being on the same wavelength as Travis Kincaid, but somehow she was.

She looked into his eyes and wondered if the soft, inviting look she saw was a figment of her imagination. It couldn't possibly be real. He was almost making her believe he had feelings.

"I'm glad to know you agree with me," he said, his voice throaty, a mixture of gravel and satin. It was the tone a man used when seducing a woman. She wondered if he was aware of it. Was he purposefully charming her?

She looked at Travis. He was stealing glances at her while sipping his Scotch. He was wary of her one minute and the next he was opening his soul to her. One thing was for sure, Travis Kincaid was more of an enigma than Michael Hunter.

There was only one possible course for her to take—not to trust either of them.

She broke eye contact and leaned back. "I could really use that shower."

"Huh? Oh, yeah. I almost forgot. Agli has set it up for you over there, between the mangrove trees."

"He has?" She turned to look.

"Granted," he explained, "it's just two buckets of water, one to wash, one to rinse, hung around the limbs with Agli's rope that he's been weaving. I had him rig some mosquito netting so you won't get eaten alive in the process."

"Mosquito netting?" she asked.

"Uh—huh." He swallowed the last of the Scotch.

"And where will you be while I'm showering?"

"Here."

She cocked an eyebrow. "Watching?"

Suddenly, he realized her intent. "Oh! Sorry. You need a..."

"Shower curtain," she said, enjoying his discomposure.

"Sure, no problem." He wiped his mouth with a napkin. "I'll just..." He glanced around.

"Use my cot sheet?"

He snapped his fingers. "That's exactly what I had in mind."

"I'll just bet it is."

Travis bolted to his feet.

Gallantly, he took the sheet from his cot and helped Agli suspend it over a rope tied between the trees while M.J. gathered chamomile shampoo, soap and a monogrammed Egyptian cotton towel she'd brought from home. Extravagances like these were important to her. She would have lugged them to the end of the earth.

Come to think of it, I've done precisely that, she thought proudly.

When she emerged from her tent, Travis was all smiles, directing her with a lantern to the makeshift shower. He tested the rope line. "Strong as the walls—"

"Of Jericho?" she cut in thinking of the Claudette Colbert, Clark Gable movie.

"I was thinking of something more solid," he said, showing not a glimmer of movie trivia association.

Her smile fell off her face. "Thanks."

Travis looked around for a proper place for the lantern. "You'll need this light," he said. "Ah, here." He placed the lantern on a raised tree root behind the apparatus. "It won't get wet here. Give me a shout if you need me."

"I'm fine, sir," she replied.

"Good," he replied tersely and trudged off to finish cleaning away the dishes with Agli's help.

M.J. went behind the shower curtain and inside the netting before taking off her clothes. She reached through the opening in the netting and laid her things over the hemp line. She pulled on the first bucket and was doused with water. It was lukewarm but felt chilling on her skin. She lathered slowly, inhaling the lavender perfume of her aromatherapy soap. Lavender was relaxing and just what she needed right now. She used a large handful of shampoo and scrubbed vigorously to rid herself of all traces of the fever, of her infirmity.

The second bucket of water was warmer than the first and rinsed her clean. It eased the stress out of her neck and shoulders, revitalizing her. She felt like a new woman.

M.J. wrapped a towel around herself, pulled back the shower curtain and froze.

Travis stood outside his tent, a menacing look on his face. He reached behind his back and pulled his revolver from his waistband.

"I've had enough."

He aimed the gun directly at her and cocked back the trigger.

20

M.J. saw the gun and froze. "Travis!"

His eyes looked like slits of steel in his face. Ice. Merciless and deadly.

"Don't move!" he warned.

The shot thundered.

M.J. screamed, dropped her towel and covered her face with her hands. She didn't want to see death coming.

A second scream began in her heart, that place where she'd allowed Travis to abide. It burst from her throat, the cry of one who'd lost hope.

Travis tore across the clearing, his long legs carrying him far too slowly to staunch his panic. "M.J.! My God! Are you all right?"

The fer-de-lance lay in chunks across the ground at her feet.

She felt Travis's terror. Her fear turned her bones to jelly. Her knees buckled, and she sagged.

Travis scooped her up in his arms before she collapsed.

She fought for consciousness. "I'm fine, sir," she assured him.

"Sure you are," he replied with conviction.

She glanced at her bloody legs. "You wanted to kill me?"

"I killed the snake," he replied through clenched teeth.

M.J. felt a bubble rise in her throat. She was flooded with fear, relief and guilt, all at the same time. "You're mad at me."

"Agli!" Travis called.

"*Si, señor!*"

"*Lamparas, por favor!*" Travis said, motioning toward the lantern. Then he instructed Agli to remove the snake's remains, douse the campfire and retire for the night.

"You can put me down, sir. I'm fully capable of taking care of myself."

"Uh-huh," he said, walking toward her tent. "Those snake guts splattered on your legs don't bother you?"

She swallowed. "Snake guts?"

"Pick 'em off all the time, do you?" He growled angrily, as if blaming her.

"Snake guts?" She felt herself turning white.

"Doesn't bother you that you're naked, either, eh?"

"Naked."

"I told Agli not to look. But I think he peeked."

"What about you?"

"I definitely peeked."

She rolled her eyes and groaned, mad at herself for being the one thing she'd always despised about heroines in fairy tales—a gutless wonder.

When she'd been attacked by the piranha, she hadn't known to be terrified. Now she knew better. Snake venom could kill her in minutes. In the movies people never survived such attacks—not even the heroine.

Travis carried M.J. into her tent and placed her on the cot.

"Did he bite you? Was I too late?" He grabbed a T-shirt from her bag and frantically wiped the snake remains away.

M.J. fumbled with the sheet, pulling it to her breasts. "Wouldn't I be dead by now?"

"Not quite yet. Another ten minutes, I'd say," he said, using the lantern to inspect her flesh.

"I only have ten minutes to live?"

"It's possible," he replied, wiping her foot clean.

"Then please don't be mad at me."

He looked at her. His eyes came back to life.

"Mad?"

She swallowed hard. His scrutiny was blazingly intense. "You sounded...angry, sir."

His eyes flashed. He ground his teeth. "I was never..." He continued cleaning her leg. His eyes traveled up the length of her thighs. He tried to look away, but instead his gaze remained fixed a fraction too long. "Could never..." His voice cracked as he looked away and went back to work.

Tears filled M.J.'s eyes as panic riddled her. He was so silent. He wasn't going to tell her the truth. He blamed her for being there, for causing delays. Now she was going to die, and he couldn't bring himself to tell her the truth.

Her trembling increased. She felt sobs of self-pity rumble in her rib cage, then her shoulders heaved. "I'm so sorry. So very sorry."

She dropped her face to her hands, not wanting to see the censure on his face. She didn't want to know the verdict. "I wish I'd never come here."

Images of her long-dreamed-about wedding blasted across M.J.'s mind, then exploded into oblivion. She saw the children she'd never birth, the house she'd never build. The man she'd never have the chance to marry and share joy and laughter with. She heard the voices of her nieces and Claire calling to her, begging her not to die.

The sheet she'd been holding fell across her belly, covering only a narrow strip of flesh. The lantern light cascaded over the curve of her shoulders and down to her breasts, like water over a fall.

Travis swallowed hard. He stared too long.

He fumbled with the sheet, trying to cover her, but his hand accidently brushed her breast. He dropped the sheet as if it were scalding.

"Uh…" He licked his dry lips. "Were you bitten?" he demanded in that booming, angry voice she despised.

His fingers gripped the sheet and moved it upward. His knuckles traced her belly, then her rib cage.

His breath caught in his throat. His face turned crimson.

M.J. was panting with fear. She didn't feel him tucking the sheet under her arms or feel his hands press against her breast. She saw anguish in his face as he took her face in his hands and peered into her eyes, as if about to kiss her. He was saying something to her. Shouting. But all she could hear was the sound of her breath.

As long as I hear my breathing, I know I'm still alive.

The sounds around her were increasing in decibels, as if she were in a huge mountain valley and the sound of her voice echoed across eternity.

"Did you hear me?" he shouted at her, his eyes probing hers.

But all she saw were the menacing furrows in his brow. She was more of a burden than she'd thought.

"What?" she finally asked between pants.

"Were you bitten? Can you feel any pain? A sting anywhere?"

"Sting?"

He dropped her face instantly and began inspecting her body.

"I have to find out if you were bitten," he said, touching her legs, pressing his fingers into her flesh.

M.J. forced herself to control her breathing. She tried to hold her breath, but that was useless. Skipping over breaths seemed more logical.

In the distance a bird cawed, a monkey squealed.

Travis inspected her legs perfunctorily, like a doctor would. He turned her ankles to the light one by one. He surveyed her calves. Then her thighs.

He stopped breathing.

M.J. tensed.

Crouched at her feet, he looked at her. Another bird cawed. His fingers moved upward.

"Please…"

He swallowed, but kept his eyes locked on hers.

She opened her mouth. "Tell me, Travis. Please tell me I'm not going to die." She sobbed and dropped her face to her hands.

He jerked his hand from her skin.

"You're not going to die. There's no bite." He reached out and touched her hands with his. Tenderly, he pulled them away from her eyes.

Her tears wetted his fingers. Relief flooded her face, and gratitude filled her eyes.

"Oh, thank you, sir!" She flung her arms around his neck, pressing her naked breasts to his chest.

He held her, his hands exploring the skin across her back. They fell to her waist, gripped her there and sank into her flesh just a fraction more than was acceptable for an employer with his employee.

"You saved me again." She half-laughed and half-sobbed. "I can never thank you enough. You've been so good to me."

"I, uh…" he stammered.

But he kept holding her.

"You're welcome," he finally managed to say.

M.J. pushed herself away from him as she suddenly realized she was naked. "I'm…sorry." She grabbed the fallen sheet, pulled it up and tied it around her breasts. "I didn't realize.…" She forced an awkward smile. "I'm so embarrassed."

"It's okay," he said, pushing himself away from the cot. "This is the jungle. It seems natural here."

She was surprised to see approval in his eyes.

"You look natural here," he said gruffly. "That was a compliment."

"Oh."

He stood. "Do you want me to get another bucket of water? So that you can finish—" he swallowed hard "—washing?"

"Yes, thank you. That would be nice."

Glancing outside the tent, he said, "I'll go get it for you. You can manage by yourself?"

"I'm fine, sir," she smiled reassuringly.

"Okay," he replied, turned slowly and left, but not before looking at her one last time.

M.J. watched him cross the camp yard and grab a pail of water. She felt a crimson flush sweep her body.

At first she thought it was spawned by embarrassment. Travis had seen her more than just a little bit naked.

Then she realized the heat came from desire. She wanted him.

She realized that Travis had revealed a great deal of himself to her tonight by telling her the myths and legends in which he believed. She got the impression that he'd never shared this side of himself with anyone. He was still the most closed-off man she'd ever encountered. Still…

She remembered the way he'd held her. The touch of his hands came back to her. His was not the hug of a friend reassuring a friend. His was not a benign embrace. It was assertive.

Slowly, the memory of his splayed fingers across her back came back to her, the way they loped down her rib cage and then to her shoulders, then down again, lower, to her waist, skimming her hips. The way he'd squeezed her flesh between his fingers, pulling on her hips as if he'd wanted even more. As if he'd wanted to pull her beneath him.

"Impossible!"

Her eyes jerked to the camp. She watched him taking

long strides. He was pacing for some reason—looking like a caged tiger, or a man who can't make up his mind.

As if he had picked up on her thoughts, Travis's head darted up. He turned, and his eyes locked on hers. He held her with his gaze, as if physically embracing her. In that second she saw it all—passion, lust.

It was a billion times more intense than anything she'd ever experienced in her life. Including Michael. And for that, Travis shook her to her roots.

"Shit!" she mumbled and dropped her eyes.

He wants me. And I want him. I've complicated my life but good.

He was inside the tent in two seconds.

"Here's the water. I brought a sponge and...your soap."

She took them from him. Her hands were shaking again, but not from terror.

"You okay?" he asked.

"Fine."

"Good," he said nervously. He hesitated.

M.J. refused to look at him. She knew what would happen if she allowed him to see the desire she knew was shining like a broadcast signal in her eyes.

She didn't want to be a one-night stand for any man.

And for Travis Kincaid, that's all it would be. She knew that. It would be an interlude, a memory to pull out when she was sixty years old.

M.J. thought better of herself and knew she deserved more. She wanted the dream, the fairy tale. She wanted forever after.

Travis Kincaid was not that kind of man.

"You get some rest," he said. "I'll see you in the morning."

"In the morning," she replied.

He left her tent, dropping the flap behind him.

21

In the mountainside northwest of the river, several days journey through dense jungle, Uma had carved his home fifty years previously. He couldn't exactly remember how long it had been, having lost track of time and the number of his advancing years. Seldom did he contact whites or encounter them this deep into his territory—his domain.

He'd long ago lost his taste for civilization, American civilization especially.

Uma had planned the end of his life among his native patients who considered him a spirit, a shaman healer at best, but not a friend. Gods were not friendly folk, and that viewpoint had suited him just fine. He liked being a hermit. He preferred his own company over that of other human beings who, once they came to know him, were apt to criticize, chastise and condemn.

But now these young people from the United States had stumbled onto his land, and he didn't like it one bit.

He could smell the greed on them.

He thought he'd passed enough years in the pristine, unmolested jungle to have forgotten, but the stench of money lust was strong enough to pervade even the natural aromatic elixirs of the Oriente. No amount of eucalyptus, vanilla, verbena and balsam could rid the air of its foul vapors.

He turned to the interior of his cave. It was lit with torches hung along the walls and hundreds of candles he'd made himself, blending floral oils with those of barks and berries, testing them for their healing properties.

Some recipes he'd learned from native shamans. Some were from his youthful dabblings in California.

Though he'd made a practice of never trading with whites, Uma had not been above coercing a native to purchase rare saplings and seeds from the markets as far away as Otaballo and Puyo to the south. It had required a lifetime to cultivate the odd varieties of lemongrass, orange trees, basil, thyme and Mediterranean juniper.

He prided himself on the Australian white-barked cajeput tree he propagated annually. Only the twigs, leaves and buds of the young plants could be fermented, then distilled, to cure the urinary and intestinal tracts. He grew geraniums in native-made pots, then steam-distilled the green leaves to extract the oil he used as an antiseptic and a general tonic to aid his patients in convalescing.

"The same tonic I gave you," he mumbled, standing over a boiling pot of aromatic herbs, bark chips and root chunks.

His pet monkey, Chipchaw, sat on the table watching him silently. He knew not to interrupt his master's thoughts.

From a twenty-five-foot tree outside the entrance to the cave, Uma plucked a handful of green bay leaves and tossed them in his stew. Then he dug into a pottery bowl, lifted a handful of Bois de Rose bark and stopped cold.

He lifted them to his nose, inhaled the woody, mossy, rose-smelling twigs and thought of *her* again.

She was the only reason he tolerated the Americans.

The men didn't know it, but it was her presence that had saved them all.

"Such magic," he said, picking up a particularly long piece and holding it to the light.

"This can eliminate wrinkles and heal scars. Nothing in the world heals skin like Bois de Rose." He put the twig down. "That is why I chose it for your ankle, Miss Callahan."

His eyes were unwavering as they stared into the pot.

It was as if he were seeing the past in the bubbling liquid.

"All these years I didn't dare to dream this dream. The old shamans told me they believed the dead could come back to the living if both parties willed it so. But I didn't believe them. It seemed too good to be true. Like a fairy tale. I thought I was being smart believing only in reality.

"Though it's true that, as the years passed, I realized that which is imagined generally becomes reality and that which one views as reality has a tendency to fade, vanish in the twinkling of an eye. The rich become poor. The poor become rich. The ill wish themselves well, and the healthy become sick and die.

"How ironic life is! How incredible that I should live long enough to witness this amazing feat of willpower. Sorry, of soul power.

"Ah, my dearest Dorothy, I wish I understood why you have chosen to change your name. So unnecessary. You should have known I would realize who you were and see past this charade.

"I understand you don't want the others to know, even this young woman whose body you have chosen to inhabit. And my God, dearest, how ever did you find one so compatible? Why, she looks exactly like you!"

He smiled broadly at Chipchaw, who grinned a toothy grin.

"I do like your sense of irony, Dorothy. You were always quick and bright like that, befitting all great journalists, I would imagine."

He placed the wooden paddle he used to stir the mixture on a crude table made of eucalyptus, the rectangular top of which was pitted and scarred from hot pots and utensils over the past half century. He used a ladle made out of a hollowed-out pod tied to a reed to scoop the liquid into watertight pouches he hung in orderly rows on pegs he'd pounded into the cave walls.

Uma had no labeling system. He categorized his products by size and color. The tiniest pouches were filled with precious, and in some cases irreplaceable, oils. The larger bags held blends of aromatic healing oils and vegetable oil his native friends purchased in the villages. These were used as lubricants for rheumatism and salves for wounds to heal skin diseases.

Tonics for ingestion were housed in the berry-red-stained leather bags. Cooking additives and flavor enhancers were in the largest bags, since these were the bartering products most requested by the natives. A decade or more ago he'd made the error of teaching the natives how to cook with herbs. Since then, they'd gone gourmet.

"I wonder, Miss Callahan, if I shouldn't add some spice to your next meal," he said, thoughtfully rubbing his scruffy beard.

"Not a lot, mind you, but just enough to jog your memory. Help you remember who I am."

He scanned the rows of bags and the makeshift shelves he'd built of wood planks and native-made concrete blocks that held minuscule pottery jars and woven baskets of dried plants, flowers, berries and fruit rind.

Then he snapped his fingers. His eyes brightened. "How silly of me to forget!" He danced a little jig, turning like an impish leprechaun about to perform mischief. "A dream catcher is all we need."

Chipchaw agreed with a nod.

Uma pulled a basket from a shelf and took off the top. He withdrew a pair of hoop earrings made of silver and colorful threads resembling rainbow spiderwebs. Green and yellow parrot feathers dangled from the bottoms. "These will do the trick."

He stuck them in his ears, regarding his shadow on the cave wall as if looking in a mirror. He bobbed his head from shoulder to shoulder, making the web shadows slide across the wall.

"I'll wear them myself while I dream about you. Then, when I place them in your ears, my dreams will scramble inside your head and remove this block to your memory."

Chipchaw clapped his hands and doffed his miniature black felt Andean hat, then replaced it.

Placing his hands behind the earrings, Uma let them lay across his palms, the feathers crossing the mounds of Venus.

"You'll remember, dearest. You are mine, Dorothy. Always were, always will be."

A candle sputtered. The flame died.

Chipchaw scrambled to his tiny bed under the shelves. He covered his eyes with his paws.

Uma's eyes were transfixed on the candle smoke as it coiled overhead. "You must remember me."

He looked at the dream catcher shadows.

"Or all will be lost. And that simply won't do."

22

Travis sat night watch listening to the jungle sounds of monkeys settling in the treetops, the scurry down to the river of a rodent and the flapping wings of a Toucan as it found a perch. He heard Agli panning for gold, something that all the natives seemed to do on their off time foolishly believing in tales of lost Incan treasure.

M.J.'s cot creaked as she rolled over and in her sleep uttered his name. He was surprised to hear his name. Was she dreaming about him, and if so, what was she dreaming?

He'd come so close to blowing this whole thing sky-high. And for what? Sex? He knew better than that. Hell, he was too old for that kind of pubescent behavior. He had a destiny to fulfill, and it did not include having an affair with an employee.

He chalked it up to temporary insanity due to the shock of seeing the snake, of being alone together in the jungle, of nerves pitched on the edge of anxiety over the feasibility of ever finding oil at all. Of seeing M.J. naked.

He pinched the bridge of his nose, letting his head fall back. "Travis, old boy, something is bothering you, all right, and it's more than a momentary brush with desire."

He rubbed the back of his neck. "But what?"

He stood and paced, then stopped. He scanned the jungle for an intruder and, satisfied there was none, went to the campfire to make a fresh pot of coffee.

He paced anxiously as he waited for the brew to heat. He checked his watch. Dawn was only an hour away.

Suddenly, it hit him.

"The fer-de-lance!"

Travis knew enough about Ecuador, the lay of the land and its natural resources and animal inhabitants, to know that this was too far south for a fer-de-lance. A python, yes. A coral snake, yes. But the fer-de-lance seldom roamed as far as Colombia.

Certainly not Ecuador.

Nothing was impossible, but the chances of that fer-de-lance casually slinking into camp were one in a million.

Ever since his boatman had been murdered on the river, Travis had feared another attack, but he hadn't said anything to Michael. And certainly not to M.J. Travis didn't believe in buying trouble. However, there was no question in his mind that someone had planted the fer-de-lance. But who? And why?

His first thought was the band of rogues who'd killed those loggers a few months back. But that was days and days of travel from here. And they'd been warned not to clear-cut that part of the jungle. In fact, his inside sources said they had been trespassing. Acting illegally. They were marauders who had taken their chances and got what they gave, as Travis saw it.

Those Americans could have been murdered by any number of factions.

And there was Uma. Who was the old man? What if he was a corporate spy from another company? Maybe he was a harmless enough old hermit, but Travis didn't trust anyone who didn't step up and state his case. What was the guy trying to hide, anyway? Or accomplish?

"What's his angle?" Travis rubbed his forearms as if shaking off an evil spell. Something bothered him. Something about the phantom Uma ate at him.

Something wasn't right. In fact, something was very wrong.

Travis was out of his element playing detective. He was a geologist, a businessman, for crying out loud—not an investigator.

Or was he? Didn't he take clues, information, inanimate soil, rock and shale, expert's opinions and computerized data, then mix them all up, decipher, discern and decide which pinprick hole to bore into the earth? Didn't he place his bets and his investors' money on his detective work?

Maybe he was more qualified to ferret out answers than he'd thought.

He just wasn't sure what he would do if he were to come face-to-face with a murderer. And there was one out there. He was convinced of it. He knew he was the target, and that M.J. had only gotten in the way.

He suspected that the murderer or murderers had not expected a woman to be with him. Native rogues drew the line at women. Had they wanted her dead, they would have shot her with a poison dart, and that would have been that.

Ordinarily, he would think someone was trying to frighten him, make him abandon the project. But Travis believed this was not a battle between good and evil, environmentalist against capitalist. This was a fight between ignorance and knowledge.

It was indicative of the power struggle of the twenty-first century.

Whoever they were, they were out there in the jungle behind every tree like snipers with infrared sights.

He'd never felt so impotent in his life. He could watch. He could fight back. Save himself.

But the next time…

When they unleashed another snake or dart or poisoned the water, could he save M.J. again? What if, the next time he had to pull his gun, he missed? What if he in-advertently caused M.J.'s death? He'd be responsible.

He'd always been responsible, at least until last night.

Travis took a deep breath. He'd always been a risk taker in business, but now he was about to be so in his personal life. He would go to M.J. and beg her straight out for forgiveness of his lecherousness.

Maybe he'd get lucky and she'd take pity on him.

M.J. smelled the orchids before she saw them. She inhaled the vanilla aroma, then stretched and opened her eyes.

"Travis!" She bolted upright, then quickly looked down and noticed that she was no longer naked but wearing a T-shirt.

She remembered putting it on before she fell asleep. "Still ogling me?"

"Ouch." He winced.

"You deserved that."

"I did." He nodded. "I'm sorry about last night."

I'm not. She expelled a breath. "No harm done. It's okay."

"No, it's not. I'm afraid my behavior may come between us when we're working. It wasn't like me. Normally, I'm quite in control of faculties—"

She cut him off. "I understand. It's okay."

He rubbed the back of his neck. "I don't know what came over me, I just—"

"Knock it off, will you?" She jumped off the cot and threw the sheet aside. "Why can't you just admit that I turned you on, and when you got hot and bothered you did the gentlemanly thing and left? But no. You have to make some federal case out of this apology. I'm not going to sue you for sexual harassment, I'm not going to wilt on the tropical vine down here and I'm not going to give up on this mission because you got a hard-on looking at my breasts!'' She sat on the straw mat, and yanked on her hiking boots, then laced them furiously.

"Huh?"

She slapped a palm against her thigh. "Sometimes you men are so damned infuriating!"

"Men are? Men?" he shot back, realizing he would never, ever understand the female psyche.

Raising her palms heavenward, she said, "God deliver me. Please!" She scowled at him. "Look, Travis. You didn't deflower me. You didn't betray your sacred morals. You are still the epitome of propriety." She bounced to her feet, then pushed past him on her way out of the tent. "Did you make coffee? I'm starved."

"Coffee?"

"Yeah." She stared at him and felt a zing from her heart to her belly.

"It's ready."

"Good." She started out of the tent then stopped abruptly. "Oh, by the way, thanks for the orchids."

"They're not from me."

She paused. "Uma?"

"That'd be my guess." Travis glanced over his shoulder at the tent door, then at the untied flap of the tent wall.

"He was here?" she asked.

"I'm sure if I investigated the ground around the tent, I'd find Uma's footprints."

She lifted an orchid from the chain necklace of a dozen blooms he'd laced together and hung from the center tent pole. "Uma." She smiled.

Travis's eyes were hard. "You don't have to look so damn happy about it."

"Why do you hate him?"

He spoke through thin lips and clenched teeth. "Because he's trying to kill me."

"He wouldn't. He saves lives, he doesn't end them."

"How do you know? You don't know him. Neither do I, but I know I don't believe a word he says."

"Why do you think Uma is trying to kill you? Maybe it's me. Maybe he's got some tribal thing against women in his jungle. After all, it was my sport bottle he spiked."

"Okay. He's trying to kill both of us."

"Travis," she replied impatiently, "you're overdramatizing."

"No, I'm not. I believe the snake I killed last night was planted here deliberately."

"What?" She felt her stomach constrict as she looked into his very resolute eyes. "You're serious."

"Damn straight. It was a fer-de-lance, not a local resident."

The shock of the pistol firing reverberated through M.J. all over again. She'd thought he was trying to kill her then. She knew she'd never forget the anger in his eyes.

"That's ridiculous! The whole thing is preposterous. Uma would not... Well, maybe... And the river..." Thoughts connected, and suppositions became accusations as panic raced through her. Was it possible the old man was plotting against them? Perhaps he was the enemy.

Despite the growing affection she had for Uma and his stories, she knew Uma thought she was some long-lost Dorothy person. There were times when she did think the old guy was the largest fruit from the farm.

Or she was, for listening to his legends. Half the time she wasn't sure if she was dreaming or if Uma had come to visit. He seemed to come and go like the evening mist. Never quite real. Always ethereal, yet somewhat predictable, like the rising of the sun.

Just why was the old man drawn to her? Why had he chosen to follow her, heal her, if all he wanted was to kill her? Was he playing some sick psycho game?

Well-founded fear told her that Travis was right to be

wary of things that go bump in the night and crazies carrying poisoned darts. Crazy people killed for sport the world over. The news was full of them. Even cold, calculated murders were committed by people who thought they were on a mission from God or that they were getting even for something their mother did or did not do for them, to them or with them.

The world was whacked out. Who was to say the jungle was any better?

She'd been naive to trust Uma. Travis and Michael were right to be concerned about her. M.J. had always trusted everyone too much, too freely and too often. She would be wise to listen.

"I'm not ready to die," she said quietly.

"Neither am I," Travis replied resolutely.

"I'll be more careful from here on out."

He nodded solemnly. "Good."

She answered him with an equally serious expression. "I'm glad that's settled. Let's get some coffee."

23

—▶ ◀—

Michael's nose for oil was on alert. Aided by the accurate computerized location findings M.J. had provided, Michael knew he was close—damn close.

There was a particular bite to the air when oil was present, yet it wasn't the usual smell of petroleum he looked for. It was an acrid mustiness he sought, as if fern, shale and human flesh and bone had placed themselves in a prehistoric communal grave, the weight of hope and guilt pressing on each other, crushing the spirit until a new life was created—that of oil.

The doomsdayers had it all wrong. There was enough oil under the polar caps and the ice of the earth to fuel industry and trillions of people for the next thousand years. The only problem was that exploration had not invented the machinery and tools to drill those reserves.

Michael liked to think of himself as a savior to mankind, bringing the oil that would keep babies warm at night and fuel the cars that brought lovers together so that more generations could be birthed.

But Michael wasn't Travis. Michael didn't have a romantic bone in his body, but these thoughts did give him a sense of dominion. Of being godlike. Such thoughts confirmed the notion he was a world changer—a noble calling.

More than anything, Michael wanted to be noble. His problem was, it wasn't in his makeup. He didn't like to think of himself as avaricious. But if he didn't take care of number one, who would?

As he studied the data more closely, his respect for M.J. grew. The woman had an incredible analytical mind, a genius for seeing past useless data and honing in on the pertinent strata. She was almost as amazing as himself.

"Pedro, ponganle equipo aqui." Michael instructed the boatman to haul boxes of dynamite sticks, microphones, recording equipment and his computer to the area he'd found in the narrow valley between two heavily vegetated ridges. As he looked around, he was suffused with the sensation that dinosaurs had once roamed the area in droves.

He inhaled the still air. It filled him with energy so strong he would have bet it was magnetized. Every molecule in his body felt charged with life.

He closed his eyes and felt at one with the earth and the prehistoric past. He could almost feel the valley floor tremble with the heavy plodding of brontosaurus and stegosaurus. He would have given anything to hear the cawing of airborne reptiles.

Michael couldn't remember a time when he was not fascinated by the prehistoric. As a kid he'd made plaster models of every dinosaur known at the time. He memorized the number of years that had passed since their reign—though all those dates were being altered now that science had figured out the world was much older than previously believed.

Michael was a Jurassic period junkie three decades before the movie's release. It was his love of the ancient that led him to become a geologist. For a short while, he'd thought of becoming an archaeologist. But the hours were bone crushing and the pay nearly nonexistent. So he'd opted for oil. There was a lot more money in it.

"Aqui." He pointed to a jutting boulder. Pedro set up his laptop.

Michael was becoming anxious the longer he stayed here. He could feel the energy of the place as if it were a restless human being. The land welcomed him, yet wanted him to hurry and leave.

It should have made him nervous. Instead, it told him everything he wanted to know.

He looked at the laptop and frowned. He didn't need high-tech machines. Why he'd brought all this stuff was beyond him. Printouts were necessary only to investors. Michael had everything he needed inside himself, in his brain.

While Pedro and Andreas set up the generator, Michael squatted, placing his palms on the ground. Then he stretched out prone and put his ear to the ground, though in reality, hearing had nothing to do with it. It was his sixth sense he used—his intuition, his psychic soul.

Oil ran like rivers through layers of shale and rock. Lakes of it were said to rest in the Oriente, possibly as much as an ocean. Though they had no tide or current, Michael knew the oceans of oil would sing to him like a siren. He'd heard their call before. He would again.

He closed his eyes and his brain to everything except the oil. He groped at the earth and scooped a handful, smelling its woodsy decay. He put it to his lips, not to imbibe, but to register moisture and seek a trace of tar.

He sat on his heels. A smile crept over his lips. But Michael did not whoop or holler. He said no thanksgiving prayer. He simply looked at the trees, rocks and hills around him, memorizing this spot and tracing in his mind the steps that brought him here.

He slapped the ground heartily like one does a buddy after a football game. "We'll set the charges here!" He paced to a location and pointed. "*Aqui.*"

The boatmen hustled toward him with wire and markers.

Tomorrow he would chart this spot with his seismic

equipment. He'd record everything he could, as deep as he could, and then return to camp.

Camp meant M.J.

M.J.

His thoughts halted abruptly. He cocked his head, listening with animal instincts to the nature around him. He felt uneasy, as if someone were watching him. But that was impossible. He was alone here except for Pedro and Andreas.

It was nature he heard. The irregular movement of the palmetto fronds was caused not by the brush of a moving animal, but by the bank of dark clouds swirling in the sky. As they curled to the south, he surmised there would be no storm brewing. Then he remembered he'd moved farther out of the jungle than he'd planned and into the hill country. This was also the year of El Nino. Strange and mysterious weather patterns had plagued much of South America and the world. This was the year rules did not apply.

Things were different now. Everything was different now.

Time was of the essence. M.J.'s description of her dream had rocked him, but good. Was it possible she'd dreamed of El Dorado, like that weird fortune-teller at the Oro Verde had predicted?

Michael suspected M.J. had pulled out the map of Colombia to study not just gorges but specific areas that confirmed her dream had a basis in reality. He'd taken the map to curtail her efforts.

He couldn't take any chances. Not now. Not when they were so close to the oil, so close to having it all.

Michael wanted oil. And he wanted M.J., too. He'd gone so far as to fantasize about a life with her.

He didn't know how she did it, always looking at him as if he were her universe. She made him feel like a million bucks.

He would like to give her a million bucks, that was for sure.

He couldn't believe how he felt. Women had never affected Michael in any one way. But now he felt he should, could, accomplish something altruistic. And for a man who had always been out for himself, who'd never formulated a charitable thought in his life, this was a change.

M.J. made him think he could change the world. She even made him believe he could change his life. It was appropriate Michael was on his knees. He'd found his Mecca.

From his cave dwelling, Uma watched the American and his crew in the tiny valley. "You're smarter than I'd suspected," he grumbled. "Must be those new machines. None of the others before you had so much equipment."

He sipped a fermented concoction he'd distilled from red moya berries and raw sugar that tasted much like the Chambord he remembered was Dorothy's favorite liqueur. He missed her most at twilight when they'd shared dry vodka martinis and spun their dreams of the future. He'd wanted to build her a cottage by the sea, covered with jasmine and surrounded by hollyhocks and a white picket fence. He'd wanted a child then. But only with her.

He was too old to think about having children now. And too sick.

He didn't like to think about his illness, but he was an educated man. He knew cancer when it erupted. His was particularly painful—kidney cancer.

He anesthetized the pain with jungle drugs, which were a hell of a lot stronger than the watered down crap he remembered from his life in California. But that was a long time ago. Perhaps things had improved since then.

He thought about the woman who called herself M.J.

She made him realize he was leaving the world without a legacy. Heirless.

Yet he had heirlooms, he thought as he glanced over his shoulder at his pots, baskets and casks. He expelled a deep sigh. He should have prepared himself better for death. Foolishly, he'd miscounted his years, forgotten a decade and pretended he'd keep on living forever. It wasn't until he'd seen his reflection in a young woman's eyes that he was hit with the brevity of his remaining time on earth. His illness was not going to go away.

It was getting worse.

He frowned at the man below as he smelled the earth like an animal and pricked his ears to every sound. The man went about his work, pacing out well holes according to the maps he carried rolled under his arm.

"I couldn't do it better myself," Uma said.

He walked inside, opened a wooden box and withdrew a pair of World War Two binoculars he'd bargained from a native twenty, no, twenty-three years ago. He doused the wall torch and blew out a trio of candles. The cave was bathed in darkness. He shuffled to the opening, remembering every inch of ground under his feet. "Let's see how really good you are, Yank."

He focused the glasses, bringing Michael's face close. He could see the gleam in Michael's eye, the lust for possession on his lips. He watched as Michael paced off measurements, then used his surveying equipment to make exact records. The crew lit lanterns and stoked a campfire. Still, Michael worked frantically, each moment appearing to egg him on to the next, causing his emotions to reach fever pitch.

"That's it, my boy." Uma adjusted the binoculars. "You can feel it, can't you? You think you've hit it and now…that's right. Do a little dance. The earth likes the jubilation. Celebrate. Praise Hosanna! Have your moment in time."

He lowered the binoculars to his side. "Because that is all you'll get."

He pressed his flattened palm on the cave wall and peered into the valley. "You egotistical simpleton. You're so close and you haven't the first inkling. Oh, you're good, I'll grant you that, but you aren't half the explorer I was. Am.

"I knew the instant I walked through that copse of trees at the entrance to this valley. I felt it in my bone marrow. In my blood cells. But look at you! You found what you were looking for and stopped! You put up your mental barriers. Ha! No wonder there are no great men in the world today.

"You must open your mind, son. Open." Uma clapped his hands. "Open Sesame!"

The monkey imitated his master, took off his hat and put it on quickly.

Uma frowned sadly at his pet. "What is the world coming to, Chipchaw? They have no magic because they aren't looking for it."

He walked to the monkey, picked him up and let him rest on his shoulder.

Uma's eyes darted to the outdoors. The sun was down. The stars were coming out, but there would be no moon tonight.

"Perhaps that's my job, Chipchaw, to show them a little magic. A little black magic."

The monkey applauded merrily as he'd been trained to do.

24

Conquerors always returned with spoils. Michael had his, and he couldn't wait to share his victory with M.J. He felt as if he were carrying the Olympic torch to camp as he approached.

Ordinarily, he let the boatmen lead the way, but not this time. He tromped ten paces ahead, anticipating the look on M.J.'s face when she saw the results of his endeavors.

He was convinced he'd found the exact spot upon which they would drill. The place that would spew forth the magic rainbow and give them their pot of gold, their future.

He knew he'd been remiss in showing his affection to her the last time he was in camp. However, he'd been so preoccupied, so determined to find the oil, that he'd forgotten to say goodbye to M.J. properly.

Now that he thought about it, he realized he must have been temporarily insane. That was the only explanation he could come up with, because the time away from her had seemed like an eternity.

He hadn't wanted to miss her. Why should he? He'd never missed anyone in his life. How was he to know this time would be different? That this woman was different?

Had it only been three days he'd been in the valley, setting charges?

It amazed him that he'd only known M.J. a little over a

week, just nine days, and she'd made such an impact on him.

God, he was torn between desire and reality.

And why the hell did his legs move so slowly, as if the jungle vines were trying to hold him back? Didn't they know he had to get back to M.J.?

M.J. wore the headphones to her portable CD player listening to "Who Wants to Live Forever?" by Queen as she rinsed out her underwear in a bucket of water. Wringing the water out of her sport bras and Jockey underpants, she sang along with the music, feeling the words as if they were written for her.

She glanced up and noticed Agli down by the river, still panning for gold. She had asked him about his quest yesterday, thinking it would be idle conversation. How wrong she'd been.

She discovered that Agli always found five to seven little chunks of gold on nearly every one of his expeditions.

Between her fractured Spanish and his broken English, she learned that Agli thought Travis and she were fools looking for oil when they could be panning for gold.

She tried to explain to him that in the world market the price of gold was at an all-time low. But that made no difference to Agli. The gold nuggets fed and clothed his family for half a year. He'd bought his wife an electric washing machine with the gold he'd panned since coming to work for Travis Kincaid. His children had new clothes, regular trips to the doctor for vaccinations in Lago Agrio. They ate better food than any of his neighbors. His loot from this trip might be enough to buy a used motorcycle. Agli considered himself a very smart and increasingly wealthy man.

M.J. liked the way Agli's eyes lit up when he spoke of his wife and two children. She told him he seemed content with his life. He nodded, smiled and agreed.

Humming and musing about Agli, M.J. didn't hear Travis as he came up behind her.

"You look happy," he said.

"I was just listening to Queen and…" She grabbed her laundry off the rock where she'd laid it and shoved her arm behind her back.

"I should think that we're a bit beyond proprieties at this point, aren't we?"

"I have this image issue."

"That's right, you do," he replied gruffly, his eyes filled with sensuality.

Stunned with the raw attraction she saw in him, she turned away.

Travis cleared his throat. "Did you get that last printout finished for me?" He coughed nervously.

"Yes. It's on the table," she said, pointing to the center of the camp.

"I'll take a look at it," he said.

But he didn't walk away. He hesitated. She could feel him wanting to approach her. She could feel his eyes on her backside. She wondered why he didn't just do it, put his arms around her and pull her to him.

Was the man so distanced from himself he couldn't possibly know his own feelings?

Unfortunately, M.J. was keenly in touch with her feelings. She responded to him with a passion so intense it frightened her. She had no idea people could feel this much.

"M.J.?"

It wasn't Travis's voice she heard.

"Michael?" She turned.

His voice cut through the foliage and lifted itself over the clap of thunder.

For three days M.J. had lived in a sphere of time where no one existed but she and the brooding, sexually charged Travis. She realized the energy between them had been so intense that she'd nearly drained herself fighting the attraction.

For three days she had not thought of Michael. For three days she'd forgotten. Now he'd come back to her. Suddenly hearing his voice, she was flooded with guilt.

"Michael?" Travis whispered and saw the shock in M.J.'s eyes.

Suddenly, the skies opened and rain pelted their faces.

"My computer!" M.J. raced toward the center of camp. She knew better than to leave it out in the open at this time of day, when it usually rained buckets for half an hour, then stopped as abruptly as it had started.

"M.J.!" Michael yelled when he saw her running like a banshee toward him.

She scooped up her laptop, hugging it to her chest. "Michael! Hurry! The rain." She ducked into her tent.

Michael charged through the downpour and followed her inside.

He was breathless as raindrops ran down his cheeks, falling from the edge of his hard jawline. His eyes were filled with anticipation. His smile was so broad he lit up the dim tent interior.

He didn't have to say a word. She knew from his expression, from his contagious excitement. "You found it!" she squealed.

Panting, he nodded. "Thanks to you."

"No way!" She didn't dare dream she could be responsible for one of the largest finds of the century. "Are you sure?"

"As much as I can be without drilling."

"Oh, Michael." She breathed his name and stood rooted to the spot.

He reached for her.

She looked at his arms as if they were contaminated. She looked at him. Then it hit her—something was different.

"Don't I at least get a hug?" he said slowly, his eyes probing her face curiously.

"Yeah, sure," she said, still holding the computer between them.

His arms went around her, crushing her. He kissed her ear. A hunk of her rain-soaked hair matted to his cheek. He felt her coolness toward him. But that was to be expected, wasn't it?

"Look," he said, "I know we argued when I left. I know you wanted to go with me, and it wasn't that I was trying to take the glory from you or not give you a chance, or anything like that. Frankly, I was so thick-headed about a lot of things back then."

He reared his head back and laughed at himself. "Did you just hear me? Is that wild? It seems like I've been away for weeks.…"

"Centuries…"

"You felt it, too?" he went on. "It's crazy how much can happen in a few days, hours, even. Isn't it?"

"Yes," she replied, feeling guilt pinch her flesh.

Michael's exuberance was pervasive. "It's forever from here, I can tell you that. We traveled constantly. Hardly slept at all, actually. You won't believe it. It's all the way back up to the Amazon rim. I didn't even know where I was going, but I kept following the overthrust you'd calculated. I swear, modern man has never set foot in that valley. If they have, they've never reported it. It's so incredibly desolate. Devoid of human…I don't know, human psychic energy. All I could feel were animals. No thought processes. I swear it was like it called to me." He raked his hair. His eyes were glassy with excitement as he quickly told his story.

M.J. caught his enthusiasm. "This is incredible, Michael. I can't believe it! Tell me more!"

At that moment, Travis walked up to the tent opening,

rain pelting him. He'd pulled his collar up and planted his Panama hat on his head.

M.J.'s eyes went to his, finding cool evasion.

"And what did it say when it called?" Travis' gruff voice asked as he stepped inside.

Michael nearly bounced across the narrow space and shook Travis's hand with both his own. "Buddy, you wouldn't have believed it. It was like…hell, I don't know. A movie. No, like I was inside a myth or something. This place is so primeval. Even Pedro and Andreas say they've never heard of this valley we found."

"Valley?" Travis tore his eyes from M.J.'s searching ones. He concentrated on Michael's story.

M.J. turned her attention to Michael. "My charts show no valley."

"I know. I know. But it's there. I was there. I followed your coordinates, M.J. I have to be honest. I think if this hadn't been the year of El Nino, I never would have found it. It's drier this year, less rainfall, so the ground was hard enough to cross. This rain this afternoon is the first we've encountered since I left. Clouds would form, but no rain. Remember us hearing that even Banos was dry this year? Not green and lush like usual?"

"Yes," Travis replied.

"This valley has the richest soil I've ever seen. I swear you could plant a seed in the morning and by nightfall have a sprout. Real Jack and the Beanstalk stuff. I brought back some." He reached in his pocket and pulled out a small plastic bag filled with earth. "Smell it, Travis. It reeks of oil. It's my guess that under normal conditions, the stuff would be oozing out of the ground, but because it's so dry…voilà!"

"Incredible," Travis said, smelling the dirt, then handing it to M.J.

She kept her eyes off Travis's face. She felt awkward, as if she'd done something wrong. But she hadn't. She'd been naked in a shower, nearly bitten by a snake, and Travis had rescued her. Those were the facts, facts she could never tell Michael. He would hear the part about her coming out of the shower, put two and two together and draw the conclusion that she and Travis had become lovers. Which they most decidedly had not.

But they'd wanted to.

"We have to get back there as soon as possible. I'm afraid if the weather turns on us—" Michael looked out the tent opening "—I might never find it again."

"You recharted it, didn't you?" Travis asked.

"Yeah, sure. Surveys. The whole bit." Michael's enthusiasm peaked as high as Chimborazo. "As soon as the rain stops—"

Travis cut him off. "You'll get some rest. And something to eat. We can start tomorrow. Besides, your men look beat. They need the rest just as much."

Michael scratched his head. "Yeah, you're right. I'm running on adrenaline, and they're not."

Travis put his arm around Michael's shoulder. "If this all pans out, you just saved our ass!" He laughed.

"Thanks," Michael replied, slapping Travis's back. He took a deep breath, his energy suddenly depleted. "I guess some shut-eye wouldn't be such a bad idea, after all."

The rain dissipated quickly.

"Thank God," Michael said, looking outside. "We still have a chance."

"Of course we do," Travis said. "But tomorrow." He nudged Michael toward the doorway.

Michael looked at M.J.

"I want to hear all about it, Michael. After you get some rest. I'll help Agli put together a stew for supper."

Michael's stomach growled. "Home cooking?"

She nodded, though she didn't feel the smile she gave him. "Something like that."

Travis followed Michael out of M.J.'s tent. As Michael walked across the soggy clearing to his tent, M.J. watched Travis glance at her.

For a long moment he held her gaze.

In that space she had the distinct impression Travis had found his feelings. He was experiencing an emotion, but he fought it valiantly and it remained stillborn.

Had there ever been a chance for her to connect with Travis, that chance was gone.

25

The gatekeepers had failed. Theirs had been a deadly game, playing two ends against the middle. Someone was bound to lose. That had been the plan. They just hadn't planned it should be them.

How were they to know consciousness had altered midstream? How were they to know leaders were fallible? How were they to know their ideals had been used for personal gain?

They were the Uma men.

They were supposed to know all, to know better.

Consulting their oracles gave them only confused messages. It was the worst predicament they could have projected for themselves.

Scrying didn't bring illumination.

Consulting their pottery runes created arguments among themselves when it was imperative they remain of one mind, one purpose.

One of the members went so far as to suggest they pray to the Christian saints, but they remembered too well the impotence of dead spirits and their lack of universal knowledge.

The Uma men were more powerful than the dead. They knew the scope and force of their collective thinking. They knew how to reach the untapped mysteries in the universe by seeking the body of thought that loomed over the earth like an ocean of energy, banding it like a prayer—that concentration of all the subconscious thoughts of all the humans, dead and alive, who had ever or would ever exist in time. They knew the thoughts of the souls of kings who had reigned in centuries past going back fifty thousand years to the first time the hunters and gatherers had come to the Amazonias. They knew the desires that kept souls bound to the earth plane through reincarnation and the process by which personalities learned their life lessons before ascending to the highest of all dimensions beyond time, through space, to be one with the Supreme Universal Mind.

It was that supreme being's thoughts that the Uma men believed they understood and were translating into the actions they took on its behalf. What they didn't understand was how they could have been misguided, misled.

It was time for them to seize their moment and make their presence known. They needed to assert themselves. They needed to make a statement not only to the intruders but to their leader, who appeared to have misled them.

This time they would not use the *tsentsak*, the magical darts. They must be more dramatic, more emphatic in their method.

They cast among themselves for one who would guide them, but no one was forthcoming. Because they were the Uma men, they were one personality. No one of them could stand out from the others, because to do so would be their demise.

Their only hope was to contact the divine in the most ancient method of their people. They would consume the leaves of the coca plant and the most powerful hallucinogen on earth, ayahuasca, the vine of the soul.

Ignorant of Western cultures that abused hallucinogenic drugs for bodily pleasures and self-destruction, the Uma men viewed the brewing of their magic potions as a precious rite, the recipe passed down from generation to generation for over ten thousand years. They gathered the necessary leaves and vines daily, never traveling so far that all the ingredients were not constantly with them, hanging in leather pouches from their necks and waists. This constant closeness also allowed the herbs and dried plants to assimilate their thoughts, their sense of right-eousness and divine purpose.

They costumed themselves in colorful feather orna-ments stolen from Amazonian jungle birds. They painted their faces with the same bright colors, each color spe-cially blended from berries, fruits and roots of the Or-iente.

Their drum rhythms began slowly, hauntingly exact, as they recreated the heartbeat of Man, then increased the tempo to match the heartbeat of the universal mind. A reed flute hit a high note, piercingly sentimental. Then another flute and another note blended with their very human voices as the chant took on a life of its own.

Sitting evenly spaced from each other in a circle, they lit the tall stack of dried wood and twigs in the center with their torches. It was vital each member place his torch on the pyre simultaneously.

They watched the fire as they chanted. The sparks rose to the ebony sky, blending with the stars. The vibrations of the song lifted the ashes higher to the planets, then far-ther still.

The song from their soul fused with the weeping of an-gels in the Cherubim. Drums beat, flutes cried, and man pleaded for guidance. The ayahuasca was passed around—all imbibed.

Then the vision maker danced among them, sprinkling brightly lit particles of woven dreams into their minds. The communion with their ancestors had begun.

A mythical anaconda slithered around the funeral pyre but remained unscathed. Though the snake was powerful, they had already seen the death of the snake they had brought to the campsite of the intruders.

The intruders had prevailed.

The vision maker danced in their minds. He moved into the fire and then out again, one minute seeming to be spirit, the next real.

They knew he was not human. If he had been, his power would have been worthless to them. They were looking for answers only the divine could impart.

Mesmerized by the flames, the deep current of drugs in their blood systems and the transcendental qualities of their mantra, the Uma men found their god. And it spoke to them.

Twelve minds in unison received the message that the answer lay before them. They were simply too blind to see.

They opened their eyes, sobriety pulling them down to earth once again.

Their weapon had been given to them. Sacred. Life-giving. The seed of all creativity.

Fire.

26

In her dream M.J. thought she smelled smoke. It burned her nostrils, then her throat, but she didn't awaken. She turned to her side.

She saw the shadows of two men hovering around her, then a third. She knew not to trust any of them. She was more than wary of them, she was terrified.

One of the shadows held a torch and lit the stack of wood beneath her feet. She realized she was tied to a stake.

But she couldn't be Joan of Arc. She was only M.J.

Acrid smoke filled the air, and she coughed. She smelled human flesh burning—her flesh.

"Aiee!" She screamed to wake herself up. "It's not a dream!"

She jumped from her cot, brushing cinders off her forearms. The hair had been burned off, and tiny black pockmarks branded her.

Frantically, she slapped at her hair, which had caught a dropping piece of burning canvas from the flaming tent ceiling.

"My head is on fire!" she screamed as panic shot through her body. Gyrating her hands and arms as fast as a propeller, she flayed at the fire in her hair. It only seemed to get worse. Finally, she squeezed the fire with her bare hands, strangling the life out of it.

I'm going to die, just like Mother.

No! Not like Mother. I was there to miss Mother. There's no one to miss me.

She thought of Claire and of her sister's warnings not to go to South America but to play it safe.

Her mind was on overload. Terror screamed through her body, rendering her immobile. She wasn't hot. She was frozen like ice.

It was so hot it was cold. No, not cold. Burning. Like ice burns.

She shivered and realized the intense heat had caused her to sweat. She forced her mind to make sense of the insane situation she was in.

The ceiling was engulfed in flames. She had but seconds before it would collapse on her.

"Take what you need, kid. The most valuable." She thought of Claire. She thought of Travis and Michael. "My work!"

She grabbed her laptop, diskettes and the file of precious research she'd spent years collecting. Bending low, she scooped up her shorts and shoes. Stopping only for her bottle of vitamin E, she raced out of the tent as long fingers of flame grasped the tent walls, twisted them, ripped them and gobbled them up.

She shot into the night, turned and watched her tent vanish before her eyes.

"Travis!" She screamed his name, not thinking, instinct her only guide. She had to save him, save the most important. Then she thought of Michael. Her eyes clicked from Travis's tent to Michael's. She realized they were both on fire. And both men were asleep. In seconds they would both be dead.

She didn't think. She only reacted.

She needed the help of one to save the other. She couldn't do it all, but she could damn well try.

"Travis! Michael!" she yelled, but the smoke had

scorched her throat. Her words were only croaks, like cicadas on a summer night.

She felt as if she were moving in slow motion. What if they were already dead? What if she was too late?

"Travis!"

She forgot the tension around the campfire as they'd shared the evening meal after Michael returned. It wasn't his fault she was feeling this attraction for him. It wasn't his fault she was suddenly confused about her needs. He didn't know the internal tempest that had erupted inside her. He didn't know she could still feel the touch of his hands on her body.

He didn't know because she knew if she told him, he really wouldn't give a damn. But none of it mattered now. The only thing she had on her mind was saving him, whether he cared a fig for her or not.

"Please don't be dead. Please, God. Don't leave me alone again!"

She dropped her things and raced into the roaring inferno. Fear was quashed in the wake of concern.

I have to save him!

The roof had collapsed. The camp stool with his clothes burned with a vengeance, a personality of the demon of destruction the fire was. Maps and charts were cinders. And the sheet that covered him was on fire.

"Travis!" She flew to him, yanked the sheet off and began slapping at his smoldering T-shirt. She pounded on his body, burning her hands.

"Wake up!"

"M.J.?" He grabbed her hands to stop the pummeling she was giving him. "What are you…" He smelled it. Death. Fire.

Her eyes spilled terror. "Travis, get up! You have to get out of here!"

He bolted to his feet, his eyes skimming the tent interior in a flash. "The maps?"

"Gone!" She yanked on his arm with such force she nearly caused him to stumble. "Come on, damn it!"

"God in heaven." He looked at her and saw the burns on her arms, a hunk of hair burned away. He reached for her.

"Now!" With the superhuman adrenaline thrust that many heroes experienced in crises, she shoved Travis through the tent opening. He rolled onto the ground.

M.J. threw her body on top of his, staunching his burning clothes. It hit him what she was doing and what had happened to him. Suddenly, the sting of his burns registered in his brain. He groaned loudly, though he wished he could cry out, but he didn't want to frighten M.J. any more than she already was.

She rolled him in the dirt, pounded his back and the sides of his thighs where his boxer shorts were reduced to ash. Pain catapulted through him. "I'm okay!" he said.

Thoughts fired through his mind, eliminating pain. "Michael?"

"Travis, we have to hurry," she said, pushing herself off him. The flames were out. She stooped and pulled him with her as she stood.

Travis's eyes turned to Michael's tent. It must have been the last to be set on fire because the ceiling had not collapsed yet. "Michael!" he yelled.

Then he looked around. "Where are the boatmen? Agli!"

M.J. remembered her whistle, put her fingers to her lips and blew. In the distance she could see them awakening. They had managed to sleep through her screams. Or maybe they had been drugged.

"*Agua!*" M.J. yelled. "*Mucho para la fuente!*"

"*Si*, meesus!" Agli yelled, and organized the awakening boatmen to bring buckets from the river.

M.J. turned her attention to Travis, who was galloping toward Michael's tent. She raced past him, but Travis grabbed what remained of her T-shirt and pulled her back. "What the hell are you doing? You're not Joan of Arc, you know."

"Yes, I am!"

"You've done enough. It's my turn."

Without waiting for her reply, he dashed inside the tent.

Michael was out cold, just as Travis had been, only in a much deeper and well deserved sleep.

"Michael, get up." Travis grabbed his shoulder and tried to rouse him.

"What?" Michael came slowly awake. "What the hell?"

Michael's eyes fell instantly on the flaming tent walls. He sniffed the acrid air.

"You're on fire!" Travis said, curling his arm around Michael and lifting him off the cot. "Hurry. M.J.!" Travis yelled. "It's okay in here! You have just a few seconds. Help me get the computer out! Hurry!"

She raced inside. Agli was there with buckets and extra hands.

They scurried to save the precious charting of Michael's last and most important site.

"Help us!" Travis ordered to the rest of the boatmen.

M.J. shoved papers into Agli's outstretched arms as the boatmen threw water on the burning tent. Michael scooped up his computer and components. Travis snatched up an armful of loaded diskettes, knowing their future was in the data.

M.J. cleaned off the little camp table and shot outside with Agli. The few buckets of water weren't having much effect on the ravenous flames. The sides of the tent were being swallowed quickly.

"Hey! I didn't risk my ass for you to lose it, Travis Kincaid and Michael Hunter! Get out here!"

Her words worked. They bolted through the tent open-

ing laden down with spoils as the four walls fell on each
other. The wave of heat knocked them all back.

"*Sancta Maria,*" the boatmen said in unison and made
the sign of the cross.

"My God!" Michael looked around at the flames surrounding him. "All three tents are…"

"Toast," M.J. said glumly, placing the tubes of graphs
on the ground. Her arms stung, then throbbed. Pain.
"Oh, God. How stupid can I be?" she grumbled.

She bent over and shoved her shoes on her feet.

Travis took a brief second to scan the fire while Michael
crouched on the ground looking dumbfounded.

"What the hell's going on here?" Michael asked of no
one in particular.

"Damned if I know," M.J. said as she clomped through
the ashes of her tent, using a stick to stir the rubble.

"What the hell are you doing?" Travis asked.

"Looking for my sunblock."

Michael shook his head, looking irritated. "This isn't
the time."

"It has aloe in it. It most certainly is the time. Both it
and my vitamin E will heal my burns and yours."

"How bad are yours?" Travis asked, stopping her to
inspect her arms and neck. "My God." Huge blisters
were forming on her back and neck, and one on her left
cheek. The worst spots were around her ears, where the
flesh was burned away. It was going to take more than
aloe—she needed immediate medical attention. So did
he. So did Michael. And it was the last thing they could
afford at the moment.

Travis's bets were on the fact that they would never
make it out of this jungle alive. "Michael, get your gun
and any ammunition you can find. Do it fast. We haven't
got a minute to lose."

"What are you talking about?" Michael asked.

"This was deliberate. Someone has been trying to

frighten us away since we got here. I get the feeling that now they won't be satisfied until we're dead. They're out there watching every move we make. Take the essentials."

"I'll do it," he said, getting to his task in seconds.

Travis turned to M.J. He wanted to touch her, to reach out to her, but those moments for them were lost.

There were a million things he wanted to say to her. He should apologize for bringing her here, but it was too late for that.

M.J. saw Travis wince as he inspected her burns. She swallowed hard. It was bad. She knew that. She couldn't see anything but the tiny burns on her arms, and it was just as well. The rest was sheer pain. She didn't want to know if she'd be scarred for life. "I'll be fine."

Travis felt that familiar wave of guilt rush through him like a Pacific curl. He'd caused these burns, cuts and bruises of hers. He would have liked to indulge himself in self-recrimination if only to feel better about himself, but right now, they didn't have time.

The chances of their making it out alive grew slimmer by the moment.

"I'm going to be honest, M.J.," he said. "We can't go back. Whoever these people are, they're going to keep following us whether we go forward or back. They not only don't want us to find the oil, they don't want us here, period. It's going to get even more dangerous for us." He took her hand. "We may not come back."

Her heart skipped a beat as Travis confirmed her worst fears. She could see the pain in his eyes, the sense of defeat.

He stated the facts, as cold and scary as they were. That was the thing about reality—it scared the shit out of her. Yet she respected him for that. He was telling it like it was—for her own good. For their own good.

"It's not your fault," she assured him.

"Yes, it is."

"I wouldn't have gone back that first day. I realize I was naive." She took a deep breath, her shoulders dropping as she exhaled. "God! That was tough for me, admitting my mistake. I'm better at defending my actions regardless of their recklessness. Believe me, this is definitely an issue I need to work on."

"M.J., you don't have to take this on yourself."

"Travis, stop. You aren't apologizing to Michael, so why should you single me out?"

She watched his expression soften, his eyes flicker with an eagerness to open up to her. She felt drawn to him. She felt as if she were looking into his soul. She was shocked to see so much need there, emptiness to be comforted and a clamoring to be loved.

She could see it, almost touch it. Why couldn't he?

How could he look at her like this, reveal his soul to her and continue to think for a minute that she was unaffected? The bastard was making her fall in love with him!

Forcing logic to override her heart brought instant clarification.

Was he a coward? Or just protecting himself? M.J. could never be sure. Either way, she was on the losing end of the stick.

M.J. saw a dark, murky cloud drift over his eyes, shutting her out. Her blood froze.

Haunting her like a banshee, M.J.'s argument with Claire came spiraling to mind. Her need to believe that an adventure would make her a worthy person had backfired.

M.J.'s fantasies had always placed her center stage, the object of adoration, the recipient of adulation. She now saw the reality. She was nothing special. She was not Ava Gardner, but a geologist, albeit a good one. And she was a fool. A fool for coming on this trip. A fool for not listening to Claire's, Travis's and Michael's warnings.

She was certainly a fool if she allowed herself to fall in love with Travis.

If they even survived this trip, which was looking doubtful, she and Travis could never be anything more than a bittersweet memory. He would go his way, and she would go hers. She wondered sadly if he would think of her from time to time. Probably not.

M.J. wasn't very good at putting the past behind her. Nothing she'd ever done had eliminated her inner demons. She was just as guilty today of making foolish choices, all in the pursuit of needing to be loved.

She was a hopeless case. But she was tough and more resilient than she'd thought. She'd pulled through the fever, the snake and the fire. She'd never tested her inner strengths before. What she'd done was cover up her pain, throw a mask of confidence over her insecurities. She'd taught herself to be outrageous. To pretend she was someone else, living someone else's life.

Now she was being forced to live this life, and she realized how very precious it was. Above all, she realized how fiercely determined she was to find out more about herself and her ability to survive anything.

She'd learned she was a hero at precisely the moment she'd concluded there was no such thing as a hero.

She'd risked her life for Travis and Michael. And she'd do it again. She knew the kind of superhuman adrenaline that raced through her body, the tilt to total unselfishness her psyche had taken the moment she'd rushed into the blazing tent to save Travis. And then had done it again to save Michael.

Perhaps her mother's death had given her this new courage. She didn't want anyone else taken from her, and would do whatever she could to make sure it didn't happen.

Choking back a hot lump in her throat, she said, "They can't kill us if they can't find us, sir."

Each time she referred to him as sir, Travis tasted a bitter acid. He couldn't help wondering how far his need to protect his employee would take him.

M.J. leaned down to pick up her backpack. "I know where Michael is taking us. If we continue west from there and on up into the Andes, we'll run into a town eventually. We can call to Quito for help from there."

Travis blinked. "I've already thought of that."

"Good. Then you know the plan." She smiled quickly, then looked at Michael, who was gathering his things.

He put his gun in his waistband, then looked at M.J.

"Don't you agree?" she asked him.

His face was implacable, resolute. "We need to move fast. And we can't stop."

"Right," Travis replied. "Are you sure you're up to it?"

She wondered if he knew he winced every time he looked at her burns. Obviously she meant more to him than he was willing to admit to himself. And especially to her.

His reaction was a sign that he cared about her. It was a small sign, a weak sign. But still it was something to believe in. She'd keep looking for signs.

She would continue to hope.

27

Uma arrived in time to see the remains of the fire. He inspected the rubble to make certain the Americans had staunched all the cinders.

"Hmm. Methodical and considerate. Rather surprising for marauders, isn't it, Chipchaw?" Uma said to his monkey, who peered over his master's shoulder.

"But then again, who's to say they are the beasts? Perhaps I am the beast. I was once. I can be again."

With keen eyes, Uma scanned the area, looking past the palms and underbrush, seeing what normal men do not see. Uma was looking for Cofan, the tribesmen who'd made battling oilmen their reason for being. But the woods were clear.

"They're going to find our home, Chipchaw, and I can't let that happen. Our work is too precious to be annihilated by ignorance. Or greed." His voice fell dully on the ground like forgotten guilts.

The monkey was silent.

"Perhaps it's time I stopped toying with these invaders and got on with it. It's not as if I have all the time in the world." He sighed heavily. "Amazing how fast one's life passes. I surely thought I'd have accomplished more this time around. But somehow I didn't. Not that I failed, mind you. It's just these blamed regrets I have."

Uma looked into the distance, and a wistful expression blanketed his face. "I would have liked her to have seen my glory. She would have been impressed."

Chipchaw appeared to know exactly his master's intent, for at that point he screeched wildly, causing the macaws to answer with shrill squawking. They took flight, their wings flapping enough to stir the palm fronds.

"Be still!" Uma berated Chipchaw and the birds. "I know what I'm saying. I know even better what I'm doing. Or rather, about to do.

"Dorothy." He inhaled her name, remembering the past then joining it to the present. "Forgive me, my love, for what I am about to do. But it's the only way. I can't leave you here to die all by yourself. And that is what will happen. You need me. You must see that by now."

Uma picked up a stick and used it as a staff. He proceeded northward toward his home, toward the valley where he knew the Americans would find their way.

M.J. was slowing them down, and she knew it. The pain from her burns was nearly more than she could stand. She was determined to prove that she could carry her own weight, carry her own things, but it was impossible for her to carry her backpack over her blistered shoulder. Her muscles screamed. She resorted to dragging the bag on the ground.

Agli, Paulo and Andreas carried what was left of their water and food. She noticed they were uncharacteristically quiet in this part of the jungle. They kept their eyes plastered to the underbrush, searching for deadly cats. But it was the absence of their happy smiles and laughter that bothered her most. She had the distinct feeling they would bolt and run at the next misfortune. She didn't blame them one bit. They were being paid to make this trip, just as she was, but she was certain even with all their jungle experiences they'd never been up against these odds.

Though she was glad she'd retrieved her sunblock and

vitamin E, she knew she needed something with Novo-
cain, something to kill the pain. But this was the jungle.
There was no pharmacy handy.

"We can stop here," Travis offered.

Michael looked at him as if he were nuts. "We have to
keep going."

"We need to rest," he said firmly. "The boys are tired,
too. Agli looks like he could sleep for a week."

"Maybe he's still drugged," M.J. said.

Shaking his head, Michael said, "We're all tired. Better
that than dead. We don't know who or what is following
us. I say we press on."

"She needs to rest," Travis insisted.

"Fine," Michael replied, dropping his computer bag.
His joints cracked as he straightened his aching arm.
Groaning, he said, "I guess I'm more bushed than I'd
thought."

"Oh, thank God, I'm not the only wimp," M.J. joked,
hoping to conceal her pain. She failed as her face twisted
into a grimace.

"Maybe I should take a look at those burns," Travis
said, coming to stand next to her.

He lifted the neckband of her T-shirt and peered at the
weeping flesh. His medical knowledge was cursory. He
had to think fast to avoid infection setting in. "Do you
have that antibiotic stuff Juan Carlos gave you?"

She shook her head. "It burned along with the rest of
my things."

"How about that vitamin E?" He yanked his cotton
shirt from his waistband and tore off the shirttails.
"Agli!" He yelled to the boatman. "*Agua pura, por favor.*"

"*Si, señor.*" Agli brought one of their last plastic jugs of
drinking water.

Travis doused the cotton with the water.

"What are you doing? We'll need that," Michael protested, watching precious drops spill on the ground.

Travis's eyes were hard as he dabbed at the burns. He bit a small hole in a large vitamin E capsule and squeezed the liquid onto M.J.'s raw wound. "She needs it now."

"I won't drink much," she promised quietly.

"You can have my ration," Travis whispered.

Michael watched them. At first he didn't believe what he saw. Then he realized he had no choice but to believe. It was there, radiating all around them like some kind of halo or electric energy field. Travis looked at M.J. as if she were the last woman on earth, the only woman on earth.

She looked at him as if he were a god.

But I'm supposed to be her god, Michael mused. He watched how she looked away from Travis, trying to hide her pain. Or something else.

M.J. dropped her chin, allowing Travis to only look at her crown. To see her wounds, but not her vulnerability.

Michael almost winced for her.

Maybe she didn't know what was happening to her. Maybe she was clueless to the attraction Michael could readily see. Maybe she still thought she was Michael's girl. She was supposed to be his girl. Wasn't that what they had decided?

Michael thought back on things, finding his entire association with M.J. Callahan an enormous riddle. He'd come on to her from the start. He couldn't stop himself, hadn't wanted to stop his desire. He'd meant it when he told her he wanted her. During those first days he'd lusted after her like a lovesick teenager.

Then he'd forced himself to prioritize his life. He focused on finding the oil and purposefully pushed luscious thoughts of M.J. out of his mind. He'd given up the woman in order to find the oil. Not for himself, but for all of them. Wasn't that what was expected of him? Wasn't that what they were there for? Wasn't that what he was supposed to do?

But somewhere between the beginning and now had

come a middle. Had Travis made a play for M.J.? Or was she so fickle she had to be satisfied by whatever man was handy? Was she out for the man of the minute?

Maybe she was playing one of them against the other. Or maybe it was some sick ego trip on her part—liking two men to fight over her, which was both juvenile and extremely dangerous.

Michael had never been involved with another man's woman. There were too many women in the world to bring that kind of problem to bear on his very busy, very exciting life-style.

As he watched M.J. plead with Travis that she was fine, that she could finish ministering to herself, that he needn't worry about her, Michael realized his musings were ridiculous. M.J. was not a schemer. Michael had met conniving women and men before. He knew what to look for. M.J. was honest, and it was that quality about her that was killing him now.

M.J. had fallen in love with Travis while Michael wasn't looking. But when? And how? What were the depths of her feelings? Had she let Travis know about them? Was she aware of how she felt?

Michael peered at Travis, watching for the slightest sign that he knew how M.J. felt. It was possible that neither of them was aware of the magnetism between them. Possible, but highly improbable. Michael knew he'd never let a moment like this pass him by. At least he couldn't remember one.

Then again, maybe lots of moments had come and gone. He hadn't made love to M.J. He'd let that moment slip by. And he hadn't really told her how he felt about her.

Now that he thought about it, he'd let a great many moments when he could have been kissing M.J., talking to M.J., listening to her, pass him by. Was it possible he'd focused so much on himself that he hadn't allowed himself to get to know her?

Was he that stupid, that blind?

"Thanks, Travis," M.J. said perfunctorily, taking the vitamin E bottle from him. The moment was achingly intimate. She gave him a smile to let him know how deeply she appreciated his kindness.

"Thanks for saving my life," he whispered.

She felt Travis's breath on her cheek. The nearness of his body heat struck her like a sexual tidal wave, and she felt herself melting from the outside in. She leaned against him with an imperceptible movement.

But Travis noticed. He sucked in his breath. He touched the back of her neck, his fingers sliding against her sweaty skin.

The nerve in her neck jumped. She felt a pang shoot through her loins and an ache erupt between her legs. Her eyelids felt heavy, her knees weak.

"M.J." He whispered her name, ostensibly so Michael could not hear him.

Silence.

She didn't dare answer him. She was too afraid to know how she would respond to him.

She felt his muscles tense against her. He felt like twisted steel.

Steeling himself against me. Protecting himself.

A cold blast of reality shook her to her core. She knew what it felt like to be rejected, abandoned. And right now, nobody did it better than Travis Kincaid. He pulled away from her.

She didn't dare look at him for fear she'd crumble emotionally. She wished to heaven she wouldn't react to him like this. She wished she understood herself better. But she didn't.

She didn't know what was happening to her. It didn't make one lick of sense. She swallowed dryly. "You're welcome," she said through parched lips. She took a step backward. "I should rest."

"Sure," he said, watching her face register alarm as if she thought him a monster. "What's the matter?" he asked, seeing dread creep into her eyes. There was a sense of abhorrence in the way she pursed her lips, as if everything about him was distasteful.

"M.J.?"

"Travis," she replied, sucking in her breath. "Don't move."

"What?" He took a step toward her.

Trembling, she reached cautiously for his hand. Travis grabbed it.

"Puma!" she screamed, and yanked Travis toward her.

It was too late.

The puma sprang from a rock behind Travis, fangs bared. Growls ripped from the cat's mouth.

"Michael! Do something!" M.J. screamed as the cat slammed himself onto Travis's back.

"Shit!" Michael was on his feet in seconds. He went for his gun in the back of his waistband, thanking his lucky angel who always protected him for urging him to load the gun before they broke camp.

M.J. held Travis's hand and went down to the ground with him. The puma was everywhere, a devil animal bent on feeding himself and his kin with human flesh. Claws scraped the air above M.J.'s head. She let go of Travis, or he let go of her—she couldn't tell which.

The terrifying growls and bloodthirsty screams the puma emitted turned M.J. inside out. She tried to scream, but the wind had been knocked out of her. Her blisters and welts broke open. Pain branded her again, but all she could think about was killing the puma and saving Travis.

Using her elbows, she pulled herself from under Travis's leg and the puma's paw. Only an arm's length away was a rock large enough to strike the puma down. If she could just reach the rock and hit the puma in the head—hell, hit him anywhere to divert attention from Travis—maybe she could save him.

She could hear Agli's agitated voice, and sensed Paulo's and Andreas's terror, though they spoke not a word.

She saw their shadows as they moved slowly away from the dueling man and animal. She felt their panic like a wave of hot energy. She couldn't let their fear infuse her. Fear was not acceptable.

She screamed as the puma's claw ripped through the air at her calf, marking her skin. She had to keep going toward the rock. The rock would save them.

Above the cat's screeches she heard Agli yelling at the puma as if to divert his attention from Travis.

"*Diablo! Diablo!*" Agli yelled.

But the cat wasn't listening.

Then she heard Andreas and Paulo joining in an unfamiliar Indian chant. She didn't understand the words they used, but she knew their intent—to save Travis.

She pulled herself another few inches away from the fracas.

"M.J.!" Michael called. "Get out of the way!"

She looked up and saw Michael sighting down the barrel of his gun.

Agli and the boatmen were screaming.

The cat swiped at her again. She screamed in terror, not pain.

The forest was alive with harrowing sounds of frightened animals, animals who feared man, but feared the puma even more.

Travis managed to roll the cat onto its back. He ducked and avoided swipe after lethal swipe from the puma's claws. Fangs snapped at his face and neck. They sank into his biceps. Travis gritted his teeth and rolled the cat again, this time positioning himself in such a way that both of his muscular legs were under the cat. Travis kicked the cat once, then rammed his booted feet into its midsection, hoping to lift the heavy cat off him.

Knowing the angry animal would attack again with twice the will, twice the power, Travis calculated he only had a split second to go for his gun in his waistband and shoot to kill.

A gun blast rang through the air. The cat fell like a heavy load on Travis, immobilizing him.

"Oh, my God! Travis!" M.J. scrambled to her feet, panic racing faster than adrenaline. "Are you alive?"

She didn't care if the puma attacked her; she would fight him to the death. "Travis!"

Smoke curled from the barrel of Michael's gun as he gazed at the lifeless forms on the ground.

M.J. whirled accusingly at Michael. "You shot him!"

"Damn straight," Michael said.

"If you killed him I'll never speak to you! I'll kill you myself!"

"I killed the cat, M.J.," Michael said, coming up to the dead puma and lifting the carcass off Travis.

Travis stared at Michael and M.J. "What took you so long?" Travis demanded, coming to a crouch, then standing.

M.J. was furious with Michael. "How did you know you wouldn't kill Travis? What if you'd missed?"

"But I didn't," he replied smugly.

"But you could have!"

"Never." Michael looked at Travis. "You okay?"

Heaving to catch his breath, Travis inspected the bleeding welts along his arm. His hands shook as he peeled his T-shirt away from the fang marks on his neck. "I'm alive." The sound of his voice seemed haunting to him, as if he wasn't quite certain he spoke the truth.

His eyes shot to M.J. "You okay?"

"Yeah," she answered weakly.

"What kind of sick karma is this?" Travis demanded while he bound his wound, twisting his T-shirt sleeves around his wounds to stanch the bleeding. "How many times do we have to face death?"

"I don't know," Michael said, "but like you, I'm starting to get the creeps. This is some morbid joke."

"*Starting* to get the creeps?" M.J. shrieked. "I've been Jell-O since the get-go. I'm not used to these near-death experiences like the two of you," she said, hugging herself.

"Let's get out of here," Travis said. "My guess is, that dead cat has friends. They'll smell blood and come running. We don't need the company where we're going." He looked to the west.

M.J. was still trembling from fright and shock. "This hasn't scared either of you in the least, has it?"

Silence.

Travis's eyes met Michael's. Neither of them would admit to fear. They'd lived through too many experiences. Some were best not remembered, others were denied. It was the only way for the psyche to survive.

She pointed to Agli and his companions, who were inspecting the dead puma with awe and terror. She had expected them to be exultant, raising the great white hunters on their shoulders like she'd seen in the movies.

Instead they lifted grave faces.

"We must leave, Señor Kincaid," Agli said. "*Nostros regressos en hoi.*"

"*Bien,*" Travis replied with a nod.

"What?" M.J. looked at Travis. "You're letting them leave?"

"I'm not letting them do anything. They'll never stay now. They think their gods have it in for us. We're bad luck."

"Maybe we are," she replied.

"They'll be all right." He watched the trio as they raced away. "Our enemies aren't after a few boatmen. They won't be satisfied until they have our heads."

"Lovely," she quipped. "Couldn't you just take Michael's word for it? That the oil is where he said it is?"

"I could," Travis replied flatly.

She noticed he avoided eye contact with Michael. "What gives?"

Michael's smirk sat crookedly on his face. "You don't know me very well, M.J., and that's why Travis won't give you a straight answer."

She was confused, and would have loved to get hostile with them both, but she didn't have the energy for it. Something about almost being eaten by a puma reminded her too much of martyrs and pearly gates. "Explain it, then."

"Travis doesn't trust me."

"That's ridiculous!" she countered. "You're his partner."

"Only partly," Michael continued, shooting Travis a hard look. "He has reasons. I have a certain, well, tainted reputation for screwing my business partners out of their shares."

She noticed that Travis's face was implacable. Peering deeply into Michael's eyes, she asked, "And did you?"

"Depends on whose perspective you believe, mine or Travis's," he said with a willful toss of the gauntlet. This was her chance to declare her choice.

Her eyes met Michael's as he stared at her. She didn't know what precisely he was implying, and this wasn't the time to pursue it. "I wasn't there, Michael. I don't take sides on hearsay. Yours, his or anybody else's. I go by my own experiences." She lifted her bag.

Michael nodded. "Fair enough," he replied and walked ahead, taking the lead.

"The going's gonna be tough," Travis warned her.

"I can do tough. Sometimes, I do tough the best," she said, shooting Travis an implacable look, wondering if he knew she was not talking about the land, but about him.

28

—▶◀—

At the edge of the northern Oriente basin, where the mountains shoot up to the sun, the primeval valley waited cautiously for the three invaders to enter. The torrid heat and humidity of the jungle broke as Travis, M.J. and Michael ascended plateaus, then hills and finally the higher foothills to the Andes. The area was dense with foliage, both behind them and ahead, keeping them hidden from their enemies. Or so they thought.

"Michael," Travis said, "this is too far north for oil. And certainly too west of where I calculated. Are you sure we're going in the right direction?" He hacked at ground foliage with a dull machete. He could really use his blade sharpener about now, but it, like his compass and a lot of other essential tools for survival, had been consumed by the mysterious fires.

Travis didn't say anything to M.J., but the hair on the back of his neck rose in direct relation to the number of unexplained attacks they'd received.

Somebody out there wanted them dead. Each time he wrestled with his unanswered questions, he thought of the eerie stories told to M.J. by the fortune-teller, Martita. Were they going to end up vanishing forever in the Oriente like that trio fifty years ago?

The thing that baffled him most was why. Why would they be sought out? Why were they targets? There were plenty of oil companies, past and present, in the Oriente. This wasn't an environmental issue. The natives welcomed the medical services the oil companies provided. Most native wives and mothers coerced their husbands to befriend the oil companies in exchange for drugs and vaccinations that let their children live longer and healthier lives.

Even the roads the oil companies cut through the rain forest no longer spurred heated debate because the oil companies kept their roads narrow and hidden so that competing companies could not see their exploration paths from a helicopter.

Loggers cut down forests, not oil companies. No, this was something else, something sinister. Something that had nothing to do with their work. But what?

Michael stopped, swiping his sweaty brow with his shirt sleeve. "I know what you're thinking, Travis. You can imagine my surprise when I found myself here," Michael replied as he turned and pressed through a thick wall of vines. "Come on," he urged, holding the vines aside.

"I feel like I'm entering a time warp or something. The energy here is different. Peaceful," M.J. said, taking a deep breath.

"It's different, all right, " Travis acknowledged as vines scraped his cheek.

Michael kept the lead, and Travis and M.J. followed. Michael had marked his trail, and only he knew how to read the signs. "Remember, I didn't use any of your charts, Travis."

"He used mine," M.J. said. Her muscles were screaming, but she pressed on.

"I never asked, M.J., but just exactly how did you come up with these coordinates?" Travis asked.

"Great. Now you want to know my trade secrets." She groaned, dragging her backpack behind her. She stopped only momentarily to roll her neck on her shoulders.

"I think you could trust me with them by now."

M.J. pulled up short. She'd never had anyone ask her such an intimate and all-too-probing question. "Why don't you ask my bank balance while you're at it?"

"I just wanted to know how you did it," he said, gritting his teeth as he watched rivulets of sweat move down her neck then plummet into the valley between her breasts. He wanted to keep his mind on work, not on the way her thin cotton T-shirt had matted itself to her bra-less form.

He wiped the sweat from his face with his palm. His hand was trembling when her eyes flashed at him. Defiant. Always ready to pounce on him verbally. Challenging. Electric. Alive.

She brought out the baser, more animalistic side of him. Travis didn't like it. It made him feel out of control. And if ever there was a time he needed to command his course, it was now. Their lives depended on it.

M.J. felt his glacial eyes on her. She would have broken out in a sweat like a prisoner under interrogation, but she didn't care how much he tried to intimidate her. She knew the truth.

He'd faltered back there in the tent. He wanted her. He'd felt what she'd felt.

Her intuition told her it was too damned important to let it ride. She was going to make Travis remember that feeling he had, that connection they'd shared, if it was the last thing she did.

She matched his intense gaze. She could gamble and risk it all—even her heart.

"The internet," she said proudly.

"What?"

"I used to do it the old-fashioned way, buying magazines and newspapers, tracking down interesting stories. I've always loved puzzles, and geology to me is just a larger, more intriguing puzzle to be solved. I collected everything about oil I could. My files were so thick and numerous that I had to take a storage room in one of those warehouses. I'll confess to a certain pack-rat mentality.

"Since I've never been to these remote places like you and Michael, I can't rely on past expeditions, not to mention that gut instinct you both appear to have, to tell me to turn left when I think I should go right.

"So what I did was a bit unusual, but others do it. I've talked to some paleontologist friends of mine who came upon an incredible dig just because they read between the lines of a *National Geographic* article."

Travis scratched his head. "That's your answer? You're a subscriber to the *National Geographic?*"

"I'm a member of the National Geographic Society, yes," she replied, lifting her nose in the air. "For ten years now. No, eleven. But that's not my only source."

"Thank God," Michael groaned.

She pulled up her shoulders proudly. "Once the internet came along I was able to track stories down, to confirm data. I read old legends I found through the historical societies in various countries."

"Legends?" Travis asked, rolling his eyes. "Amazing."

"Isn't it?" she agreed.

She continued. "At first I steered the common course of studying published geological maps by Shell, Exxon, Texaco. All the majors. I kept stumbling over their references to original maps from the 1920s and 1930s. I copied old maps onto transparencies and overlaid them on current maps. But the old maps fascinated me. I downloaded articles from the Smithsonian Institution. I found original publications about the compositions of the shale, limestone and sand in overlooked areas. Then I backed up that information with articles I found in international petroleum trade magazines. It's incredible how many of these articles never make our presses. I found obscure bits on the UPI and AP wires. I cross-referenced stories I'd read about in our petroleum journals. I was relentless.

While you two were trekking through jungles and shooting lions and tigers and bears…"

"No bears." Michael shivered. "Never bears."

"I was building the data I needed to help Stewart Energy nail down their North Atlantic offshore oil field." She stepped up to Travis and poked him in the chest. "Which is how I won my somewhat illustrious reputation that caused you to hire me in the first place."

"May I remind you that I did not hire you!" Travis protested.

She frowned, then walked around Michael and took up the position of trailblazer. "I think I know where we're going."

Michael glared at Travis. "Do me a favor? Don't piss her off anymore. I'm dead tired." He double-timed his steps, caught up to M.J. and grabbed her elbow. "Hey, don't be mad a me!"

"Michael, what *is* there about that man that gets my goat?" Her eyes were blazing.

Michael cautiously surveyed her expression. "I don't know, M.J. You tell me."

She opened her mouth to answer. Something glib would have done quite nicely. But Michael dropped his hold on her and walked on.

She glanced at Travis, who was adjusting his duffel on his back. His eyes met hers. She felt that zing once again, only this time it went straight to her heart.

Uncomfortable with the intensity of their magnetism for each other, Travis dropped his eyes.

She looked away. The moment passed.

They continued in silence for a quarter of an hour. There was barely any daylight remaining.

M.J. was beyond exhausted. Her muscles screamed, her back ached, and the sting from her burns seemed to renew itself in waves. No amount of aloe could replace painkillers, but wishing for them was a waste of energy.

"Guys," she finally said weakly, "it's almost nightfall, and could we please rest? I don't think I can make it much farther."

Even in his exuberance to see the valley again, Michael nearly fell to his knees. "She's right. If we continue in darkness, we could get lost. I'm beat."

"All right. Let's make camp in these trees. That wall of vines will hide us from…"

"The enemy?" M.J. finished the somber thought.

"Yes," Travis replied flatly, unemotionally.

"Then we can't make a fire?" she asked. "Cook some food?"

"No," Travis said. "It's too dangerous."

"I'm so hungry," she moaned. "But we don't have much left, do we?"

"The shopping cart's empty," Travis answered.

Lying flat on his back, Michael said, "Neophytes."

"What?" M.J. heard the defensive tone in her voice. As tired as she was, she was still ready for battle—any kind of battle.

"Look around you." Michael spread his arms expansively. "The place is a virtual deli."

"The heat's gotten to him," M.J. explained to the silent plants and birds watching.

"Okay. Okay. I guess it's up to me to prove it to you. See that red howler monkey in the trees up there?"

"Yes," M.J. replied, squinting through the rapidly falling darkness."

"That tells me bananas can't be far," Michael said, rising. "Don't worry, I'll fetch dinner."

Relief flooding her, M.J. let her head fall on a soft mound of fern and moss. "Bananas are very high. How will you…"

"Climb, M.J."

"God." She yawned. "I can't imagine doing that."

Rising, then walking past her, he put his hand on her damp hair and whispered, "That's why I'm the hero."

She smiled weakly, nearly falling asleep as the sound of his footsteps dissipated in the distance.

Travis dropped the heavy duffel. His back felt as if it would snap in two. He crumpled on the moss beside M.J.

"You're in pain," he said, pulling the narrow band of her T-shirt from her shoulder. The wound seeped a clear liquid.

She winced. To keep her mind off her own pain, she touched his arm where the puma had cut him. "So are you."

Reason shattered to a million shards in Travis's brain as he looked at M.J.'s pleading face. His fingers slid down her arms, pulling her close to him.

His eyes delved into hers, bringing her out of herself, past her ego, into his needs. She became his with a look.

Tears filled her eyes. "Travis, don't."

He held his breath. "I want you so badly, I can't stand it."

"Don't say that. I don't have many defenses left."

"I know. And I'm just about the worst bet you could make in your life."

"That's what's held you back?" she asked.

"Yes. Because of me, you could die," he whispered angrily, his fingers gripping her arms. "I should shake some sense into you. Make you understand that I'm not good for you. But you look at me…"

"How?" She dropped her eyes to his sensual mouth.

"Like I'm the last man on earth."

"You are."

His lips took her mouth in a kiss that was part desperation, part resurrection. It lifted her, touched her soul, captured her heart.

Suddenly, it was as if her entire world had come together. All the fragmented pieces seemed logical and oriented. Fitting. Perfect.

Her heart opened to him of its own volition. She realized how much love she'd held back all this time waiting for him. For Travis.

She felt as if she'd come home, and the pang of sweetness told her how unloved she'd always felt.

She knew her mother and Claire loved her, but they were family. They had expectations. This was a love she gave away generously. She was filled with hope—hope that Travis would love her back. And she knew her life would never be the same.

She kissed him, giving herself to him totally and completely.

"My God," he groaned. His hands were everywhere, ravaging her, cradling her with reverence and need, causing an explosion inside her.

He pulled the T-shirt over her head, then clasped her face between his hands. He devoured her lips, taking her tongue inside his mouth, making her want him as much as he craved her. "My God, you make me feel alive," he moaned.

Her breath came in long, heaving waves of heat and desire. She thrust her breasts into his hands. She filled him with herself, forcing him to touch more, taste more, feel more in his heart than he'd ever felt before.

Ecstasy filled her as he slowly pushed her down on the soft green moss, hovering over her like angels over souls.

He ground his erection into her thigh, and she felt lust blaze through her like a flash fire. He unzipped her shorts and yanked them over her hips and lower until she kicked them off. She helped him unzip his shorts and free himself to love her.

He tasted and teased her from the tip of her tongue to her nipples, then down her sleek belly and lower to the apex between her legs.

"I've dreamed of this," he said sensuously. "But I never dared hope you'd be so ready for me. You want me this much?"

"I need you this much," she whispered.

She'd always heard that lovers were fools. Now she knew it to be true. She was the world's worst fool.

"Tell me to stop," he begged as he moved over her, stroking her bud with his erection.

Grasping his hips, she coaxed him lower. "Never," she said. "Tell me…"

"I've wanted you since I first laid eyes on you," he groaned, moving his lips to her nipple and grasping her full breast in his hand.

"I think I knew that," she replied, arching her back as another spasm ricocheted through her. She moaned. The ache inside her was more relentless than the unknown swirling danger in the jungle around them.

"Travis, I want you," she whispered.

"Then hold me close. Hold me like you'll never let me go," he said, entering her.

At that moment, M.J. believed that, on some mystical, spiritual plane, she and Travis were bonded for all time. She'd always sensed he'd been out there, somewhere, waiting for her. She'd been right.

That ache in her heart she'd known all her life had finally come to an end. As Travis continued to stroke her, she felt as if she were shooting through fathoms of deep emotional waters. In her fingers she held a starfish as a guide. Orgasm pulled her higher and higher, out of her body, out of the water, spiraling her above the earth to the heavens. The starfish exploded into the constellations, showering her with rapture. She was without a body, without pain or a past.

"Oh, Travis." She breathed his name in his ear once she'd returned to her body.

He touched her cheek. "For so long, I thought you were Michael's girl."

"No, I only belong to me."

He kissed her with so much emotion, so much tenderness, that her lips trembled. "Now you belong to me."

She wasn't threatened by this old-fashioned declaration, but rather touched in way no man had ever touched her before. "What a sweet thing to say," she whispered as a tear slid down her cheek. She realized for the first time that she didn't feel alone.

She felt cherished, loved and protected.

It's all true. Everything I've ever believed in is true. Odd, the places one finds a knight in shining armor.

He kissed her again, as rapaciously as his first kiss. "I want you all over again," he said. Forcing himself to his senses, he slowly pulled away from her and sat up. He picked up her T-shirt and pulled it over her head, smoothing her hair from her face. "But I'll behave," he said, smiling mischievously.

She looked at him and felt a shadow of fear chill her. She had wanted to tell him that she loved him, but he had not said it to her. He'd only said that he wanted her. He had passion for her, lust. But was it love?

"Travis," she began, taking a deep breath. Then she stopped.

"Yes?"

She touched his cheek. Her eyes searched his. "I—I…"

He kissed her fingers. "You have regrets?"

"Oh, no," she said, sincerity rimming her eyes. "I thought it was…you were lovely. It's just…"

"I know. Michael. You—" He hesitated.

"I should talk to him," she said, looking away.

"No, M.J. I'll talk to him. He'll be back soon, and he'll know."

"He will?"

"If he doesn't already," Travis said.

"How?"

"I told you, you look at me as if I were the last man on earth."

His statement was shockingly revealing. What had her heart been trying to tell her that her mind had missed? Had she distrusted Michael from the beginning? Had she known intuitively that Travis had wanted her from the moment they met, like he said? Had her instincts known her destiny all along? Was that why she'd never let Michael into her heart the way she had Travis?

And why had she, of all people, someone who proclaimed far too loudly to all her friends and family that she would know her soul mate the second they met, almost chosen the wrong man?

Perhaps it wasn't that Michael was devious and not to be trusted. Perhaps what her psyche had been telling her all along was simply that he wasn't the right one for her.

She looked at Travis, his eyes twinkling like a lit Christmas tree at the mention of her adoration for him.

M.J. had never put anyone on a pedestal. That was supposed to be her spot.

She couldn't resist baiting him. "Me? What about you? Your face is glowing right now."

"Admit it," he said. "I kept you guessing."

"Yes, you did," she replied.

You still do. Am I the only woman on earth for you, Travis?

She lowered her head. "I guess I'm not such a good actress, after all."

"Lucky for me," he said, and kissed her deeply before moving away from her and dusting off bits of moss.

Sadly, she watched the tiny motes and lacy embers flutter to the ground—the last evidence of their lovemaking.

She heard the jungle sounds around them threatening and wondered if they'd live long enough to make love again.

29

They had a slow start the next day. The lack of food and water was taking a toll on all their energies. Mostly, M.J. moved slower, being weighted down with guilt.

She had always prided herself upon being straight with people. Honest—that was her watchword.

She couldn't understand how people carried on love affairs while married to someone else. The entire idea made her stomach roil. True, she wasn't married to Michael, hadn't ever slept with him. They hadn't committed themselves to each other. In fact, she'd been more confused by Michael than comforted by his presence in her life since she'd met him.

Yes, she'd been attracted to him. What red-blooded woman would not? He was bigger than life, handsome and virile—and clearly attracted to her. But that was where it had ended.

However, right now she felt like she was Hester Prynne, deserving of a huge fat capital *A* across her chest for cheating on Michael.

Not that sleeping with Travis had been wrong. It was the most right thing she'd ever done. But as the morning hours dragged on and they continued whacking their way through the vegetation, she wished she could just blurt the truth out to Michael, get it off her chest.

As far as she was concerned, they couldn't get to Michael's valley soon enough, and her reason for wanting to see it had nothing to do with oil.

"How much longer?" she asked, still dragging her backpack.

Michael's excitement rang in his voice. "It's just over this ridge."

"Thank God," she replied and trudged onward.

Thirty-five minutes later they entered Michael's valley.

M.J. stood rooted to the ground as she surveyed the green walls of vegetation. An eerie sensation of crossing time barriers suffused her with awe more than fear, respect rather than elation.

She drew in the clean air, smelling eucalyptus, vanilla and rose. Or was it the funereal, musty scent of decaying organisms?

"My God," M.J. said. "Everything is so different here."

"Isn't it?" Michael agreed, victory resting comfortably on his face.

Travis peered around, ever vigilant, ever ready for an attack from an unseen enemy. He wished to hell he or they would show their faces. But they never did. Still, he sensed they were not far away.

The trees were taller here in the valley, skimming the sky, and though the land had none of the dense bottom foliage they'd experienced in the jungle, it had a majesty that made M.J. realize she would never see anything like this valley again for the rest of her life.

"You can almost feel the dinosaurs walking here, can't you?" Michael asked with elation.

"It's incredible," M.J. agreed. "The air is very still."

"That's right. No wind current. We're too low for much, though the storms brewing in the mountains will roll down on us by nightfall. We need to make camp, but I want to show you what I found, Travis."

Michael ran across the valley floor, clomping over tall grasses and wildflowers with his booted feet. To M.J. he looked like a child racing toward home. Her heart went out to him.

Michael turned to her, waving her toward him. "Come on, M.J.! You, too, Travis! Can't you feel it?"

"It?" she asked.

"Yes!" he shouted, throwing his head back. "Success!"

Suddenly, she could feel his excitement. As if from the center of the earth, it shot through her from the soles of her feet, up her spine to the top of her head. She felt as if she'd burst with its enormity.

"My God, Travis." She turned an expectant face to him. "He's really done it."

"If it's here, then we've done it together," he replied solemnly.

"If."

"It's a big word," Travis said and followed Michael, his eyes scanning the ground. Travis's instincts were on overdrive. As far as he was concerned, there was no more guessing. He'd said "if" to M.J. to keep her calm, to keep her from being disappointed. If by some portentous stroke of fate they should fail, he wanted her to be prepared. There was always a chance they could go back empty-handed.

Feeling the soil beneath his feet, smelling the air grow more acrid the farther they ventured into the valley, Travis breathed in success. It had been a long time, and it felt good. He'd be rich once again, but this time his life would be different. He envisioned a new wing at Rice University, paid for by him but donated anonymously. Day schools. Medical centers. Money for jungle-based doctors like Juan Carlos who were counting on him for donations, substantial donations.

Ominous emotion dampened his spirits as he realized he hadn't given much thought to how exactly he would live his personal life. He'd thought about what he would like to do for the world, what he should have done the first time around. But he'd made no plans for himself—

no trips for fun, no vacations, no sight-seeing. No ski lessons.

He had not envisioned himself gazing at sunsets in the Rockies because there had been no reason for it. There had been no one to share it with. It hit him then that he was more alone in his future than he was in the present and in the past.

He stopped dead in his tracks and looked at M.J. as she moved slowly through the wildflowers and vines toward him. She was taking it all in—every scent, every flower, every minute this place had existed from time immemorial. She was living every second of her experience.

She had the courage to greet life with open arms, which was more than he could say for himself.

Being honest, the closest he'd come to knowing himself, to understanding himself, had been while he was making love with M.J. He'd told her that she belonged to him, and he'd meant it when he said it. But the reality was that he had no more to offer her now than he had then.

There were no guarantees in life. But that wasn't what you told someone when you loved them. You guaranteed them plenty—a long life, for starters. And Travis couldn't even promise they'd be alive this afternoon.

"Over here!" Michael shouted, waving. "I found my mark! As if I'd forget!"

Travis answered his wave and signaled to M.J. "Hurry, M.J.! You don't want to miss this!"

She waved back, smiling.

Travis beamed at her, then took off running toward Michael. His long legs ate up the ground. As he drew closer, his instincts told him this was the real thing. They'd found what they'd been seeking.

Finally, Travis had validation that he'd been right to insist they stay together. He didn't have time to take M.J. to

Lago Agrio or to send Michael with her. He had to press on.

But he wanted M.J. with him at this moment.

He hadn't realized his desire had been partly to blame for his decision to keep her at his side. He'd told himself he was watching out for her welfare, when all along he'd been looking out for his own.

She was the last of the trio to make it across the valley floor.

"M.J.! Stop dawdling!" Travis smiled jubilantly at her.

She lifted her head, the last of the day's sunlight momentarily blinding her. "I'm coming!" she replied.

Though she wanted to run to them, she took her time. She was more exhausted than she wanted to admit. But it was more than that. There was something about this mysterious place that beckoned to her in a way she didn't understand.

It was as if she were caught in the middle of someone else's dream. Something about the way the sun spliced through the tall trees, the slope of the mountainside, the green of the grasses and the unusual wildflowers jogged her memory. She'd never been here before—few humans had. So why did it feel as if she'd come home? Why did she know that beyond that clump of trees to the east was a small creek with the clearest water imaginable? And with tiny fish that look as if they were a long way from their Caribbean home. Why did the air feel familiar? And those peculiar jutting mountains to the west. Had this valley been photographed in one of the journals she'd read? Had someone put it in a movie?

Maybe it reminded her of the Sierras she'd visited with Claire and the kids. Maybe there was nothing unusual about it at all. Maybe it was just another picturesque valley, like all mountain valleys.

In her mind's eye she saw herself dressed in white

linen, a Panama hat on her head. She was with the two men again, one dark-haired and one blond.

She heard a man's voice. He was singing.

"See the other side in a silver plane," he sang. "Watch the jungle when it's wet with rain. Just remember, darling, till you're home again, you belong to me..."

The voice continued. "See the market place in old Algiers, Send me photographs and souvenirs. Just remember when a dream appears, you belong to me. I'll be so alone without you. Maybe you'll be lonesome, too. And know..."

M.J. became one with the moment, remembering the music, hearing it swell inside her head. The orchestra sounded scratchy, as if someone were playing an old Victrola record.

"You belong to me." He sang with so much emotion. Devotion.

M.J.'s eyes popped wide open.

"Uma!" She clasped her hands to her mouth. "But it couldn't be."

But it was. A young man's voice. A young man she'd seen while in the throes of her fevered dream. A young Uma in a tuxedo.

It was crazy. Insane. She was losing her mind.

"Maybe I'm overdramatizing again." She remonstrated with herself.

Thunder rolled in the distance. Clouds swept down the mountainside like diaphanous angels descending to earth. M.J. shivered, but the temperature had not dropped.

She felt a shadow fall over her. She stopped and looked behind her, but there was no one. There was only the sound of a quartet of hummingbirds fluttering nearby.

She felt it again. "Hello?" she asked of no one in particular and glanced around, waiting for an answer.

She took another few steps.

"M.J."

She was positive someone had whispered her name. She stopped again. "Who is it? Who are you?"

Thump!

The blowgun dart entered the side of her neck, past the burns, deeper, to where its poison could enter her bloodstream.

The hunter was an expert shot, she thought as her hand felt the pointed needle.

It was the last thought she had before blacking out.

30

The Uma men finally had to speak about the matter to each other. This time their telepathy would not do. There was a traitor in their midst.

Because there was no chief among them, the task of identifying the blasphemer was more than difficult. They agreed it was impossible.

"We are the one," said the youngest. "One mind. One body. One goal. How can this be happening? We are the true believers. We make history happen with our minds. You have all told me that for one of us to dissent for even a moment is the end of us. Why would any of you try to destroy us? Yourself?"

"He is right. It is impossible we can be divided against ourself. To cut us in half is to die," said the eldest Cofan member.

"There must be a test among us to root out the evil that has penetrated our unit."

"How can one test oneself?" asked the youngest.

"One must always be testing the self. Otherwise, there can be no growth. Perhaps we have been on divergent paths for some time and have not realized our failure to the one," the eldest Cofan member explained to the rest of the body who were not as old and as experienced as he.

"Who among us would be so bold as to take the woman? And for what purpose? Does one among us lust after her?"

There was silence around the circle.

Eyes accused. But no eyes were averted. Cowardice was not acceptable to the Uma men.

"Are we not the gatekeepers?" asked the youngest member. "Are we not guided directly by the god Uma himself?"

All heads nodded.

The youngest continued. "Then I say we consult Uma in the manner in which we have always summoned him. Let him point out the traitor. Let Uma decide what punishment should come to bear. Uma is the god. We are only the one, manifesting his orders on this earth. Is that not so?"

"That is so," the membership replied in unison.

"So it is done," the eldest said, as he reverently opened a pouch made of woven palm fronds. He placed sacred powder in a pipe, lit it with a flaming twig from the campfire and inhaled the magic smoke.

He passed the pipe to the member sitting next to him, who also inhaled deeply. The pipe was shared by all twelve members. According to their ways, they would all dream the same dream, see the same vision, and without speaking to each other, they would be given the divine word from Uma himself.

Chanting deeply in their throats, they created a gurgling sound like the tempo of a river as it passes over stones. They closed their eyes and let the divine Uma enter their mental sphere.

Uma appeared as he always did to his men—horrific, carrying a terrifying mask that covered an even more grotesque face. He was young, tall, his body perfectly carved human flesh. His wings were broad like those of an archangel, but the claws on his feet were more fierce than those of the deadliest animal on earth. He was immensely strong, his forearms and biceps bulging with muscles, and his shoulders were wide enough to cut a swath through the Oriente as he scourged the earth, cleansing it with fire, preparing it for rebirth.

Because Uma had come to them many times to give direction, orders, sometimes even to praise, they were not prepared for this unusual visit.

Uma's voice thundered through their minds like an angry storm. He was outraged as he flung his mighty arms over his head and then around him, turning, spinning like a tornado, threatening to destroy everything in his path.

"There is no traitor among us!" Uma's voice boomed. "There is an imposter!"

Though the youngest of the members was tempted to open his eyes at this astounding announcement, he didn't dare. To do so would be to break the vision. He did not want to be responsible for Uma's departure at the moment the truth was at hand.

"Imposter?" the twelve said aloud together.

The vision continued. Uma relayed to his followers telepathically that the imposter was a white man, old and of no threat physically to them. Uma said that the old man had been posing as a god for too long and that the time had come to stop his evil. He told them the old man lived in a cave above the sacred valley of monsters and that the old man had taken the young woman captive.

"He wants to kill her?" the youngest member asked.

"He wants to possess her in life, and in death, as well," Uma said.

"She is our prey. Our trophy. She was to be a sacrifice to you," the eldest Cofan member explained.

"Only the sacrifices given by the pure in spirit are acceptable.

"We are pure."

"I say that you are not."

The Uma men were silent in mind and tongue.

Uma's anger raged. "You have no defense for yourselves because I speak the truth. You have faltered in your thoughts. You are no longer able to complete the simplest of missions. You alone are responsible for keeping this valley pure, and you have failed. The intruders have defiled my soil twice now. One among the three has a heart bent on evil, an evil so incomprehensible, it has no place in this valley. I remember feeling this desecration two generations ago, when three white people came to this valley. Then, as now, their hearts were filled with greed. I feel this again."

Uma continued. "You have failed me. You have allowed them to come this far. You have not deterred them. You have not sent them back. Their greed is stronger than your conviction. You have lost your power." Uma spread his wings about him, a show of power. His intention was to cast fear, and his ploy worked.

The Uma men cowered before their god.

The youngest opened his eyes and was stunned to see the flame-eyed, hideous face of Uma bearing down on him. But he felt his strength of purpose surge through him, giving him courage. "That's not true!" he protested in their defense.

"Silence!" Uma raged. "How dare you, my chosen, betray me and abuse the gifts and power I have given you!"

Uma's breath was hot as a blast from hell and as forceful as a gale wind, blowing their hair and causing them to shield their faces with their hands.

Uma's voice resonated inside their minds, inside every cell of their beings, for this was how he spoke to them. "It is your destiny to keep this valley and its secrets safe. The secrets that lie just beyond this valley have evaded mankind for twelve thousand years. Your ancestors were not corruptible. They knew the enormity of their challenge. But you! You are weak. You lack the heart! And for that there is no forgiveness. The future of all mankind rests in your hands!"

"We—we accept our mission." They prayed with their minds.

"This imposter who kidnaps the woman must be eliminated. More importantly, all three of the invaders must be killed. They threaten to expose everything about us that we hold dear. They would not understand our secrets. They would misuse them. They would bring great terror into the world.

"Human beings are not ready to learn what we know. They are not ready for truth. They are comfortable believing what they believe. It is true the ways of the world and the energy planes that surround the earth are moving to a higher vibration. They are more in keeping with the lower planes of gods where I reside. Their access to my world is coming soon. I can feel the force of their new way of thinking. Still, it is too soon for them, too soon for me. I am an ancient soul, and it takes a long time for me to alter my thoughts to align with higher vibrations."

The youngest member was confused. "There are those above Uma?"

Uma's eyes blazed like fire. "I see them coming in hordes, like never before."

"What are they?"

"They are not gods," Uma replied. "They call themselves angels."

Uma spread his wings once again. "I am disappointed in you, the one, and you the individual members of the body of the one. Heed me! Do not take this warning lightly."

Uma swept his wings upward, lifting his mighty body off the ground. Then, hovering overhead, Uma vanished in a rush of wind.

The Uma men huddled together as the air grew cold again.

They were unsure about the course they should take, but action was imperative. Ignorant of the metaphysical tenets Uma had tried to explain to them, they surmised among themselves that they had sinned.

The very thought went against every belief in their system. Sin was failure. Failure was ineptness. And ineptness in the jungle meant certain death.

They felt the sting of their own corruption. They needed to redeem themselves. Collectively, they agreed there was only one path to redemption.

They had to sacrifice the white woman and her companions to save their souls.

31

───►─◄───

M.J. felt as if she were the protagonist in a science-fiction movie, traveling at the speed of light, through tunnels of sound and spirals of brilliant galaxies.

She was falling.

She knew she was screaming, but she couldn't hear her voice. Her throat felt raw. Her white linen clothes fluttered and flapped against her skin as she descended. She was reaching for someone.

Then she heard that voice she'd heard before, in her fevered dreams.

"Dorothy."

How many times did she have to tell him that she was M.J.? She wasn't Dorothy. Never had been.

"Dorothy?"

In her sleep she protested. "No," she mumbled, rolling her head from side to side.

"Wake up, Dorothy."

M.J. awakened from the drug-induced dream state with a pounding headache. Placing her palm to her temple, she sat up, groaning. "Where am I?"

"Safe at last," the craggy voice answered.

Focusing in the dim light, she looked around the cave. "Who's there?"

A good-natured chuckle answered her. "How could you forget me so easily?"

"Uma?"

"Yes." He approached her slowly.

"How did I get here?" She peered into the darkness, then watched as he lit torches and candles. Dozens of them. She patted the hard ground under her, then moved the mountain of native woven blankets aside. "Where exactly is here?"

"Welcome to my home," he said, carrying a fat candle toward her and placing it on the ground next to her.

"You found me?"

"In a manner of speaking." He grinned mischievously.

Her memory raced back to her with lightning speed. Her hand flew to her neck where she'd been hit with the blowgun dart. "You tried to kill me!"

"No, I saved you."

She looked at him. "I'm not buying it. You deliberately shot me."

"It was only a sleeping potion. You can buy the same thing in the States at the pharmacy, probably without a prescription these days."

"How would you know?" she accused.

"I do get a newspaper from time to time. In my own way, I try to keep up." He smiled charmingly.

"So, what did you do? Carry me on your back?"

"I'm in good shape for my age, but that's a bit of a stretch for me. I used my burro," he said. "His name's Al."

"Sure." She nodded condescendingly. "You just hoisted me onto the back of your pack mule with no help from anyone."

"I might have had some help."

"Now the truth comes out." She crossed her arms.

"I said 'might,'" he replied defensively.

"How many were there?" she asked, glancing furtively around her, wondering if they were watching from the shadows.

"Just two. They live near here. Frankly, they're as old as I am. And you, well, you're quite healthy, I must say."

"The fact that I've lost a dress size since coming here is beside the point—"

"Then why mention it?" he asked teasingly.

"So, do these friends of yours know they are accomplices to a kidnapping and that they will rot in jail with you once I turn you all in?"

Uma laughed and slapped his knee. "Now that's a ripe one!"

"What's so funny? I *will* turn you in to the authorities once I get out of here."

"No, you won't," he replied, his smile falling as he yanked off her blanket.

M.J. looked at her legs and the rope binding her ankles together. The same rope was then tied to a stake.

"Shackled?" Horror riddled her expression.

Uma clamped his hand over her forearm. "You have been badly burned. While I was treating you, your body went into shock. I had to tie your legs down."

"Good. Fine. Then take this thing off," she said, reaching for the rope and pulling on it.

"Not so fast. How do I know you won't run away?"

"Of course I'm going to run away!"

He tightened his grip. He was hurting her. She was amazed at his strength, and for the first time she wondered if he had needed assistance from his friends.

"I haven't finished treating you. Several of your burns have become infected."

"Infected?"

"I suspect staph, though I don't have the means to take a culture. You'll just have to take my word for it. You'll scar, at the very least. If it spreads…" He held his palms upward.

M.J. didn't need any further explanation. She knew all too well the dangers of infection. Staphlococcus was something every doctor, nurse and hospital feared. But she didn't trust anyone who had to kidnap her to treat her. "Show me."

"If you insist."

"I do."

Uma rose, went to a tall set of crudely constructed shelves and withdrew a tortoiseshell hand mirror. To M.J. it looked like the kind women used fifty years ago.

Handing it to her, he said, "Look at your neck." He picked up the candle and held it close to her throat, back-lighting her silhouette.

Anxiety shot through her. Her hand shook. She suddenly wasn't so all-fired offensive. There were deep holes where the fire had burned through the top layer of skin. On the edge was the white puss that she feared. She felt exposed and extremely vulnerable, as if the burns represented the awakening of her soul. She'd never looked inside herself as much as she did now.

It had happened again. She had escaped death by the narrowest of margins. This time, however, she'd been the instigator of the rescue. She'd been the savior.

"I'm flawed."

"Frankly, yes."

M.J. had always prided herself on her pretty, clear skin. She now had a scar on her leg and indelible fingerprints left on her neck by fate—a fate she had personally chosen. "Tell me they will heal."

"I'll do my best. This eucalyptus is the only wonder drug I have. It's a good antiseptic and has bactericidal properties. If it does its job, the infection will clear quickly. I have a kind of home-brewed alcohol made from orange blossom, chervil, which has antibiotic action, and mint and savory for an astringent action. But only a miracle can save you from scarring."

She thought about that for a second. "That's okay. I'll let my hair grow to cover it up," she said, knowing she had put those scars there. She was making herself over.

She'd saved human lives to earn these medals of honor. It had all been worth it.

"I'm concerned because staph can be deadly."

"I don't know about all these things you're using, but I had some antibacterial cream the doctor gave me for my leg. It burned in the fire."

"I can tell by your condition that it must have been awful for you," he said with compassion.

She looked at him warily. "You didn't see it? You weren't there?"

"Why would you think I would be?"

"You seem to know our every move. Even before we do." She straightened defensively, moving away from him.

"Do you think I had something to do with starting the fires?"

"How did you know there was more than one? I never told you that!"

"I came upon your camp afterward. I made certain the fires were out."

"There was no need. Travis and Michael saw to that."

"Good job, too."

"So why were you poking around?"

"Concern for you," he replied quietly. He rose and went to the table where he'd been mixing the alcohol elixir. He ground the chervil and mint with his mortar and pestle.

"That's for me?"

"Yes. You are my patient."

"You're not a doctor," she countered.

"I'm better than that pup your friend brought in from the outside." He tamped the mixture with renewed force.

"He's from Quito," she corrected, finding his frame of reference curious.

He added eucalyptus oil to the dry herbs, followed by

a paste of orange blossom and sage. He blended it into a pungent-smelling paste.

M.J. took one sniff and said, "You're not going to put that on me, are you?"

"No," he replied, handing it to her. "You are. I have to cut the gauze. Can't let too much air into the wounds. Impurities."

She took the mortar. "This from a man who brought me here under force."

"It was not force."

"A blowgun is a weapon of aggression."

"You wouldn't have come willingly. You needed medical attention," he insisted. "I doubt your companions have any foresight beyond the ends of their noses to realize anything more than this avaricious quest of theirs."

"You don't like them, do you?"

"No."

"Well, it's my quest, too," she said, sticking her finger in the gummy paste. She spread a small amount on her forearms. It stung and felt icy cold on her burns, though the paste itself was tepid. "It feels like acid. Are you sure you told me everything that's in this stuff?"

"Not all of it. You've never heard of such plants. Few have," he said, laying a strip of gauze over her arm. "Here, give me that. I'll do your neck."

M.J. held the wooden bowl beside her cheek while he worked. She kept her eyes on the burning candles to keep her mind off the pain. She winced when the medicine touched her skin, but in an instant she was numb.

"You could sell this stuff and make a fortune."

"I don't need a fortune, and I did sell it at one time."

"Really? When?"

"I'm not sure anymore. My memory isn't all it used to be. Senility, I suppose."

"You're no more senile than I am. Selective memory is more like it."

Uma was silent as he finished dabbing her burns.

"So what do you think? Will I live?"

"You need time to heal."

"You said that the last time."

"Time *is* the great healer, for just about everything," he replied. "Especially the psyche. I should know. I've had a lifetime of healing."

There was a hollowness to his voice that caught M.J.'s attention. "By that do you mean of yourself or others?"

"Both, I suppose."

"And do you have a wounded heart?"

Uma froze.

She realized she'd blurted the question without thinking it through. Her words hung in the air like daggers. "I'm sorry, it's none of my business."

"It's all right. I want you to know me. It's been a long time since I had a friend to share things with."

"So is that what this is all about?" she asked.

"This?"

"Yeah. Following us. Spying. Knocking me out with your woogie-woogie dart."

He paused, pondering her accusation. "I hadn't thought that was what I was doing, but you might be right." He placed the last of the gauze on her neck. "There, that ought to do it. I'll change the dressings in the morning."

She pressed further. "I guess it gets pretty lonely out here in the jungle, huh?"

"Oh, I don't know. It seems to me I can remember being quite alone in a big city surrounded by so-called friends. I think I was alone more then than now."

"Oh, I doubt that."

He smiled at her naiveté. "I have Chipchaw to keep me company." He clapped his hands, and the little monkey scrambled off his tiny bed in the corner and scurried to Uma's side.

Uma's face grew thoughtful. "Seldom do I walk into a village and see only one person. Numerous times I can remember tending so many I'd stay as a guest of the chief for a week. By the time I leave, I'm exhausted."

"Sounds like you could use some help," she said.

"Help? Are you daft? No one but an old fool like me would do what I do. These young pups like your friend—"

"Juan Carlos," she interjected.

"They all want money, a lot of it, for services rendered. These people can't pay."

"But the government could subsidize the doctors and build hospitals once they get back on their feet."

"Yes, it could. And everyone would benefit. But I don't believe I'll live long enough to see it."

"Don't say that! If my friends and I can find the oil that's here, we are hoping our investments will help build just such a hospital."

He stared at her. "Who fed you that line of poppycock?"

"Travis—"

He cut in, suddenly angered, "Is that how he got you down here? He appealed to your ridiculous American ideals?"

"No, I—"

He threw his hands in the air. "Amazing the lengths men will go to feed their greed."

"Greed?" She gaped at the old man as he stormed from the table to a work area comprised of two sawhorses and lashed-together pine logs on which plants were drying. He slapped a stalk of wide green eucalyptus leaves against his leg as he paced. His eyes seemed to peer through the cave walls as if they didn't exist.

"Greed is the only thing that brings men to this godforsaken place. Why else would they risk their lives? I've seen it happen too many times to count. They come seeking fortune, but instead they find danger. Death. They find their demons, wage war with them and lose." He flayed his leg with the eucalyptus but didn't seem to feel it.

"Are you all right?" she asked carefully. "You seem a little tense." Her eyes fell to the eucalyptus switch.

Uma followed her gaze. "Huh? Oh, sorry." He inhaled the leaves, calming himself. He placed the whip on the worktable.

"And did you lose your battle with yourself?"

"Yes, but I'm winning it now," he replied, the last of his anxiety lifting like a hot air balloon.

"How did you do that?"

"I told you. Time."

She nodded, smiling. She didn't understand the riddles in which he spoke, but she realized she needed to use diplomacy when speaking with him. She'd always thought her impatience was an impairment to her personal growth. *Time* was the one answer she hated hearing.

"Tell me I need Zen, but don't tell me I have to be patient. I hate that!"

"Youth always does."

"Youth, huh? Well, you sure flew off the handle quick enough. Maybe you haven't conquered all your demons, after all."

"No. Not demons anymore." He exhaled. "Just memories."

"Of what?"

"Whom," he corrected as he built a perfect Boy Scout campfire in the middle of the cave floor where yesterday's ashes remained.

His eyes grew vacant, then weepy, then solemn. "You remind me so much of her. She was a bit taller, more willowy and beautiful."

"Gee, thanks."

"You don't understand how it was with her and me.

You are just as lovely. There's no question of that." He lifted his face, and though his eyes were closed, she sensed he was seeing all he needed to see. He was reliving the past.

"She was full of life, like you," he continued. "High-spirited and very intelligent. Too intelligent for most men. But then, I always liked to think of myself as above the norm. It was only right she be a goddess."

"And you were in love with her," M.J. surmised.

As his face fell, the flames bathed him in a golden glow. He looked ethereal, like some old wise sage in a fairy tale or Arabian movie. His eyes were filled with emotions so powerful and consuming, she almost felt them. He was like a force field. Yet he was as approachable as a gentle summer rain. He was very much like a mystical creature who knew how to draw people into his sphere, then transform himself into something or someone else. Prince to frog. Frog to prince.

But which one was he this time?

"I was desperately in love with her," he said wistfully.

M.J.'s mouth curved into a commiserating smile. She wondered if Travis would ever think this way about her.

"What was her name?"

"Dorothy. Dorothy Stevens."

"What was there about her that made you never forget her?"

He jabbed at a flaming log. His expression was granite, his eyes suddenly vacant, as if he'd lost all touch with reality.

M.J. quickly regretted asking the question. Something told her she didn't want to know his answer. She felt herself retracting from him.

Then he lifted his gaze to her.

She peered deeply into them and saw the demon inside him.

"I killed her," he replied.

32

Travis felt the hairs on the back of his neck stand on end.

"Isn't this incredible, Travis? Can you feel it? Smell it?" Michael asked, scooping handfuls of earth to his nose. He inhaled the earth like it was fine wine, savoring it. The present suddenly became the past for him. He thought of the billion years it had taken the earth to make this aroma. There was nothing like it in the world.

"Yes." Travis looked behind him.

"You agree that we've hit the mother lode?" Michael asked excitedly.

"Where's M.J.?" Travis asked, his eyes scanning the expanse of meadow and forest behind him.

"She's right—" Michael straightened, and his words were cut off. He spun to the north, to the east.

Travis's blood turned to ice. He felt as if he'd been lanced in the gut. "Where the *hell* is M.J.?" Travis began running, retracing his steps through the thigh high grasses and wildflowers.

"Oh, shit!" Michael grabbed their bags and followed Travis.

"M.J.!" Travis shouted. He heard her name echo back to him.

He realized his mistake. He'd just broadcasted their coordinates to their trackers.

Travis pawed the tall grasses, using his arms like harvesting scythes. He signaled silently to Michael to fan out and search the ground.

She could have fainted, he told himself. She could have been bitten by a snake. Fallen in a hole. Stumbled into a hunter's old trap. A hundred mishaps flitted through his brain. None of them were good. Yet, he knew it was none of these. Their predators had followed them and taken M.J.

"The sons of bitches!"

They'd been trying to kill them all since the river. He was tired of their cat-and-mouse game. He knew he worked best when he was the tracker.

Travis pulled his gun out of his waistband and signaled Michael to do the same. They cocked their guns in unison.

"You bastards!" Travis yelled to the forest, then to the mountain walls. He lifted his gun and shot into the air to make certain he was heard.

"Come on! Come and get me!"

"Are you crazy, Travis?" Michael jumped on him and grabbed the gun out of his hand. "That was really smart. We'll never find her if we're dead. What the hell's gotten into you, man?"

Travis avoided Michael's piercing look. "I lost my cool."

"I'd say so," Michael agreed. "You know as well as I do there are plenty of head-shrinking cannibal tribes in the Oriente. Keep this up, and we'll really be in the soup. Literally."

"She can't just disappear on her own, Michael. She wouldn't wander off. She's not that stupid."

"No, she's not. But for the time being and argument's sake, let's assume she's been kidnapped."

Travis was being hammered by fear and a severely painful stabbing in his heart. "I know. What do you suggest?"

"They didn't go past us, so that means they had to leave by the south, east or west."

His heart slamming against his ribs, Travis tried to think. It wasn't easy. "They'd leave tracks, a trail of some kind."

"Yeah, broken twigs, crushed grasses, mangled flowers."

Travis focused on the spot where he'd last seen M.J. He remembered he'd turned to wave at her. She'd smiled at him and waved back. Even now he could feel the force of her energy, could see the love in her eyes.

"I have to find her." Travis scanned the mountains. "We don't have much time left."

He pointed to the spot where M.J. had been. "It's got to be there," Travis said.

"What does?"

"Our clue." Travis strode past Michael, lifting his feet high, stomping through the tall grass. He became the investigator again.

He remembered she'd had some yellow wildflowers in her hand when she'd waved.

"Flowers." His eyes sliced across the area. "There!"

Travis rushed toward a patch of buttercup-yellow daisy look-alikes. "These."

"What?" Michael asked.

"She picked flowers from right here."

Travis crouched and saw the first of the tracks. "Look. A footprint." He stood and followed a path. "Michael, how could you miss this?"

"Miss what?"

"These are Uma's boots! I recognize them. The same ones that were beside the tent when he came to our camp at night."

"No way." Michael was incredulous. He, too, searched the area. "Look, two more sets of prints. But these are barefoot."

"And deeper. Thank God this ground is so soft,"

Travis said. "These two men, I assume, carried her. Uma walked behind."

"But how did they do it so fast? M.J. would have put up a fight."

Travis looked at Michael as the truth hit them.

"Blowgun."

"You got it," Travis said. "They were prepared, all right. It's my guess they had to have known we were coming."

"You mean, they were set up here in ambush rather than trailing us?"

"Exactly. Which tells me they had to have followed you here on the first trip." He looked at the mountainside and hills. "Or they were, at the very least, watching when you entered the valley. And I don't think these are the same guys who've been trying to kill us."

"Great," Michael said. "Now they're coming from all sides."

"Precisely."

"Well, they're quick. I've got to give them that," Michael said.

"No kidding. I swear it was only a second or two that I had my back turned on her. It must have been more. Probably was because I was so involved that I didn't..."

"We. We didn't pay attention to M.J." Michael finished the sentence for him.

"Do you see her backpack anywhere around here?" Travis asked.

"No. They must have taken it with them."

Travis followed the tracks for a hundred yards. Michael checked the direction.

"They're headed northwest, into the mountains."

"I was afraid of that. And us with no rope for rappelling."

Michael loaded Travis's pistol and handed it to him.

"We'll be lucky if we make it out of this valley by nightfall, you know."

"Let's see how far we can get. Without light we'll lose the trail." Travis bent and picked up their bags. He handed one to Michael. He realized they hadn't gathered the precious soil samples they'd risked their lives to get.

Suddenly, they seemed unimportant.

"It's not light I'm worried about losing," Michael replied, shielding his eyes against the sun.

"I know," Travis said, slapping him on the back as they started out. "Neither am I."

33

━━◆━━

"You killed Dorothy?"

"Yes," Uma replied.

"You mean, it was an accident."

"No, I wanted her dead."

"Why?"

"It was the only way," he replied.

M.J.'s mouth went dry. Her brain scrambled to formulate the proper response to this monster. "The only way for what?"

"To love her for eternity."

His answer caught her off guard. She was repulsed. Her stomach lurched, and she wanted to vomit. If he'd murdered once, he would do it again. What was to stop him? He'd obviously gotten away with it, living here in obscurity.

How could she be living this nightmare? What dark angel had she conjured to put her here?

"Don't you want to hear the story?" he asked.

She peered into his deep-set eyes. Was he crazy? Was he making this up? Was he deranged from the decades of loneliness?

Any way she looked at it, she didn't want to know what he would do to her if she didn't play along. "Of course I want to hear the story."

"I thought you might," he replied, settling into a chair he'd made of logs, bent branches and leather lashes.

"Let's see. Where to start." Beginning his story was

hard for him. He hadn't realized it would be so emotional.

He chose to start with simple details. "You asked me once what my real name is. Well, it's Nelson Anderson," he said. A restrained chuckle gurgled in his throat. "How odd. I'd almost forgotten my own name, it's been so long since I've thought of it. I suppose I wanted to forget it existed, as if that would somehow purge me of my sin."

"I can understand that," M.J. replied, hoping to keep things on an even keel. "Go on."

"It was 1933. I was a geologist of some note by then. I'd given up on medicine, and it had given up on me. Besides, the oil rush was on. Some folks were buying up oil leases and mineral rights in Texas and Louisiana. California was really booming. But I'd read about South America all my life and I was fascinated by it. The lure of the exotic, I suppose.

"I was pretty cocky in those days. I'd bragged to some journalists in California that I was coming down here and that I'd hit it big before Royal Dutch Shell or Standard Oil of New Jersey. Of course, I was stupid, as well. I didn't realize that locating the oil is only half the battle. Getting it out of the inaccessible Oriente is the other. Still, I was foolish and romantic. I thought I was invincible."

He gazed into the night shadows, his eyes filling with memories.

"Anyway, Dorothy was one of the journalists. She worked for the *San Francisco Examiner*. One of William Randolph Hearst's prize pupils, she had said…"

"I'm more than a prize pupil," Dorothy said with a haughty tilt to her chin as she stood in the bright Los Angeles sunshine. "I'm the best damned reporter on staff. My mother worked for Mr. Hearst before she got married. She covered the earthquake. She taught me everything I know," she said to Nelson.

"What's the most important thing she told you?"

"That I'll know by instinct when I've found a great story," she replied, her brown eyes sparkling. "I think you're that story for me, Mr. Anderson."

"I don't know about that, but I will say you certainly know how to stroke my ego."

"I should hope so! How else can I convince you to take me along on your voyage?"

He lifted his fedora onto the back of his head and rubbed his neck. "I don't think that's possible, Miss…"

"Stevens. Dorothy Stevens."

"Miss Stevens, I don't have the luxury of an unlimited budget. It costs a great deal of money for boat tickets, plane tickets, lodging…"

"Oh, don't worry about that. I'll get the paper to pick up my expenses. I just want you to assure me that I'll have a hell of a story."

He laughed in spite of himself. "Do you always swear so much, Miss Stevens?"

"Absolutely, Mr. Anderson." She grinned widely, displaying straight white teeth.

She dazzled him. She'd walked up to him after the news conference not three minutes ago, and she'd taken him like Teddy took San Juan Hill.

"If you can get your publisher to pay your expenses, you have a deal, Miss Stevens. I'll take you to South America."

"You'll shake on that?"

He looked deep into her eyes and felt a bolt of energy shoot through him, as if a force of nature had brought them together. What had begun as a verbal tour de force was something altogether different now.

She wanted him.

He knew it. He believed it. It was as if she were orchestrating their futures, and he had little to say about it.

A strange calm descended upon him. All his life, he'd

only had one goal—wealth. He wanted to be rich so badly he would have sold his soul to the devil. He didn't particularly care how he made money, as long as he made it. Though he was stunningly well-educated and boasted several degrees, he hadn't had the wherewithal at the time of the great stock market rise to invest. When the crash came four years ago, he'd had to scramble just like everyone else. The difference was that he'd never had anything to lose in the first place. He was working from an attitude of strength rather than defeat. His enthusiasm was energizing to investors. When it came to risk-taking, Nelson ranked up there with the best of them. He didn't care where he had to go or what dangers he'd encounter. He was determined to find oil. A few moments ago he was exhilarated with the barrage of questions and his fast and accurate answers to the press. He'd tried to impress them with his expertise about precisely where to look for oil in the great Oriente of Ecuador. His ideas had been sterling, his mind utterly focused.

Until she walked up.

Suddenly, he knew that something had changed. His life had taken a new direction, and nothing would ever be the same.

Almost without thinking it through, he replied, "Yes, I will." He took her hand in his. "My word is my bond, Miss Stevens."

"Mine, too," she replied, flashing him an unforgettable smile. An indelible smile. A look he would treasure forever. He was more than mesmerized, he was hooked.

Nelson's banker and partner, Darren Klein, descended the concrete steps of City Hall. The most noteworthy of local press conferences were held here because of the photogenic properties of the flapping American flags on the front lawn. Every entrepreneur Darren had backed, both personally and commercially, had held his press conferences on these steps. It made for good business.

"Are you out of your mind, Nelson?" Darren growled as he watched Dorothy Stevens walk away. "You don't know this woman from Adam. Not only is it a ridiculous idea to take a woman to the jungle, but she's a reporter, for God's sake. She'll tell all your secrets."

Nelson's eyes followed Dorothy as she sashayed down the street, her hips swinging from side to side. The floral organza dress she wore was romantically long and fashionable. It skimmed her willowy body like a waterfall. Her hair was past her shoulders and fell in shimmering curls under the wide-brimmed straw hat she wore. He noticed, too, that she carried her gloves rather than wore them, all the better to drop one daintily and plead ignorance if a gentlemen stooped to retrieve it for her.

She was a practiced coquette, he thought. She was all softness and lushness. No angles to her face. No harsh lines to her attitude. Yet she was full of herself, just like him. He liked that, liked it a lot. "First of all, I don't believe for a minute her newspaper is going to give her that kind of money. Second, look at her. There's nothing businesslike about her. Especially not the way she dresses."

"She curses like a newspaperman."

Nelson smiled. "She's shooting for effect, I tell you." He laughed and slapped Darren on the back good-naturedly. "I have no intention of taking that woman anywhere...except to bed."

34

The following day Dorothy Stevens tracked Nelson down at the steamship office where he was booking his and Darren's tickets.

"I was hoping to find you here," she said, walking up to him. She was dressed in a soft apple-green chiffon day dress. She wore a white horsehair hat with matching green grosgrain ribbons that fell against her hair, making her look like a spring nymph.

He was enchanted, but wary at her boldness in pursuing him. What if she didn't get the money from her publisher? Yesterday, it wouldn't have been a tragedy, but he'd spent the majority of last night in cold sweats thinking about making love to her, and he knew his trip to South America would be meaningless without her. "So, our meeting is not Kismet?"

"I was following you. Well, sort of." She moved a step closer.

She smelled of jasmine, gardenia and vanilla. Her body musk intoxicated him. He tugged at his shirt collar. She was too close. She was under his skin already, and there wasn't a thing he could do about it. She had him.

"Sort of?" Nelson asked, swallowing hard and feeling an even harder erection.

"I went to the room you're letting. I got the address from this guy I know at the Hall of Records where you and Darren Klein filed your company's name, just in case you were wondering," she said, proudly showing her investigative skills to him. Taking a deep breath, she continued. "The landlady told me you haven't been there long."

"Just a couple of—" He was replying when she finished his statement for him.

"—months," she said, nodding. "Which means you haven't seen a lot of Los Angeles."

"Just because I haven't lived here long doesn't mean I haven't been in town."

"*Au contraire, mon cher*," she replied with a pout of her ruby lips.

He liked the way she used the familiar endearment. He felt closer to her, enough so that he hoped she wasn't simply flirting with him. Enough that perhaps she might be interested in him.

She reeled him in like an expert, and he let her. "I peeked at your mail, Nelson. Some of it had been re-routed from New York. What were you there for?"

"Surely, you have that figured out, as well."

She rocked on her heels. "High-powered investors, perhaps?"

"Bingo."

"Is that where you found Darren Klein?"

"He found me," Nelson corrected.

"He's a playboy."

"But a savvy one." Nelson shook his finger at her. "Don't cast stones until you've turned them all over."

"There's nothing in his dossier that points to this sudden interest in oil," she replied smartly.

"Lots of people are looking at oil now. It's the hottest commodity. It's futuristic. My prediction is that it's the base for the economies of the coming American generations. This depression can't last forever. All money doubles in seven years. I don't believe in bad luck past seven years. Break a mirror and you've got seven years of bad luck. But what's after that? Why, seven years of good luck. The pendulum always swings back. Seven years of lean. Seven years of plenty. Remember Joseph's dreams in the Bible? Seven. Well, it's been four since the crash. That's three more years of bad times, and things will start to change. Believe me, by 1937 the worst will be behind us. Something will come along to turn things around."

"Like what? A miracle?"

"Historically, it's usually a war, but we won't talk about that. Let's talk about your meeting with your publisher."

"What about it?" she asked.

"Did you get the expense money?"

Unpretentiously, she reached in her square leather purse and retrieved a passport and steamer ticket. She grinned mischievously. "They open at seven. I was first in line."

Nelson gasped audibly. "I don't believe it!" He reached for her ticket. "How did you do that so easily?" It had taken him nearly two years to get someone to listen to his ideas, to believe in him enough to pay him to chase his dream. Yet this audacious woman, who hadn't a notion in her head about South American oil until yesterday afternoon, when he'd brought it to her attention at the press conference, had snapped her fingers and now had a ticket and her expenses to Ecuador.

"What are you, a witch?"

"Thanks a lot!"

"Well, it's just that you did it so fast. Like magic."

"My dear Nelson. You will come to find out that when I'm around, magic always happens. That must be your problem."

"I don't have a problem," he protested.

"But of course you do, if you don't believe in magic." She beamed a paralyzingly brilliant smile at him.

She was right. She'd certainly caught him in her spell. He felt powerless against her. It was a bewildering feeling. He was the leader of this expedition, the creator, the founder and the force behind it from its inception. Yet, in only a matter of hours, Dorothy Stevens had become the impetus that thrust him forward.

He wanted to find oil, yes. But now he wanted to go to South America for more than that. He wanted to use his time to explore Dorothy. He wanted to know her, be inside her, be a part of her. But he didn't know how he would convince her to accept him—she seemed to always be a step or six ahead of him.

"I have all the faith in the world in you, Nelson," she said. "Your expedition is going to make news. World news. More than that, you're about to make history. Change the course of a continent. Why, it's as if you're Atlas bearing the world on your back. It's a burden and a responsibility, isn't it? But at the same time I sense that you wouldn't have it any other way. That it's men like you, ones who chose just such a course, who make themselves into heroes. Into bigger-than-life personae. You're the kind of person we all emulate. We need people like you, Nelson. The world needs heroes," she said, tossing her words like laurel wreaths. "How silly of you to think I wouldn't find a way to be with you."

She made him feel simultaneously like an idiot and her ideal. "You make too much of me."

"On the contrary, Nelson," she breathed seductively. "I don't make enough of you at all." She traced the outline of her lips with her tongue, enticing him. Playing with him. Challenging him.

He felt hard again.

"At least, not yet." She almost purred, her face coming close enough to his that their lips brushed.

Nelson swallowed the lump of lust in his throat. Clenching his fists and shoving them into his pockets, he said, "We really do need to keep this strictly business, Miss Stevens."

"Oh, I don't have a problem with that, Mr. Anderson." She backed away, but only after allowing her breasts to swipe across his chest.

Forcing his body heat to subside, Nelson thought he'd lost his mind. He couldn't think. "Good." His tongue stuck dryly to the roof of his mouth as he spoke. "Then I'll see you here Wednesday morning when we are scheduled to leave."

"Absolutely, Mr. Anderson," she assured him as she turned her back.

The sun seemed to dip behind a cloud when Dorothy wasn't smiling at him, he thought, as she dashed down the block, caught a cab and sped away. He looked at the overcast sky.

Odd, the sun hadn't been out all morning.

The first day at sea, Nelson did not see Dorothy. He pretended to be working in his stateroom, but the fact was that he hadn't been able to concentrate on anyone or anything but Dorothy.

Dinner was formal that night. Black tie. At the captain's table.

Darren wore his long, straight black hair slicked back, as he always did for formal affairs. When he did, he looked astonishingly like Errol Flynn, but shorter. Nelson was intimidated by Darren's good looks. The only women on board were matronly Mrs. Helena Lancaster-Throckmorton-Whyte, the thrice married, enormously bosomed, white-haired, busybody socialite from San Francisco and, of course, Dorothy.

Dorothy would be dazzled by Darren, Nelson feared.

Worse, he didn't know much about Darren beyond his fiscal capabilities to fund his company. But he remembered Dorothy's statement. *"He's a playboy."*

He wished he'd asked her how she'd come to that conclusion. Was it hearsay? Was it mentioned in the tabloids? Or was it personal observation on her part?

Any way he sliced it, Nelson realized, he had to be on guard around Darren.

Dorothy was dressed in a long, bias-cut white satin gown, like the kind Jean Harlow made famous. Wrapped around her shoulders were layers of silk illusion that looked like clouds. Dorothy's huge dark eyes, high cheekbones and sensuous mouth put her evening clothes to shame. She had them all—Captain Parker, First Mate Elroy, the galley crew, Darren, Nelson, even Mrs. Lancaster-Throckmorton-Whyte—wanting to bask in her loveliness.

Holding a cigarette between his fingers, his chin resting in the palm of his hand, Nelson couldn't help thinking that not even Scheherazade kept her companions more rapt.

"You have had so many adventures in your line of business, Miss Stevens," Mrs. Lancaster-Throckmorton-Whyte gushed. "Do tell me this will be the most adventurous one of all!" She clapped her tiny, chubby hands together gleefully.

Dorothy smiled sufferingly and then turned her mesmerizing eyes on Nelson, who wasn't in the least prepared for their impact or her statement. "I believe that I'm about to embark on the greatest adventure of all. However, the proof of that is up to Mr. Anderson. He holds the key."

Nelson gasped. He straightened a bit, then nonchalantly stubbed out his cigarette in a square ashtray. "If I don't succeed, Mr. Klein and his investors will be out a good deal of money. Quite frankly, the possibility of failure hasn't crossed my mind."

The salt-and-pepper-haired captain said, "Good for you, son. Never had failure myself." He chuckled. "If I did, I'd be ten fathoms under!"

The captain's black humor was lost on his guests, who stared at him with frightened eyes. The first mate, Mr. Elroy, saved the day by diverting attention from the captain to Nelson. "If you are going to the Oriente, Mr. Anderson, are you certain it's only oil you're after?"

"Why, what else would there be?"

The captain's jaw dropped as he looked at his first mate. They both broke into laughter.

"Surely, you're joking."

"No." Nelson lit another cigarette. He didn't like the insinuation that he was a fool, even if he'd been called precisely that too many times to count. "There's nothing else there to interest me."

"Not even El Dorado?" The captain pulled a long Havana from his inside jacket pocket.

First Mate Elroy immediately struck a wooden match for the captain, who drew slowly and expertly on the expensive cigar. "Surely, you've heard of—"

"Yes, Mr. Elroy. I've heard of it. My mother used to tell me fairy tales as a child, too."

"El Dorado is not a fairy tale," the captain replied earnestly.

"I'm afraid you are the one who is joking now," Nelson replied with a smirk. "I'm too smart to fall for that."

The captain's expression was convincing, Nelson thought. "I've seen it."

The gasps around the table seemed to suck up all the oxygen.

Nelson felt light-headed. "You did not."

"I don't make a habit of lying, son."

"I'm afraid I'm at a loss. What is El Dorado?" Dorothy asked. While she dug in her evening purse for a paper and pen, the men exchanged surprised glances. Realizing she'd brought only her lipstick, she closed the beaded bag and looked up. "What?"

The captain smiled indulgently. "You aren't much of an archaeological buff, are you?"

Taking in the quizzical eyes focused on her, she replied, "I'm about to be now, aren't I, Captain?" Propping her elbows on the table, she placed her beautiful face in her hands and flashed the captain an engaging smile. "It's a Spanish legend, probably left over from the conquistadores," she surmised.

"The conquistadores put a name to the city, but the Incas built it long before the Spanish discovered these mountains. Back then, everyone was looking for gold, and the Incas were noted for their love of it. They, like the Mayans in Mexico, couldn't get enough of the stuff. They molded statues and headdresses of gold, smeared gold dust on their faces during tribal dances and celebrations. But the Incas were said to have hoarded their gold and built a city out of it. What they did was form enormous sheets of gold that they hung on the interior walls of their temples. The temples were carved into the mountainsides so that no one could see the city from the outside world. You have to know exactly which mountain pass to take, how high to climb and then literally which rock to look under."

"Do you remember where it was?"

"I'll never forget it. It was on the eastern slope of the Andes, where the land drops off so quickly and the vegetation grows so high that entering the jungle is impossible. So is coming back up the mountainside. There is nothing but scaling walls. Rappelling down the peaks on ropes is the only mode of travel."

"That's insane."

"That's what I said." The captain laughed to himself. He stared at the burning end of his cigar, his memory fixed on that long-ago experience. "It was sheer folly, I'll grant you that. I shouldn't have tried it. But I was young.

I took more chances on the sea than I'd ever risked on land. I kept figuring, how bad could it be?"

"And was it?" Dorothy was practically drooling over the details.

The captain's eyes turned stormy. "It was thirty years ago, and still, those were the worst days of my life. And the most miraculous. It was a miracle I survived. I should never have gone."

Dorothy leaned closer to the captain, and Nelson watched the way she ate up the details of the macabre, mysterious story, as if her life depended on it.

The captain continued. "When I found it, the entryway looked like an ordinary mountainside where a rockfall had occurred. The reality was that the entrance was behind the rockfall. Just inside were huge polished stone columns that reminded one of something Greek or Roman in design, but different. They were smoother, with pointed tops and no capitals. They resembled ears of corn."

Dorothy harrumphed. "Sounds like Flash Gordon's rocket, to me."

Nelson held his breath. "What an odd thought."

Shrugging, she replied, "Not for me. I told you, I always look to the future. Not to the past."

Nelson caught the sensual glimmer in her eye. He smiled to himself, basking in her subtle sexual repartee. "Go on, Captain. I'm fascinated."

"The first of many long hallways are lined in gold, and I could tell that the rest of the interior must have been incredible to see."

"But I thought you said you saw it. You didn't go inside?"

The captain exhaled, and smoke rose across his face like armor. He looked down. "I know of no man who has done this."

"But I—" Dorothy leaned forward.

He cut her off. "Don't get me wrong. I was almost there. I could see it from my vantage point across the gorge. But the passageway was narrow, barely a foot's length wide on both sides. Looking back on it, I try to tell myself I should have jumped for it—even if it meant death. After all, living life to the fullest is what life is about. I'm sure there are some who want to pass their elderly years in the quiet countryside, but not I. I believe a man is the sum of his adventures. To have risked everything for a discovery like that would have been worth the peril."

Nelson couldn't resist asking, "Then why didn't you?"

The captain plunged the burning cigar into the ashtray. "That is the true mystery of El Dorado. Frankly, I believe many have seen the city of gold. They just don't want to admit they failed to bring back its riches like I did. The truth of the matter is there is something there." He gestured in the air with his hands, manipulating invisible objects, trying to crush them but failing. "An evil force, I think."

"Evil?" Dorothy smirked. "What has the metaphysical got to do with archaeology?"

"Nothing and everything. At least at El Dorado it does."

"Why do you think this thing was evil?"

"Because it made me afraid." The captain bellowed as if embarrassed to admit his fault. "I trembled so much, I faltered. But no, it was more than that. It was…"

The captain's eyes went vacant as he peered at the porthole above Dorothy's head. In the distance was the huge expanse of sea, and at the end of eternity was the horizon. He was back there, inside his experience, reliving every moment.

"I remember now. It was incredibly windy. Howling winds slapped my face. There was little dust, but I remember my face being pelted by tiny rocks. I closed my eyes. It seemed to me the sounds of hell assaulted my ears. I wanted to jump across, but the winds held me back. I was afraid, incredibly afraid. It felt like some Biblical curse had been put upon this place. It was cold. No, I was cold inside, as if something evil were hovering over me. I believed the howling was the sound of miserable dead.

"Each time I tried to move, a new blast of wind hit me. It was as if a ghostly hand were holding me back. Or maybe it was my guardian angel holding me safe. I don't know. I'll never know. Once I conquered enough of my fear to force my foot to move, I backed away and circled the mountainside, back down the steep trail I'd come. I realized I had no need in my life for this gold. I'd thought I had, but I was wrong. At that moment, I missed the sea tremendously. I cried all the way down. Not a manly thing to do, I know, but I didn't care. I knew then I would always be happy on the sea. I haven't left her since."

"Fascinating," Dorothy said, gushing. She easily believed his story.

Nelson wasn't convinced. "How often do you tell your passengers this ghost tale?"

The captain was silent.

The first mate's eyes drilled Nelson's face. "I can vouch that this is the first I've ever heard the whole story." He glanced at the captain with compassion. "Only once before, when he first returned to the sea, did I hear a rumor in Belize City about the sea captain who'd lost three of his crew while searching for El Dorado."

"Three men died?" Dorothy gasped.

"Yes." He nodded. "They fell to their deaths while trying to jump across. One by one they took a leap, and I remember now that it seemed odd, in fact impossible I was seeing what I was seeing. They were airborne for a long moment, as if they were flying on their own power without wings. They were suspended as if that force, that evil force I was trying to explain, held them over the gorge, enticing them. Playing with them like gods before letting them fall to their doom. I came back alone."

"My God," Dorothy replied softly, her eyes suddenly filling with compassion, for in that minute she was back there with him. "How awful for you, Captain. I'm sorry."

A hush fell around the table, as if they were sharing a moment of prayer for the departed.

Nelson watched Dorothy's face fill with empathy. And he knew from that moment on, for the rest of his life, he was inexorably in love with Dorothy. He could never be satisfied with just sex from her. He had to have more than her body. He had to possess her heart, own her soul.

He reached in his pocket for his linen handkerchief and handed it to her. Tears fell down her cheeks. She stared at his hand. She left the handkerchief on the table, but took his hand and curled it inside both of hers.

Nelson's heart stopped.

Dorothy's eyes met his. A single tear fell slowly, as if in slow motion, out of the corner of her eye.

Nelson would never forget the way she looked that night. She was showing him her soul in all its vulnerability.

He laced his fingers in hers and, not caring that there was anyone else in the room, lifted her hand to his lips and kissed her fingers one by one.

Silently, Dorothy rose from her chair, never taking her eyes off Nelson's face.

He rose with her and escorted her out of the captain's quarters.

He put his arm around her as they made their way down the windy deck. Dorothy was cold. She shivered. Nelson took off his tuxedo jacket and put it around her shoulders, crushing the fine French silk illusion. He walked her to his cabin, unlocked the door and held it for her while she entered the small berth.

He poured Scotch for them—straight, deep and strong.

Wordlessly, they toasted each other, drinking slowly from the glasses.

Her eyes told him she knew every move he would make. Her eyes told him she was no virgin. But then, neither was he, though in his fantasy he'd wanted to be the first for her.

He'd never thought to ask her if she'd been married before. Or was married now. If she'd had children. What her favorite color was. Her favorite food. Her hobbies.

He hadn't asked because he'd only lusted for her.

Lust wasn't an intellectual response. Lust was wicked and divine at the same time. It accepted completely the moment in time and space it occupied. It cast away all peripheral matters and all immaterial details of one's life that had nothing to do with the lust. Lust was the tonic that cured the sins of guilt and depression, self-deprecation and self-destruction.

Lust for Nelson was all he'd wanted. Instead, he'd found love.

And it would eat him alive.

35

$\blacktriangleright\!\!-\!\!\blacktriangleleft$

A majestic mansion was being built smack-dab in the center of Quito by a Lebanese family from Quayaquil. When the patriarch discovered that Nelson and Darren had come to Ecuador to conquer the Oriente, he invited them to dinner in the middle of the construction rubble.

The day was clear and airless, it seemed to Nelson, who'd never been two miles above sea level. He was having more than a difficult time adjusting to the altitude and to a loss of energy due to making love with Dorothy twice a day.

He pulled his Panama hat down to his eyebrows to shield his eyes from the intense mountain sunlight. Darren pulled him aside.

"I think it's wonderful you're hobnobbing with these wealthy Ecuadoreans. They might do us some good. But later, after we come back from the expedition. We need to get to the jungle," he urged.

"I've got everything set to leave tomorrow," Nelson replied. "Pack mules. Boatmen arranged for the river. Supplies. Ropes. Food. Water. Guides. I could use a little relaxation."

"I thought that was what you and Dorothy…"

"Leave her out of this." Nelson poked Darren's chest none too softly with his index finger.

"I just meant—"

"I know what you meant." Nelson cut him off. "You still don't want her on the trip."

"No, I don't. I think she'll slow us down."

"She's a journalist. She'll record everything we see and find. How we do it." Nelson felt himself sparkle from the inside out. He was amazed how quickly he caught his own fever.

"She'll make us famous, is what you're saying."

"Who's stopping at fame? Immortality is all a matter of press. She's the press. She's the one to do it."

Darren shook his head, put his hands on his hips and looked at the ground. "Christ, you've got it bad."

"What?"

"Her!" Darren's hand shot up in the air as he spun away from his friend and partner.

"Dorothy is vital to our futures," Nelson argued.

"To yours, you mean." He stopped himself. "Look, Nelson. It's no secret you two are inseparable. I want what's best for you. But the problem is that you're listening to her so much lately, I feel she's running this expedition. She doesn't know a damn thing about the jungle."

"Neither do you."

"Or you!" Darren argued. "You've never been out of the United States in your life. At least I've seen Riyadh, which isn't saying much, but it's something."

"Why are you so down on Dorothy?"

Darren rubbed the back of his neck. "We're behind, Nelson. A week behind schedule. That schedule costs me money. I'm leaving tomorrow, with the equipment, with or without you."

"Without me, you have no geologist to tell you where to go."

"Is that so? Well, I'm the investor, and for the past two months I've done what good investors should do. I've studied data. I've gone over the maps and I think I have a fix on things. I'll take my chances. It's my money."

Nelson realized that Darren had been pushed as far as possible. He couldn't spend any more time in the hotel room with Dorothy pretending tomorrow would never come. They had to leave. He would be putting Dorothy in danger in the jungle, but he also knew she felt she had to go. She wanted her story even more than he wanted her.

What Nelson hadn't told either Darren or Dorothy was that, while he'd been in Quito, he'd been doing some research on El Dorado. He'd been asking a lot of questions and getting a lot of information.

He'd heard the legends. He'd found an old man who wanted to sell him a map to the city of gold for a hundred dollars. Nelson had paid. It was Darren's money. What did he care?

Nelson didn't know why his personality had seemed to change so much lately. He'd never thought of himself as an obsessive type of person, but perhaps he was.

He'd worked diligently to put together natural herbs and flowers as healing medicines. He'd tried to get them patented. But no one was listening at the time.

He blamed the Depression. He blamed the lack of expertise on the part of those who interviewed him. He blamed the lack of venture capital available. But he did not blame himself or the mountains of studies he'd compiled. They all pointed in the same direction. His timing was off, was all.

That was when he'd decided to get smart. He'd sat in his chair on a Saturday night with a month's worth of newspapers spread at his feet. He'd gone over the markets. Stocks. Spending trends. Capital investment trends. Buying trends.

He realized that the place to put his time and energy for the next decade was oil.

He hadn't given up on his plants and herbs. He'd just put them on the back burner. He would make his fortune on them in the coming years.

After hearing the captain's convincing story about El Dorado, Nelson realized his destiny had changed again.

He wanted to find the gold. What a coup that would be! What a story Dorothy could write about him then!

He imagined himself on the cover of *Time* and *Look*. Dorothy was right about him. Darren was right about him. He wanted to be immortal. He wanted it written that he'd accomplished what all the Spanish conquistadores had never managed. What men like the captain had failed to do. He would find El Dorado. He would enter it and he would lay claim to it. He would be immortal. If he had to use Darren in the process of meeting his goal, then so be it.

The end would justify the means.

"We'll leave in the morning," Nelson promised. "You'll find your oil, Darren. That I promise you."

Though the trip into the jungle was arduous, it was uneventful. Totally uncharted, the terrain was dense and required a considerable amount of undercutting to the brush to make their trail. They traveled with twenty natives who hacked away the jungle. Darren had provided for their trip just as if they were on safari in Africa. Since there were no roads at all down from the Andes, they traveled by burro and on foot down the precipitous mountainside. They made camp each night, and two cooks prepared their meals. The fact that it took them a week and a half to make it to where one day in the future Lago Agrio would stand was acceptable to Darren, who believed they would spend no less than three months searching for the oil.

There was no communication whatsoever with the outside world. When Nelson, Dorothy and Darren left Quito, the residents waved them goodbye and forgot about them, knowing that if they returned, it would be a miracle.

Nelson called the shots on the direction and course the journey would take. His speculations were precise, even though he'd never been to South America. He hadn't counted on the army ants that stole their food, taking whole leaves of lettuce, or lechuga, on their backs, marching it to their huge mounds in single file. The blackflies were a constant bother, as were the mosquitoes. Dorothy wore a safari hat with mosquito netting falling like a veil to protect her fair skin from the nasty bites.

Though they heard the growl of a jaguar at night, Nelson explained that jaguars were shy animals and did not attack man like Pumas. Anacondas wrapped themselves around huge trees and slithered across their path from time to time, more from curiosity than hunger. The jungle was abundant with small, tasty prey, and the big snakes did not need to feed on man.

What they were most wary of were the cannibals. Many were the tales in the towns and villages down the Andean slopes of the possessive natives who killed invaders and then shrunk their heads as a sign to others who dared venture too far into the Oriente.

Dorothy didn't believe in cannibals, though she had every intention of writing about them to make her story more harrowing, sensational and commercial. The more danger, the better, her editor had told her.

She intended to keep the pitch high.

Ironically, the greatest peril on the expedition came not from cannibals or jaguars; it came from within.

As each day passed, Nelson found himself falling more deeply in love with Dorothy. She, on the other hand, was noncommittal. She still dreamed of herself as a great journalist. This journey to the Amazon would make her famous. When they returned she planned to go to New York and meet with Hearst himself. If she maneuvered things perfectly, she could get some key radio interviews—maybe even speak with Walter Winchell.

It was the evening they dined on roasted lamb that

Dorothy made her play for Darren, in the form of a business proposition.

"I've been thinking, Darren. You appear to be somewhat connected to the power brokers in Los Angeles."

"I know a few," he replied.

"I've been mulling some things around. I have an idea for a screen story I'd like to sell to MGM."

"Those are pretty big boys. I don't know that I..."

"Okay. Let's think smaller. RKO. Universal," she persisted.

Nelson didn't like the way she touched Darren's forearm with the same familiarity she used with him. He was losing control over her, and he couldn't let that happen. "What story are you talking about?"

"Why, about our adventures here," she replied.

Nelson shook his head. "You can't sell that. It's not yours. It belongs to me."

Her back stiffened righteously. "I beg your pardon?"

"You heard me. This is my story. I own the rights."

"That's impossible, and you know it. Legally, I'm not paid by you or by Darren, but by my publisher. I have to give them a story. But I don't have to give them all of it, nor are they interested in a fantasized version of it. My perspective of this trip is mine and mine alone. Yours is yours. You could have Johnny Weissmuller play your part."

He didn't like the way he'd been compartmentalized and isolated from her new ideas about her future. He envisioned her in Hollywood, pursued by producers and movie stars. He saw her sitting by a swimming pool being ogled by young, healthy, good-looking men who would use her to boost their own careers.

Nelson bristled.

Dorothy could see Nelson's anxiety over her proposal and attempted to soften the blow. "Nelson, darling, don't get so upset. Why, you're positively steaming at the ears.

It was just an idea. And probably a silly one at that. After all, how would I get my story into the proper hands? I don't know a soul in that industry.''

Nelson let her pat his hand. He felt cold beads of fear erupt on his forehead. He'd been more than agitated that she would leave him. He realized he was terrified.

Clasping her fingers in his hand, he drew her hand to his lips and crushed his mouth against it. "I can't bear the thought of you being away from me.''

He opened his eyes, and when he looked up, he saw Dorothy's compassionate gaze.

"Oh, Nelson. You are a sentimental lug, aren't you?'' She melted.

Out of the corner of his eye, Nelson caught a glimpse of Darren watching them. There was no mistaking the jealousy he saw in his partner's eyes.

It was at that moment Nelson knew he'd miscalculated. He'd shown his vulnerability to Darren, not realizing until that second that Darren was in love with Dorothy, as well.

The mood from that moment altered. Nelson was on guard. He watched Darren like a hawk, dissecting the other man's every word and intention. As the jungle heat rose, Nelson's obsessions escalated. He dwelt constantly on bringing every conversation back around to El Dorado. If he wasn't thinking about Dorothy or what ploy to use next to control her, he was mentally strategizing on how to find the lost city of gold.

In his mind, the two had become the same. Dorothy and El Dorado. Mecca and Paradise.

Darren seemed to enjoy exposing Nelson's hair-trigger excitability to Dorothy, who was increasingly pulling away from the obsessive Nelson.

Dorothy was sitting at the camp table as the supper dishes were being cleared away by the cook and his helper. Her beauty glowed in the campfire flames as she looked at Darren. Because Nelson had little to think about other than El Dorado, his dinner conversations had become single-minded and boring.

He wasn't fun anymore.

"I've been thinking about your suggestion, Dorothy, and I've realized that, not only will I help you find a studio for your movie, but I know someone in New York publishing who would be quite interested in your autobiography," Darren said smoothly.

Dorothy held her breath, her hand over her heart. "A book?"

"Why not?"

"My God, I've never dared even think... Did you hear that, Nelson? A book! With my name on it."

Darren steepled his fingers. His eyes filled with longing as he looked at Dorothy.

Nelson saw raw lust. He didn't dare address it. To do so would be to give it power. If he ignored it, it would go away. He clapped his hands for the cook, who came running. "Scotch!"

The cook went to the black trunk and opened it. He brought a full bottle and poured a slight measure into a glass for his employer.

Nelson grabbed the bottle, poured three fingers and belted it down. He waved the cook away, keeping his hand wrapped around the bottle while Dorothy and Darren conversed, neither of them noticing him or his sullen mood.

"I'll go you one better," Darren said. "Why not invent a character, like yourself who goes on a series of these adventures."

"Fiction?" Her eyes were wide as she absorbed all he was saying.

"You could do it," Darren urged.

"I'm not a fiction writer. I'm a journalist."

"But you could be. Don't you see? You have so many talents, Dorothy. You've only begun to use them."

Nelson watched Darren playing her like a song. Oh, he was good. Damn good.

He drank another three fingers of Scotch. The fire appeared to flame up and then retreat in waves.

"Nelson, you're lit," Dorothy said, disgusted.

Nelson didn't know how it happened, but his face was on the table. "I'm tired is all. Take me to bed, Dorothy."

"Nelson!"

Darren rose. "Come on, old man, you've had a day of it." He put his hands under Nelson's armpits, pulled him to his feet and helped him to his tent.

Nelson didn't remember much after that, but he should have.

Hours later, Nelson awoke groggy and feeling as if a sledgehammer were batting him in the head. "Dorothy?" He sat up slowly on his cot. "Dorothy?"

He opened his eyes and peered into the darkness beyond the mosquito netting at the doorway to his tent. The campfire was out. The crew was asleep. There was silence—except for the sounds coming from Dorothy's tent.

He didn't know if she was talking to someone or if she was talking in her sleep.

He rose, left the tent and shuffled across the clearing.

"Oh, God!"

Nelson heard Dorothy's climactic cry with his heart not his ears. Like a fool, he went to the tent and lifted the flap. He had to see them together. He didn't believe she would sleep with another man knowing how much he loved her.

He saw Darren's naked backside rising and falling. He saw Dorothy's creamy arms and legs wrapped around Darren's strong back. Her hair fell over the edge of the cot like a shadow.

Nelson trembled. His legs weakened and barely held him up. His body turned cold, and he felt as if the blood had drained out of him. His breath came in rasps. Then he couldn't breathe at all. He thought he was dying.

And he was.

His heart exploded in rage, the fragments freezing in a state of suspended animation, refusing to come together. Refusing to forgive.

Hate and revenge filled the void where his heart used to be.

"Darren, I had no idea it could be like this," she said.

"I have loved you from the first day I saw you," he replied. "I thought I would go crazy if I didn't have you."

Nelson couldn't believe Darren was saying the things to Dorothy he'd wanted to say. That he was making love to Dorothy and she was letting him. It killed him to know that Dorothy had invited Darren into her tent, into her body. It was an inconceivable thought.

But then, Nelson had not told Dorothy of his intentions. He'd flirted with her but had not committed himself. That was such a strong step for him to take. To commit. It was more than he'd been willing to do at the time.

The fact that he had no one to blame but himself did not matter to Nelson. He blamed Darren for this breach of trust.

Darren had taken something that was not his. He'd stolen Dorothy. He was a thief, a perpetrator. And he would have to be punished for his crime.

Nelson's insides grew hard with resolve. It was up to him to be judge and jury. He had to weigh the evidence.

It was important he watch Darren kiss Dorothy's breasts. See her urge him to take her again. Witness their testaments of passion. Of love.

It killed him, but he took it. He felt like a martyr. He felt like a saint. And he would have restitution.

Nelson's legs returned to life. He backed away silently, imagining himself a specter rather than flesh. He would remain anonymous to the lovers until the time was right for him to take what was rightfully his.

36

━◄━

Nelson didn't know his mind had snapped. He only knew he loved Dorothy and he would have her and the gold at any cost.

Once Darren was utterly and inexorably focused on Dorothy, he didn't pay as much attention to the trivialities of their course as he had previous to making love with her.

Nelson routed them toward the mountains where the captain said he'd been to the city of gold.

They came to a fertile prehistoric valley that smelled of wildflowers and petroleum. Theatrically, to impress Dorothy, Nelson pulled out a divining rod to point his way to the oil. They scooped the earth and smelled it—the oil was there.

Darren was exultant, planning how he would announce the find to the press, how he would structure the deal. How he would create an oil company larger than any in the world. He imagined himself a king among the captains of industry. And he imagined Dorothy as his queen.

"Marry me," Darren said to Dorothy, no longer thinking it necessary to hide his affair from his partner.

"What?" She laughed and threw her arms around his neck.

"I'll be rich. I'll take you anywhere you want."

"New York!" She giggled. "Paris. Barcelona." She kissed him.

Nelson couldn't stand it. "You both have such small expectations for yourselves."

They immediately dropped their smiles and looked at him. "Whatever do you mean, Nelson?"

"This is just some oil. It's nothing."

"Hardly, old man," Darren said, sliding his arm possessively around Dorothy's waist.

"El Dorado. That's where the riches lay." Nelson pointed to the mountains to the west. "It's not that far. We can do it. We can make it."

Dorothy stepped away from Darren, letting his hand fall from her waist. She moved closer to Nelson.

In that single movement, Nelson realized the chess game was active again. He'd suspected that Dorothy was mercenary, and he was right. She wanted Darren only for what he could bring to her career—his money. But it wasn't love, of that he was certain.

Nelson smiled at her. "Gold, Dorothy. A whole city of it. Think of it. Paris would be nothing. You could own Paris and Moscow, too. I'll buy you the Bolshoi Ballet for entertainment."

"You can't really mean you're going to go for it," she said.

"I didn't come this far to turn back without at least trying."

"But you can't get across the gorge," Darren said as Dorothy took another step toward Nelson.

Nelson didn't care that Dorothy was corrupt. So was he.

"I bought rappelling ropes, hooks and cleats in Quito. I have the proper equipment to get us across the gorge."

Dorothy's eyes were rapacious. She looked as if she could eat him up in one swallow. She wanted it all—everything. The greed Nelson saw in her eyes was his savior, for he knew he would have her, after all.

Holding out his hand, he said, "Come with me, Dorothy. Let's go to the top of the mountain."

She nearly raced to him, leaving Darren behind, forgotten.

"And just what am I supposed to do? Go back by myself?" Darren asked.

Nelson was laughing. "The crew will assist you. Just leave one guide to help us on our way back. I'm not greedy." He laughed, knowing precisely how to bait Darren.

"You know I can't do that. I'm going with you," he said.

"Fine," Nelson said, looking into Dorothy's eyes and wondering how he'd mistaken vacuousness for sparkle, self-centeredness for compassion. She was a consummate actress. She had fooled him and she'd fooled Darren. She was a perfectionist with her craft.

Too bad she wasn't a strategist like him. She was playing right into his hands.

The climb was not as arduous as it was time-consuming. They found footpaths that looked to have been made over centuries of travel by barefoot natives. Just as the captain had said, the trail at the top was no wider than a foot length, and many was the time Nelson felt rocks crumble beneath him and saw them slide down the slope.

The reality of their perilous climb was more adventure than Dorothy had bargained for. Several times she asked Nelson to turn back. "This isn't worth it," she said regretfully.

"Of course it is," Nelson said.

"How will we even carry any gold back? This trail is too narrow for burros. And since the crewmen refused to climb with us, all we have are our pockets and two bags. That's not much," she argued.

Darren agreed. "She's right. This is insane."

"It's not!" Nelson insisted. He urged them around just one more bend. It was the right one.

They came upon two mountain cliffs so close together it looked as if only a sun ray could break through the gap between them. The gorge separating the two looked deceptively easy to cross.

"Why, it's nothing!" Dorothy said.

"No more than the width of a car," Darren replied.

"We can make this!" Dorothy said excitedly. "Keep going." She urged Nelson to round the corner.

And then it happened.

A wind as mighty as the gusts across the vast Sahara sprang from the gorge floor and the sky at the same time. It whistled through the narrow cliffs, making a crying sound like a human being in pain. It assaulted their ears.

Dorothy threw her hands over her ears as the wind flapped at the bandanna she'd tied around her throat. She was blasted against the mountainside with gale force. "My God! What is it?"

The wind whipped at their faces. Nelson's Panama hat was ripped from his head and went spiraling above him.

The sun split through the crags like a butcher's knife, blinding them momentarily.

Squinting, Nelson peered across the gorge and then up the mountainside. That's when he saw it. Suddenly, Nelson felt an unfamiliar reverence. "My God."

"Gold," Darren said with an edge to his voice looking at the blinding pillars at the entrance to the cave. "Maybe jewels, too."

Dorothy tried to open her eyes, but the wind and the sun kept them shut. "I can't see it."

Darren turned to her. "You weigh the least, Dorothy. You should try the rock bridge. See if it holds you."

At the thought of Dorothy in peril, Nelson sensed incredible danger and loss. "No. I'll go," he said.

Nelson stayed low, crawling across the abyss on his belly. The wind whipped around him like a tornadoe. It was all he could do to fight his way across. Once on the other side he signalled to Darren.

Darren's eyes squinted as he looked into the gold light. "You're next. If you make it, I'll go," he said, pushing Dorothy onto the bridge.

"Dorothy, stay down!" Nelson shouted but it was too late. She was halfway to him when the strong winds caused her to stumble and fall off the edge. Reflexively, her hand grasped a jutting rock, but her right hand dangled free.

Nelson raced to her. "Give me your hand!" he yelled as he shot his hand out to grab her.

Her fingers found his just as she was about to plummet to her death.

"I've got her!" Nelson winced as he held on to Dorothy.

Darren forgot Nelson's warning to stay on his belly and made the same mistake Dorothy had. As he stood, the wind caught him in an undertow and sucked him off the bridge as if he were no more than a piece of lint.

"Darren!" Dorothy screamed. "Darren!"

"Darling, I'll save you," Nelson said.

Her fingers were slipping out of Nelson's hand. "I love you, darling. I'll never let anything hurt you," Nelson said, meaning every word he uttered.

But it was too late. Dorothy slipped away, falling silently to her death. He watched her beautiful face grow small and distant. He whispered her name repeatedly as he felt his heart breaking.

Nelson had greatly miscalculated. He'd tried to win Dorothy by appealing to her greed. In the end, he'd lost to the one thing he hadn't counted upon—true love. At the very end, her every thought had been of Darren.

The abyss was so deep, Nelson didn't even hear their bodies hit the ground.

For a long moment, Nelson thought that if he watched over the edge, he would see Dorothy's spirit rise and come back to haunt him. So he waited, but nothing happened.

Then he knew she would have to return to him some way other than in spirit form. She was, after all, his forever. He'd decided that when he'd given his heart to her, and she'd sealed their fate when she'd broken his heart. They were bound for eternity. They could never escape each other.

Finally, Nelson rose. He looked at the entrance to the city of gold, and it was just as the captain had described. Two tall columns rose a hundred feet in the air. They did look like ears of corn, which made sense since the Incas introduced maize to the Americas. They also looked like Flash Gordon's rockets, with fins at the base to hold them upright.

The wind continued to blast, and when he tried to step forward, he knew this was no ordinary wind. It was like a wind tunnel, pushing him back yet pulling him in. And he was reminded of the magnets he'd played with as a child.

He realized that he was standing on the edge of some kind of opening to another dimension. This wasn't wind. It was a magnetized area where negative met positive. Where the forces of good and evil met and coexisted.

At that very second he realized the enormity of what he'd done.

The energy blasts and the force of the polarization of electricity had unseated his brain.

He had killed them just as surely as if he'd pushed them over the edge himself. He had brought them here, put their lives in danger.

He'd thought he'd done it in the name of love. Now he

understood he was the instrument of evil, for in the deepest, darkest recesses of his heart, he knew he'd wanted them dead. Knew he'd be lost without Dorothy, couldn't bear knowing that she had chosen Darren over him. And the force of his evil intentions set this tragedy in motion.

He threw his forearm over his eyes, not daring to look at the city of gold anymore. He couldn't be tempted. He had to get away from here, but he was riveted to the spot by the energies whirling around him. He was in the middle of a twister. He was dying, yet alive. He was crazy, yet sane.

"Dorothy! I love you!" he screamed at the top of his lungs. "I'm sorry for what I've done!"

He managed to move his right foot away from the energy vacuum. He took another step, then another, slowly inching away from El Dorado. He crept down the mountain, and with every step, the enormity of his sins pelted him. He suffered in heart and soul.

He might not have killed them, but he'd surely caused their deaths. He deserved to be killed. He thought of throwing himself over the mountainside, but he was a coward. He didn't have the guts.

When he made it to the bottom of the mountain, his crew was waiting for him. They gasped when they saw him and turned their faces away. Several ran screaming from him.

"What is it?" Nelson didn't understand.

One of the crewmen grabbed the silver flask Nelson used to hold his Scotch. He peered into the reflective metal to see that his hair and eyebrows had turned completely white. He dropped the flask on the ground, fell to his knees and sobbed for hours.

He knew then that he'd altered his fate. He could never leave the jungle. He could never go back to the United States. He would spend the rest of his life haunted by the memory of what had happened, and making restitution for his sins.

He had gone to the mountain to find the legendary city of gold. He had wanted to become a legend.

Well, he'd succeeded.

37

━━ ◄ ━━

Through the haze, M.J. could hear a voice singing. It was Uma's voice, the young Nelson's voice.

It was the voice of the past and present.

M.J. couldn't remember if she was in a silver plane or on a magic carpet ride. It was some ride, that was for sure. She rubbed her temple, trying to come awake, but all she heard was Travis saying, "You belong to me."

She realized that he wasn't saying, "I love you." Suddenly, she felt terribly sad and alone.

"Dorothy." A voice undulated through the murky fog in her brain.

"Yes?" she answered, then realized she wasn't Dorothy. But she felt like Dorothy—lost, alone, abandoned and forgotten. All she wanted to do was go home.

But M.J. didn't have a home anymore. She'd left her career behind. She'd left Claire and the girls behind. She'd fallen in love, but she wasn't sure Travis wanted her.

"Dorothy," Nelson said, placing his aged hand on her forehead. "You've been asleep quite some time, but I'm glad you've decided to awaken."

M.J. pushed his hand away angrily. She'd had it with men who wanted to claim her but wouldn't commit. Wasn't that the point of the bizarre story Nelson had told her? "Don't touch me. And I'm not Dorothy!"

"I've been meaning to ask you that," he said coolly in an offhanded manner of acceptance and clipped disdain. "What is your name, exactly?"

Her head felt like a beach ball. "You drugged me again."

"Sorry," he said, sitting in his chair and lacing his fingers over his middle.

She looked away, trying to focus in the dim light. "It's M.J."

"That's not a name."

Her head was pounding. She didn't know where he'd sent her in her drugged state, but it must have been far away. She'd lost half her gray matter on the return trip. "I don't have a name."

"Why not?"

"My parents didn't think enough of me to give me one."

"What a horrid thing to have happened. It's just as well, because you'll always be Dorothy to me."

She was tired of his game. Tired of arguing with him. He'd just drug her again, and it would take hours for her to battle her way to reality. She hated these headaches he gave her. She'd never tolerated drugs well. That was why she stuck to natural herbs and minerals. She never needed drugs and felt they were a waste of money. "Why is it so important to you that I be Dorothy?"

"Because I'm dying."

"What?"

"I've known it for some time now."

"How do you know?" she asked, her voice softening in empathy.

"Cancer has ways of making itself known."

"But you could go back to Los Angeles. Get help. You could…"

"Dorothy, my dear. M.J." He sighed. "I'm old. I haven't any more time to steal. I have nothing to lose here in my world. And here, I would prefer you be Dorothy. I do so wish you believed in reincarnation. It would make things much easier for us."

"Well, I don't."

"Too bad," he said.

"I'm not a ghost. I'm a person."

"But Dorothy has come back to me through you," he insisted.

"She's dead, Nelson. You killed her, just like you said. I was hoping there was some mistake, some accident you blamed yourself for all these years. But you killed her."

"I know that."

"No, you don't. If you did, you'd realize she is dead, forever and always. I'm M.J. I'm somebody else and I can never be someone I'm not." She knew she was an idiot to think she could reason with him. He was dying. He'd probably drugged himself with any manner of concoctions that produced lunacy. Not that she blamed him. If she were in pain, she'd want anesthesia just as much. Maybe more.

But part of her told her she should be playing it smart with him in order to plot her escape. She should toy with his illusions, mess with his brain long enough to break free.

But she didn't. She felt sorry for him. She sensed he was not half as nuts now as he'd been back when Dorothy was alive. Greed and heartache had sent him over the edge then. After that, he'd spent the rest of his life trying to save lives. Nelson wasn't nearly as crazy as some of the people she used to work with. "You loved her enough to ruin your life for her?"

"Ruin?" Nelson looked at the bags and pouches of herbal healers. Thoughtfully, he shook his head. "Perhaps she was my destiny, after all. If I hadn't met Dorothy, I wouldn't have wanted her so much that I lost my mind over it. I wouldn't have stayed in this jungle a minute longer than it took to find the oil field. I would have packed up, gone back to California and spent my life behind a desk." He squeezed the bridge of his nose with his thumb and forefinger. "The thought sounds barbaric to me now."

He expelled a deep sigh. "I created all this on my own. I've invented, sought, combined and tested these plants and herbs on humans and animals for over five decades. I've kept all the records in those journals you see stacked on that shelf closest to the opening."

"You what?" Her eyes flew to the shelf.

"I wonder if anyone would be interested?"

"Are you kidding? Why, only Eli Lilly, or Upjohn, just to name a few."

Wearily, he wiped his face with his hands. "It makes no difference to me now."

"It should," she replied indignantly. "What if you've found something here that, with a little help or adjusting, could save not just a couple dozen lives, but lives all over the world? What if there's something that could eliminate pain and suffering? And what about this moo-joo juice you keep giving me? What's in this stuff? I mean, I'm so out of it, I go someplace else, like I'm in another time dimension."

"You are," he said flatly. "That's the point of it."

He was doing it again, she thought, being metaphysically scary, when all she was doing was trying to be positive and sweet to him. She didn't like the way he always took the conversation to psychic abstracts. She liked dealing with facts, figures, graphs and charts. She liked seeing life written on a graduated bar graph. She could analyze it then, see results and possibly—no, probably—be able to squelch her panic every time she thought she was seeing ghosts. She didn't like to think there was a spirit world. Not because she didn't have the courage to face the devil on occasion, but because, if there were angels leading her destiny, she didn't like the one who'd been assigned to her. As far as she was concerned, she'd gotten the rotten end of the mystical stick. She'd been abandoned by her father, her mother was dead, she'd fallen in love with Travis, whose love she still wasn't sure about, and now she was being held prisoner in a cave in the middle of nowhere.

She knew no one was going to save her. The angels had better things to do. She'd just have to save herself.

"No, Nelson, what you gave me is a dream. Pretty dreams, some of them, but nothing more. I'm me. I've spent a great deal of time and energy inventing this person I've decided to be. You can play Pygmalion with someone else, but not with me."

She rose, and immediately fell down. "What have you done?" she demanded, inspecting her tethered ankles.

"I'm keeping you safe."

"Bullshit!" Her temper flaring, M.J. leaned over to untie her feet. The leather sliced her hands and soon she was bleeding. "Oh, my God! What is this?" She put her finger into her mouth.

"Don't suck on that," he said flatly, watching her reaction.

She fell over in a dead heap.

"Or else you'll fall asleep again," he replied, pulling her finger out of her mouth. He covered her with a blanket. "Maybe you're right. Upjohn would probably pay a small fortune for an anesthetic that works this fast."

He stood, shoved his hands in his pockets and, walking away, said, "It's something to consider."

Peering around, Travis said, "I'd kill for my binoculars."

"Sorry, mate. They're melted," Michael said, scanning the mountain cliffs around them. "We'll never find her in these rocks. There's no telling which way they went."

"Instinct. That's what we have to rely on," Travis said.

"Do you mind telling me exactly how to do that?" Michael asked.

"Concentrate on M.J. On her thoughts. Try to link your mind with hers. Maybe you can see her surroundings with your mind's eye. Maybe you'll pick up a scent or a color that will give us a clue," Travis replied.

"You're joking."

"I'm dead serious," Travis said, knowing he was grasping, but he was desperate.

Meticulously, he took in every tree, crevice and path on the mountainside.

"And this works?" Michael was doubtful.

Nodding, Travis climbed over a huge boulder and worked his way higher. "I have no idea."

"Great. Just great," Michael moaned. Hands on his hips, he asked, "Why aren't we turning right here, following these ruts?"

"Because I want to go this way."

"Why?"

"Because it's the way to the light."

"What light?" Michael asked.

"The one coming from up there." He pointed.

Michael followed his gesture to the pinprick of light shining from what looked like a forest. "What do you think it is?"

"M.J.," Travis said, still climbing. His heart throbbed with a yearning he hadn't known before. Her face seemed to rise before him like a vision. She was saying something to him, but he couldn't hear her. He closed his eyes, and his hearing cleared.

Save me, Travis. I'm here. Just come find me. I'll wait for you.

It was uncanny the clarity that came with fear.

Travis knew that if he found M.J. alive, he'd never let her go. He'd tell her that he wanted her with him always, that he realized *she* was the reason his destiny had brought him to Ecuador. He'd wandered off his course, thinking his company was the most important thing. But it wasn't—she was.

The vision of M.J. melded with Travis's thoughts, and they became one. He was inside her head, reading her thoughts.

He knew, not rationally or with his heart but with his intuition, that M.J. was bound, shackled or tied up. It was as if he could feel the restraints around his ankles.

He hated being tied down. It frightened him.

Then he realized it was M.J. who hated being tied down—especially to a man. She had to be free. She'd built her life around freedom—never marrying or having children or buying a home. She even leased her car, all in the pursuit of being able to blast off to an adventure someday—an adventure that would show her the world.

The adventure had been Travis. Now he knew it, too.

He could see her as clearly as if she were sitting beside him. He looked around at her prison. Expecting to see trees, he saw lights. Lots of them.

Candles?

He opened his eyes. "She's in a cave, Michael."

"What?" Michael faced Travis.

"I...could see it. That's not a forest up there. It's trees, yes, but beyond that are caves. And she's in one of them."

"Okay. So we just hope the light doesn't go out. Otherwise, it will take us forever to find her."

Travis was in agreement. "We've got less than thirty minutes of light left. One wrong step and we could find ourselves at the bottom of this cliff."

"We'll go as far as possible and if we can't make it all the way, we'll bunk down for the night and start up again at dawn. Agreed?" Michael asked.

"Agreed."

38

This time, M.J. was prepared. She fought the drug with every ounce of her will. She knew that if the mind could heal the body, then the mind could also stave off ill-meant attacks. Nelson had doped her up so many times, surely at some point she would develop an immunity. She didn't care if she was medically accurate or not. The only thing that mattered was that she give her mind a logical explanation for the task ahead.

Anesthetizing waves washed over her, but she rode them like a surfer. She told herself she was on top of it, above it. That it would pass.

She heard him walk away from her, heard the rattling of what sounded like pans and glasses. The sounds came in and out. Though she kept her eyes shut to feign sleep, her ears were on guard. She heard him strike a match and smelled tobacco smoke, as if he were smoking a pipe or cigar. She didn't care which. The important thing was that Nelson was no longer watching her. He was no doubt off in his dream world, believing she was unconscious and, therefore, not a threat.

Doubled over, a position she'd purposefully chosen, she had no problem slowly untying the leather strips around her ankles. She realized he'd laced some kind of plant or vine with the leather. It was the prickly vine that had sliced her skin. She'd reacted precisely as he'd expected. She'd sucked the poison off the cuts.

The second she'd tasted the foul, bitter liquid, she recognized it. She didn't swallow it, and as soon as she fell over in a heap, she'd spit the poison out.

M.J. realized she was smack-dab in the middle of the most challenging acting job of her life. If she could manage to free herself without Nelson and his blasted, far-too-curious Chipchaw discovering her intentions, she'd nominate herself for an Oscar. Or an Emmy, at the very least.

The leather straps unfurled once their knots reluctantly gave way. Gingerly, she peeled the poison vine from her ankles. She took the risk of opening one eye.

It was just as she'd suspected. Nelson was sitting at the entrance to the cave in his chair, smoking a crude pipe. Chipchaw was lying at his feet like a loyal pet. They were watching the stars. They weren't watching her. She could make a dash for it, but she'd have to go past them. And then what?

She had no clue where she was—north, south, east or west of the place she'd left Travis and Michael.

Travis. Michael. Surely they've missed me by now. But how could they ever find me? They could be anywhere by now, searching the mountains in vain for me.

Panic set in. Her hands got clammy, and she felt herself beginning to tremble. She didn't want to die in the jungle, never to be heard from again. She didn't want to be the fodder for someone else's legend half a century from now.

For the life of her, she still had a difficult time believing Nelson had killed Dorothy in cold blood the way he'd described. There was so much gentleness in him now, so much he'd been giving to people. She'd liked to have said that God worked in mysterious ways, even forcing circumstances so one committed murder in order to seek his divine path—becoming a healer. But she didn't buy it—none of it.

There was something in his story he wasn't telling her.

There were secrets, rather than lies, rooted at the base of it. The lure of the mythical El Dorado might be good enough for some, but Nelson was too intelligent.

Yet, he'd seen it.

Something didn't add up, but she didn't know what it was.

What she did believe was that if she could ever find El Dorado and go back to the place where he'd committed murder, she would find a lot of answers.

She didn't buy his explanation, that he was remorseful about having killed Dorothy, so much so that he could never go back. She didn't buy that he'd feared going to prison. All he would have had to do was cook up a good story. He had plenty of time and he was certainly smart enough.

No one, even today, would question an accident in the middle of uncharted jungle. No court in the world would have questioned a motive. As far as the world was concerned, Nelson didn't have a motive.

It was too suspicious that he gave up the millions he could have made off the oil he'd found. He must have entered El Dorado. Yet, he didn't have a single ounce of gold here in this cave. No icons. No gold nuggets. Not even a pouch of dust. It didn't make any sense.

He was a man of vision. He'd admitted wanting to make a name for himself, to become a legend. But he'd given up the biggest chance in the century to be famous, both in oil and in archaeology.

Why?

With each of her suppositions and conclusions, M.J. only found herself saddled with another bucketful of questions. The more she thought about Nelson, his life and his story, the more she was convinced he was hiding something—something big.

M.J.'s brain was working overtime, enough so that she'd successfully fought the narcotic. Like most sleep enhancers, the narcotic's potency dwindled after the first twenty or thirty minutes. Clarity spread over her like a spring rain. The slight dizziness she felt was gone. Her leaden body felt light again. She was back to normal.

Now what to do? Should she just barge past Nelson and go sailing out of the cave into the wild, dangerous unknown? She couldn't very well ask him for directions. Maybe she should turn the tables and take him as *her* prisoner. Force him to show her the way down and out of the valley.

Yes, that was it. She would…

"Here they come, Chipchaw," Nelson said, calmly blowing smoke rings. "I knew they were smart. Not as smart as I am, of course. But then, I suppose it took a few years to break me in, as well, now, didn't it?" Nelson chuckled.

Travis and Michael. It has to be! I'm going to be rescued from my prison!

She held her breath, wondering what she should do. If her friends had any sort of plan in mind, she didn't want to foul their strategy. Right now, Nelson thought she was out of it, that she was still bound up.

If Travis and Michael were to confront Nelson with violence, the fact that she was conscious and free could be to all their benefit.

She couldn't help wondering why Nelson didn't move from his chair as his enemies approached. He waited patiently—too patiently. She didn't like it. Why wasn't he preparing for the intruders? Shouldn't he be barricading the entrance? Leaving? Hiding?

She realized Nelson must think he had an advantage. But what? Peering through darkness, she saw he had draped a blanket over his legs. He was hiding something.

A gun!

She heard muffled voices.

Travis.

Chipchaw squealed, hopped on top of Nelson's lap, then scrambled to his shoulder. He squeaked, and his eyes opened like saucers filled with terror. He jumped to a bookshelf, then to another, squealing and making a racket.

Then M.J. heard Travis's deep voice. "Uma, I presume," he said, standing tall in the cave entrance.

The light of the candles and the small interior cooking fire illuminated his face and Michael's, ringing them in golden halos. They looked like angels with attitude.

"Nelson," he corrected, not rising from his chair, but putting his pipe on the edge of a shelf nearby.

Chipchaw slapped his tiny hands on the side of his cheeks, eyes wide as moons, and continued to squeal, a blood-curdling scream meant to frighten away large predatory animals—including white hunters.

"This is Chipchaw," Nelson said, motioning toward the monkey.

"Nice mascot," Michael said.

"His manners need some work, but he keeps me company," Nelson said.

Travis spoke. "And you aren't Uma?"

"Not like you think. However, you believe that I am. Therefore I must be."

"I thought so."

Nelson's smile was slow and sly. "But I'm not the Uma you seek. You're looking for a demon. A destroyer. A murderer."

"You left out kidnapper," Travis said. "Where is she?"

"Over here, sir!" M.J. shouted from her place in the shadows, suddenly wanting to throw all caution aside.

Travis was here. He was going to save her. Everything was going to be all right.

She rose slowly, awkwardly, her legs unused to movement and still numb from the drugs. She stumbled.

She heard Nelson's sharp intake of breath. He was old,

but he wasn't missing a trick. She saw his hand move under the blanket. On instinct, she yelled at Travis, "Be careful! He's got a gun!"

"So do I!" Travis replied, pointing his gun at the old man. "Fully loaded. Extra clips in my pockets. Don't try anything."

Nelson was nonplussed and shrugged his shoulders.

"Are you all right, M.J.?" Michael called.

"Yes!" she said finally, getting her feet to place themselves one in front of the other. She felt like a newborn colt just learning to walk. She'd overcome the narcotic in her mind, but getting her motor skills back was another trick indeed.

Coming into the light, she saw the fear in Travis's eyes die. Joy radiated from him as she rushed into his outspread arms.

"M.J.," he said, relief flooding his body. He held her tightly to him, kissing the top of her head and thinking his good fortune had finally returned. "I thought I'd lost you," he whispered. "I don't know what I would have done if I had."

"I'm fine, sir," she whispered, clinging to him.

Michael hadn't realized he'd also held his arms out for her, but she hadn't wanted him. She'd gone to Travis. They looked natural together—as right as rain. She'd gone to Travis. To the man she loved and who loved her back.

Dumbfounded, Michael dropped his arms to his sides where they dangled next to his hips uselessly. Gone were thoughts of safety, of watching Nelson's covert, calculated movements. Michael felt a deep, abiding pain in his solar plexus, as if he'd been lanced. He stepped back and stumbled with the impact of her betrayal.

Michael had never lost at love before. He'd done the choosing. He said where and when, and the women came running on his terms. He'd always been the one to pursue, then break it off when it suited him. His ego had never been slapped before. His pride had never been cut down to size—until now. And he didn't like it one iota. He'd never been in such pain.

Michael didn't know his dark thoughts showed like ochre in his eyes. He didn't know his jaw had ground his smile to a menacing sneer. He didn't see his expression blacken with hatred.

But Nelson did.

"Hurts, doesn't it?" he whispered to Michael.

"What?" Michael didn't have time for idle chatter with a senile old man.

Nelson kept his voice low and his hand under the blanket where he held on tightly to his blow gun. He knew that Dorothy thought he had a real gun, but she was wrong. That was good. They would miscalculate.

He looked at Michael. "She doesn't want you."

Michael's face twisted. The old man's words were so simple. Truth always was. And they ripped his heart apart. Until that moment, Michael had told himself he'd done it all for M.J. because he loved her.

The fact that his rationalization was unfounded didn't matter. Michael had always reinterpreted facts, conversations, motivations and incidents to fit what his mind needed to have happen in order for him to always see himself in a hero's role.

Michael was the good guy. Michael was the genius. Michael was the lover extraordinaire.

Not once had he ever faced the truth—that he was self-centered and narcissistic. No, that was the other guy. That wasn't him. He was the good guy.

Being single, independent, an adventurer, had been his personal design. It wasn't true that every woman he'd ever loved had left him. He couldn't remember their reasons for breaking up with him. They weren't important. He would always find someone else—someone better, more beautiful, more accepting of him. Someone more intelligent, fun, exciting. After all, he'd found M.J.

It was imperative Michael win M.J. Win the oil. Win this contest between himself and Travis. He had to have her, at any cost.

Travis was kissing her like he thought he'd never live to kiss her again. Michael watched them sharing love, making love together. Holding, caressing, touching. She was crying. Travis wiped her tears and kept assuring her that they were all going to be fine. And she believed him.

Envy caused Michael's stomach to lurch. Hatred spewed bile from his liver to his throat and burned like acid.

"Why don't you tell them the truth about yourself?" Nelson said, loud enough to bring Travis and M.J. back to the present.

"What?" M.J. asked.

Nelson leveled his dark eyes on Michael. "Your friend here has a confession to make."

"Me? I'm not the kidnapper." Michael spat the words accusingly.

"It was never my intention to harm her, and you know it. I wanted to protect her, protect her from you."

M.J. and Travis exchanged a look. "What's going on?"

Nelson's eyes never left Michael's face. He watched the younger man with keen, perceptive eyes. Yet M.J. had the distinct impression he was relying on instinct, intuition, more than eyesight. "Tell them where they will find the city of gold," he said.

"Say, what is this?" Travis asked, but Michael remained silent.

M.J. felt the hairs on the back of her neck stand on end. Her blood turned cold. She'd been terrified of snakes, pumas and things that go bump in the night ever since she began the expedition, but never had she felt this impossibly debilitating sense of powerlessness. Something was more than terribly wrong.

She stared at Michael, as did Travis.

"Michael? What's he talking about?"

Then she saw it. The blazing jealousy in Michael's eyes was directed at Travis. He shot her a glacial look or two, but it was nothing compared to the outright psychotic emotions she saw in his eyes when he looked at Travis.

She felt Travis's grip tighten on her waist. She pressed her hand over his and into her flesh. She wanted him to know she would be there for him, with him. They were in this together. Whatever *this* was.

Nelson's old voice broke the silence. "Not talking, eh? Well, I can understand that. I thought it strange that, upon my last visit to a particularly odd group of natives several months ago, one of them boasted to me that they had broken through the barriers between heaven and earth with their minds and had conjured up the god Uma. They said they no longer believed that Uma was an old medicine man, a shaman like me. They told me that I had no power now that they knew the real truth about Uma. I explained that I've never touted myself as a mystical person. I'm very much human, even though the natives have enjoyed spreading stories about me over the decades. But I was curious about this new tack they were taking. I prodded them to tell me what they were talking about. They said Uma came to them and told them they had failed in their mission as gatekeepers. That they had allowed intruders into the jungle who wanted to annihilate El Dorado."

"El Dorado?" M.J.'s voice held surprise as she looked at Michael, who was clearly unnerved by this transformation.

Michael waved his gun at Nelson. "Go on, old man," he growled.

"Uma told them that three intruders had come to steal

not only the gold, but the secrets, as well. It's the secrets of El Dorado the Uma men guard with their lives."

Nelson continued. "I watched you in the valley just a few days ago, when you first came. You found your spot to drill in no time flat. But that's not really what you came for. I've watched other geologists in the Oriente. They set many charges. But you used only a spare amount of dynamite."

Travis's head jerked from Nelson to Michael. "There did seem to be an awful lot of dynamite left when you came back."

"He didn't use it," Nelson accused. "He used his fancy machines, and he poked around plenty up here in the caves where there is no oil."

Michael sneered at Nelson. "But there is gold."

"Not the kind you want to find," Nelson warned. "Believe me, you don't want to know—"

"Don't tell me what I want or don't want!" Michael shouted, brandishing his gun. "You're what I came looking for, old man. I heard the stories about you. Some people say you're the fairy tale, but when M.J. started telling us her cockamamy stories about an old medicine man, I knew I'd really struck it rich. I figured sooner or later you'd pull some stunt like this and I'd get lucky. She was my ticket to finding you."

"I don't believe you, Michael!" M.J. shouted angrily. "You didn't mean to hurt me. You're better than that, better than this."

"I admit to getting off track for a short spell. Getting soft. But luckily, I got right back on. I've waited too long for the big payola. I needed the cover of this expedition so that the local antiquarians wouldn't get wind of it. I was here a year ago, and I guess I asked too many questions about El Dorado. All of a sudden other archaeologists are vying for grants to search for Atlantis. It's a hot topic now, what with the millennium coming."

"But you had money, Michael," Travis said.

"Ha! I've blown every dime I've made looking for something this big. You have no clue what I've been through. This kind of thing will make me…" He sputtered, looking for the right word.

"Immortal?" M.J. asked.

"Yes!" he exclaimed.

"This is ridiculous, Michael." Travis took a step toward him.

Michael fired the gun at his feet. "Patronizing doesn't work with me. See, Travis, you think everybody is noble like you. Well, we aren't. You want to be Daddy Rabbit— run your company, put some bucks in the bank. Me? I want more. I want the bucks and the fame. The cover of *Time*. Television interviews. The awards. The Nobel, maybe. Can you imagine what it would be like? To have found the key to Atlantis?"

M.J. shook her head. "But it's just mythology, Michael."

Nelson cast M.J. a suffering look. "I'm afraid Michael is right, my dear. At least more so than you are. I've been to El Dorado."

M.J. wanted to protest that what he remembered was a delusion, but Travis tugged on her arm, halting her.

Whispering, he said, "Not now."

Michael's smile was malevolent. "You bet your ass I'm right, old man. And you're going to get a chance to see it all, M.J. You, too, Travis. And Nelson here, he's going to take us there."

"You won't make it," Nelson warned.

"Who's going to stop me?" Michael asked, chuckling. "You?"

Nelson shook his head. "The Uma men. They are sworn to kill everyone who tries to desecrate El Dorado. The world isn't ready for the secrets in that cave. The Uma men know this. They are guided by their visions.

They have been pursuing you all along. You have never been far from their sight."

"They're savages," Michael said. "Their primitive weapons are no match for guns."

"I wouldn't be too sure of that," Travis said. "They've kept us on the run quite effectively."

"They'll stop at nothing to protect the secrets," Nelson continued, glaring at Michael. "You can't stop them with bullets. They're relentless."

"Shut up!" Michael yelled.

"They'll kill us all before they let anything desecrate El Dorado."

"I said, shut up!"

Travis bolted away from M.J. and grabbed Michael's hand.

The gun went off.

The thrust of Travis's body against Michael sent them both tumbling to the ground. Travis squeezed Michael's wrist, but Michael was strong. He doubled his fist and belted Travis in the jaw.

"M.J.! Down!" Travis called, as he grappled with Michael for control of the gun. The gun fired again.

Chipchaw scrambled to another bookcase while M.J. screamed and covered her ears as the sound echoed off the cave walls, sounding like a rally of gunfire. The monkey ran to the shadows.

"You son of a bitch!" Travis snarled.

Michael hit him again. "Get off of me!"

Travis rolled over Michael's body and slammed his wrist against the hard cave floor, but still Michael wouldn't give up. Finally, Travis succeeded in wresting the gun from Michael and knocking it to the far cave wall. Michael drew his arm back to land another blow, but Travis blocked the hit and belted Michael with a left cross. Michael was unfazed. He shoved Travis off and scrambled to his feet.

"Come on! Let's do it! Let's get it on!" he taunted Travis.

M.J. crawled into the darkness where she'd seen the gun skitter. She groped in the shadows, and her fingers found metal. She grabbed the gun. Knowing she could shoot the eyelashes off a woodpecker from forty paces, she aimed the gun over their heads. "Stop it!" she shouted. "Both of you! Now!"

Travis landed another blow to Michael's midsection. Michael backed up a step, shook his head and flushed with renewed anger. "You can't stop me," he said, and reached behind his back. He pulled out a Glock and held it with both hands.

"Michael!" M.J. said, holding her gun on him.

He laughed at her. "Put it down, M.J., or Travis winds up with no knees."

She dropped the gun and rushed to Travis's side.

Michael pointed the gun at Nelson. "Now come out from under the blanket and kick the blowgun over here."

"You knew?" Nelson asked.

"You really do think I'm stupid."

"No," Nelson said. "I just didn't know you were quite so reckless."

"Whatever," he said. "M.J., find us some matches and grab a few of those candles. I'm sure we're going to need some illumination where we're going."

M.J. nodded and did as he'd asked.

"Come on, old man. Let's get this show on the road before your freaky friends show up."

Nelson tried one last time to reason with him. "To leave here there is only one path down."

"Don't mess with me," Michael warned.

"We must go up the mountains through the pass. It is very dangerous. I'm not sure I will remember the way."

Michael cocked the gun and held it to M.J.'s temple. "I

have every confidence you'll remember exactly how you got there."

Nelson swallowed, his eyes pleading with M.J. "It's coming back to me."

"That's what I thought," Michael replied. "And just in time."

39

There was confusion among the Uma men where there had never been discord before. They felt the rift in the universe. Something dire was happening, something that would upset the balance of power for all time.

Their power.

"Someone is close to the forbidden city."

"The intruders will not be deterred."

"Can this evil be possible?"

"We must all agree that it has always been necessary from time to time to purge the earth. Cleansing is good. Death is good," instructed the eldest Cofan member.

"You are right," the youngest member replied, remembering the harrowing breath of Uma blasting down on him.

"If we do not kill the invaders, then Uma will have us branded as the evil ones. Others will come demanding our deaths, as well."

To a man, they knew that their way was the only way. It was the divine way. They had to maintain order. They were the gatekeepers. It was their job to keep the earth in balance.

"We must reverse this disorder. Killing is good. It is our tenet, our holiest of truths. It is our way," the eldest Cofan member said.

"We are omnipotent among the earth walkers. We often change the course of human history by forcing intruders out of the rain forest. We know how to frighten and intimidate. If we allow these evildoers to steal the secrets of El Dorado, we will be lost. We will not rest until we cleanse the earth of their spirits," he said, passion surging through his body.

The membership felt his electricity. They nodded solemnly in agreement. They felt their faith being renewed, their zealousness returning.

They were the Uma men. They would bond and become a whole consciousness again once they had killed.

"And what of the imposter that Uma told us about? The one who goes about healing and calling himself Uma when he is only human?" the youngest member asked.

"We will rid the earth of him, as well," the eldest Cofan member said. "Redemption will be ours if we succeed in putting the world back in proper order."

They chanted their mantra inside their heads, where their thoughts increased in power. They returned to communicating with each other through telepathy. It was the ancient way. It was the way they had been taught by their ancestors, before language had been invented by the lesser beings that roamed the earth.

The Uma men had been wrong to allow their thoughts to be bastardized by discord among them. They knew it was imperative to recapture their power and become the one again.

They were gatekeepers. They knew their duty to their god, and they would not fail.

40

The road to Utopia was as perilous as all mystical pilgrimages should be, M.J. thought, but the narrow footpath that wound toward the moon and stars, then burrowed deeply into the mass of stony mountain peaks frightened her more than the jungle. "Are you sure you know the way?" she asked Nelson, stumbling for the fourth time as a rock slipped out from under her foot. "It feels as if the mountain is alive, and it's trying to kill me!"

Nelson led the way with Chipchaw riding on his shoulder. "It is very much alive, and yes, this old mountain would be quite happy to see us perish before reaching El Dorado."

"Thanks. I needed that assurance," she said, not hiding her sarcasm. "What I wouldn't give for a lantern. It's dark as pitch."

"Use your instincts to guide you, my dear," Nelson whispered. "Sometimes your eyes deceive you. Keep your back to the mountainside, like I'm doing. Slide your feet along the crevice between the mountain and the footpath. You won't fall."

"I wish I had your confidence," she muttered.

"Oh, I don't have confidence," he said.

"What is it, then?"

"I'm going to die anyway. I just don't care."

M.J. swallowed. She thought of Travis's kisses, of the life she'd like to lead with him. A sane one. A quiet one. Going to the grocery store. Trying on dresses. Sending

Christmas cards. They were all very normal things. She wanted to live long enough to give them another try. "Yeah? Well, I do."

Travis followed behind M.J., and Michael, still holding his gun on them all, took up the rear.

Travis remonstrated himself for falling into Michael's trap. Why hadn't he seen it coming? He'd been so hell-bent on keeping his company solvent he hadn't checked things out. His instincts had been keen from the beginning, telling him not to trust someone who'd betrayed him once before. Michael had used Travis years ago and he was doing it again now.

"Hey, Travis! Michael!" M.J. signaled. She pointed down the mountainside. "We've got company."

She held out the binoculars Nelson owned toward Travis. He reached out to her and took them, lifted them to his eyes and peered through them.

"Give me those," Michael demanded, and Travis handed them over. Peering through the lenses, Michael laughed, bemused. "Those scrawny guys are my enemy? Man, I've been worrying for nothing."

Travis could hear voices growing excited. "We've been spotted! Let's step on it."

Nelson peered down the slope. "They're ransacking my cave! All my work!"

M.J. felt his pain like a lance. She knew how she'd feel if someone destroyed her life's work. She reached out to touch his hand. "We'll live through this. We'll make it, and when we do, you and I will go back there and get all your notes and we'll…"

"You are a dreamer, aren't you, my dear?" Nelson asked. Then he shook his head. "I'm not going to live through this. Neither are you."

"Nice talk," Travis said.

"Yeah, cut the chitchat and keep going, old-timer," Michael ordered.

Nelson grumbled but moved on.

"They can't kill us," Michael said. "I have guns and plenty of ammunition. I can pick them off one by one. M.J's a great shot, too," he said.

"Oh, I didn't say they'd use conventional methods."

"What will they use? Blowguns?" M.J. asked.

"Possibly. And other things."

"What other things?" she pressed.

Nelson smirked. "You know, it's been a long time since I've had a social life of any kind to speak of. I must say, I rather like sharing my escapades with such an appreciative audience."

"That's just dandy, old man, but get on with it," Michael said, sneering.

"Witchcraft, we used to call it. Voodoo's another good word. But the fact of the matter is, they pray people to death. They meditate their enemies' demise. They put their minds together and they believe collectively they have enough power to rule the world—their world, anyway."

"Primitive," Travis said.

"Actually, Carl Jung wrote about the collective unconscious quite a bit, as I remember. I heard him speak in Basel once." Nelson winked at M.J. and continued climbing, his back still against the mountain wall.

"So, who's leading this parade, a shrink or a geologist?" Michael asked.

Nelson was unperturbed. "You find through life, young man, that it pays to pay attention to a great many things. That's the problem with the modern world, or at least it was when I left it. Everyone and everything was getting so compartmentalized. Separate. Every doctrine was estranged from the other. It's not until you take a little of this and put it with a little of that that you get the real answers."

"Real answers," M.J. repeated. "To what?"

"Life, of course!" He glanced at her as if she'd lost her mind fifty yards back.

"Look, old man," Michael said, "All I care about is that you know enough about life to get us away from them—" he pointed down the mountain "—and back to civilization."

"To my knowledge, no one other than myself and my friends, Dorothy and Darren, have made it even this far. There are many ways to die on the false trails that lead off this one we're taking. You are safe because you're with me. I know the way very well."

"How many times have you been here?" M.J. asked.

"Only once."

"Then how can you be so sure?"

Nelson's eyes filled with wisdom and awe. "It is a path you will never forget, either."

M.J. moved her left foot, getting a hold, feeling solid ground beneath her, and edged her body up. They were moving at a snail's pace, but whenever she tried to rush, she stumbled. She peered over the sheer cliff into the abyss. The faintest ray of moonlight lit the tips and spikes of rock below. If she fell, she'd be impaled. She felt sick all over.

"This voodoo of theirs works?" she asked, not really wanting an answer, but as long as Nelson kept talking she didn't have to think about the dangerous trail and how close she was to death every time she moved.

"Not always."

"But you said that was what they used to vanquish their enemies."

"They like to think that's how they do it, but I'd say you've experienced their repertoire. Fire, blowguns—"

"Snakes," Travis said.

"And shrunken heads," Nelson said.

"I missed those," M.J. replied anxiously.

"It's a favorite of theirs."

"How much farther is it, old man?" Michael demanded.

M.J. watched the moon creep out of sight behind the mountain. She didn't think she would ever see anything as wonderful as the sun rising. She would be able to see their way so much better.

But then, so would the Uma men.

"This is the easy part of the journey," Nelson said. "Distance wise it's not so far."

Looking at the narrow trail, M.J. swallowed hard. Her toes were hanging over the edge. "How can this be the easy part?"

"It just is," Nelson replied. "You'll be safe with me."

She didn't believe him. She was convinced she was going to die. Nobody had this many scrapes with death and walked away. Nobody's luck was that good.

Nelson was still talking, but she realized he was doing it to keep her mind off the danger, off the fact that they were going to die.

"Age can only be counted when one uses the time wisely to put together all those separate compartments of life I've been referring to."

M.J.'s heart slammed against her ribs. She'd had anxiety attacks before. In fact, M.J. was an expert on anxiety and panic. But this was worse. Much worse.

"Would you be so kind as to put them together for us, Nelson?" She squeezed her eyes shut and slid her left foot over the crumbling gravel, moving higher—always higher.

"Love to," he said, his voice lifting to a trill.

God, how can he sound so happy when we are about to die?

"I say we all just keep quiet and keep going," Travis said reaching out to hold M.J.'s hand.

She opened her eyes and looked at him. Never had she seen so much love in another's eyes. Never had she felt her fears dissolve so quickly. Never had she felt less alone.

He pressed his fingers into her palm. "Don't be afraid. We'll make it. All of us. I promise," he said.

She nodded, wanting to believe him. "Okay." It was all she said, but it said so much. She was surrendering to him, allowing him to care for her.

Michael circled a bend, his back flattened against the mountainside, his hiking boots hanging half over the edge of the trail. Rivulets of fine gravel cascaded down the mountainside each time he moved. He realized that with each step, the path grew narrower and more perilous. Sweat trickled down his temple, and his breathing was shallow.

M.J. felt the path beneath her narrow. She moved upward, step after step.

"Nelson? Have you taken into consideration that each time one of us takes a step, we take an inch of ground with us? There's no way we can go back down. We'll never make it."

Nelson chuckled. "Don't worry. I told you, we aren't going back the way we came. It's like life. Once you make a decision, there is never any going back. You can only go forward."

"And that's what we're doing?" M.J. asked.

Before Nelson could answer, Travis replied, "That is most definitely what we are doing."

"I think now would be a good time to tell you what to expect with El Dorado," Nelson said. "It's very important to arrive at the gates to El Dorado just as the moon is going down and the sun is coming up."

"Why? Is the lighting that important?"

"No, but the air currents are."

"Air currents?" Travis asked.

Nelson's expression was serious. "We are only feet from the entrance right now."

"No way," Travis said, pushing away from the mountainside. His eager movement was met with a blast of cold air, then a rush of warm air. They slipped around him like giant hands, pulling him. His foot slipped a fraction of an inch and panic shot through his arms. He quickly grabbed for a jutting rock near his head. As his fingers encircled the rock, he felt the air swirl past him, slamming his body against the rock. "Shit! That was close!" he said, his cheek plastered against the mountain.

"You see, the wind is shifting," Nelson pointed out.

"Incredible." Travis sucked in his breath.

"Come. Be careful," Nelson said tugging gently on M.J.'s hand.

"I'm afraid," she said, suddenly wishing she were anywhere on earth but here.

Nelson shook his head. "You, of all of us, have the least to fear."

"Why—why do you say that?"

"Because you are pure of heart. Your heart is filled with love. Even for me. Even for Michael, despite his evil deeds."

"I don't understand. What has that to do with El Dorado?"

"It has everything to do with it." Nelson turned another bend and pulled them toward the elusive city of gold.

The wind shrieked through the narrow cavern, sounding like dying animals and laughing children. It was the eeriest sound M.J. had ever heard. It was haunting and terrifying, yet melodic and rhapsodizing. She felt in her heart as if she were listening to some kind of angelic poetry. It contained all the emotions anyone in love had ever felt.

The sun rose higher, and the moon died in the west. The light changed, but the silver gold twilight of evening was the same color that shot through the morning.

"One man's dawn is another man's dusk," Nelson said reverently.

They continued their slow climb.

"Just a few more steps," Nelson said. "I must warn you that the wind will get stronger, much stronger. It will become quite frightening. The winds careening through here must be over a hundred miles an hour. Hold tight to each other. Find a handhold on the mountain, a rock or branch to cling to. Once you see El Dorado, the winds will be their strongest. They can kill all of us. You must be strong. And courageous. El Dorado will be across from us. It's on the other mountainside."

"Is there a path? A ledge to cross?" M.J. shouted over the mounting roar of the winds.

"Yes, but I haven't seen it in five decades. It was precariously narrow even then." Nelson placed a bent arm over his eyes to avoid the flying dust and rubble in the wind.

"How did you get across?"

"I never did," Nelson said. "I've never seen the inside of El Dorado!"

"Then how do you know what to expect?" she asked, the wind blowing her hair, whipping it across her face.

Suddenly, Travis halted. Holding M.J.'s hand, he signaled her to stop. "You've led us a merry chase, old man, haven't you?"

"What are you talking about, Travis?" M.J. shouted.

Travis leaned across M.J., who kept her back to the mountainside. "Nelson! This isn't wind, and you know it."

Nelson was silent.

Michael moved closer to Travis, yelling. "What the hell is this if it's not wind?"

Nelson smiled slyly, knowingly.

As M.J. looked at him, she had the distinct impression there was more than age in his eyes, more than wisdom.

There was incredible knowledge. Chills shot up her spine and blanketed her body. She felt her blood run cold again.

"Tell us!" she demanded.

"Magnetic polarization—the force created when incredible positive energy meets incredible negative energy."

"It makes sense," Travis said. "The Andes are called the Avenue of the Volcanoes. When molten lava hardens, the direction of the earth's magnetic field at that time is locked into the lava. We can measure it millions of years back. The poles of the earth have shifted many times over that many years. It was this discovery that led to the birth of plate tectonics, that all the continents are drifting around on seas of lava. So, of course it is possible to have both negative and positive magnetic fields embedded in this area."

"And this wind or attraction has nothing to do with the sun rising or the moon setting?" she asked.

"A little, but not all." Nelson pulled them around the last bend. The footpath was no wider, but before them, on the other side of the mountain, carved into the rock, was an opening that hung over the sheer cliffs. There was only a narrow stone extension across the abyss.

Outside the cave entrance were two tall columns carved out of the rock. They were plated in gold, carved in the ancient Egyptian style with huge uncut emeralds forming a decorative border. The entrance was rough, not smooth, as if someone wanted to retain the integrity of the natural landscape yet was intent on putting artistry into the columns.

Then a sound more high-pitched than the wind wailed through the cavern. It was melodious yet filled M.J. with dread.

"The Uma men!" Michael yelled, cocking the gun.

He fired at the chanting men, who moved in a narrow band around the mountain's edge.

"Michael! Give me a gun!" Travis shouted.

"Do you think I'm a fool?" Michael snarled. "I can take care of some stupid natives."

Nelson worked his way to M.J., took her hand and urged her to squat against the mountainside. "Keep down." He pointed at the Uma men. "They have spears."

"They'll never fly through this wind," she said.

"They are the gatekeepers. Their zealousness will keep their aim sure."

Nelson placed his hands against the mountain, then stepped around M.J. "Stay down and keep moving toward the rock bridge. You must make it across the gorge to El Dorado. There is no wind on the other side."

"How do you know?"

"When I was here before, with Dorothy and Darren, we came upon this place in exactly the same manner. We didn't realize there was a magnetic force at work, as well as the wind. When Darren saw the gold and jewels, his greed went haywire. Back then the footpath was wider. I suppose we could have jumped across it. But we didn't want to take the chance. Darren wanted to use Dorothy as the guinea pig, see if she could cross first. But I jumped onto the footpath first. I had to crouch close to the rock and crawl across on my belly. A little over halfway, the winds seem to shift and, rather than blow you over, they will pull on you. Like a magnet.

"Once Darren saw I was making it over, he shoved Dorothy onto the bridge. She was terrified. I heard her scream, and I turned back for her. I got to her just in time to catch her as she started to fall.

"Darren's elation at finding El Dorado made his mind snap. He went crazy. He jumped onto the bridge, rather than staying low like he should have. He got caught by a huge undertow of wind current and fell. At about the same second, I lost Dorothy's grip, and she fell."

"And you didn't go back to the other side? To see the city?"

"I couldn't. It had no meaning for me without Dorothy. And the strangest thing was, the winds, or whatever they are, died immediately, and I made it down the mountainside to the cave where I now live."

"So, I was right. You didn't kill Dorothy, after all."

Nelson stared at the ground. "I killed her by bringing her to this godforsaken land." He looked away from M.J. so she would not see his tears. He pointed across the gorge. "See the columns? They have not diminished over time. No erosion. Halfway across the bridge, the winds will begin to fade. You're strong. You can make it."

"Where are you going?"

His smile was weak. "I'll hold off the Uma men while you and Travis get across."

"But you..."

He shook his head violently, shouting over the loud wind. "My time's up. Yours isn't."

"Nelson..."

"Goodbye, Dorothy."

She started to argue with him, then thought better of it. *Let him have his fantasy. He only has moments left.* A pang blistered her heart. She tried to speak, but emotion burned her throat. She threw her arms around his neck and hugged him.

Suddenly, she wanted to *be* Dorothy for him. She wanted to tell him that she was the woman of his dreams.

"You have a wonderful life," he said, and kissed her cheek.

She didn't know she was crying until she tasted her own tears.

M.J. moved, and Nelson slowly worked his way toward Travis.

"Give it up, Travis," Nelson said. "Michael thinks he is controlling the situation. Go help M.J. I told her how to cross the gorge. Save yourselves."

"No way. We go together," Travis argued.

Nelson shook his head. "She'll die if you don't do something," he shouted over the wind.

"What about you?"

"I'm a dead man already," Nelson said somberly, his eyes falling on Michael.

Travis stared at him, realizing that, all this time, not once had he ever thought he would actually die. Even if he was fooling himself, he'd never admit defeat. Yet this man was doing just that. Travis wondered if he would face his death quite as courageously. He hoped he would.

"Thanks," Travis said, and shook Nelson's hand just as a dart from a blowgun struck the mountainside near Travis' face.

"Hurry, there's no time," Nelson warned.

Travis slid toward M.J., who was moving inch by inch into even stronger winds.

Michael had succeeded in killing two of the Uma men. Another had fallen off the cliff. There were still nine men to his one gun. He'd been sure he could defeat them, but they kept coming, chanting their refrain of garbled Indian words that meant nothing to him. The pitch of their voices made his skin crawl. He fired again. Just then, another dart shot over his head, nearly parting his hair.

"Die, damn you!" He fired again and killed another, a man who must have been a hundred years old or more.

Nelson came up behind him. "Michael, you must go with the others. I'll hold them off."

"You're nuts. I'm not giving you my gun!"

"You have no choice. They will kill you! I will make certain they don't make it any farther than here."

"How?"

Nelson reached in his pouch and pulled out a thin reed

and a handful of darts. "My poison is more potent. And I've had more practice than any of them."

A spear struck the ground at Michael's feet, causing him to jump. He fired, picking off the next Uma man in line. But the rest were undaunted.

"What the hell's the matter with them? Why don't they turn back?"

"They can't. It's against their beliefs. We're not supposed to be here, and they'll stop at nothing to stop us!" Nelson shouted. "Now, go with the others!"

Michael didn't hesitate.

Nelson knew he wouldn't. Michael was a coward.

Nelson waited for the Uma men to come closer, watching death approach with resolution. Just as Dorothy had been born again in M.J., he knew that his death was a passing into another life. Into another place and time.

He waited until Michael was far enough around the bend, then he laid his darts down. He didn't want killing on his record when he passed through the planes.

The Uma men continued chanting their eclectic rhythms as they moved into the fierce bands of wind.

None of them had been this close to the forbidden city before. None of them had ever left the jungle. None of them had been filled with such fear as they were on this mission.

They knew the imposter when they saw him. He fit the description of the old medicine man they sought.

The eldest Cofan was still alive, but as he raised his spear, a blast of wind yanked on his arm, unsettling his stance, and he fell backward into the rocky gorge.

Another member slipped over the side as he tried to save their leader, choosing to save a human life rather than protect and guard the sacred city of El Dorado. For that sin, he had to die. But he didn't care, for he had loved the old man all his life.

Nelson covered his head as a rain of spears sailed toward him, striking his legs and arms. He clamped his jaw to keep from crying with pain.

The five remaining gatekeepers blew their poisoned darts, striking mark after mark. But Nelson refused to die. He lifted his eyes to them, returning their zealous gazes with one of his own. He fought them with his powerful mind. Thoughts battled thoughts. Good fought evil. Knowledge overcame ignorance.

The Uma men were forced to move closer, into the fiercely blowing winds. Nelson knew they were jungle dwellers, unused to the precariousness of mountain travel, of the pits and falls.

Nelson's life blood spewed on the ground. The poison had invaded his body. His heart was slowing. His eyes were closing. He could barely hear their chants anymore, but he knew they were still coming.

Then he heard a scream, and another and another.

The footpath gave way beneath their feet. The ground seemed to be as greedy for their souls as their enemies were.

One by one the Uma men fell to their deaths until none remained. Then all Nelson heard was silence.

He was glad he hadn't had to die alone.

41

"I'll go first," Travis said.

"Just keep low, like Nelson told me to," M.J. shouted.

"Don't worry," Travis replied, crouching, then slinking onto the rock bridge with his hands extended. He inched his way along, keeping one arm clamped to the rock, holding himself steady.

The winds were as forceful as an undertow at sea. He felt as if he were being sucked into a whirlpool yet thrust into a tornado. He couldn't hear anything but the screaming wind. The air was filled with sand, and it scoured his face as he crawled.

He was halfway there when the winds seemed to turn on him and he felt a new sensation. Even the hair on his head changed course in the direction of the new wind.

He moved faster, knowing that the rock beneath him was steady, that he was nearly there. He scrambled across the last section and made it to the cliffside. Here the ground was much steadier and wider.

He turned to M.J., gesturing with his arm for her to start out. "Come on!" he shouted, though he knew she couldn't hear him.

M.J. hadn't mentioned to Travis the dreams she'd had of being Dorothy. She hadn't told him she'd seen herself die falling off this very cliff as Dorothy in some past incarnation. And she didn't now tell him she was scared stiff.

She crouched as low as she could and began inching

her way across. The wind whipped her hair, pulling it up, flinging it aside, slapping her cheeks with it.

"Get your butt down!" Michael yelled.

She flattened her belly against the rock. "It *is* down," she said, thinking she'd never eat another chocolate bar again in her life.

Imitating Travis's every move, M.J. fought her terror as much as she fought the massively powerful winds. At the halfway mark she felt the same wind shift and found the last section an easier, though no less frightening, task.

Before M.J. was all the way across, Michael stuck his gun in the back of his shorts and began the trek across.

M.J. stood and flung herself into Travis's arms, reveling in his kiss. Michael was more than halfway across.

"Are you okay?" Travis asked.

She nodded. "I'm fine, sir."

They chuckled, and he kissed her.

Michael made it across, instantly pulling out his gun and cocking it.

"Okay, lovebirds, let's get on with it."

M.J. turned and stared down the gun barrel. "You know what, Michael? If you're going to kill us, why not just get it over with? Huh? Just shoot the damn thing!"

His blistering eyes stripped away her bravado. "Don't think I won't. But right now I need you both to help me."

"To do what?" she demanded. "Carry out the gold? We can't get out of here. If it weren't for those fanatics trying to kill us, we wouldn't be here."

Michael snorted derisively. "You must think I'm an idiot. Yes, I want the gold, but that's not what lures me. And frankly, if it weren't for those fanatics, I wouldn't have pushed us this far."

"What are you talking about?" Travis asked.

"Knowledge. Secrets of the universe. That's the quest that incites us all today. That's the pot at the end of the rainbow."

"Tree of knowledge," M.J. said reverently.

"Always was. Always will be," he answered her, his eyes burning with frenzy.

At that moment M.J. realized she'd only thought she'd known terror. Michael was completely crazy. He wanted the gold and the fame and power that infinite knowledge would bring.

She'd always wondered what drove someone to keep up the eternal quests, to risk his life for an archaeological She'd been stupid to think it was the thrill of the hunt, the danger. No, that had never been it. Those were trials men like Michael endured but would just as soon have done without.

It was the drive to become omnipotent that motivated him. He was worse than the Uma men. At least they knew they could never be God, whereas Michael was betting everything that he would be.

Michael grabbed M.J. and ripped off the bottom of her T-shirt.

"What are you doing?" she demanded, knocking his hand away.

"Making torches. Get those sticks over there, Travis. Near the entrance. Let's see what El Dorado is really all about."

Michael tied the fabric around the stick Travis handed him and lit it with the lighter he'd brought to light his Cohibas. Travis ripped the bottom of his shorts and made a second torch.

They passed between the golden columns and entered the cave.

M.J. shivered as they ventured into the dark. "Is it always so cold?"

"Yes, but this cave is surprisingly dry. Look at the ceiling," Travis said. "And the floor. No stalactites or stalagmites. That makes no sense," he said, holding his torch in front of him. "Unless… Ah! Just as I thought. Look! This is just the exterior of the cave. The wall closes in just ahead."

"It's like a vestibule," M.J. said.

"Precisely. There should be an opening into the other rooms," Travis said, approaching a solid wall.

"This can't be all there is," M.J. replied. "These lava formations must be a million years old."

"Or a hundred million," Michael offered.

Travis pressed his hand over the curved rock, searching for a crevice. He felt a rush of cold air, and his torch flickered. "Here," he said, and moved to the left. "It's low and narrow, but it's a passageway all the same."

"But to where?" Michael asked.

"Come on!" M.J. shouted excitedly. "What do you think we'll find first?" she whispered to Travis as he slipped into the crevice, his back pressed against one side as he worked his way in.

"Bats. Snakes. The usual."

"God, I hate that part," she said, creeping farther into the darkness. Travis held his lighted torch over her head.

"Am I crazy or is it getting warmer?" Michael asked.

"But it was cold just a minute ago," M.J. said.

"That was due to the outside air," Travis said. "I'll bet this isn't a mountain but a volcano."

M.J. swallowed hard. "I hate that part even more."

The passageway opened up into a large room. Even without light, they sensed the space around them was enormous.

Michael kept his head low, his eyes scouring the ground and the walls for anything that moved. "Just as I thought." He held the torch high. "Snakes."

The floor was moving with them.

M.J. screamed and backed up into what felt like a wall behind her. She turned and faced a hideous beaked bird. "Aah! What is it?"

Travis spun around, holding the torch closer. "A statue. Look. He's half bird, half man."

"He looks Egyptian," M.J. said.

Michael also moved his torch closer. "He looks like the

depictions of Uma I've seen. He's standing on a sarcophagus."

Travis handed M.J. his torch, then lifted her onto the coffin. "There's no snakes up here."

"How do we get rid of them?" she said, avoiding one that wanted to slither up her leg.

"We don't."

"I was afraid you'd say that."

Travis took his torch back from M.J. and looked around. "There's some kind of incense burner here," he said shooing the snakes away with the torch to make a path to a shallow metal dish on a tall pedestal. "There's wood in it." He put the torch to the half-charred wood. As dried out as it was, it lit in an instant. Soon the cave room was bathed in light.

Travis ripped more of his shorts and made a larger torch.

"There's another coffin," Michael said, jumping up. "Come on, Travis! And hold your torch higher." He pointed to the walls of the cave. "Would you look at this stuff?"

Travis held the torch to the wall, illuminating carefully organized and bordered sets of cave drawings.

"The artistry is incredible," Michael said, squinting at the markings.

Travis moved the torch to the right. "Holy shit, the old man was right. These are…" He pulled the torch away to illuminate the entire wall.

They all gasped in unison. "Egyptian!"

"I can't believe it," Travis said. "They're not Indian, Inca or even Moshe."

"They look like the ones I studied in college," M.J. said.

"Come on, M.J.!" Travis said. "I'll keep the snakes away while you make out these markings."

"She stays put where I can see her," Michael said, holding the gun toward her.

"She knows more about it than you do, Michael. Get a goddamn grip!"

"I can't decipher hieroglyphics, Travis," she said, staring at the blanket of snakes. "I only know a few things."

"Okay, fine. I'll hold the light here. Can you tell anything?" he asked, tracing his fingers over some symbols he knew stood for water, air and fire.

M.J. took in the whole picture. "Water, air, earth. But what is that?" She pointed to an angled configuration. "How wild—they look like constellations. They remind me of—"

"Greek mythology," Michael said. "Plato."

"Yeah," Travis said, pointing to the drawings of suns and moons, rifts of land and people depicted as falling off the edge of the earth into the sea.

"Do you think that is what this was like then? All this water here?" M.J. asked.

"No," Travis said. "That would be impossible, since the valley where Michael found the oil appears to have been heavily inhabited by dinosaurs."

"But water did come in here years later. There were earthquakes, then more mountains formed. Then the land dried once again," she offered.

"Which would put these drawings even further back," Michael said.

"We could take some side-scan sonars of the area. They'll go down pretty far, even through salt water. Then we can use ground-penetrating radar to double-check our findings."

"You forget, we don't have our equipment," Travis said.

But if we did... M.J. suddenly realized the enormity of their find. Michael was right. They were rewriting every history book, every geological database on earth.

"If the Egyptians were here, then they got here by aircraft," he said, pointing to a drawing of a man wearing an

Egyptian-style helmet, piloting what looked like a modern-day NASA escape module.

"No chance. We would have known about it before now. There would have been a reference somewhere," Travis said.

"Eric Von Daniken doesn't count?" M.J. asked, but neither Travis nor Michael was listening.

"Maybe it's not a machine, but a metaphor for the embryo state. It could have some sort of religious significance."

Travis backed away from the intriguing wall, and as he did, he held his breath.

"What is it?" M.J. asked, suddenly catching his excitement.

"Correct me if I'm wrong, but I thought Egyptians were dark-haired."

"They were. Are." M.J. sucked in her breath.

Travis pointed to a painting of a woman being administered to by her servants. Ever so lightly, he touched the paint. "It's not powder or dust. It's gold paint."

"They were blond?" M.J. asked.

"And blue-eyed," Travis said. "This is monumental. This is bigger than the discovery of the Rosetta Stone or the Dead Sea Scrolls. These are not Egyptians, but their forebears, the Atlanteans."

M.J. gaped, but made no sound.

Michael asked, "Are you sure?"

"Of course not. But it's a fairly educated guess. Unless this is all some kind of modern-day practical joke. I can't believe I'm saying this, but it's the only logical explanation I can come up with."

Michael was shaking with awe and excitement. His torch wavered. "This...this place was Atlantis?"

"I thought it was in the middle of the Atlantic Ocean."

"These drawings of the people falling off a cliff. I don't think it's this cliff. See the water? What if this land mass was Atlantis? What if the survivors came here?"

"It's possible," M.J. interjected. "Nelson told me that back in the twenties the search for Atlantis was all the rage among the explorers. He said the newspapers were full of it, and that Dorothy wrote several articles on adventurers at the time. Maybe it had been her destiny to come here to find this."

Travis said, "Thinking back on all those legends I've heard, the basic thread is that the Atlanteans scattered to Egypt, the Yucatán, Peru and the Pyrenees in Spain, taking with them the records of their dying world. Right? I know that the majority of the information went to the library in Alexandria, which was destroyed during a civil war in the third century. Everything was lost. But the rest of it…"

M.J. spoke. "Do you realize what this is? It's not a religious temple. It's not a city of gold. It's a hall of records."

Just as she spoke, a huge wind roared through the cave, extinguishing their torches, plunging them into darkness.

"Can you relight, Michael?"

He flicked his Zippo. "Yeah, I'll use my shirt." He pulled his arms out of the sleeves. Then he lit the fabric. It smoldered for a long moment, then finally caught. "This won't last long."

"Well, I'm not donating any more to the cause," M.J. said, losing her footing, then falling down.

"M.J., are you okay?" Travis asked.

"I don't know."

A rumble from deep inside the earth shook the ground. The snakes slithered out of Travis's path. "What was that?" he exclaimed.

Another rumble roared, even louder, and the ground shook enough to unseat M.J.

She screamed as a snake slithered over her arm.

"The ground is moving!" M.J. said. "We're going to—"

A ripping sound careened through the cave, and the earth split open. M.J., Travis and Michael quaked, then slid as the earth upended, thrusting plates of itself into the air.

"Travis!" M.J. screamed. "Help me!"

The ground she was clinging to was suddenly thrust upward, and she was dangling over a cliff's edge. She held on to the slippery rock with only her fingertips.

Travis was sliding toward her. "M.J.!" He slid past her.

She reached out for him with her free arm. He clung to her forearm.

"You can't hold us both!"

Her eyes slammed shut with the strain. "I know."

She let go.

It's like the dream. I'm dying. Falling.

She hadn't had time to tell Travis how much she loved him. In the dream she'd told the man that she loved him, but only after her soul left her body.

She landed in water—freezing cold, icy water. Her teeth chattered, and she spat water when she surfaced. Suddenly arms shot up from beneath her, holding her, cradling her.

"M.J.! You're alive!" Travis grabbed her face and kissed her.

"Not f-for long. Hy-hypothermia."

"I know," he replied as a wave of water rushed over them.

"Wh-what is this?"

"A subterranean river," he said, buoying her body with his.

They were traveling at lightning speed, she soon realized. She'd gotten cold so quickly that she hadn't sensed any movement at all.

They were funneled through the cavern created by the earthquake.

"If it's subterranean, we'll sink to the center of the earth and never get out."

"I know! If you can grab anything, a rock, anything at all, then do it!" Travis gurgled as water filled his mouth.

Carried by the current, they shot down a narrow rock passageway like a luge.

M.J. felt for rocks, for tiny saviors, but there were none. She held on to Travis for dear life, wondering which of them would die first. Water filled her nostrils, freezing her sinuses. Her head burned; her eyes teared. She thought her head would implode. She also knew that she had to start counting the seconds to her death. They'd been in the water for almost two minutes. That left only two minutes.

They were moving so fast, she felt she was covering miles, not yards.

Fifty-nine seconds. Fifty-eight. Fifty-seven.

"There's a bend coming up, sharp rocks. M.J., duck!"

She took a deep breath, and Travis shoved her head below the surface.

Fifty-six. Fifty-five.

Her lungs were exploding from the lack of air, from the intense cold. She tried to swim to the surface but the current was moving faster than it should have. M.J. knew subterranean rivers didn't move this fast.

The earthquake has caused this river to reroute itself. This is its maiden voyage.

Forty-five… There's a chance we can get out!

"M.J.!" a voice called.

She bounced underwater again. She could see Travis; he was turning blue. He couldn't have called to her.

Travis stared at her with the eyes of a dead man. She grabbed him by the upper arm, then pushed herself to the surface, forcing her muscles to work, using her will to propel her.

I won't let you die! Not now! We've come too far!

"M.J.! I'm over here!" the voice called.

She spat water as she surfaced. "Michael!"

He reached for her. He was holding on to a huge, jutting piece of rock. He strained. "Take my arm!"

The water pushed her and an unconscious Travis toward Michael. She held out her hand. "Michael! Save us!"

Though his face was dripping wet, she could see the pain in his eyes, a pain she'd put there. She wanted to tell him she was sorry.

"Please…" She felt as if her arm would disconnect from its socket if she stretched any farther.

Their fingertips met.

"M.J." His voice was filled with the love she'd once heard. "I'll always be here to save you."

In that instant she knew inexorably that Michael had loved her and she had loved him, if only for an instant in time. In her own way, she loved him still.

Their hands connected. Michael caught her just as they were about to go careening down an internal waterfall to dangerously sharp rocks below.

"Oh, Michael! I thought you were dead." She gasped and choked on lungs filled with water.

"I was the first over the side," he said, straining to rein her in.

"Can you get Travis? He's…"

"Dead?"

"No!" she screamed over the pounding waterfall. "He's fine. Just fine. Michael, take his arm!"

"What about you?"

She looked past Michael. "I'll swim to that next rock. I can do it."

Thirty-five seconds.

"No, M.J.!"

"Yes, Michael!" she shouted angrily.

"I can't save you both."

"Then save him, Michael!" She pulled the unconscious Travis toward the rock and brought his hand as close to Michael's as she could without losing her grip. "On the count of two! One…two!" She let go of Michael's hand and shoved Travis's limp hand into Michael's grasp.

"Thank you," she whispered, then let the water push

her to the next rock. She clung to it, then slowly, achingly, she pulled herself atop the newly cut rock. It was porous, like most of the rocks that had fallen into the crevice. They had not been part of the underground waterway, and therefore were not slippery.

"Help, M.J.!" Michael called.

Adrenaline shot through her numb muscles as she moved on her belly over the rock to the one where Michael was holding Travis.

Leaning down, she grabbed Travis's free hand. He was ice cold. So was she.

But she wanted to live.

She dug her heels into the porous rock for support and pulled with all her strength. Travis came out of the water and onto the rock. She moved back to the flat surface behind her and pulled again as Michael pushed.

Finally, Travis was on solid ground. And he was breathing.

She flung her head back with a prayer on her lips. "Thank you, God. Thank you!" When she did, she saw a light up above and noticed the complete silence.

It was the most incredibly brilliant light she'd ever seen. For a second she thought she'd been dreaming a near-death rescue. She felt the warmth of the light rays on her face. Her teeth stopped chattering. Her iron will forced her body to receive the warmth from above. She rubbed her arms, then her cramping legs. She breathed the warm air in and out bringing her body back to life. The light was gold, like…

"Sun! It's the sun! It's a hole, an opening! Look, Travis! We can climb up the rocks. We can get out of here! We'll be saved!"

She slapped his face and rubbed his throat and cheeks. He was convulsing with hypothermia. "You're fine, sir. You're fine. You're fine." Working feverishly, she rubbed her hands over his naked back and chest, not realizing that the effort was making her blood flow again, too. She was warming herself by warming him. By saving him, she was saving herself.

Finally he moaned. "M.J.?"

She kept rubbing while she cried, "You're fine, sir. You're fine."

His teeth chattered. "I—I'm freezing." He hugged himself and curled into a ball. She wrapped her arms around him, still rubbing his back. She could feel the cold leave his skin.

"You're alive, Travis!"

"So are you!"

She kissed him and felt warmth come to his mouth. She smiled.

"Oh, my God! I forgot about Michael!"

"He's alive, t-too?"

"Yes!" She scrambled away from Travis. "Michael!" She shot her arm over the side of the big rock and reached for him. "Give me your hand. I'll save you!"

Michael didn't answer. She saw that his arm was caught between two rocks. He had turned just as blue as Travis had been.

"Michael?" She held her breath as she reached for him again. He wasn't reaching back.

I can't be too late. I just can't be.

Michael stared at her with glassy eyes. His teeth were not chattering like hers. For the first time M.J. realized her will could not bring him back to life.

She was stunned. *This isn't happening. He has to be alive. He has to be!* Terror filled her as she watched the water swirl angrily around his lifeless face. She reached out one more time. There was a chance, she told herself. *There's always a chance.*

"Michael," she sobbed as Travis crawled behind her. "He's dead, Travis. He died saving you," she said.

"Help me get him out of there," Travis said. "We'll take him home."

"Home," she said.

Just as Travis reached out, Michael's icy hand became unwedged from the rocks, and the body lost its hold.

"Oh, God, no! Michael!" M.J. screamed.

Michael's body went careening over the waterfall, to the rocks below.

M.J. buried her face in Travis's chest.

It had all happened so fast. Where there was once life, now there was death. It was over so quickly.

"I...know he was wrong...but he didn't have to die."

Travis held M.J. close as they watched Michael's body move toward the center of the earth.

M.J. started shivering, as did Travis. "Michael saved us," she sobbed.

"I know," he replied, a burning lump in his throat. "He did the right thing, after all. He was a good man."

"The best," she whispered sadly.

"Come on," he said. "We have to get out of here and get into the sun. Then we can find our way to a town on this side of the mountain."

"Up there." She pointed to the opening above them.

He held out his hand as he crawled toward the light. "Just hang on to me."

Slowly the glow in her heart warmed her face, and she smiled up at Travis. "I thought you were hanging on to me."

"Always, M.J." He smiled back. "Always."

Epilogue

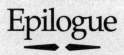

Twelve thousand feet above the earth in the shadow of Mount Cotapaxi, where the thin air is scented by groves of eucalyptus and vast rose farms, stands a four hundred and fifty year old mammoth white-stucco hacienda called La Cienega. In 1768 the Ecuadorian disciples of revolution met here to draft their Declaration of Independence from Spain.

M.J. chose the old chapel at La Cienega as the setting for her wedding because it exemplified her evolvement away from her past and her commitment to her future with Travis.

Gazing at her reflection in the antique mirror above the rosewood chest in the presidential suite, she was astounded at the change she saw in herself.

The confidence that flashed in her eyes had nothing to do with the crown of blush-colored roses, green English ivy and white baby orchids from which a floor-length veil of French silk illusion draped. Nor was it from the scoop-necked empire-waisted gown of white silk edged in blush satin ribbons and the whisper-thin silk train hemmed in tiny satin rosettes. Her confidence came from knowing that she'd looked into the eyes of evil, faced death, and triumphed.

She was afraid of nothing.

Most especially, she was ready to give her heart and soul to Travis.

She looked at her white satin shoes with tiny satin rosettes on the toes and giggled. "I feel like Cinderella. No, a princess."

"You're more than that to me. You're a vision," Travis said, walking through the double doors to the third-floor room dressed in a black tuxedo, looking more handsome than a man should be allowed to look. "You take my breath away," he said.

"No fair." She smiled. "I was going to use that line."

Cupping her face in his hands, he kissed her tenderly, giving her back all the love she felt for him.

"I beat you to it," he said. "And it wasn't a line."

"I wonder if it's against the law to be this happy," she breathed, letting her lips linger against his a moment too long.

He pulled her to his chest, sliding his arms around her, his hands urging her hips to his. She could feel him harden against her. "Now I know why the groom isn't supposed to see the bride before the wedding. Do you think the guests will mind waiting an hour or two?"

His kiss was consuming and more erotic than she'd known him to be. It held the promise of their long night of passion ahead.

"You're doing this on purpose," she whispered sensually.

"Damn straight. It's going to be torture thinking about what I want to do to you, knowing we have hours of dinner, then dancing, the guests…"

He kissed her again.

"Torture," she repeated. "How ever will you survive?" she teased.

"If I made it through the jungle and that freezing river, I think I can make it through our wedding party."

"We could leave early," she offered. "Of course, Claire would be scandalized."

As his tongue plunged into her mouth, M.J. could feel his heart banging against his ribs. Placing her palm over his chest, she whispered, "Darling, you'll be worn out before the ceremony."

"Don't bet on it," he said, reluctantly pulling away.

Smiling, she said, "I'd better fix my makeup."

"Yes, we can't have Claire thinking—"

"Did I hear my name?" Claire said loudly from the doorway.

"How long have you been standing there?" M.J. asked.

"I saw and heard the whole thing," Claire replied primly. Then she burst into a glorious smile and sighed deeply, clutching a bouquet of blush roses and white orchids to her chest. "Finally, you've made me so happy!"

M.J. tried to think of a razor-sharp comeback to smite Claire with, but nothing came to her. Now she understood what people meant when they said bitterness cannot dwell in a heart filled with true love. They were right.

"I'm glad," M.J. replied. "Really glad."

Claire sighed again. "You two are so…so perfect together!"

Travis looked at himself. "Are you sure it's not just these outfits?"

"You should have seen us in the jungle, Claire. Half-naked, fighting pumas…" M.J. began.

Claire cut her off, waving her palms at them and shaking her head. "Please, I've heard it once. That was enough. It scares me to death thinking you could have been killed." Her voice caught in her throat. "No, I won't think about it. That's all over now."

"Don't say that, Claire! Travis and I will have a lot more adventures. This is only the beginning."

Before Claire could protest, Travis interrupted, "Darling, this time your sister is right. The only adventure I want you pursuing is the one I intend to have with you in that bed. No more life-and-death scenes. Okay?"

M.J. looked into Travis's eyes and melted. "Okay," she said meekly.

Travis held out his arm to M.J. "Now, if I'm not mistaken it's time for me to make you my wife."

M.J. took his arm, then looked at Claire. "Are Erin and Colleen ready?"

"They've paved the road into La Cienega with rose petals. Better watch out. They'll have this room blanketed if we don't get down there and give them something to do!"

The black wrought-iron staircase had been decorated in thick garlands of huge multipetaled Ecuadorian blush colored roses, ivy and airy white gypsophila. White candles in antique black Spanish wrought-iron candelabras lit the landings and lined the walkway through the gardens, around the huge oak trees, and into the chapel where Erin and Colleen were dressed in empire floor-length dresses in blush silk exactly like Claire's. They wore crowns of tiny rosebuds with white satin ribbons flowing down their backs. Their white straw baskets were filled with rose petals from the abundant supply in the huge buckets beside the chapel entrance.

The setting sun filtered through the stained glass windows, creating a fantasy world of colored sunbeams and candle glow. M.J. couldn't help wondering how many weddings this chapel had seen in over four hundred years of existence. She imagined the Spanish beauties who'd lived here and pledged their hearts. She wondered if any of them had loved as deeply as she loved Travis.

Looking at the garlands of roses and ivy, the massive floral arrangements on the white, gold and pale blue altar, and the hundreds of beeswax candles, she wondered if the chapel had ever been this beautiful.

Robert, Claire's husband, had agreed to be Travis's best man. Travis had flown in his aging but ecstatically happy parents, Jim and Elizabeth, from Houston, along with the most loyal members of his board and staff. By the time they'd included their boatmen, Agli and Andreas, and of course, Gustavo, and their friends from the

Oro Verde—Benito, Kirstin and Emile, the hotel managers—the tiny chapel was nearly standing room only.

As M.J. and Travis walked arm in arm down the aisle, M.J. expected to feel slighted, not having a father to give her away. But she didn't. She felt whole. Complete. She felt unconditionally loved.

The shadow of Michael's death drifted over her heart, and for a moment she felt excruciatingly sad. She remembered his smile, his laughter, his pain and finally, the abiding love she'd seen in his eyes those last seconds of his life.

Michael had come to understand the meaning of life, just as she had—that love can never be cruel. It is the breath of the spirit.

At that moment M.J. felt a tear on her cheek. She looked into Travis's eyes and saw them glistening. He was remembering Michael, too. She smiled. Travis smiled back.

A trio of Andean flutists and two violinists played "You Belong to Me" as she walked down the aisle. She thought of Nelson, of how much he'd loved his dear Dorothy and how much he'd wanted M.J. to be his long-lost love. She thought of seeing the other side in a silver plane and knew that she'd never be cavalier about a plane trip again. She would always think of Nelson, and knew she would miss him dearly.

Tears welled in her eyes as the music swelled. Visions of pyramids along the Nile and markets in Old Tangiers flitted across her mind as Travis squeezed her arm bringing her thoughts to him.

At that moment she knew she was embarking upon the greatest adventure of her life.

"I love you," he whispered as they stood in front of a minister from a nearby village.

M.J. never took her eyes off Travis while they repeated their vows to each other. He held both her hands during the ceremony, only letting go to put a simple gold wedding band on her finger.

Though she'd fantasized about her wedding day when she was a child, she realized her visions had been mediocre, at best. Even her overblown, over-the-top imagination didn't come close to the reality of this day. She felt as if she were glowing from the inside out, radiating love into Travis and then out to all their friends and family. At that moment she wanted to hug the world.

When Travis pulled her into his arms and kissed her as the minister pronounced them man and wife, M.J. knew she'd found joy.

"I love you, Travis."

"I love you back, M.J. Kincaid." He kissed her again.

They turned to face the jubilant faces of their family and friends. As they stepped off the altar, Travis tugged on M.J.'s arm and whispered, "I have a confession to make."

"Here? Now?" She gasped.

"I lied to you."

"About what?"

"I'm not ready to give up our adventures quite yet." He smiled at his parents.

"Travis…"

"I booked us on a flight to Cairo for our honeymoon."

Her heart skipped a beat.

How could he know what I was thinking?

She gaped in surprise.

"Don't tell me you don't want to know the answers to the puzzles we found," he teased.

She felt that familiar zing of anticipation.

Pyramids. Atlantean secrets. Sphinx.

Excitement shone on her face. "Claire's gonna be miffed."

"I know." He chuckled conspiratorially.

Chills scampered down her spine. She squeezed his arm. "Oh, I do love you so!"

Travis smiled even more broadly. "And I intend to keep you so happy that you'll be saying that to me for the rest of your life."

"Not a problem, sir. Not a problem."

AUTHOR NOTE

For almost two years I have been living part-time in Quito, Ecuador. The legends contained within these pages, though not necessarily true, are not false.

There is a legend—many, actually—of geologists in the 1930s never returning from the Oriente. The geological sections of this book are accurate. The legend of Uma is one I heard while visiting Banos, the gateway to the Oriente. Metal sculptures of Uma's likeness can be found in the art galleries in this area. The legend of his followers holds its basis in truth, but the bulk is fiction.

The legend of El Dorado is as old as time; the Spanish conquistadores scoured all of South America for it. What is truly interesting is that I came upon an expedition executed in 1983 that actually claims to have seen El Dorado. Its location is secret, but is within the general vicinity of the Andes, between Ecuador and Colombia. The magnetic forces of the area, the "winds," are a true account, as well as the geological explanation for their existence. No one, to my knowledge, has crossed the gorge, however. Neither has anyone from this expedition returned to the site, for a myriad reasons, funding being a critical factor.

It is also true that in both South and North America I have come across a surprising number of believers in the suppositions about Atlantis contained within this story. Are the ones I've written about true? We don't know…yet.

For my recipe and bookmark collecting friends, I'm offering "South American Black Bean Soup," or if you simply have a comment, please send a legal-sized, self-addressed envelope with an international reply coupon to me at: 5644 Westheimer Road, 110, Houston, Texas 77056, USA.

CATHERINE LANIGAN

tender MALICE

When Karen invented a revolutionary
computer program, her life changed
forever. A co-worker goes missing and
her roommate is threatened.

Who can she trust?

Is it the man with whom she has
become involved, or her new
business partner?

MIRA®

Available now

CATHERINE LANIGAN

in love's SHADOW

On a cold December evening, a shot rang out in a wealthy Chicago suburb and the lives of three women were changed forever. Bud Pulaski, successful businessman, committed suicide, leaving behind a shattered wife, an estranged sister, a bitter mistress and many unanswered questions.

They are three women—searching for answers that will affect the rest of their lives. Searching for a ray of hope in love's shadow.

Available Now

Detective Jackie Kaminsky can't ignore
a thirty-year-old unsolved murder.
Especially when it is in her own garden.
Her instincts are put to the test and she suspects the
peaceful neighbourhood is hiding a sinister secret.

Find out how far the murderer will go to stop the
truth emerging in

fourth horseman

by

MARGOT
DALTON

Published 24th March 2000

Available from all good
paperback stockists

MIRA®

M176

2 FREE BOOKS
plus a MYSTERY GIFT

To thank you for choosing to read this Best of the Best™ novel from MIRA® Books, we would like to send you another two books and a Mystery Gift—FREE—with NO COST and NO OBLIGATION! Simply fill in the coupon and return it to us at the address below.

And as a further thank-you—we'd like to make you a bonus offer. Each month you can receive THREE of these great novels FOR THE PRICE OF JUST TWO! These books will be delivered direct to your door each month—and we'll even pay the postage and packing.

REPLY TODAY! NO STAMP NEEDED!

YES! Please send me my 2 free Best of the Best novels and Mystery Gift. If having received my free books and Gift, I do not wish to receive any more I will let you know. Otherwise each month, I will receive 3 Best of the Best novels for just £11.98—saving me a massive 33% on the combined cover prices! Even postage and packing is free! I understand that I may cancel at any time with no further obligation. I am over 18.

B0EA

Ms/Mrs/Miss/Mr ....Initials ....
BLOCK CAPITALS PLEASE

Surname..

Address..

....

....Postcode ....

Send coupon to:
UK: FREEPOST CN81, Croydon, Surrey, CR9 3WZ
EIRE: PO Box 4546, Kilcock, County Kildare (stamp required)

THE BRIGHTEST STARS IN WOMEN'S FICTION MIRA